THE VERY BEST OF
DALE CARNEGIE

Dale Harbison Carnegie (1888–1955) was an American writer and lecturer and the developer of famous courses in self-improvement, salesmanship, corporate training, public speaking and interpersonal skills. Born into poverty on a farm in Missouri, he was the author of the bestselling *How to Win Friends and Influence People* (1936), *How to Stop Worrying and Start Living* (1948) and many more self-help books.

THE VERY BEST OF
DALE CARNEGIE

~The Man Who Transformed Lives~

selected non-fiction

RUPA

Published by
Rupa Publications India Pvt. Ltd 2018
7/16, Ansari Road, Daryaganj
New Delhi 110002

Sales centres:
Allahabad Bengaluru Chennai
Hyderabad Jaipur Kathmandu
Kolkata Mumbai

Edition copyright © Rupa Publications India Pvt. Ltd 2018
The contents are based on public domain sources.

ISBN: 978-93-5304-092-5

First impression 2018

10 9 8 7 6 5 4 3 2 1

CONTENTS

HOW TO WIN FRIENDS AND INFLUENCE PEOPLE

PART 1

1. You Can't Win an Argument 3
2. How to Avoid Making Enemies 8
3. If You're Wrong, Admit It 11
4. A Drop of Honey 16
5. The Secret of Socrates 19
6. The Safety Valve in Handling Complaints 22
7. How to Get Cooperation 25
8. The Magic Formula 27
9. What Everybody Wants 29
10. An Appeal That Everybody Likes 33
11. The Movies Do It. TV Does It. Why Don't You Do It? 36
12. When Nothing Else Works, Try This 38

PART 2

13. Do This and You'll Be Welcome Anywhere 41
14. Make a Good First Impression 46
15. If You Don't Do This, You Are Headed for Trouble 49
16. Become a Good Conversationalist 53
17. How to Interest People 57
18. How to Make People Like You Instantly 59

PART 3

19. If You Must Find Fault, This is the Way to Begin 62
20. How to Criticise—and Not Be Hated For It 65
21. Talk About Your Own Mistakes First 68
22. No One Likes to Take Orders 70

23. Let the Other Person Save Face   72
24. How to Encourage People   75
25. Give a Dog a Good Name   78
26. Make the Fault Seem Easy to Correct   81
27. Making People Glad to Do What You Want   83

PART 4
28. Think Before You Criticize   85
29. The Big Secret of Dealing with People   88
30. Understand the Other's Point of View   95

DEVELOP SELF-CONFIDENCE, IMPROVE PUBLIC SPEAKING

1. Increase Courage and Self-Confidence   101
2. How to Open a Talk   110
3. How to Close a Talk   119
4. Self-Confidence Through Preparation   123
5. How Famous Speakers Prepared Their Addresses   128
6. Essential Elements of Successful Speaking   134
7. The Improvement of Memory   139
8. The Secret of Good Delivery   149
9. Platform Presence and Personality   157
10. How to Make Your Meaning Clear   166
11. Improving Your Diction   173
12. How to Interest Your Audience   181
13. Capturing Your Audience at Once   189

THE QUICK & EASY WAY TO EFFECTIVE SPEAKING

PART 1: Basic Principles of Effective Speaking
1. Acquiring the Basic Skills   199
2. Develop Confidence   207
3. Speak Effectively, the Quick and Easy Way   215

PART 2: Techniques of Effective Speaking
4. Introducing Speakers, Presenting and Accepting Awards 223
5. Organizing the Longer Talk 230
6. Applying What You Have Learned 244

PART 3: The Three Aspects of Every Speech
7. Earning the Right to Talk 251
8. Vitalizing the Talk 261
9. Delivering the Talk 267
10. Sharing the Talk with the Audience 271

PART 4: The Two Methods of Delivering a Talk
11. The Short Talk to Get Action 282
12. The Talk to Inform 294
13. The Talk to Convince 296
14. Impromptu Talks 306

HOW TO STOP WORRYING AND START LIVING

PART 1
1. How to Analyse and Solve Worry Problems 315
2. How to Eliminate Fifty Per Cent of Your
   Business Worries 322
3. 'Seventy Per Cent of All Our Worries...' 327

PART 2
4. Live in 'Day-tight Compartments' 335
5. What Worry May Do to You 340

PART 3
6. How to Crowd Worry Out of Your Mind 345
7. Don't Let the Beetles Get You Down 350
8. A Law That Will Outlaw Many of Your Worries 355
9. Co-operate with the Inevitable 359

PART 4

10. How to Add One Hour a Day to Your Waking Life   363
11. Avoid Fatigue and Look Young   366
12. How to Keep from Worrying about Insomnia   372

PART 5

13. Remember That No One Ever Kicks a Dead Dog   376
14. Do This—and Criticism Can't Hurt You   378
15. How My Mother and Father Conquered Worry   381

PART 6

16. Eight Words That Can Transform Your Life   389
17. Never Worry about Ingratitude   401
18. Would You Take a Million Dollars for What You Have?   408
19. Find Yourself and Be Yourself: Remember
There Is No One Else on Earth Like You   415
20. If You Have a Lemon, Make Lemonade   422
21. How to Cure Melancholy in Fourteen Days   430
22. One of the Two Major Decisions of Your Life   444

HOW TO ENJOY YOUR LIFE AND YOUR JOB

PART 1: Stop Worrying

1. Four Good Working Habits That Will
Help Prevent Fatigue and Worry   455
2. How to Banish the Boredom That Produces Fatigue,
Worry and Resentment   460
3. How to Overcome Tiredness   468

HOW TO WIN FRIENDS AND INFLUENCE PEOPLE

PART 1

1

YOU CAN'T WIN AN ARGUMENT

Shortly after the close of World War I, I learnt an invaluable lesson one night in London. I was manager at the time for Sir Ross Smith. During the war, Sir Ross had been the Australian ace out in Palestine; and shortly after peace was declared, he astonished the world by flying halfway around it in thirty days. No such feat had ever been attempted before. It created a tremendous sensation. The Australian government awarded him $50,000; the King of England knighted him; and, for a while, he was the most talked-about man under the Union Jack. I was attending a banquet one night given in Sir Ross's honour; and during the dinner, the man sitting next to me told a humorous story which hinged on the quotation: 'There's a divinity that shapes our ends, rough-hew them how we will.'

The raconteur mentioned that the quotation was from the Bible. He was wrong. I knew that. I knew it positively. There couldn't be the slightest doubt about it. And so, to get a feeling of importance and display my superiority, I appointed myself as an unsolicited and unwelcome committee of one to correct him. He stuck to his guns. What? From Shakespeare? Impossible! Absurd! That quotation was from the Bible. And he knew it.

The storyteller was sitting on my right; and Frank Gammond, an old friend of mine, was seated at my left. Mr Gammond had devoted years to the study of Shakespeare. So the storyteller and I agreed to submit the question to Mr Gammond. Mr Gammond listened, kicked me under the table, and then said: 'Dale, you are wrong. The gentleman is right. It is from the Bible.'

On our way home that night, I said to Mr Gammond: 'Frank, you knew that quotation was from Shakespeare.'

'Yes, of course,' he replied, 'Hamlet, Act Five, Scene Two. But we were guests at a festive occasion, my dear Dale. Why prove to a man he is wrong? Is that going to make him like you? Why not let him save his face? He didn't ask for your opinion. He didn't want it. Why argue with him? Always avoid the acute angle.' The man who said that taught me a lesson I'll never forget. I not only had made the storyteller uncomfortable, but had put my friend in an embarrassing situation. How much better it would have been had I not become argumentative.

It was a sorely needed lesson because I had been an inveterate arguer. During my youth, I had argued with my brother about everything under the Milky Way. When I went to college, I studied logic and argumentation and went in for debating contests. Talk about being from Missouri, I was born there. I had to be shown. Later, I taught debating and argumentation in New York; and once, I am ashamed to admit, I planned to write a book on the subject. Since then, I have listened to, engaged in and watched the effect of thousands of arguments. As a result of all this, I have come to the conclusion that there is only one way under high heaven to get the best of an argument—and that is to avoid it. Avoid it as you would avoid rattlesnakes and earthquakes.

Nine times out of ten, an argument ends with each of the contestants more firmly convinced than ever that he is absolutely right.

You can't win an argument. You can't because if you lose it, you lose it; and if you win it, you lose it. Why? Well, suppose you triumph over the other man and shoot his argument full of holes and prove that he is non compos mentis. Then what? You will feel fine. But what about him? You have made him feel inferior. You have hurt his pride. He will resent your triumph. And:

A man convinced against his will is of the same opinion still.

Years ago Patrick J. O'Haire joined one of my classes. He had had little education, and how he loved a scrap! He had once been a chauffeur, and he came to me because he had been trying, without much success, to sell trucks. A little questioning brought out the fact that he was continually scrapping with and antagonizing the very people he was trying to do business with. If a prospect said anything derogatory about the trucks he was selling, Pat saw red and was right at the customer's throat. Pat won a lot of arguments in those days. As he said to me afterwards, 'I often walked out of an office saying: "I told that bird something." Sure I had told him something, but I hadn't sold him anything.'

My first problem was not to teach Patrick J. O'Haire to talk. My immediate task was to train him to refrain from talking and to avoid verbal fights.

Mr O'Haire became one of the star salesmen for the White Motor Company in New York. How did he do it? Here is his story in his own words: 'If I walk into a buyer's office now and he says: "What? A White truck? That's no good! I wouldn't take one if you gave it to me. I'm going to buy the Whose-It truck," I say, "The Whose-It is a good truck. If you buy the Whose-It, you'll never make a mistake. The Whose-Its are made by a fine company and sold by good people."

'He is speechless then. There is no room for an argument. If he says the Whose-It is best and I say sure it is, he has to stop. He can't keep on all afternoon saying, "It's the best", when I'm agreeing with him. We then get off the subject of Whose-It and I begin to talk about the good points of the White truck.

'There was a time when a remark like his first one would have made me see scarlet and red and orange. I would start arguing against the Whose-It; and the more I argued against it, the more my prospect argued in favour of it; and the more he argued, the more he sold himself on my competitor's product.

'As I look back now I wonder how I was ever able to sell anything.

I lost years of my life in scrapping and arguing. I keep my mouth shut now. It pays.'

As wise old Ben Franklin used to say:

> If you argue and rankle and contradict, you may achieve a victory sometimes; but it will be an empty victory because you will never get your opponent's goodwill.

So figure it out for yourself. Which would you rather have, an academic, theatrical victory or a person's goodwill? You can seldom have both.

The Boston Transcript once printed this bit of significant doggerel:

> Here lies the body of William Jay, Who died maintaining his right of way—He was right, dead right, as he sped along. But he's just as dead as if he were wrong.

You may be right, dead right, as you speed along in your argument; but as far as changing another's mind is concerned, you will probably be just as futile as if you were wrong.

Buddha said: 'Hatred is never ended by hatred but by love,' and a misunderstanding is never ended by an argument but by tact, diplomacy, conciliation and a sympathetic desire to see the other person's viewpoint.

Lincoln once reprimanded a young army officer for indulging in a violent controversy with an associate. 'No man who is resolved to make the most of himself,' said Lincoln, 'can spare time for personal contention. Still less can he afford to take the consequences, including the vitiation of his temper and the loss of self-control. Yield larger things to which you show no more than equal rights; and yield lesser ones though clearly your own. Better give your path to a dog than be bitten by him in contesting for the right. Even killing the dog would not cure the bite.'

Opera tenor Jan Peerce, after he was married nearly fifty years, once said: 'My wife and I made a pact a long time ago, and we've kept it no matter how angry we've grown with each other. When one yells, the other should listen—because when two people yell, there is no communication, just noise and bad vibrations.'

Rule 1: Avoid arguments.

Don't raise your voice, improve your argument.
—Desmond Tutu

Act enthusiastic and you will be enthusiastic.
—Dale Carnegie

2

HOW TO AVOID MAKING ENEMIES

When Theodore Roosevelt was in the White House, he confessed that if he could be right 75 per cent of the time, he would reach the highest measure of his expectation.

If that was the highest rating that one of the most distinguished men of the twentieth century could hope to obtain, what about you and me?

If you can be sure of being right only 55 per cent of the time, you can go down to Wall Street and make a million dollars a day. If you can't be sure of being right even 55 per cent of the time, why should you tell other people they are wrong?

You can tell people they are wrong by a look or an intonation or a gesture just as eloquently as you can in words—and if you tell them they are wrong, do you make them want to agree with you? Never! For you have struck a direct blow at their intelligence, judgement, pride and self-respect. That will make them want to strike back. But it will never make them want to change their minds. You may then hurl at them all the logic of a Plato or an Immanuel Kant, but you will not alter their opinions, for you have hurt their feelings.

Never begin by announcing: 'I am going to prove so-and-so to you.' That's bad. That's tantamount to saying: 'I'm smarter than you are. I'm going to tell you a thing or two and make you change your mind.'

That is a challenge. It arouses opposition and makes the listener want to battle with you before you even start.

It is difficult, under even the most benign conditions, to change people's minds. So why make it harder? Why handicap yourself?

If you are going to prove anything, don't let anybody know it.

Do it so subtly, so adroitly, that no one will feel that you are doing it. This was expressed succinctly by Alexander Pope:

Men must be taught as if you taught them not, and things unknown proposed as things forgot.

Socrates said repeatedly to his followers in Athens:

One thing only I know, and that is that I know nothing.

Well, I can't hope to be any smarter than Socrates, so I have quit telling people they are wrong. And I find that it pays.

If a person makes a statement that you think is wrong—yes, even that you know is wrong—isn't it better to begin by saying: 'Well, now, look. I thought otherwise but I may be wrong. I frequently am. And if I am wrong, I want to be put right. Let's examine the facts.'

There's magic, positive magic, in such phrases as: 'I may be wrong, I frequently am. Let's examine the facts.'

Nobody in the heavens above or on the earth beneath or in the waters under the earth will ever object to your saying: 'I may be wrong. Let's examine the facts.'

You will never get into trouble by admitting that you may be wrong. That will stop all argument and inspire your opponent to be just as fair and open and broad-minded as you are. It will make him want to admit that he, too, may be wrong.

I once employed an interior decorator to make some draperies for my home. When the bill arrived, I was dismayed.

A few days later, a friend dropped in and looked at the draperies. The price was mentioned, and she exclaimed with a note of triumph: 'What? That's awful. I am afraid he put one over on you.'

True? Yes, she had told the truth, but few people like to listen to truths that reflect on their judgement. So, being human, I tried to defend myself. I pointed out that the best is eventually the cheapest, that one can't expect to get quality and artistic taste at bargain-basement prices, and so on and on.

The next day another friend dropped in, admired the draperies, bubbled over with enthusiasm and expressed a wish that she could afford such exquisite creations for her home. My reaction was totally different. 'Well, to tell the truth,' I said, 'I can't afford them myself. I paid too much. I'm sorry I ordered them.'

When we are wrong, we may admit it to ourselves. And if we are handled gently and tactfully, we may admit it to others and even take pride in our frankness and broad-mindedness. But not if someone else is trying to ram the unpalatable fact down our oesophagus.

Horace Greeley, the most famous editor in America during the time of the Civil War, disagreed violently with Lincoln's policies. He believed that he could drive Lincoln into agreeing with him by a campaign of argument, ridicule and abuse. He waged this bitter campaign month after month, year after year. In fact, he wrote a brutal, bitter, sarcastic and personal attack on President Lincoln the night Booth shot him.

But did all this bitterness make Lincoln agree with Greeley? Not at all. Ridicule and abuse never do.

Martin Luther King was asked how, as a pacifist, he could be an admirer of Air Force General Daniel 'Chappie' James, then the nation's highest-ranking black officer, Dr King replied, 'I judge people by their own principles—not by my own.'

In other words, don't argue with your customer or your spouse or your adversary. Don't tell them they are wrong, don't get them stirred up. Use a little diplomacy.

Rule 2: Never tell the other person, 'You're wrong.'

Take no thought of who is right or wrong
or who is better than. Be not for or against.
—Bruce Lee

Any fool can criticize, condemn and complain—and most fools do.
—Dale Carnegie

3

IF YOU'RE WRONG, ADMIT IT

Within a minute's walk of my house there was a wild stretch of virgin timber, where the blackberry thickets foamed white in the springtime, where the squirrels nested and reared their young, and the horse weeds grew as tall as a horse's head. This unspoiled woodland was called Forest Park—and it was a forest, probably not much different in appearance from what it was when Columbus discovered America. I frequently walked in this park with Rex, my little Boston bulldog. He was a friendly, harmless little hound; and since we rarely met anyone in the park, I took Rex along without a leash or a muzzle.

One day we encountered a mounted policeman in the park, a policeman itching to show his authority.

'What do you mean by letting that dog run loose in the park without a muzzle and leash?' he reprimanded me. 'Don't you know it's against the law?'

'Yes, I know it is,' I replied softly, 'but I didn't think he would do any harm out here.'

'You didn't think! You didn't think! The law doesn't give a tinker's damn about what you think. That dog might kill a squirrel or bite a child. Now, I'm going to let you off this time; but if I catch this dog out here again without a muzzle and a leash, you'll have to tell it to the judge.'

I meekly promised to obey.

And I did obey—for a few times. But Rex didn't like the muzzle, and neither did I; so we decided to take a chance. Everything was lovely for a while, and then we struck a snag. Rex and I raced over the brow of a hill one afternoon and there, suddenly—to my dismay—I saw the majesty of the law, astride a bay horse. Rex was out in front, heading straight for the officer.

I was in for it. I knew it. So I didn't wait until the policeman started talking. I beat him to it. I said: 'Officer, you've caught me red-handed. I'm guilty. I have no alibis, no excuses. You warned me last week that if I brought the dog out here again without a muzzle you would fine me.'

'Well, now,' the policeman responded in a soft tone. 'I know it's a temptation to let a little dog like that have a run out here when nobody is around.'

'Sure it's a temptation,' I replied, 'but it is against the law.'

'Well, a little dog like that isn't going to harm anybody,' the policeman remonstrated.

'No, but he may kill squirrels,' I said.

'Well now, I think you are taking this a bit too seriously,' he told me. 'I'll tell you what you do. You just let him run over the hill there where I can't see him—and we'll forget all about it.'

That policeman, being human, wanted a feeling of importance; so when I began to condemn myself, the only way he could nourish his self-esteem was to take the magnanimous attitude of showing mercy.

But suppose I had tried to defend myself—well, did you ever argue with a policeman?

But instead of breaking lances with him, I admitted that he was absolutely right and I was absolutely wrong; I admitted it quickly, openly and with enthusiasm. The affair terminated graciously in my taking his side and his taking my side. Lord Chesterfield himself could hardly have been more gracious than this mounted policeman, who, only a week previously, had threatened to have the law on me.

If we know we are going to be rebuked anyhow, isn't it far better to beat the other person to it and do it ourselves? Isn't it much easier to listen to self-criticism than to bear condemnation from alien lips?

Say about yourself all the derogatory things you know the other person is thinking or wants to say or intends to say—and say them before that person has a chance to say them. The chances are a hundred to one that a generous, forgiving attitude will be taken and your mistakes will be minimized just as the mounted policeman did with me and Rex.

Ferdinand E. Warren, a commercial artist, used this technique to win the goodwill of a petulant, scolding buyer of art.

'It is important, in making drawings for advertising and publishing purposes, to be precise and very exact,' Mr Warren said as he told the story.

'Some art editors demand that their commissions be executed immediately; and in these cases, some slight error is liable to occur. I knew one art director in particular who was always delighted to find fault with some little thing. I have often left his office in disgust, not because of the criticism, but because of his method of attack. Recently I delivered a rush job to this editor, and he phoned me to call at his office immediately. He said something was wrong. When I arrived, I found just what I had anticipated—and dreaded. He was hostile, gloating over his chance to criticize. He demanded with heat why I had done so and so. My opportunity had come to apply the self-criticism I had been studying about. So I said: "Mr So-and-so, if what you say is true, I am at fault and there is absolutely no excuse for my blunder. I have been doing drawings for you long enough to know better, I'm ashamed of myself."

'Immediately he started to defend me, "Yes, you're right, but after all, this isn't a serious mistake. It is only—"

'I interrupted him. "Any mistake," I said, "may be costly and they are all irritating."

'He started to break in, but I wouldn't let him. I was having a grand time. For the first time in my life, I was criticizing myself—and I loved it.

'"I should have been more careful," I continued. "You give me a lot of work, and you deserve the best; so I'm going to do this drawing all over."

'"No! No!" he protested. "I wouldn't think of putting you to all that trouble." He praised my work, assured me that he wanted only a minor change and that my slight error hadn't cost his firm any money; and, after all, it was a mere detail—not worth worrying about. 'My eagerness to criticize myself took all the fight out of him. He ended up by taking me to lunch; and before we parted, he gave me a cheque and another commission.'

There is a certain degree of satisfaction in having the courage to admit one's errors. It not only clears the air of guilt and defensiveness, but often helps solve the problem created by the error.

Michael Cheung, who teaches our course in Hong Kong, told of how the Chinese culture presents some special problems and how sometimes it is necessary to recognize that the benefit of applying a principle may be more advantageous than maintaining an old tradition. He had one middle-aged class member who had been estranged from his son for many years. The father had been an opium addict, but was now cured. In Chinese tradition an older person cannot take the first step. The father felt that it was up to his son to take the initiative towards a reconciliation. In an early session, he told the class about the grandchildren he had never seen and how much he desired to be reunited with his son. His classmates, all Chinese, understood his conflict between his desire and long-established tradition. The father felt that young people should have respect for their elders and that he was right in not giving in to his desire, but to wait for his son to come to him.

Towards the end of the course the father again addressed his class. 'I have pondered this problem,' he said. 'Dale Carnegie says, "If you are wrong, admit it quickly and emphatically." It is too late for me to admit it quickly, but I can admit it emphatically. I wronged my son. He was right in not wanting to see me and to expel me from his life. I may lose face by asking a younger person's forgiveness, but I was at fault and it is my responsibility to admit this.' The class applauded and gave him their full support. At the next class he told how he went to his son's house, asked for and received forgiveness and was now embarked on a new relationship with his son, his daughter-in-law and the grandchildren he had at last met.

What could you say to a man who treated you like that? When we are right, let's try to win people gently and tactfully to our way of thinking, and when we are wrong—and that will be surprisingly often, if we are honest with ourselves—let's admit our mistakes quickly and with enthusiasm. Not only will that technique produce astonishing results; but, believe it or not, it is a lot more fun, under the circumstances, than trying to defend oneself. Remember the old proverb: 'By fighting you never get enough, but by yielding you get more than you expected.'

Rule 3: If you are wrong, admit it.

Truth is always the strongest argument.
—Sophocles

Are you bored with life? Then throw yourself into some work you believe in with all your heart, live for it, die for it, and you will find happiness that you had thought could never be yours.
—Dale Carnegie

4

A DROP OF HONEY

It is an old and true maxim that 'a drop of honey catches more flies than a gallon of gall.' So with men, if you would win a man to your cause, first convince him that you are his sincere friend. Therein is a drop of honey that catches his heart, which, say what you will, is the great high road to his reason.

Daniel Webster, who looked like a god and talked like Jehovah, was one of the most successful advocates who ever pleaded a case; yet he ushered in his most powerful arguments with such friendly remarks as: 'It will be for the jury to consider', 'This may, perhaps, be worth thinking of', 'Here are some facts that I trust you will not lose sight of', or 'You, with your knowledge of human nature, will easily see the significance of these facts'. No bulldozing. No high-pressure methods. No attempt to force his opinions on others. Webster used the soft-spoken, quiet, friendly approach, and it helped to make him famous.

You may never be called upon to address a jury, but you may want to get your rent reduced. Will the friendly approach help you then? Let's see.

O.L. Straub, an engineer, wanted to get his rent reduced. And he knew his landlord was hard-boiled. 'I wrote him,' Mr Straub said in a speech before the class, 'notifying him that I was vacating my apartment as soon as my lease expired. The truth was, I didn't want to move. I wanted to stay if I could get my rent reduced. But the situation seemed hopeless. Other tenants had tried—and failed. Everyone told me that the landlord was extremely difficult to deal with. But I said to myself, "I am studying a course in how to deal with people, so

I'll try it on him—and see how it works."

'He and his secretary came to see me as soon as he got my letter. I met him at the door with a friendly greeting. I fairly bubbled with goodwill and enthusiasm. I didn't begin talking about how high the rent was. I began talking about how much I liked his apartment house. Believe me, I was "hearty in my approbation and lavish in my praise." I complimented him on the way he ran the building and told him I should like so much to stay for another year but I couldn't afford it.

'He had evidently never had such a reception from a tenant. He hardly knew what to make of it.

'Then he started to tell me his troubles. Complaining tenants. One had written him fourteen letters, some of them positively insulting. Another threatened to break his lease unless the landlord kept the man on the floor above from snoring. "What a relief it is," he said, "to have a satisfied tenant like you." And then, without my even asking him to do it, he offered to reduce my rent a little. I wanted more, so I named the figure I could afford to pay, and he accepted without a word.

'As he was leaving, he turned to me and asked, "What decorating can I do for you?"

'If I had tried to get the rent reduced by the methods the other tenants were using, I am positive I should have met with the same failure they encountered. It was the friendly, sympathetic, appreciative approach that won.'

Years ago, when I was a barefoot boy walking through the woods to a country school out in Northwest Missouri, I read a fable about the sun and the wind. They quarrelled about which was the stronger, and the wind said, 'I'll prove I am. See the old man down there with a coat? I bet I can get his coat off him quicker than you can.'

So the sun went behind a cloud, and the wind blew until it was almost a tornado, but the harder it blew, the tighter the old man clutched his coat to him.

Finally, the wind calmed down and gave up, and then the sun came out from behind the clouds and smiled kindly on the old man.

Presently, he mopped his brow and pulled off his coat. The sun then told the wind that gentleness and friendliness were always stronger than fury and force.

The use of gentleness and friendliness is demonstrated day after day by people who have learnt that a drop of honey catches more flies than a gallon of gall. Aesop was a Greek slave who lived at the court of Croesus and spun immortal fables 600 years before Christ. Yet the truths he taught about human nature are just as true in Boston and Birmingham now as they were 26 centuries ago in Athens. The sun can make you take off your coat more quickly than the wind; and kindliness, the friendly approach and appreciation can make people change their minds more readily than all the bluster and storming in the world.

Rule 4: Begin in a friendly way.

Without contraries is no progression. Attraction and repulsion, reason and energy, love and hate, are necessary to human existence.
—William Blake

For better or worse, you must play your own instrument in the orchestra of life.
—Dale Carnegie

5

THE SECRET OF SOCRATES

In talking with people, don't begin by discussing the things on which you differ. Begin by emphasizing—and keep on emphasizing—the things on which you agree. Keep emphasizing, if possible, that you are both striving for the same end and that your only difference is one of method and not of purpose.

Get the other person saying 'Yes, yes' at the outset. Keep your opponent, if possible, from saying 'No'.

The skilful speaker gets, at the outset, a number of 'Yes' responses. This sets the psychological process of the listeners moving in the affirmative direction. It is like the movement of a billiard ball. Propel in one direction, and it takes some force to deflect it; far more force to send it back in the opposite direction.

It is a very simple technique—this yes response. And yet, how much it is neglected! It often seems as if people get a sense of their own importance by antagonizing others at the outset.

Get a student to say 'no' at the beginning, or a customer, child, husband or wife, and it takes the wisdom and the patience of angels to transform that bristling negative into an affirmative.

Eddie Snow, who sponsors our courses in Oakland, California, tells how he became a good customer of a shop because the proprietor got him to say 'yes, yes'. Eddie had become interested in bow hunting and had spent considerable money in purchasing equipment and supplies from a local bow store. When his brother was visiting him he wanted to rent a bow for him from this store. The sales clerk told him they didn't rent bows, so Eddie phoned another bow store. Eddie described what happened:

'A very pleasant gentleman answered the phone. His response to my question for a rental was completely different from the other place. He said he was sorry but they no longer rented bows because they couldn't afford to do so. He then asked me if I had rented before. I replied, "Yes, several years ago." He reminded me that I probably paid $25 to $30 for the rental. I said "yes" again. He then asked if I was the kind of person who liked to save money. Naturally, I answered "yes." He went on to explain that they had bow sets with all the necessary equipment on sale for $34.95. I could buy a complete set for only $4.95 more than I could rent one. He explained that is why they had discontinued renting them. Did I think that was reasonable? My "yes" response led to a purchase of the set, and when I picked it up I purchased several more items at this shop and have since become a regular customer.'

Socrates, 'the gadfly of Athens', was one of the greatest philosophers the world has ever known. He did something that only a handful of men in all history have been able to do: he sharply changed the whole course of human thought; and now, 24 centuries after his death, he is honoured as one of the wisest persuaders who ever influenced this wrangling world.

His method? Did he tell people they were wrong? Oh, no, not Socrates. He was far too adroit for that. His whole technique, now called the 'Socratic method', was based upon getting a 'yes, yes' response. He asked questions with which his opponent would have to agree. He kept on winning one admission after another until he had an armful of yeses. He kept on asking questions until finally, almost without realizing it, his opponents found themselves embracing a conclusion they would have bitterly denied a few minutes previously.

The next time we are tempted to tell someone he or she is wrong, let's remember old Socrates and ask a gentle question—a question that will get the 'yes, yes' response.

Rule 5: Get the other person to agree with you immediately.

There can be no progress without head-on confrontation.
—Christopher Hitchens

*Develop success from failures. Discouragement and
failure are two of the surest stepping stones to success.*
—Dale Carnegie

6

THE SAFETY VALVE IN HANDLING COMPLAINTS

Most people trying to win others to their way of thinking do too much talking themselves. Let the other people talk themselves out. They know more about their business and problems than you do. So ask them questions. Let them tell you a few things.

If you disagree with them you may be tempted to interrupt. But don't. It is dangerous. They won't pay attention to you while they still have a lot of ideas of their own crying for expression. So listen patiently and with an open mind. Be sincere about it. Encourage them to express their ideas fully.

Letting the other person do the talking helps in family situations as well as in business. Barbara Wilson's relationship with her daughter, Laurie, was deteriorating rapidly. Laurie, who had been a quiet, complacent child, had grown into an uncooperative, sometimes belligerent teenager. Mrs Wilson lectured her, threatened her and punished her, but all to no avail.

'One day,' Mrs Wilson told one of our classes, 'I just gave up. Laurie had disobeyed me and had left the house to visit her girl friend before she had completed her chores. When she returned I was about to scream at her for the ten-thousandth time, but I just didn't have the strength to do it. I just looked at her and said sadly, "Why, Laurie, Why?"

'Laurie noted my condition and in a calm voice asked, "Do you really want to know?" I nodded and Laurie told me, first hesitantly, and then it all flowed out. I had never listened to her. I was always telling her to do this or that. When she wanted to tell me her thoughts, feelings, ideas, I interrupted with more orders. I began to realize that she needed me—not as a bossy mother, but as a confidante, an outlet for all her confusion about growing up. And all I had been doing was talking when I should have been listening. I never heard her.

'From that time on I let her do all the talking she wanted. She tells me what is on her mind, and our relationship has improved immeasurably. She is again a cooperative person.'

A large advertisement appeared on the financial page of a New York newspaper calling for a person with unusual ability and experience. Charles T. Cubellis answered the advertisement, sending his reply to a box number. A few days later, he was invited by letter to call for an interview. Before he called, he spent hours on Wall Street finding out everything possible about the person who had founded the business. During the interview, he remarked: 'I should be mighty proud to be associated with an organization with a record like yours. I understand you started twenty-eight years ago with nothing but a desk room and one stenographer. Is that true?'

Almost every successful person likes to reminisce about his early struggles. This man was no exception. He talked for a long time about how he had started with $450 in cash and an original idea. He told how he had fought against discouragement and battled against ridicule, working Sundays and holidays, twelve to sixteen hours a day; how he had finally won against all odds until now the most important executives on Wall Street were coming to him for information and guidance. He was proud of such a record. He had a right to be, and he had a splendid time telling about it. Finally, he questioned Mr Cubellis briefly about his experience, then called in one of his vice presidents and said: 'I think this is the person we are looking for.'

Mr Cubellis had taken the trouble to find out about the accomplishments of his prospective employer, He showed an interest in the other person and his problems. He encouraged the other person to do most of the talking—and made a favourable impression.

Rule 6: Let the other person do more of the talking.

In comedy laughter settles all arguments.
—Robert McKee

7

HOW TO GET COOPERATION

Don't you have much more faith in ideas that you discover for yourself than in ideas that are handed to you on a silver platter? If so, isn't it bad judgement to try to ram your opinions down the throats of other people? Isn't it wiser to make suggestions—and let the other person think out the conclusion?

Adolph Seltz of Philadelphia, sales manager in an automobile showroom and a student in one of my courses, suddenly found himself confronted with the necessity of injecting enthusiasm into a discouraged and disorganized group of automobile salespeople. Calling a sales meeting, he urged his people to tell him exactly what they expected from him. As they talked, he wrote their ideas on the blackboard. He then said: 'I'll give you all these qualities you expect from me. Now I want you to tell me what I have a right to expect from you.' The replies came quick and fast: loyalty, honesty, initiative, optimism, teamwork, eight hours a day of enthusiastic work. The meeting ended with a new courage, a new inspiration— one salesperson volunteered to work fourteen hours a day—and Mr Seltz reported to me that the increase of sales was phenomenal.

Twenty-five centuries ago, Lao-tse, a Chinese sage, said some things that readers of this book might use today:

> The reason why rivers and seas receive the homage of a hundred mountain streams is that they keep below them. Thus they are able to reign over all the mountain streams. So the sage, wishing to be above men, putteth himself below them; wishing to be before them, he putteth himself behind them. Thus, though his

place be above men, they do not feel his weight; though his place be before them, they do not count it an injury.

Rule 7: Let the other person have ownership of the idea.

By the very act of arguing, you awake the patient's reason; and once it is awake, who can foresee the result?
—C.S. Lewis

Do the hard jobs first. The easy jobs will take care of themselves.
—Dale Carnegie

8

THE MAGIC FORMULA

Remember that other people may be totally wrong. But they don't think so. Don't condemn them. Any fool can do that. Try to understand them. Only wise, tolerant, exceptional people even try to do that.

There is a reason why the other man thinks and acts as he does. Ferret out that reason—and you have the key to his actions, perhaps to his personality.

Try honestly to put yourself in his place.

If you say to yourself, 'How would I feel, how would I react if I were in his shoes?' you will save yourself time and irritation, for 'by becoming interested in the cause, we are less likely to dislike the effect.' And, in addition, you will sharply increase your skill in human relationships.

Sam Douglas of Hempstead, New York, used to tell his wife that she spent too much time working on their lawn, pulling weeds, fertilizing, cutting the grass twice a week when the lawn didn't look any better than it had when they moved into their home four years earlier. Naturally, she was distressed by his remarks, and each time he made such remarks the balance of the evening was ruined.

After taking our course, Mr Douglas realized how foolish he had been all those years. It never occurred to him that she enjoyed doing that work and she might really appreciate a compliment on her diligence.

One evening after dinner, his wife said she wanted to pull some weeds and invited him to keep her company. He first declined, but then thought better of it and went out after her and began to help her pull weeds. She was visibly pleased, and together they spent an hour in hard work and pleasant conversation.

After that he often helped her with the gardening and complimented her on how fine the lawn looked, what a fantastic job she was doing with a yard where the soil was like concrete. Result: a happier life for both because he had learnt to look at things from her point of view—even if the subject was only weeds.

Tomorrow, before asking anyone to buy your product or contribute to your favourite charity, why not pause and close your eyes and try to think the whole thing through from another person's point of view? Ask yourself: 'Why should he or she want to do it?' True, this will take time, but it will avoid making enemies and will get better results—and with less friction and less shoe leather.

'I would rather walk the sidewalk in front of a person's office for two hours before an interview,' said Dean Donham of the Harvard Business School, 'than step into that office without a perfectly clear idea of what I was going to say and what that person—from my knowledge of his or her interests and motives—was likely to answer.'

It is enormously important to think always in terms of the other person's point of view, and see things from that person's angle, as well as your own.

Rule 8: Try to see things from the other's point of view.

Arguments, like men, are often pretenders.
—Plato

Do the thing you fear to do and keep on doing it…that is the quickest and surest way ever yet discovered to conquer fear.
—Dale Carnegie

9

WHAT EVERYBODY WANTS

Wouldn't you like to have a magic phrase that would stop arguments, eliminate ill feeling, create goodwill and make the other person listen attentively?

Yes? All right. Here it is: 'I don't blame you one iota for feeling as you do. If I were you I would undoubtedly feel just as you do.'

An answer like that will soften the most cantankerous old cuss alive. And you can say that and be 100 per cent sincere, because if you were the other person you, of course, would feel just as he does. Take Al Capone, for example. Suppose you had inherited the same body and temperament and mind that Al Capone had. Suppose you had his environment and experiences. You would then be precisely what he was—and where he was. For it is those things—and only those things—that made him what he was. The only reason, for example, that you are not a rattlesnake is that your mother and father weren't rattlesnakes.

You deserve very little credit for being what you are—and remember, the people who come to you irritated, bigoted, unreasoning, deserve very little discredit for being what they are. Feel sorry for the poor devils. Pity them. Sympathize with them. Say to yourself: 'There, but for the grace of God, go I.'

Three-fourths of the people you will ever meet are hungering and thirsting for sympathy. Give it to them, and they will love you.

I once gave a broadcast about the author of *Little Women*, Louisa May Alcott. Naturally, I knew she had lived and written her immortal books in Concord, Massachusetts. But, without thinking what I was saying, I spoke of visiting her old home in Concord, New Hampshire.

If I had said New Hampshire only once, it might have been forgiven. But, alas and alack! I said it twice. I was deluged with letters and telegrams, stinging messages that swirled around my defenceless head like a swarm of hornets. Many were indignant. A few insulting. One Colonial Dame, who had been reared in Concord, Massachusetts, and who was then living in Philadelphia, vented her scorching wrath upon me. She couldn't have been much more bitter if I had accused Miss Alcott of being a cannibal from New Guinea. As I read the letter, I said to myself, 'Thank God, I am not married to that woman,' I felt like writing and telling her that although I had made a mistake in geography, she had made a far greater mistake in common courtesy. That was to be just my opening sentence. Then I was going to roll up my sleeves and tell her what I really thought. But I didn't. I controlled myself. I realized that any hotheaded fool could do that—and that most fools would do just that.

I wanted to be above fools. So I resolved to try to turn her hostility into friendliness. It would be a challenge, a sort of game I could play. I said to myself, 'After all, if I were she, I would probably feel just as she does.' So, I determined to sympathize with her viewpoint. The next time I was in Philadelphia, I called her on the telephone. The conversation went something like this:

ME: Mrs So-and-So, you wrote me a letter a few weeks ago, and I want to thank you for it.

SHE: (in incisive, cultured, well-bred tones) To whom have I the honour of speaking?

ME: I am a stranger to you. My name is Dale Carnegie. You listened to a broadcast I gave about Louisa May Alcott a few Sundays ago, and I made the unforgivable blunder of saying that she had lived in Concord, New Hampshire. It was a stupid blunder, and I want to apologize for it. It was so nice of you to take the time to write me.

SHE: I am sorry, Mr Carnegie, that I wrote as I did. I lost my temper. I must apologize.

ME: No! No! You are not the one to apologize; I am. Any school

child would have known better than to have said what I
said. I apologized over the air the following Sunday, and
I want to apologize to you personally now.

SHE: I was born in Concord, Massachusetts. My family has been
prominent in Massachusetts affairs for two centuries, and
I am very proud of my native state. I was really quite
distressed to hear you say that Miss Alcott had lived in
New Hampshire. But I am really ashamed of that letter.

ME: I assure you that you were not one-tenth as distressed as I
am. My error didn't hurt Massachusetts, but it did hurt me.
It is so seldom that people of your standing and culture
take time to write people who speak on the radio, and I
do hope you will write again if you detect an error in my
talks.

SHE: You know, I really like very much the way you have accepted
my criticism. You must be a very nice person. I should like
to know you better.

So, because I had apologized and sympathized with her point
of view, she began apologizing and sympathizing with my point of
view. I had the satisfaction of controlling my temper, the satisfaction
of returning kindness for an insult. I got infinitely more fun out of
making her like me than I could ever have gotten out of telling her
to go and take a jump in the Schuylkill River.

Dr Arthur I. Gates said in his splendid book *Educational
Psychology*: 'Sympathy the human species universally craves. The child
eagerly displays his injury; or even inflicts a cut or bruise in order to
reap abundant sympathy. For the same purpose adults... show their
bruises, relate their accidents, illness, especially details of surgical
operations. "Self-pity" for misfortunes real or imaginary is, in some
measure, practically a universal practice.'

So, if you want to win people to your way of thinking, put in
practice...

Rule 9: Be sympathetic to the other person's ideas and desires.

Friendship improves happiness and abates misery, by the doubling of our joy and the dividing of our grief.
—Marcus Tullius Cicero

Don't be afraid to give your best to what seemingly are small jobs. Every time you conquer one it makes you that much stronger. If you do the little jobs well, the big ones will tend to take care of themselves.
—Dale Carnegie

10

AN APPEAL THAT EVERYBODY LIKES

I was reared on the edge of the Jesse James country out in Missouri, and I visited the James farm at Kearney, Missouri, where the son of Jesse James was then living. His wife told me stories of how Jesse robbed trains and held up banks and then gave money to the neighbouring farmers to pay off their mortgages.

Jesse James probably regarded himself as an idealist at heart, just as Dutch Schultz, 'Two Gun' Crowley, Al Capone and many other organized crime 'godfathers' did generations later. The fact is that all people you meet have a high regard for themselves and like to be fine and unselfish in their own estimation.

J. Pierpont Morgan observed, in one of his analytical interludes, that a person usually has two reasons for doing a thing: one that sounds good and a real one.

The person himself will think of the real reason. You don't need to emphasize that. But all of us, being idealists at heart, like to think of motives that sound good. So, in order to change people, appeal to the nobler motives.

Is that too idealistic to work in business? Let's see. Let's take the case of Hamilton J. Farrell of the Farrell-Mitchell Company of Glenolden, Pennsylvania. Mr Farrell had a disgruntled tenant who threatened to move. The tenant's lease still had four months to run; nevertheless, he served notice that he was vacating immediately, regardless of lease.

'These people had lived in my house all winter—the most expensive part of the year,' Mr Farrell said as he told the story to the class, 'and I knew it would be difficult to rent the apartment again before fall. I could see all that rent income going over the hill and believe me, I saw red.

'Now, ordinarily, I would have waded into that tenant and advised him to read his lease again. I would have pointed out that if he moved, the full balance of his rent would fall due at once—and that I could, and would move to collect.

'However, instead of flying off the handle and making a scene, I decided to try other tactics. So I started like this: "Mr Doe," I said, "I have listened to your story, and I still don't believe you intend to move. Years in the renting business have taught me something about human nature, and I sized you up in the first place as being a man of your word. In fact, I'm so sure of it that I'm willing to take a gamble.

'"Now, here's my proposition. Lay your decision on the table for a few days and think it over. If you come back to me between now and the first of the month, when your rent is due, and tell me you still intend to move, I give you my word I will accept your decision as final. I will privilege you to move and admit to myself I've been wrong in my judgement. But I still believe you're a man of your word and will live up to your contract. For after all, we are either men or monkeys—and the choice usually lies with ourselves!"

'Well, when the new month came around, this gentleman came to see me and paid his rent in person. He and his wife had talked it over he said—and decided to stay. They had concluded that the only honourable thing to do was to live up to their lease.'

When Cyrus H.K. Curtis, the poor boy from Maine, was starting on his meteoric career, which was destined to make him millions as owner of *The Saturday Evening Post* and the *Ladies' Home Journal*, he couldn't afford to pay his contributors the prices that other magazines paid. He couldn't afford to hire first-class authors to write for money alone. So he appealed to their nobler motives. For example, he persuaded even Louisa May Alcott, the immortal author of *Little Women*, to write for him when she was at the flood tide of her fame; and he did it by offering to send a cheque for a hundred dollars, not to her, but to her favourite charity.

Right here the sceptic may say: 'Oh, that stuff is all right for Farell and Curtis or a sentimental novelist. But, I'd like to see you make it work with the tough babies I have to collect bills from!' You may be right. Nothing will work in all cases—and nothing will work with all people. If you are satisfied with the results you are now getting, why change? If you are not satisfied, why not experiment?

Rule 10: Appeal to the nobler motives.

Criticism, like rain, should be gentle enough to nourish a man's growth without destroying his roots.
—Frank A. Clark

Try honestly to see things from the other person's point of view.
—Dale Carnegie

11

THE MOVIES DO IT. TV DOES IT.
WHY DON'T YOU DO IT?

Many years ago, the *Philadelphia Evening Bulletin* was being maligned by a dangerous whispering campaign. A malicious rumour was being circulated. Advertisers were being told that the newspaper was no longer attractive to readers because it carried too much advertising and too little news. Immediate action was necessary. The gossip had to be squelched.

But how?

This is the way it was done.

The *Bulletin* clipped from its regular edition all reading matter of all kinds on one average day, classified it and published it as a book. The book was called *One Day*. It contained 307 pages—as many as a hard-covered book; yet the *Bulletin* had printed all this news and feature material on one day and sold it, not for several dollars, but for a few cents.

The printing of that book dramatized the fact that the *Bulletin* carried an enormous amount of interesting reading matter. It conveyed the facts more vividly, more interestingly, more impressively, than pages of figures and mere talk could have done.

This is the day of dramatization. Merely stating a truth isn't enough. The truth has to be made vivid, interesting, dramatic. You have to use showmanship. The movies do it. Television does it. And you will have to do it if you want attention.

Rule 11: Dramatize your ideas.

With the new day comes new strength and new thoughts.
—Eleanor Roosevelt

Each nation feels superior to other nations.
That breeds patriotism—and wars.
—Dale Carnegie

12

WHEN NOTHING ELSE WORKS, TRY THIS

Charles Schwab had a mill manager whose people weren't producing their quota of work.

'How is it,' Schwab asked him, 'that a manager as capable as you can't make this mill turn out what it should?'

'I don't know,' the manager replied. 'I've coaxed the men, I've pushed them, I've sworn and cussed, I've threatened them with damnation and being fired. But nothing works. They just won't produce.'

This conversation took place at the end of the day, just before the night shift came on. Schwab asked the manager for a piece of chalk, then, turning to the nearest man, asked:

'How many heats did your shift make today?'

'Six.'

Without another word, Schwab chalked a big figure '6' on the floor, and walked away.

When the night shift came in, they saw the '6' and asked what it meant.

'The big boss was in here today,' the day people said. 'He asked us how many heats we made, and we told him six. He chalked it on the floor.'

The next morning Schwab walked through the mill again. The night shift had rubbed out '6' and replaced it with a big '7'.

When the day shift reported for work the next morning, they saw a big '7' chalked on the floor. So the night shift thought they were better than the day shift, did they? Well, they would show the night shift a thing or two. The crew pitched in with enthusiasm, and when they quit that night, they left behind them an enormous, swaggering '10'. Things were stepping up.

Shortly this mill, which had been lagging way behind in production, was turning out more work than any other mill in the plant.

The principle?

Let Charles Schwab say it in his own words: 'The way to get things done,' says Schwab, 'is to stimulate competition. I do not mean in a sordid money-getting way, but in the desire to excel.'

The desire to excel! The challenge! Throwing down the gauntlet! An infallible way of appealing to people of spirit.

Without a challenge, Theodore Roosevelt would never have been President of the United States. The Rough Rider, just back from Cuba, was picked for governor of New York State. The opposition discovered he was no longer a legal resident of the state, and Roosevelt, frightened, wished to withdraw. Then Thomas Collier Platt, then U.S. Senator from New York, threw down the challenge. Turning suddenly on Theodore Roosevelt, he cried in a ringing voice: 'Is the hero of San Juan Hill a coward?'

Roosevelt stayed in the fight—and the rest is history. A challenge not only changed his life; it had a real effect upon the future of his nation.

Frederic Herzberg, one of the great behavioural scientists, studied in depth the work attitudes of thousands of people ranging from factory workers to senior executives. What do you think he found to be the most motivating factor—the one facet of the jobs that was most stimulating? Money? Good working conditions? Fringe benefits? No—not any of those. The one major factor that motivated people was the work itself. If the work was exciting and interesting, the worker looked forward to doing it and was motivated to do a good job.

That is what every successful person loves: the game. The chance for self-expression. The chance to prove his or her worth, to excel, to win. That is what makes foot-races, and hog-calling, and pie-eating contests. The desire to excel. The desire for a feeling of importance.

Rule 12: Challenges generate excitement.

He has a right to criticize, who has a heart to help.
—Abraham Lincoln

Fear doesn't exist anywhere except in the mind.
—Dale Carnegie

PART 2

13

DO THIS AND YOU'LL BE WELCOME ANYWHERE

Why read this book to find out how to win friends? Why not study the technique of the greatest winner of friends the world has ever known? Who is he? You may meet him tomorrow coming down the street. When you get within ten feet of him, he will begin to wag his tail. If you stop and pat him he will almost jump out of his skin to show you how much he likes you. And you know that behind this show of affection on his part, there are no ulterior motives: he doesn't want to sell you any real estate, and he doesn't want to marry you.

Did you ever stop to think that a dog is the only animal that doesn't have to work for a living? A hen has to lay eggs, a cow has to give milk and a canary has to sing. But a dog makes his living by giving you nothing but love.

When I was five years old, my father bought a little yellow-haired pup for fifty cents. He was the light and joy of my childhood. Every afternoon about four-thirty, he would sit in the front yard with his beautiful eyes staring steadfastly at the path, and as soon as he heard my voice or saw me swinging my dinner pail through the buck brush, he was off like a shot, racing breathlessly up the hill to greet me with leaps of joy and barks of sheer ecstasy.

Tippy was my constant companion for five years. Then one tragic night—I shall never forget it—he was killed within ten feet of my head, killed by lightning. Tippy's death was the tragedy of my boyhood.

You never read a book on psychology, Tippy. You didn't need to. You knew by some divine instinct that you can make more friends in two months by becoming genuinely interested in other people than you can in two years by trying to get other people interested in you. Let me repeat that. You can make more friends in two months by becoming interested in other people than you can in two years by trying to get other people interested in you.

Yet I know and you know people who blunder through life trying to wigwag other people into becoming interested in them.

Of course, it doesn't work. People are not interested in you. They are not interested in me. They are interested in themselves—morning, noon and after dinner.

The New York Telephone Company made a detailed study of telephone conversations to find out which word is the most frequently used. You have guessed it: it is the personal pronoun 'I.' 'I.' 'I.' It was used 3,900 times in 500 telephone conversations. 'I.' 'I.' 'I.' 'I.'

When you see a group photograph that you are in, whose picture do you look for first?

If we merely try to impress people and get people interested in us, we will never have many true, sincere friends. Friends, real friends, are not made that way.

That, too, was one of the secrets of Theodore Roosevelt's astonishing popularity. Even his servants loved him. His valet, James E. Amos, wrote a book about him entitled *Theodore Roosevelt, Hero to His Valet*. In that book Amos relates this illuminating incident:

> My wife one time asked the President about a bobwhite. She had never seen one and he described it to her fully. Sometime later, the telephone at our cottage rang. [Amos and his wife lived in a little cottage on the Roosevelt estate at Oyster Bay.] My wife answered it and it was Mr Roosevelt himself. He had called her, he said, to tell her that there was a bobwhite outside her window and that if she would look out she might see it. Little things

like that were so characteristic of him. Whenever he went by our cottage even though we were out of sight, we would hear him call out: 'Oo-oo-oo, Annie?' or 'Oo-oo-oo, James!' It was just a friendly greeting as he went by.

How could employees keep from liking a man like that? How could anyone keep from liking him?

Roosevelt called at the White House one day when the President and Mrs Taft were away. His honest liking for humble people was shown by the fact that he greeted all the old White House servants by name, even the scullery maids.

'But when he saw Alice, the kitchen maid,' writes Archie Butt, 'he asked her if she still made corn bread. Alice told him that she sometimes made it for the servants, but no one ate it upstairs.

'"They show bad taste," Roosevelt boomed, "and I'll tell the President so when I see him."

'Alice brought a piece to him on a plate, and he went over to the office eating it as he went and greeting gardeners and labourers as he passed...

'He addressed each person just as he had addressed them in the past. Ike Hoover, who had been head usher at the White House for forty years, said with tears in his eyes: "It is the only happy day we had in nearly two years, and not one of us would exchange it for a hundred-dollar bill."'

All of us, be it workers in a factory, clerks in an office or even a king upon his throne—all of us like people who admire us. Take the German Kaiser, for example. At the close of World War I he was probably the most savagely and universally despised man on this earth. Even his own nation turned against him when he fled over into Holland to save his neck. The hatred against him was so intense that millions of people would have loved to tear him limb from limb or burn him at the stake. In the midst of all this forest fire of fury, one little boy wrote the Kaiser a simple, sincere letter glowing with kindliness and admiration. This little boy said that no matter what the others thought, he would always love Wilhelm as his Emperor. The Kaiser was deeply touched by this letter and invited the little boy to come to see him. The boy came, so did his mother—and the Kaiser married her. That little boy didn't need to read a book on how to win friends and influence people. He knew how instinctively.

If we want to make friends, let's put ourselves out to do things for other people—things that require time, energy, unselfishness and thoughtfulness. When the Duke of Windsor was Prince of Wales, he was scheduled to tour South America, and before he started out on that tour he spent months studying Spanish so that he could make public talks in the language of the country; and the South Americans loved him for it.

For years I made it a point to find out the birthdays of my friends. How? Although I haven't the foggiest bit of faith in astrology, I began by asking the other party whether he believed the date of one's birth has anything to do with character and disposition. I then asked him or her to tell me the month and day of birth. If he or she said 24 November, for example, I kept repeating to myself, '24 November, 24 November.' The minute my friend's back was turned I wrote down the name and birthday and later would transfer it to a birthday book. At the beginning of each year, I had these birthday dates scheduled in my calendar pad so that they came to my attention automatically. When the natal day arrived, there was my letter or telegram. What a hit it made! I was frequently the only person on earth who remembered.

If we want to make friends, let's greet people with animation and enthusiasm. When somebody calls you on the telephone use the same psychology. Say 'Hello' in tones that bespeak how pleased you are to have the person call. Many companies train their telephone operators to greet all callers in a tone of voice that radiates interest and enthusiasm. The caller feels the company is concerned about them. Let's remember that when we answer the telephone tomorrow.

Showing a genuine interest in others not only wins friends for you, but may develop in its customers a loyalty to your company.

A show of interest, as with every other principle of human

relations, must be sincere. It must pay off not only for the person showing the interest, but for the person receiving the attention. It is a two-way street—both parties benefit.

If you want others to like you, if you want to develop real friendships, if you want to help others at the same time as you help yourself, keep this principle in mind:

Rule 13: Show a genuine interest in other people.

All the effort in the world won't matter if you're not inspired.

—Chuck Palahniuk

Fear not those who argue but those who dodge.

—Dale Carnegie

14

MAKE A GOOD FIRST IMPRESSION

At a dinner party in New York, one of the guests, a woman who had inherited money, was eager to make a pleasing impression on everyone. She had squandered a modest fortune on sables, diamonds and pearls. But she hadn't done anything whatever about her face. It radiated sourness and selfishness. She didn't realize what everyone knows: namely, that the expression one wears on one's face is far more important than the clothes one wears on one's back.

Actions speak louder than words, and a smile says, 'I like you. You make me happy. I am glad to see you.'

That is why dogs make such a hit. They are so glad to see us that they almost jump out of their skins. So, naturally, we are glad to see them.

A baby's smile has the same effect.

Have you ever been in a doctor's waiting room and looked around at all the glum faces waiting impatiently to be seen? Dr Stephen K. Sproul, a veterinarian in Raytown, Missouri, told of a typical spring day when his waiting room was full of clients waiting to have their pets inoculated. No one was talking to anyone else, and all were probably thinking of a dozen other things they would rather be doing than 'wasting time' sitting in that office. He told one of our classes: There were six or seven clients waiting when a young woman came in with a nine-months-old baby and a kitten. As luck would have it, she sat down next to a gentleman who was more than a little distraught about the long wait for service. The next thing he knew, the baby just looked up at him with that great big smile that is so characteristic of babies. What did that gentleman do? Just what you and I would do, of course; he smiled back at the baby. Soon he struck up a conversation with the woman about her baby and his grandchildren, and soon the entire reception room joined in, and the boredom and tension were converted into a pleasant and enjoyable experience.'

An insincere grin? No. That doesn't fool anybody. We know it is mechanical and we resent it. I am talking about a real smile, a heartwarming smile, a smile that comes from within, the kind of smile that will bring a good price in the marketplace.

The effect of a smile is powerful—even when it is unseen.

You must have a good time meeting people if you expect them to have a good time meeting you.

I have asked thousands of business people to smile at someone every hour of the day for a week and then come to class and talk about the results. How did it work? Let's see... Here is a letter from William B. Steinhardt, a New York stockbroker. His case isn't isolated. In fact, it is typical of hundreds of cases.

'I have been married for over eighteen years,' he wrote.

Mr Steinhardt, 'and in all that time I seldom smiled at my wife or spoke two dozen words to her from the time I got up until I was ready to leave for business. I was one of the worst grouches who ever walked down Broadway.'

'When you asked me to make a talk about my experience with smiles, I thought I would try it for a week. So the next morning, while combing my hair, I looked at my glum mug in the mirror and said to myself, "Bill, you are going to wipe the scowl off that sour puss of yours today. You are going to smile. And you are going to begin right now." As I sat down to breakfast, I greeted my wife with a "Good morning, my dear," and smiled as I said it.

'You warned me that she might be surprised. Well, you underestimated her reaction. She was bewildered. She was shocked. I told her that in the future she could expect this as a regular occurrence, and I kept it up every morning.

'This changed attitude of mine brought more happiness into our home in the two months since I started than there was during the last year.

'As I leave for my office, I greet the elevator operator in the apartment house with a "Good morning" and a smile. I greet the doorman with a smile. I smile at the cashier in the subway booth when I ask for change. As I stand on the floor of the Stock Exchange, I smile at people who until recently never saw me smile.

'I soon found that everybody was smiling back at me. I treat those who come to me with complaints or grievances in a cheerful manner. I smile as I listen to them and I find that adjustments are accomplished much easier. I find that smiles are bringing me dollars, many dollars every day.'

Everybody in the world is seeking happiness—and there is one sure way to find it. That is by controlling your thoughts. Happiness doesn't depend on outward conditions. It depends on inner conditions.

The ancient Chinese were a wise lot—wise in the ways of the world; and they had a proverb that you and I ought to cut out and paste inside our hats. It goes like this: 'A man without a smiling face must not open a shop.'

Your smile is a messenger of your goodwill. Your smile brightens the lives of all who see it. To someone who has seen a dozen people frown, scowl or turn their faces away, your smile is like the sun breaking through the clouds. Especially when that someone is under pressure from his bosses, his customers, his teachers or parents or children, a smile can help him realize that all is not hopeless—that there is joy in the world.

Rule 14: A smile is the best ornament you can wear.

It was only a sunny smile, and little it cost in the giving, but like morning light it scattered the night and made the day worth living.
—F. Scott Fitzgerald

Be sympathetic with the other person's ideas and desires.
—Dale Carnegie

15

IF YOU DON'T DO THIS, YOU ARE
HEADED FOR TROUBLE

I once interviewed Jim Farley and asked him the secret of his success. He said, 'Hard work,' and I said, 'don't be funny.'

He then asked me what I thought was the reason for his success. I replied: 'I understand you can call ten thousand people by their first names.'

'No. You are wrong,' he said. 'I can call fifty thousand people by their first names.'

Make no mistake about it. That ability helped Mr Farley put Franklin D. Roosevelt in the White House when he managed Roosevelt's campaign in 1932.

During the years that Jim Farley travelled as a salesman for a gypsum concern, and during the years that he held office as town clerk in Stony Point, he built up a system for remembering names.

In the beginning, it was a very simple one. Whenever he met a new acquaintance, he found out his or her complete name and some facts about his or her family, business and political opinions. He fixed all these facts well in mind as part of the picture, and the next time he met that person, even if it was a year later, he was able to shake hands, inquire after the family, and ask about the hollyhocks in the backyard. No wonder he developed a following!

For months before Roosevelt's campaign for President began, Jim Farley wrote hundreds of letters a day to people all over the western and northwestern states. Then he hopped onto a train and in 19 days covered 20 states and 12,000 miles, travelling by buggy, train, automobile and boat. He would drop into town to meet his people at lunch or breakfast, tea or dinner, and give them a 'heart-to-heart talk'. Then he'd dash off again on another leg of his journey.

As soon as he arrived back East, he wrote to one person in each town he had visited, asking for a list of all the guests to whom he had talked. The final list contained thousands and thousands of names: yet each person on that list was paid the subtle flattery of getting a personal letter from James Farley. These letters began 'Dear Bill' or 'Dear Jane,' and they were always signed 'Jim'.

Jim Farley discovered early in life that the average person is more interested in his or her own name than in all the other names on earth put together. Remember that name and call it easily, and you have paid a subtle and very effective compliment. But forget it or misspell it—and you have placed yourself at a sharp disadvantage. For example, I once organized a public-speaking course in Paris and sent form letters to all the American residents in the city. French typists with apparently little knowledge of English filled in the names and naturally they made blunders. One man, the manager of a large American bank in Paris, wrote me a scathing rebuke because his name had been misspelled.

Sometimes it is difficult to remember a name, particularly if it is hard to pronounce. Rather than even try to learn it, many people ignore it or call the person by an easy nickname. Sid Levy called on a customer for some time whose name was Nicodemus Papadoulos. Most people just called him 'Nick.' Levy told us: 'I made a special effort to say his name over several times to myself before I made my call. When I greeted him by his full name: "Good afternoon, Mr Nicodemus Papadoulos," he was shocked. For what seemed like several minutes there was no reply from him at all. Finally, he said with tears rolling down his cheeks, "Mr Levy, in all the fifteen years I have been in this country, nobody has ever made the effort to call me by my right name."'

People are so proud of their names that they strive to perpetuate them at any cost. Even blustering, hard-boiled old P.T. Barnum, the greatest showman of his time, disappointed because he had no sons to carry on his name, offered his grandson, C.H. Seeley, $25,000 dollars if he would call himself 'Barnum' Seeley.

For many centuries, nobles and magnates supported artists, musicians and authors so that their creative works would be dedicated to them.

Libraries and museums owe their richest collections to people who cannot bear to think that their names might perish from the memory of the race. The New York Public Library has its Astor and Lenox collections. The Metropolitan Museum perpetuates the names of Benjamin Altman and J.P. Morgan. And nearly every church is beautified by stained-glass windows commemorating the names of their donors. Many of the buildings on the campus of most universities bear the names of donors who contributed large sums of money for this honour.

Most people don't remember names, for the simple reason that they don't take the time and energy necessary to concentrate and repeat and fix names indelibly in their minds. They make excuses for themselves; they are too busy.

But they were probably no busier than Franklin D. Roosevelt, and he took time to remember and recall even the names of mechanics with whom he came into contact. Roosevelt knew that one of the simplest, most obvious and most important ways of gaining goodwill was by remembering names and making people feel important—yet how many of us do it?

Half the time we are introduced to a stranger, we chat a few minutes and can't even remember his or her name by the time we say goodbye.

Napoleon the Third, Emperor of France and nephew of the great Napoleon, boasted that in spite of all his royal duties he could remember the name of every person he met.

His technique? Simple. If he didn't hear the name distinctly, he said, 'So sorry. I didn't get the name clearly.' Then, if it was an unusual name, he would say, 'How is it spelled?'

During the conversation, he took the trouble to repeat the name several times, and tried to associate it in his mind with the person's features, expression and general appearance.

If the person was someone of importance, Napoleon went to even further pains. As soon as His Royal Highness was alone, he wrote the name down on a piece of paper, looked at it, concentrated on it, fixed it securely in his mind and then tore up the paper. In this way, he gained an eye impression of the name as well as an ear impression.

We should be aware of the magic contained in a name and realize that this single item is wholly and completely owned by the person with whom we are dealing...and nobody else.

The name sets the individual apart; it makes him or her unique among all others. The information we are imparting or the request we are making takes on a special importance when we approach the situation with the name of the individual. From the waitress to the senior executive, the name will work magic as we deal with others.

Rule 15: A person's name is the sweetest and most important sound in any language to him or her.

A single day is enough to make us a little larger or,
another time, a little smaller.
—Paul Klee

Everybody in the world is seeking happiness—and there is one sure way
to find it. That is by controlling your thoughts. Happiness doesn't depend
on outward conditions. It depends on inward conditions.
—Dale Carnegie

16

BECOME A GOOD CONVERSATIONALIST

Some time ago, I attended a bridge party. I don't play bridge—and there was a woman there who didn't play bridge either. She had discovered that I had once been Lowell Thomas's manager before he went on the radio and that I had travelled in Europe a great deal while helping him prepare the illustrated travel talks he was then delivering. So she said: 'Oh, Mr Carnegie, I do want you to tell me about all the wonderful places you have visited and the sights you have seen.'

As we sat down on the sofa, she remarked that she and her husband had recently returned from a trip to Africa. 'Africa!' I exclaimed. 'How interesting! I've always wanted to see Africa, but I never got there except for a twenty four-hour stay once in Algiers. Tell me, did you visit the big-game country? Yes? How fortunate. I envy you. Do tell me about Africa.'

That kept her talking for 45 minutes. She never again asked me where I had been or what I had seen. She didn't want to hear me talk about my travels. All she wanted was an interested listener, so she could expand her ego and tell about where she had been.

Was she unusual? No. Many people are like that.

For example, I met a distinguished botanist at a dinner party given by a New York book publisher. I had never talked with a botanist before, and I found him fascinating. I literally sat on the edge of my chair and listened while he spoke of exotic plants and experiments in developing new forms of plant life and indoor gardens (and even told me astonishing facts about the humble potato). I had a small indoor garden of my own—and he was good enough to tell me how to solve some of my problems.

As I said, we were at a dinner party. There must have been a dozen other guests, but I violated all the canons of courtesy, ignored everyone else and talked for hours to the botanist.

Midnight came. I said good night to everyone and departed. The botanist then turned to our host and paid me several flattering compliments. I was 'most stimulating'. I was this and I was that, and he ended by saying I was a 'most interesting conversationalist'.

An interesting conversationalist? Why, I had said hardly anything at all. I couldn't have said anything if I had wanted to without changing the subject, for I didn't know any more about botany than I knew about the anatomy of a penguin. But I had done this: I had listened intently. I had listened because I was genuinely interested. And he felt it. Naturally that pleased him. That kind of listening is one of the highest compliments we can pay anyone. 'Few human beings,' wrote Jack Woodford in Strangers in Love, 'few human beings are proof against the implied flattery of rapt attention.' I went even further than giving him rapt attention. I was 'hearty in my approbation and lavish in my praise.'

Listening is just as important in one's home life as in the world of business. Millie Esposito of Croton-on- Hudson, New York, made it her business to listen carefully when one of her children wanted to speak with her. One evening she was sitting in the kitchen with her son, Robert, and after a brief discussion of something that was on his mind, Robert said: 'Mom, I know that you love me very much.'

Mrs Esposito was touched and said: 'Of course I love you very much. Did you doubt it?'

Robert responded: 'No, but I really know you love me because whenever I want to talk to you about something you stop whatever you are doing and listen to me.'

One morning years ago, an angry customer stormed into the office of Julian F. Detmer, founder of the Detmer Woollen Company, which later became the world's largest distributor of woollens to the tailoring trade.

'This man owed us a small sum of money,' Mr Detmer explained to me. 'The customer denied it, but we knew he was wrong. So our credit department had insisted that he pay. After getting a number of letters from our credit department, he packed his grip, made a trip to Chicago, and hurried into my office to inform me not only that he was not going to pay that bill, but that he was never going to buy another dollar's worth of goods from the Detmer Woollen Company.

'I listened patiently to all he had to say. I was tempted to interrupt, but I realized that would be bad policy. So I let him talk himself out. When he finally simmered down and got in a receptive mood, I said quietly: "I want to thank you for coming to Chicago to tell me about this. You have done me a great favour, for if our credit department has annoyed you, it may annoy other good customers, and that would be just too bad. Believe me, I am far more eager to hear this than you are to tell it."

'That was the last thing in the world he expected me to say. I think he was a trifle disappointed, because he had come to Chicago to tell me a thing or two, but here I was thanking him instead of scrapping with him. I assured him we would wipe the charge off the books and forget it, because he was a very careful man with only one account to look after, while our clerks had to look after thousands. Therefore, he was less likely to be wrong than we were.

'I told him that I understood exactly how he felt and that, if I were in his shoes, I should undoubtedly feel precisely as he did. Since he wasn't going to buy from us anymore, I recommended some other woollen houses.

'In the past, we had usually lunched together when he came to Chicago, so I invited him to have lunch with me this day. He accepted reluctantly, but when we came back to the office he placed a larger order than ever before. He returned home in a softened mood and, wanting to be just as fair with us as we had been with him, looked over his bills, found one had been mislaid, and sent us a cheque with his apologies.

'Later, when his wife presented him with a baby boy, he gave his son the middle name of Detmer, and he remained a friend and customer of the house until his death twenty-two years afterwards.'

Remember that the people you are talking to are a hundred times more interested in themselves and their wants and problems than they are in you and your problems. A person's toothache means more to that person than a famine in China which kills a million people. A boil on one's neck interests one more than 40 earthquakes in Africa. Think of that the next time you start a conversation.

Rule 16: Be a good listener.

You must not ever stop being whimsical. And you must not, ever, give anyone else the responsibility for your life.
—Mary Oliver

Feeling sorry for yourself, and your present condition, is not only a waste of energy but the worst habit you could possibly have.
—Dale Carnegie

17

HOW TO INTEREST PEOPLE

Everyone who was ever a guest of Theodore Roosevelt was astonished at the range and diversity of his knowledge. Whether his visitor was a cowboy or a Rough Rider, a New York politician or a diplomat, Roosevelt knew what to say. And how was it done? The answer was simple. Whenever Roosevelt expected a visitor, he sat up late the night before, reading up on the subject in which he knew his guest was particularly interested.

For Roosevelt knew, as all leaders know, that the royal road to a person's heart is to talk about the things he or she treasures most.

As I write this chapter, I have before me a letter from Edward L. Chalif, who was active in Boy Scout work.

'One day I found I needed a favor,' wrote Mr Chalif. 'A big Scout jamboree was coming off in Europe, and I wanted the president of one of the largest corporations in America to pay the expenses of one of my boys for the trip.

'Fortunately, just before I went to see this man, I heard that he had drawn a cheque for a million dollars, and that after it was cancelled, he had it framed.

'So the first thing I did when I entered his office was to ask to see the cheque. A cheque for a million dollars! I told him I never knew that anybody had ever written such a cheque, and that I wanted to tell my boys that I had actually seen a cheque for a million dollars. He gladly showed it to me; I admired it and asked him to tell me all about how it happened to be drawn.'

You notice, don't you, that Mr Chalif didn't begin by talking about the Boy Scouts, or the jamboree in Europe, or what it was he wanted? He talked in terms of what interested the other man. Here's the result:

'Presently, the man I was interviewing said: "Oh, by the way, what was it you wanted to see me about?" So I told him.

'To my vast surprise,' Mr Chalif continues, 'he not only granted immediately what I asked for, but much more. I had asked him to send only one boy to Europe, but he sent five boys and myself, gave me a letter of credit for a thousand dollars and told us to stay in Europe for seven weeks. He also gave me letters of introduction to his branch presidents, putting them at our service, and he himself met us in Paris and showed us the town. Since then, he has given jobs to some of the boys whose parents were in want, and he is still active in our group.

'Yet I know if I hadn't found out what he was interested in, and got him warmed up first, I wouldn't have found him one-tenth as easy to approach.'

Rule 17: Talk in relation to the other person's interests.

When we give cheerfully and accept gratefully, everyone is blessed.
—Maya Angelou

18

HOW TO MAKE PEOPLE LIKE YOU INSTANTLY

I was waiting in line to register a letter in the post office at Thirty-third Street and Eighth Avenue in New York. I noticed that the clerk appeared to be bored with the job—weighing envelopes, handing out stamps, making change, issuing receipts—the same monotonous grind year after year. So I said to myself: 'I am going to try to make that clerk like me. Obviously to make him like me, I must say something nice, not about myself, but about him. So I asked myself, "What is there about him that I can honestly admire?"' That is sometimes a hard question to answer, especially with strangers; but, in this case, it happened to be easy. I instantly saw something I admired no end.

So while he was weighing my envelope, I remarked with enthusiasm: 'I wish I had your head of hair.'

He looked up, half-startled, his face beaming with smiles. 'Well, it isn't as good as it used to be,' he said modestly. I assured him that although it might have lost some of its pristine glory, nevertheless it was still magnificent. He was immensely pleased. We carried on a pleasant little conversation and the last thing he said to me was: 'Many people have admired my hair.'

I'll bet that person went to lunch that day walking on air. I'll bet he went home that night and told his wife about it. I'll bet he looked in the mirror and said: 'It is a beautiful head of hair.'

I told this story once in public and a man asked me afterwards: 'What did you want to get out of him?'

What was I trying to get out of him!!! What was I trying to get out of him!!!

If we are so contemptibly selfish that we can't radiate a little happiness and pass on a bit of honest appreciation without trying to get something out of the other person in return—if our souls are no bigger than sour crab apples, we shall meet with the failure we so richly deserve.

Oh yes, I did want something out of that chap. I wanted something priceless. And I got it. I got the feeling that I had done something for him without his being able to do anything whatever in return for me. That is a feeling that flows and sings in your memory long after the incident is past.

There is one all-important law of human conduct. If we obey that law, we shall almost never get into trouble. In fact, that law will bring us countless friends and constant happiness. The law is this: Always make the other person feel important.

So let's obey the Golden Rule, and give unto others what we would have others give unto us.

How? When? Where? The answer is: All the time, everywhere.

David G. Smith of Eau Claire, Wisconsin, told one of our classes how he handled a delicate situation when he was asked to take charge of the refreshment booth at a charity concert.

'The night of the concert I arrived at the park and found two elderly ladies in a very bad humour standing next to the refreshment stand. Apparently each thought that she was in charge of this project. As I stood there pondering what to do, one of the members of the sponsoring committee appeared and handed me a cash box and thanked me for taking over the project. She introduced Rose and Jane as my helpers and then ran off.

'A great silence ensued. Realizing that the cash box was a symbol of authority (of sorts), I gave the box to Rose and explained that I might not be able to keep the money straight and that if she took care of it I would feel better. I then suggested to Jane that she show two teenagers who had been assigned to refreshments how to operate the soda machine, and asked her to be responsible for that part of the project.

'The whole evening was very enjoyable with Rose happily

counting the money, Jane supervising the teenagers, and me enjoying the concert.'

You don't have to wait until you are ambassador to France or chairman of the Clambake Committee of your lodge before you use this philosophy of appreciation. You can work magic with it almost every day.

If, for example, the waitress brings us mashed potatoes when we have ordered French fries, let's say, 'I'm sorry to trouble you, but I prefer the French fries.' She'll probably reply, 'No trouble at all' and will be glad to change the potatoes, because we have shown respect for her.

Little phrases such as 'I'm sorry to trouble you,' 'Would you be so kind as to—?' 'Won't you please?' 'Would you mind?' 'Thank you'—little courtesies like these oil the cogs of the monotonous grind of everyday life—and incidentally, they are the hallmark of good breeding.

Rule 18: Make the other person feel important.

In the end, those who demean others only disrespect themselves.
—D.B. Harrop

First ask yourself: What is the worst that can happen? Then prepare to accept it. Then proceed to improve on the worst.
—Dale Carnegie

PART 3

19

IF YOU MUST FIND FAULT,
THIS IS THE WAY TO BEGIN

A friend of mine was a guest at the White House for a weekend during the administration of Calvin Coolidge. Drifting into the President's private office, he heard Coolidge say to one of his secretaries, 'That's a very pretty dress you are wearing this morning, and you are a very attractive young woman.'

That was probably the most effusive praise Silent Cal had ever bestowed upon a secretary in his life. It was so unusual, so unexpected, that the secretary blushed in confusion. Then Coolidge said, 'Now, don't get stuck up. I just said that to make you feel good. From now on, I wish you would be a little more careful with your punctuation.'

His method was probably a bit obvious, but the psychology was superb. It is always easier to listen to unpleasant things after we have heard some praise of our good points.

A barber lathers a man before he shaves him; and that is precisely what McKinley did back in 1896, when he was running for President. One of the prominent Republicans of that day had written a campaign speech that he felt was just a trifle better than Cicero and Patrick Henry and Daniel Webster all rolled into one. With great glee, this chap read his immortal speech aloud to McKinley. The speech had its fine points, but it just wouldn't do. McKinley didn't want to hurt the man's feelings. He must not kill the man's splendid enthusiasm, and yet he had to say 'no'. Note how adroitly he did it.

'My friend, that is a splendid speech, a magnificent speech,' McKinley said. 'No one could have prepared a better one. There are many occasions on which it would be precisely the right thing to say, but is it quite suitable to this particular occasion? Sound and sober as it is from your standpoint, I must consider its effect from the party's standpoint. Now go home and write a speech along the lines I indicate, and send me a copy of it.'

He did just that. McKinley blue-pencilled and helped him rewrite his second speech, and he became one of the effective speakers of the campaign.

Dorothy Wrublewski, a branch manager of the Fort Monmouth, New Jersey, Federal Credit Union, reported to one of our classes how she was able to help one of her employees become more productive.

'We recently hired a young lady as a teller trainee. Her contact with our customers was very good. She was accurate and efficient in handling individual transactions. The problem developed at the end of the day when it was time to balance out.

'The head teller came to me and strongly suggested that I fire this woman. "She is holding up everyone else because she is so slow in balancing out. I've shown her over and over, but she can't get it. She's got to go."

The next day I observed her working quickly and accurately when handling the normal everyday transactions, and she was very pleasant with our customers.

'It didn't take long to discover why she had trouble balancing out. After the office closed, I went over to talk with her. She was obviously nervous and upset. I praised her for being so friendly and outgoing with the customers and complimented her for the accuracy and speed used in that work. I then suggested we review the procedure we use in balancing the cash drawer. Once she realized I had confidence in her, she easily followed my suggestions and soon mastered this function. We have had no problems with her since then.'

Beginning with praise is like the dentist who begins his work with Novocain. The patient still gets a drilling, but the Novocain is pain-killing.

Rule 19: Begin with praise.

It is easier to be critical than correct.

—Benjamin Disraeli

20

HOW TO CRITICIZE—AND NOT BE HATED FOR IT

Charles Schwab was passing through one of his steel mills one day at noon when he came across some of his employees smoking. Immediately above their heads was a sign that said 'No Smoking'. Did Schwab point to the sign and say, 'Can't you read?' Oh no, not Schwab. He walked over to the men, handed each one a cigar, and said, 'I'll appreciate it, boys, if you will smoke these on the outside.' They knew that he knew that they had broken a rule—and they admired him because he said nothing about it and gave them a little present and made them feel important. Couldn't keep from loving a man like that, could you?

Public officials are often criticized for not being accessible to their constituents. They are busy people, and the fault sometimes lies in overprotective assistants who don't want to overburden their bosses with too many visitors. Carl Langford, who has been mayor of Orlando, Florida, the home of Disney World, for many years, frequently admonished his staff to allow people to see him. He claimed he had an 'open-door' policy; yet the citizens of his community were blocked by secretaries and administrators when they called.

Finally the mayor found the solution. He removed the door from his office! His aides got the message, and the mayor has had a truly open administration since the day his door was symbolically thrown away.

Simply changing one three-letter word can often spell the difference between failure and success in changing people without giving offence or arousing resentment.

Many people begin their criticism with sincere praise followed by the word 'but' and ending with a critical statement. For example, in trying to change a child's careless attitude toward studies, we might say, 'We're really proud of you, Johnnie, for raising your grades this term. But if you had worked harder on your algebra, the results would have been better.'

In this case, Johnnie might feel encouraged until he heard the word 'but'. He might then question the sincerity of the original praise. To him, the praise seemed only to be a contrived lead-in to a critical inference of failure. Credibility would be strained, and we probably would not achieve our objectives of changing Johnnie's attitude toward his studies.

This could be easily overcome by changing the word 'but' to 'and'. 'We're really proud of you, Johnnie, for raising your grades this term, and by continuing the same conscientious efforts next term, your algebra grade can be up with all the others.'

Now, Johnnie would accept the praise because there was no follow-up of an inference of failure. We have called his attention to the behaviour we wished to change indirectly, and the chances are he will try to live up to our expectations.

Calling attention to one's mistakes indirectly works wonders with sensitive people who may resent bitterly any direct criticism. Marge Jacob of Woonsocket, Rhode Island, told one of our classes how she convinced some sloppy construction workers to clean up after themselves when they were building additions to her house.

For the first few days of the work, when Mrs Jacob returned from her job, she noticed that the yard was strewn with the cut ends of lumber. She didn't want to antagonize the builders, because they did excellent work. So after the workers had gone home, she and her children picked up and neatly piled all the lumber debris in a corner. The following morning she called the foreman to one side and said, 'I'm really pleased with the way the front lawn was left last night; it is nice and clean and does not offend the neighbours.' From that day forward the workers picked up and piled the debris to one side, and the foreman came in each day seeking approval of the condition the lawn was left in after a day's work.

An effective way to correct others' mistakes is...

Rule 20: Call attention to people's mistakes indirectly.

Criticism is something we can avoid easily by saying nothing, doing nothing, and being nothing.

—Aristotle

Flaming enthusiasm, backed up by horse sense and persistence, is the quality that most frequently makes for success.

—Dale Carnegie

21

TALK ABOUT YOUR OWN MISTAKES FIRST

My niece, Josephine Carnegie, had come to New York to be my secretary. She was nineteen, had graduated from high school three years previously, and her business experience was a trifle more than zero. She became one of the most proficient secretaries west of Suez, but in the beginning, she was—well, susceptible to improvement. One day when I started to criticize her, I said to myself: 'Just a minute, Dale Carnegie; just a minute. You are twice as old as Josephine. You have had ten thousand times as much business experience. How can you possibly expect her to have your viewpoint, your judgement, your initiative—mediocre though they may be? And just a minute, Dale, what were you doing at nineteen? Remember the asinine mistakes and blunders you made? Remember the time you did this... and that...?'

After thinking the matter over, honestly and impartially, I concluded that Josephine's batting average at nineteen was better than mine had been—and that, I'm sorry to confess, isn't paying Josephine much of a compliment.

So after that, when I wanted to call Josephine's attention to a mistake, I used to begin by saying, 'You have made a mistake, Josephine, but the Lord knows, it's no worse than many I have made. You were not born with judgement. That comes only with experience, and you are better than I was at your age. I have been guilty of so many stupid, silly things myself, I have very little inclination to criticize you or anyone. But don't you think it would have been wiser if you had done so and so?'

It isn't nearly so difficult to listen to a recital of your faults if the person criticizing begins by humbly admitting that he, too, is far from impeccable.

Admitting one's own mistakes—even when one hasn't corrected them—can help convince somebody to change his behaviour. This was illustrated more recently by Clarence Zerhusen of Timonium, Maryland, when he discovered his fifteen-year-old son was experimenting with cigarettes.

'Naturally, I didn't want David to smoke,' Mr Zerhusen told us, 'but his mother and I smoked cigarettes; we were giving him a bad example all the time. I explained to Dave how I started smoking at about his age and how the nicotine had gotten the best of me and now it was nearly impossible for me to stop. I reminded him how irritating my cough was and how he had been after me to give up cigarettes not many years before.

'I didn't exhort him to stop or make threats or warn him about their dangers. All I did was point out how I was hooked on cigarettes and what it had meant to me.

'He thought about it for a while and decided he wouldn't smoke until he had graduated from high school. As the years went by David never did start smoking and has no intention of ever doing so.

'As a result of that conversation I made the decision to stop smoking cigarettes myself, and with the support of my family, I have succeeded.'

A good leader follows this principle:

Rule 21: Before criticizing the other person, talk about your own mistakes.

If you have no critics you'll likely have no success.
—Malcolm X

If only the people who worry about their liabilities would think about the riches they do possess, they would stop worrying.
—Dale Carnegie

22

NO ONE LIKES TO TAKE ORDERS

I once had the pleasure of dining with Miss Ida Tarbell, the dean of American biographers. When I told her I was writing this book, we began discussing this all-important subject of getting along with people, and she told me that while she was writing her biography of Owen D. Young, she interviewed a man who had sat for three years in the same office with Mr Young. This man declared that during all that time he had never heard Owen D. Young give a direct order to anyone. He always gave suggestions, not orders. Owen D. Young never said, for example, 'Do this or do that' or 'Don't do this or don't do that'. He would say, 'You might consider this' or 'Do you think that would work?' Frequently he would say, after he had dictated a letter, 'What do you think of this?' In looking over a letter of one of his assistants, he would say, 'Maybe if we were to phrase it this way it would be better.' He always gave people the opportunity to do things themselves; he never told his assistants to do things; he let them do them, let them learn from their mistakes.

A technique like that makes it easy for a person to correct errors. A technique like that saves a person's pride and gives him or her a feeling of importance. It encourages cooperation instead of rebellion.

Resentment caused by a brash order may last a long time—even if the order was given to correct an obviously bad situation. Dan Santarelli, a teacher at a vocational school in Wyoming, Pennsylvania, told one of our classes how one of his students had blocked the entrance way to one of the school's shops by illegally parking his car in it. One of the other instructors stormed into the classroom and asked in an arrogant tone, 'Whose car is blocking the driveway?' When the student who owned the car responded, the instructor screamed: 'Move that car and move it right now, or I'll wrap a chain around it and drag it out of there.'

Now that student was wrong. The car should not have been parked there. But from that day on, not only did that student resent the instructor's action, but all the students in the class did everything they could to give the instructor a hard time and make his job unpleasant.

How could he have handled it differently? If he had asked in a friendly way, 'Whose car is in the driveway?' and then suggested that if it were moved, other cars could get in and out, the student would have gladly moved it and neither he nor his classmates would have been upset and resentful.

Asking questions not only makes an order more palatable; it often stimulates the creativity of the persons whom you ask. People are more likely to accept an order if they have had a part in the decision that caused the order to be issued.

An effective leader will use...

Rule 22: Ask questions instead of giving direct orders.

The individual must not merely wait and criticize,
he must defend the cause the best he can.
The fate of the world will be such as the world deserves.
—Albert Einstein

23

LET THE OTHER PERSON SAVE FACE

Years ago the General Electric Company was faced with the delicate task of removing Charles Steinmetz from the head of a department. Steinmetz, a genius of the first magnitude when it came to electricity, was a failure as the head of the calculating department. Yet the company didn't dare offend the man. He was indispensable—and highly sensitive. So they gave him a new title. They made him Consulting Engineer of the General Electric Company—a new title for work he was already doing—and let someone else head up the department.

Steinmetz was happy.

So were the officers of G.E. They had gently manoeuvred their most temperamental star, and they had done it without a storm—by letting him save face.

Letting one save face! How important, how vitally important that is! And how few of us ever stop to think of it! We ride roughshod over the feelings of others, getting our own way, finding fault, issuing threats, criticizing a child or an employee in front of others, without even considering the hurt to the other person's pride. Whereas a few minutes' thought, a considerate word or two, a genuine understanding of the other person's attitude, would go so far toward alleviating the sting!

Let's remember that the next time we are faced with the distasteful necessity of discharging or reprimanding an employee.

'Firing employees is not much fun. Getting fired is even less fun.' (I'm quoting now from a letter written me by Marshall A. Granger, a certified public accountant.) 'Our business is mostly seasonal.

Therefore we have to let a lot of people go after the income tax rush is over.

'It's a byword in our profession that no one enjoys wielding the axe. Consequently, the custom has developed of getting it over as soon as possible, and usually in the following way: "Sit down, Mr Smith. The season's over, and we don't seem to see any more assignments for you. Of course, you understood you were only employed for the busy season anyhow, etc., etc."

'The effect on these people is one of disappointment and a feeling of being "let down". Most of them are in the accounting field for life, and they retain no particular love for the firm that drops them so casually.

'I recently decided to let our seasonal personnel go with a little more tact and consideration. So I call each one in only after carefully thinking over his or her work during the winter. And I've said something like this:

"Mr Smith, you've done a fine job (if he has). That time we sent you to Newark, you had a tough assignment. You were on the spot, but you came through with flying colours, and we want you to know the firm is proud of you. You've got the stuff—you're going a long way, wherever you're working. This firm believes in you, and is rooting for you, and we don't want you to forget it."

'Effect? The people go away feeling a lot better about being fired. They don't feel "let down". They know if we had work for them, we'd keep them on. And when we need them again, they come to us with a keen personal affection.'

Even if we are right and the other person is definitely wrong, we only destroy ego by causing someone to lose face. The legendary French aviation pioneer and author Antoine de Saint-Exupéry wrote: 'I have no right to say or do anything that diminishes a man in his own eyes. What matters is not what I think of him, but what he thinks of himself. Hurting a man in his dignity is a crime.'

A real leader will always follow...

Rule 23: Let the other person save face.

Even if I knew that tomorrow the world would go to pieces, I would still plant my apple tree.

—Martin Luther

If you believe in what you are doing, then let nothing hold you up in your work. Much of the best work of the world has been done against seeming impossibilities. The thing is to get the work done.

—Dale Carnegie

24

HOW TO ENCOURAGE PEOPLE

Pete Barlow was an old friend of mine. He had a dog- and-pony act and spent his life travelling with circuses and vaudeville shows. I loved to watch Pete train new dogs for his act. I noticed that the moment a dog showed the slightest improvement, Pete patted and praised him and gave him meat and made a great to do about it.

That's nothing new. Animal trainers have been using that same technique for centuries.

Why, I wonder, don't we use the same common sense when trying to change people that we use when trying to change dogs? Why don't we use meat instead of a whip? Why don't we use praise instead of condemnation? Let us praise even the slightest improvement. That inspires the other person to keep on improving.

I can look back at my own life and see where a few words of praise have sharply changed my entire future. Can't you say the same thing about your life? History is replete with striking illustrations of the sheer witchery of praise.

In the early 19th century, a young man in London aspired to be a writer. But everything seemed to be against him. He had never been able to attend school more than four years. His father had been flung in jail because he couldn't pay his debts, and this young man often knew the pangs of hunger. Finally, he got a job pasting labels on bottles of blacking in a rat-infested warehouse, and he slept at night in a dismal attic room with two other boys—guttersnipes from the slums of London. He had so little confidence in his ability to write that he sneaked out and mailed his first manuscript in the dead of night so nobody would laugh at him. Story after story was refused.

Finally the great day came when one was accepted. True, he wasn't paid a shilling for it, but one editor had praised him. One editor had given him recognition. He was so thrilled that he wandered aimlessly around the streets with tears rolling down his cheeks.

The praise, the recognition, that he received through getting one story in print, changed his whole life, for if it hadn't been for that encouragement, he might have spent his entire life working in rat-infested factories. You may have heard of that boy. His name was Charles Dickens.

Another boy in London made his living as a clerk in a dry-goods store. He had to get up at 5 a.m., sweep out the store and slave for fourteen hours a day. It was sheer drudgery and he despised it. After two years, he could stand it no longer, so he got up one morning and, without waiting for breakfast, tramped fifteen miles to talk to his mother, who was working as a housekeeper.

He was frantic. He pleaded with her. He wept. He swore he would kill himself if he had to remain in the shop any longer. Then he wrote a long, pathetic letter to his old schoolmaster, declaring that he was heartbroken, that he no longer wanted to live. His old schoolmaster gave him a little praise and assured him that he really was very intelligent and fitted for finer things and offered him a job as a teacher.

That praise changed the future of that boy and made a lasting impression on the history of English literature. For that boy went on to write innumerable best-selling books and made over a million dollars with his pen. You've probably heard of him. His name: H.G. Wells.

Let me repeat: The principles taught in this book will work only when they come from the heart. I am not advocating a bag of tricks. I am talking about a new way of life.

Talking about changing people. If you and I will inspire the people with whom we come in contact to a realization of the hidden treasures they possess, we can do far more than change people. We can literally transform them.

Exaggeration? Then listen to these sage words from William

James, one of the most distinguished psychologists and philosophers America has ever produced:

Compared with what we ought to be, we are only half awake. We are making use of only a small part of our physical and mental resources. Stating the thing broadly, the human individual thus lives far within his limits. He possesses powers of various sorts which he habitually fails to use.

Yes, you who are reading these lines possess powers of various sorts which you habitually fail to use; and one of these powers you are probably not using to the fullest extent is your magic ability to praise people and inspire them with a realization of their latent possibilities.

Abilities wither under criticism; they blossom under encouragement. To become a more effective leader of people, apply...

Rule 24: Praise every improvement.

To be in one's own heart in kindly sympathy with all things; this is the nature of righteousness.
—Confucius

25

GIVE A DOG A GOOD NAME

What do you do when a person who has been a good worker begins to turn in shoddy work? You can fire him or her, but that really doesn't solve anything. You can berate the worker, but this usually causes resentment. Henry Henke, a service manager for a large truck dealership in Lowell, Indiana, had a mechanic whose work had become less than satisfactory. Instead of bawling him out or threatening him, Mr Henke called him into his office and had a heart-to-heart talk with him.

'Bill,' he said, 'you are a fine mechanic. You have been in this line of work for a good number of years. You have repaired many vehicles to the customers' satisfaction. In fact, we've had a number of compliments about the good work you have done. Yet, of late, the time you take to complete each job has been increasing and your work has not been up to your own old standards. Because you have been such an outstanding mechanic in the past, I felt sure you would want to know that I am not happy with this situation, and perhaps jointly we could find some way to correct the problem.'

Bill responded that he hadn't realized he had been falling down in his duties and assured his boss that the work he was getting was not out of his range of expertise and he would try to improve in the future.

Did he do it? You can be sure he did. He once again became a fast and thorough mechanic. With that reputation Mr Henke had given him to live up to, how could he do anything else but turn out work comparable to that which he had done in the past.

In short, if you want to improve a person in a certain respect, act as though that particular trait were already one of his or her outstanding characteristics. Shakespeare said 'Assume a virtue, if you have it not.' And it might be well to assume and state openly that other people have the virtue you want them to develop. Give them a fine reputation to live up to, and they will make prodigious efforts rather than see you disillusioned.

Georgette Leblanc, in her book Souvenirs, My life with Maeterlinck, describes the startling transformation of a humble Belgian Cinderella.

'A servant girl from a neighbouring hotel brought my meals,' she wrote. 'She was called "Marie the Dishwasher" because she had started her career as a scullery assistant. She was a kind of monster, cross-eyed, bandy-legged, poor in flesh and spirit.

'One day, while she was holding my plate of macaroni in her red hand, I said to her point-blank, "Marie, you do not know what treasures are within you."

'Accustomed to holding back her emotion, Marie waited for a few moments, not daring to risk the slightest gesture for fear of a catastrophe. Then she put the dish on the table, sighed and said ingenuously, "Madame, I would never have believed it." She did not doubt, she did not ask a question. She simply went back to the kitchen and repeated what I had said, and such is the force of faith that no one made fun of her. From that day on, she was even given a certain consideration. But the most curious change of all occurred in the humble Marie herself. Believing she was the tabernacle of unseen marvels, she began taking care of her face and body so carefully that her starved youth seemed to bloom and modestly hide her plainness.

'Two months later, she announced her coming marriage with the nephew of the chef. "I'm going to be a lady," she said, and thanked me. A small phrase had changed her entire life.'

Georgette Leblanc had given 'Marie the Dishwasher' a reputation to live up to—and that reputation had transformed her.

If you want to excel in that difficult leadership role of changing the attitude or behaviour of others, use...

Rule 25: Give the other person a good reputation to live up to.

What distinguishes modern art from the art of other ages is criticism.

—Octavio Paz

If you can't sleep, then get up and do something instead of lying there worrying. It's the worry that gets you, not the lack of sleep.

—Dale Carnegie

26

MAKE THE FAULT SEEM EASY TO CORRECT

A bachelor friend of mine, about forty years old, became engaged, and his fiancée persuaded him to take some belated dancing lessons. 'The Lord knows I needed dancing lessons,' he confessed as he told me the story, 'for I danced just as I did when I first started twenty years ago. The first teacher I engaged probably told me the truth. She said I was all wrong; I would just have to forget everything and begin all over again. But that took the heart out of me. I had no incentive to go on. So I quit her.

'The next teacher may have been lying, but I liked it. She said nonchalantly that my dancing was a bit old-fashioned perhaps, but the fundamentals were all right, and she assured me I wouldn't have any trouble learning a few new steps. The first teacher had discouraged me by emphasizing my mistakes. This new teacher did the opposite. She kept praising the things I did right and minimizing my errors. "You have a natural sense of rhythm," she assured me. "You really are a natural-born dancer." Now my common sense tells me that I always have been and always will be a fourth-rate dancer; yet, deep in my heart, I still like to think that maybe she meant it. To be sure, I was paying her to say it; but why bring that up?

'At any rate, I know I am a better dancer than I would have been if she hadn't told me I had a natural sense of rhythm. That encouraged me. That gave me hope. That made me want to improve.'

Tell your child, your spouse or your employee that he or she is stupid or dumb at a certain thing, has no gift for it and is doing it all wrong, and you have destroyed almost every incentive to try to improve. But use the opposite technique—be liberal with your encouragement, make the thing seem easy to do, let the other person know that you have faith in his ability to do it, that he has an undeveloped flair for it—and he will practise until the dawn comes in the window in order to excel.

Rule 26: Use encouragement.

Act enthusiastic and you will be enthusiastic.
—Dale Carnegie

27

MAKING PEOPLE GLAD TO DO WHAT YOU WANT

The effective leader should keep the following guidelines in mind when it is necessary to change attitudes or behavior of people:

1. Be sincere. Do not promise anything that you cannot deliver. Forget about the benefits to yourself and concentrate on the benefits to the other person.
2. Know exactly what it is you want the other person to do.
3. Be empathetic. Ask yourself what is it the other person really wants.
4. Consider the benefits that person will receive from doing what you suggest.
5. Match those benefits to the other person's wants.
6. When you make your request, put it in a form that will convey to the other person the idea that he personally will benefit. We could give a curt order like this: 'John, we have customers coming in tomorrow and I need the stockroom cleaned out. So sweep it out, put the stock in neat piles on the shelves and polish the counter.' Or we could express the same idea by showing John the benefits he will get from doing the task: 'John, we have a job that should be completed right away. If it is done now, we won't be faced with it later. I am bringing some customers in tomorrow to show our facilities. I would like to show them the stockroom, but it is in poor shape. If you could sweep it out, put the stock in neat piles on the shelves and polish the counter, it would make us look efficient and you will have done your part to provide a good company image.'

Will John be happy about doing what you suggest? Probably not very happy, but happier than if you had not pointed out the benefits. Assuming you know that John has pride in the way stockroom looks and is interested in contributing to the company image, he will be more likely to be cooperative. It also will have been pointed out to John that the job would have to be done eventually and by doing it now, he won't be faced with it later.

It is naïve to believe you will always get a favourable reaction from other persons when you use these approaches, but the experience of most people shows that you are more likely to change attitudes this way than by not using these principles—and if you increase your success by even a mere 10 per cent, you have become 10 per cent more effective as a leader than you were before—and that is your benefit.

People are more likely to do what you would like them to do when you use...

Rule 27: Make the other person happy about doing whatever you suggest.

Let us be grateful to people who make us happy,
they are the charming gardeners who make our souls blossom.
—Marcel Proust

PART 4

28

THINK BEFORE YOU CRITICIZE

On 7 May 1931, the most sensational manhunt New York City had ever known had come to its climax. After weeks of search, 'Two Gun' Crowley—the killer, the gunman who didn't smoke or drink—was at bay, trapped in his sweetheart's apartment on West End Avenue.

One hundred and fifty policemen and detectives laid siege to his top-floor hideaway. They chopped holes in the roof; they tried to smoke out Crowley, the 'cop killer', with teargas. Then they mounted their machine guns on surrounding buildings, and for more than an hour one of New York's fine residential areas reverberated with the crack of pistol fire and the rat-tat-tat of machine guns. Crowley, crouching behind an overstuffed chair, fired incessantly at the police. Ten thousand excited people watched the battle. Nothing like it had ever been seen before on the sidewalks of New York.

When Crowley was captured, Police Commissioner E.P. Mulrooney declared that the two-gun desperado was one of the most dangerous criminals ever encountered in the history of New York. 'He will kill,' said the Commissioner, 'at the drop of a feather.'

But how did 'Two Gun' Crowley regard himself? We know, because while the police were firing into his apartment, he wrote a letter addressed 'To whom it may concern.' And, as he wrote, the blood flowing from his wounds left a crimson trail on the paper. In this letter Crowley said: 'Under my coat is a weary heart, but a kind one—one that would do nobody any harm.'

A short time before this, Crowley had been having a necking party with his girlfriend on a country road out on Long Island. Suddenly a policeman walked up to the car and said: 'Let me see your licence.'

Without saying a word, Crowley drew his gun and cut the policeman down with a shower of lead. As the dying officer fell, Crowley leapt out of the car, grabbed the officer's revolver and fired another bullet into the prostrate body. And that was the killer who said: 'Under my coat is a weary heart, but a kind one—one that would do nobody any harm.'

Crowley was sentenced to the electric chair. When he arrived at the death house in Sing Sing, did he say, 'This is what I get for killing people'? No, he said: 'This is what I get for defending myself.'

The point of the story is this: 'Two Gun' Crowley didn't blame himself for anything.

If 'Two Gun' Crowley or the desperate men and women behind prison walls don't blame themselves for anything—what about the people with whom you and I come in contact?

John Wanamaker, founder of the American stores that bear his name, once confessed: 'I learned thirty years ago that it is foolish to scold. I have enough trouble overcoming my own limitations without fretting over the fact that God has not seen fit to distribute evenly the gift of intelligence.'

Wanamaker learnt this lesson early, but I personally had to blunder through this old world for a third of a century before it even began to dawn upon me that ninety-nine times out of a hundred, people don't criticize themselves for anything no matter how wrong it may be.

Criticism is futile because it puts a person on the defensive and usually makes him strive to justify himself. Criticism is dangerous, because it wounds a person's precious pride, hurts his sense of importance and arouses resentment.

B.F. Skinner, the world-famous psychologist, proved through his experiments that an animal rewarded for good behaviour will learn much more rapidly and retain what it learns far more effectively than an animal punished for bad behaviour. Later studies have shown that the same applies to humans. By criticizing, we do not make lasting changes and often incur resentment.

There you are; human nature in action, wrongdoers, blaming everybody but themselves. We are all like that. So when you and I are tempted to criticize someone tomorrow, let's remember 'Two Gun' Crowley. Let's realize that criticisms are like homing pigeons. They always return home. Let's realize that the person we are going to correct and condemn will probably justify himself or herself, and condemn us in return; or, like the gentle Taft, will say: 'I don't see how I could have done any differently from what I have.'

Mark Twain lost his temper occasionally and wrote letters that turned the paper brown. For example, he once wrote to a man who had aroused his ire: 'The thing for you is a burial permit. You have only to speak and I will see that you get it.' On another occasion he wrote to an editor about a proofreader's attempts to 'improve my spelling and punctuation.' He ordered: 'Set the matter according to my copy hereafter and see that the proofreader retains his suggestions in the mush of his decayed brain.'

The writing of these stinging letters made Mark Twain feel better. They allowed him to blow off steam, and the letters didn't do any real harm, because Mark's wife secretly lifted them out of the mail. They were never sent. When dealing with people, let us remember we are not dealing with creatures of logic. We are dealing with creatures of emotion, creatures bristling with prejudices and motivated by pride and vanity.

Bitter criticism caused the sensitive Thomas Hardy, one of the finest novelists ever to enrich English literature, to give up forever the writing of fiction. Criticism drove Thomas Chatterton, the English poet, to suicide.

Rule 28: Don't condemn, complain or criticize.

You never have to change anything you
got up in the middle of the night to write.
—Saul Bellow

29

THE BIG SECRET OF DEALING WITH PEOPLE

There is only one way under high heaven to get anybody to do anything. Did you ever stop to think of that? Yes, just one way. And that is by making the other person want to do it.

Remember, there is no other way.

Of course, you can make someone want to give you his watch by sticking a revolver in his ribs. You can make your employees give you cooperation—until your back is turned—by threatening to fire them. You can make a child do what you want it to do by a whip or a threat. But these crude methods have sharply undesirable repercussions.

The only way I can get you to do anything is by giving you what you want.

What do you want?

Sigmund Freud said that everything you and I do springs from two motives: the sex urge and the desire to be great.

John Dewey, one of America's most profound philosophers, phrased it a bit differently. Dr Dewey said that the deepest urge in human nature is 'the desire to be important'. Remember that phrase: 'the desire to be important.' It is significant. You are going to hear a lot about it in this book.

What do you want? Not many things, but the few things that you do wish, you crave with an insistence that will not be denied. Some of the things most people want include:

1. Health and the preservation of life.
2. Food.
3. Sleep.

4. Money and the things money will buy.
5. Life in the hereafter.
6. Sexual gratification.
7. The well-being of our children.
8. A feeling of importance.

Almost all these wants are usually gratified—all except one. But there is one longing—almost as deep, almost as imperious, as the desire for food or sleep—which is seldom gratified. It is what Freud calls 'the desire to be great'. It is what Dewey calls the 'desire to be important'.

The desire for a feeling of importance is one of the chief distinguishing differences between mankind and the animals. It was this desire for a feeling of importance that led an uneducated, poverty-stricken grocery clerk to study some law books he found in the bottom of a barrel of household plunder that he had bought for fifty cents. You have probably heard of this grocery clerk. His name was Lincoln.

It was this desire for a feeling of importance that inspired Dickens to write his immortal novels. This desire inspired Sir Christopher Wren to design his symphonies in stone. This desire made Rockefeller amass millions that he never spent! And this same desire made the richest family in your town build a house far too large for its requirements.

This desire makes you want to wear the latest styles, drive the latest cars and talk about your brilliant children.

It is this desire that lures many boys and girls into joining gangs and engaging in criminal activities. The average young criminal, according to E.P. Mulrooney, one-time police commissioner of New York, is filled with ego, and his first request after arrest is for those lurid newspapers that make him out a hero. The disagreeable prospect of serving time seems remote so long as he can gloat over his likeness sharing space with pictures of sports figures, movie and TV stars and politicians.

History sparkles with amusing examples of famous people

struggling for a feeling of importance. Even George Washington wanted to be called 'His Mightiness, the President of the United States'; and Columbus pleaded for the title 'Admiral of the Ocean and Viceroy of India'. Catherine the Great refused to open letters that were not addressed to 'Her Imperial Majesty'; and

Mrs Lincoln, in the White House, turned upon Mrs Grant like a tigress and shouted, 'How dare you be seated in my presence until I invite you!'

Our millionaires helped finance Admiral Byrd's expedition to the Antarctic in 1928 with the understanding that ranges of icy mountains would be named after them; and Victor Hugo aspired to have nothing less than the city of Paris renamed in his honour. Even Shakespeare, mightiest of the mighty, tried to add lustre to his name by procuring a coat of arms for his family.

People sometimes become invalids in order to win sympathy and attention, and get a feeling of importance. For example, take Mrs McKinley. She got a feeling of importance by forcing her husband, the President of the United States, to neglect important affairs of state while he reclined on the bed beside her for hours at a time, his arm about her, soothing her to sleep. She fed her gnawing desire for attention by insisting that he remain with her while she was having her teeth fixed, and once created a stormy scene when he had to leave her alone with the dentist while he kept an appointment with John Hay, his secretary of state.

Some authorities declare that people may actually go insane in order to find, in the dreamland of insanity, the feeling of importance that has been denied them in the harsh world of reality. There are more patients suffering from mental diseases in the United States than from all other diseases combined.

What is the cause of insanity?

Nobody can answer such a sweeping question, but we know that certain diseases, such as syphilis, break down and destroy the brain cells and result in insanity. In fact, about one-half of all mental diseases can be attributed to such physical causes as brain lesions, alcohol, toxins and injuries. But the other half—and this is the appalling part of the story—the other half of the people who go insane apparently have nothing organically wrong with their brain cells. In post-mortem examinations, when their brain tissues are studied under the highest-powered microscopes, these tissues are found to be apparently just as healthy as yours and mine.

Why do these people go insane?

I put that question to the head physician of one of our most important psychiatric hospitals. This doctor, who has received the highest honours and the most coveted awards for his knowledge of this subject, told me frankly that he didn't know why people went insane. Nobody knows for sure. But he did say that many people who go insane find in insanity a feeling of importance that they were unable to achieve in the world of reality. Then he told me this story:

'I have a patient right now whose marriage proved to be a tragedy. She wanted love, sexual gratification, children and social prestige, but life blasted all her hopes. Her husband didn't love her. He refused even to eat with her and forced her to serve his meals in his room upstairs. She had no children, no social standing. She went insane; and, in her imagination, she divorced her husband and resumed her maiden name. She now believes she has married into English aristocracy, and she insists on being called Lady Smith.

'And as for children, she imagines now that she has had a new child every night. Each time I call on her she says: "Doctor, I had a baby last night."'

Life once wrecked all her dream ships on the sharp rocks of reality; but in the sunny, fantasy isles of insanity, all her barkentines race into port with canvas billowing and winds winging through the masts.

Tragic? Oh, I don't know. Her physician said to me: 'If I could stretch out my hand and restore her sanity, I wouldn't do it. She's much happier as she is.'

If some people are so hungry for a feeling of importance that they actually go insane to get it, imagine what miracle you and I can achieve by giving people honest appreciation this side of insanity.

I have among my clippings a story that I know never happened, but it illustrates a truth, so I'll repeat it:

According to this silly story, a farm woman, at the end of a heavy day's work, set before her menfolk a heaping pile of hay. And when they indignantly demanded whether she had gone crazy, she replied: 'Why, how did I know you'd notice? I've been cooking for you men for the last twenty years and in all that time I ain't heard no word to let me know you wasn't just eating hay.'

When a study was made a few years ago on runaway wives, what do you think was discovered to be the main reason wives ran away? It was 'lack of appreciation'. And I'd bet that a similar study made of runaway husbands would come out the same way. We often take our spouses so much for granted that we never let them know we appreciate them.

A member of one of our classes told of a request made by his wife. She and a group of other women in her church were involved in a self-improvement programme. She asked her husband to help her by listing six things he believed she could do to help her become a better wife. He reported to the class: 'I was surprised by such a request. Frankly, it would have been easy for me to list six things I would like to change about her—my heavens, she could have listed a thousand things she would like to change about me—but I didn't. I said to her, "Let me think about it and give you an answer in the morning."

'The next morning I got up very early and called the florist and had them send six red roses to my wife with a note saying: "I can't think of six things I would like to change about you. I love you the way you are."

'When I arrived at home that evening, who do you think greeted me at the door: That's right. My wife! She was almost in tears. Needless to say, I was extremely glad I had not criticized her as she had requested.

'The following Sunday at church, after she had reported the results of her assignment, several women with whom she had been studying came up to me and said, "That was the most considerate thing I have ever heard." It was then I realized the power of appreciation.'

I once succumbed to the fad of fasting and went for six days and nights without eating. It wasn't difficult. I was less hungry at the end of the sixth day than I was at the end of the second. Yet I know, as you know, people who would think they had committed a crime if they let their families or employees go for six days without food; but they will let them go for six days, and six weeks, and sometimes sixty years without giving them the hearty appreciation that they crave almost as much as they crave food.

We nourish the bodies of our children and friends and employees, but how seldom do we nourish their self-esteem? We provide them with roast beef and potatoes to build energy, but we neglect to give them kind words of appreciation that would sing in their memories for years like the music of the morning stars.

Some readers are saying right now as they read these lines: 'Oh, phooey! Flattery! Bear oil! I've tried that stuff. It doesn't work— not with intelligent people.' The difference between appreciation and flattery? That is simple. One is sincere and the other insincere. One comes from the heart out; the other from the teeth out. One is unselfish; the other selfish. One is universally admired; the other universally condemned.

King George V had a set of six maxims displayed on the walls of his study at Buckingham Palace. One of these maxims said: 'Teach me neither to proffer nor receive cheap praise.' That's all flattery is— cheap praise.

One of the most neglected virtues of our daily existence is appreciation. Somehow, we neglect to praise our son or daughter when he or she brings home a good report card, and we fail to encourage our children when they first succeed in baking a cake or building a birdhouse. Nothing pleases children more than this kind of parental interest and approval.

Try leaving a friendly trail of little sparks of gratitude on your daily trips. You will be surprised how they will set small flames of friendship that will be rose beacons on your next visit.

Pamela Dunham of New Fairfield, Connecticut, had among her responsibilities on her job the supervision of a janitor who was doing a very poor job. The other employees would jeer at him and litter the hallways to show him what a bad job he was doing. It was so bad, productive time was being lost in the shop.

Without success, Pam tried various ways to motivate this person. She noticed that occasionally he did a particularly good piece of work. She made a point to praise him for it in front of the other people. Each day the job he did all around got better, and pretty soon he started doing all his work efficiently. Now he does an excellent job and other people give him appreciation and recognition. Honest appreciation got results where criticism and ridicule failed.

Rule 29: Appreciation should be honest, not flattery.

Everyone should be respected as an individual, but no one idolized.
—Albert Einstein

If you want to be enthusiastic, act enthusiastic.
—Dale Carnegie

30

UNDERSTAND THE OTHER'S POINT OF VIEW

I often went fishing up in Maine during the summer. Personally I am very fond of strawberries and cream, but I have found that for some strange reason, fish prefer worms. So when I went fishing, I didn't think about what I wanted. I didn't bait the hook with strawberries and cream. Rather, I dangled a worm or a grasshopper in front of the fish and said: 'Wouldn't you like to have that?'

Why not use the same common sense when fishing for people? The only way on earth to influence other people is to talk about what they want and show them how to get it.

Remember that tomorrow when you are trying to get somebody to do something. If, for example, you don't want your children to smoke, don't preach at them, and don't talk about what you want; but show them that cigarettes may keep them from making the basketball team or winning the hundred-yard dash.

This is a good thing to remember regardless of whether you are dealing with children or calves or chimpanzees. For example: one day Ralph Waldo Emerson and his son tried to get a calf into the barn. But they made the common mistake of thinking only of what they wanted: Emerson pushed and his son pulled. But the calf was doing just what they were doing: he was thinking only of what he wanted; so he stiffened his legs and stubbornly refused to leave the pasture. The Irish housemaid saw their predicament. She couldn't write essays and books; but, on this occasion at least, she had more horse sense, or calf sense, than Emerson had. She thought of what the calf wanted; so she put her maternal finger in the calf's mouth and let the calf suck her finger as she gently led him into the barn.

Andrew Carnegie, the poverty-stricken Scotch lad who started to work at two cents an hour and finally gave away $365 million, learned early in life that the only way to influence people is to talk in terms of what the other person wants. He attended school only four years; yet he learnt how to handle people.

To illustrate: His sister-in-law was worried sick over her two boys. They were at Yale, and they were so busy with their own affairs that they neglected to write home and paid no attention whatever to their mother's frantic letters.

Then Carnegie offered to wager a hundred dollars that he could get an answer by return mail, without even asking for it. Someone called his bet; so he wrote his nephews a chatty letter, mentioning casually in a postscript that he was sending each one a five-dollar bill.

He neglected, however, to enclose the money.

Back came replies by return mail thanking 'Dear Uncle Andrew' for his kind note and—you can finish the sentence yourself.

Tomorrow you may want to persuade somebody to do something. Before you speak, pause and ask yourself: 'How can I make this person want to do it?'

That question will stop us from rushing into a situation heedlessly, with futile chatter about our desires.

At one time I rented the grand ballroom of a certain New York hotel for twenty nights in each season in order to hold a series of lectures.

At the beginning of one season, I was suddenly informed that I should have to pay almost three times as much rent as formerly. This news reached me after the tickets had been printed and distributed and all the announcements had been made.

Naturally, I didn't want to pay the increase, but what was the use of talking to the hotel about what I wanted? They were only interested in what they wanted. So a couple of days later I went to see the manager.

'I was a bit shocked when I got your letter,' I said, 'but I don't blame you at all. If I had been in your position, I should probably have written a similar letter myself. Your duty as the manager of the hotel is to make all the profit possible. If you don't do that you will be fired and you ought to be fired. Now, let's take a piece of paper and write down the advantages and the disadvantages that will accrue to you, if you insist on this increase in rent.'

Then I took a letterhead and ran a line through the centre and headed one column 'Advantages' and the other column 'Disadvantages'.

I wrote down under the head 'Advantages' these words: 'Ballroom free'. Then I went on to say: 'You will have the advantage of having the ballroom free to rent for dances and conventions. That is a big advantage, for affairs like that will pay you much more than you can get for a series of lectures. If I tie your ballroom up for twenty nights during the course of the season, it is sure to mean a loss of some very profitable business to you.

'Now, let's consider the disadvantages. First, instead of increasing your income from me, you are going to decrease it. In fact, you are going to wipe it out because I cannot pay the rent you are asking. I shall be forced to hold these lectures at some other place.

'There's another disadvantage to you also. These lectures attract crowds of educated and cultured people to your hotel. That is good advertising for you, isn't it? In fact, if you spent $5,000 advertising in the newspapers, you couldn't bring as many people to look at your hotel as I can bring by these lectures. That is worth a lot to a hotel, isn't it?'

As I talked, I wrote these two 'disadvantages' under the proper heading, and handed the sheet of paper to the manager, saying: 'I wish you would carefully consider both the advantages and disadvantages that are going to accrue to you and then give me your final decision.'

I received a letter the next day, informing me that my rent would be increased only 50 per cent instead of 300 per cent.

Mind you, I got this reduction without saying a word about what I wanted. I talked all the time about what the other person wanted and how he could get it.

Suppose I had done the human, natural thing; suppose I had

stormed into his office and said, 'What do you mean by raising my rent 300 per cent when you know the tickets have been printed and the announcements made? Three hundred per cent! Ridiculous! Absurd! I won't pay it!'

What would have happened then? An argument would have begun to steam and boil and sputter—and you know how arguments end. Even if I had convinced him that he was wrong, his pride would have made it difficult for him to back down and give in.

Here is one of the best bits of advice ever given about the fine art of human relationships. 'If there is any one secret of success,' said Henry Ford, 'it lies in the ability to get the other person's point of view and see things from that person's angle as well as from your own.'

That is so good, I want to repeat it: 'If there is any one secret of success, it lies in the ability to get the other person's point of view and see things from that person's angle as well as from your own.'

That is so simple, so obvious, that anyone ought to see the truth of it at a glance; yet 90 per cent of the people on this earth ignore it 90 per cent of the time.

Rule 30: Arouse in the other person a desire for the object.

What you do makes a difference, and you have to decide what kind of difference you want to make.
—Jane Goodall

If you want to conquer fear, don't sit home and think about it. Go out and get busy.
—Dale Carnegie

DEVELOP SELF-CONFIDENCE, IMPROVE PUBLIC SPEAKING

Part 1

1

INCREASE COURAGE AND SELF-CONFIDENCE

Courage is one step ahead of fear.
—Coleman Young

More than eighteen thousand businesspersons, since 1912, have been members of the various public speaking courses conducted by me. Most of them have, at my request, written stating why they had enrolled for this training and what they hoped to obtain from it. Naturally, the phraseology varied; but the central desire in these letters, the basic want in the vast majority, remained surprisingly the same: 'When I am called upon to stand up and speak,' man after man wrote, 'I become so self-conscious, so frightened, that I can't think clearly, can't concentrate, can't remember what I had intended to say. I want to gain self-confidence, poise, and the ability to think on my feet. I want to get my thoughts together in logical order and I want to be able to say my say clearly and convincingly before a business group or audience.' Thousands of their confessions sounded about like that.

For example—to quote one specific instance—years ago, a Brooklyn physician, whom we will call Dr Curtis, spent the winter in Florida near the training grounds of the Giants. Being an enthusiastic baseball fan, he often went to see them practise. In time, he became quite friendly with the team, and was invited to attend a banquet given in their honour.

After the coffee and nuts were served, several prominent guests were called upon to 'say a few words'. Suddenly, with the abruptness and unexpectedness of an explosion, he heard the toast-master remark: 'We have a physician with us tonight, and I am going to ask Dr Curtis to talk on a baseball player's health.'

Was he prepared? Of course. He had had the best preparation in the world: He had been studying hygiene and practising medicine for almost a third of a century. He could have sat in his chair and talked about this subject all night to the man seated on his right or left. But to get up and say the same things to even a small audience—that was another matter. That was a paralysing matter. His heart doubled its pace and skipped beats at the very contemplation of it. He had never made a public speech in his life, and every thought that he had had now took wings.

What was he to do? The audience was applauding. Everyone was looking at him. He shook his head. But that served only to heighten the applause, to increase the demand. The cries of 'Dr Curtis! Speech! Speech!' grew louder and more insistent.

He was in positive misery. He knew that if he got up he would fail, that he would be unable to utter half a dozen sentences. So he arose and, without saying a word, turned his back on his friends and walked silently out of the room, a deeply embarrassed and humiliated man.

Small wonder that one of the first things he did after getting back to Brooklyn was to come to the Central YMCA and enrol in the course in Public Speaking. He didn't propose to be put to the blush and be stricken dumb a second time.

He was the kind of student that delights an instructor: He was in dead earnest. He wanted to be able to talk, and there was no half-heartedness about his desires. He prepared his talks thoroughly, he practised them with a will, and he never missed a single session of the course.

He did precisely what such a student always does: He progressed at a rate that surprised him, that surpassed his fondest hopes. After the first few sessions his nervousness subsided, and his confidence mounted higher and higher. In two months he had become the star speaker of the group. He was soon accepting invitations to speak elsewhere; he now loved the feel and exhilaration of it, the distinction and the additional friends it brought him.

The gaining of self-confidence and courage and the ability to think calmly and clearly while talking to a group is not one-tenth as difficult as most men imagine. It is not a gift bestowed by Providence on only a few rarely endowed individuals. It is like the ability to play golf. Any man can develop his own latent capacity if he has sufficient desire to do so.

Is there the faintest shadow of a reason why you should not be able to think as well in a perpendicular position before an audience as you can when sitting down? Surely, you know there is not. In fact, you ought to think better when facing a group of men. Their presence ought to stir you and lift you. A great many speakers will tell you that the presence of an audience is a stimulus, an inspiration, that drives their brains to function more clearly, more keenly. At such times, thoughts, facts, ideas, that they did not know they possessed, drift smoking by, as Henry Ward Beecher said; and they have but to reach out and lay their hands hot upon them. They ought to be your experience. It probably will be if you practise and persevere.

Of this much, however, you may be absolutely sure: Training and practise will wear away your audience-fright and give you self-confidence and an abiding courage.

Do not imagine that your case is unusually difficult. Even those who afterwards became the most eloquent representatives of their generation were, at the outset of their careers, afflicted by this blinding fear and self-consciousness.

Mark Twain, the first time he stood up to lecture, felt as if his mouth were filled with cotton and his pulse were speeding for some prize cup.

Charles Stewart Parnell, the great Irish leader, at the outset of his speaking career, was so nervous, according to the testimony of his brother, that he frequently clenched his fists until his nails sank into his flesh and his palms bled.

Disraeli admitted that he would rather have led a cavalry charge than have faced the House of Commons for the first time. His opening speech there was a ghastly failure. So was Sheridan's.

In fact, so many of the famous speakers of England have made poor showings at first that there is now a feeling in Parliament that it is rather an inauspicious omen for a young man's initial talk to be a decided success. So take heart.

After watching the careers and aiding somewhat in the development of so many speakers, the author is always glad when a student has, at the outset, a certain amount of flutter and nervous agitation.

There is a certain responsibility in making a talk, even if it is to only two dozen men in a business conference—a certain strain, a certain shock, a certain excitement. The speaker ought to be keyed up like a thoroughbred straining at the bit. The immortal Cicero said, two thousand years ago, that all public speaking of real merit was characterized by nervousness.

Speakers often experience this same feeling even when they are talking over the radio. 'Microphone fright', it is called. When Charlie Chaplin went 'on the air', he had his speech all written out. Surely he was used to audiences. He toured America back in 1912 with a vaudeville sketch entitled 'A Night in a Music Hall'. Before that he was on the legitimate stage in England. Yet, when he went into the padded room and faced the microphone, he had a feeling in the stomach not unlike the sensation one gets when he crosses the Atlantic during a stormy February.

Some men, no matter how often they speak, always experience this self-consciousness just before they commence; but in a few seconds after they have got on their feet, it disappears.

Even Lincoln felt shy for the few opening moments. In a few moments he gained composure and warmth and earnestness, and his real speech began.

Your experience may be similar to his.

In order to get the most out of this training, and to get it with rapidity and dispatch, four things are essential:

FIRST: START WITH A STRONG AND PERSISTENT DESIRE

This is of far more importance than you probably realize. If your instructor could look into your mind and heart now and ascertain the depth of your desires, he could foretell, almost with certainty, the swiftness of the progress you will make. If your desire is pale and flabby, your achievements will also take on that hue and consistency. But, if you go after this subject with persistence, and with the energy of a bulldog after a cat, nothing underneath the Milky Way will defeat you.

Therefore, arouse your enthusiasm for this study. Enumerate its benefits. Think of what additional self-confidence and the ability to talk more convincingly in business will mean to you. Think of what it may mean to you socially; of the friends it will bring, of the increase of your personal influence, of the leadership it will give you. And it will give you leadership more rapidly than almost any other activity you can think of or imagine.

It is an attainment that almost every person of education longs for. After Andrew Carnegie's death there was found, among his papers, a plan for his life drawn up when he was thirty-three years of age. He then felt that in two more years he could so arrange his business as to have an annual income of fifty thousand dollars; so he proposed to retire at thirty-five, go to Oxford and get a thorough education, and 'pay special attention to speaking in public'.

Think of the glow of satisfaction and pleasure that will accrue from the exercise of this new power. The author has travelled round over no small part of this terrestrial ball; and has had many and varied experiences; but for downright, and lasting inward satisfaction, he knows of few things that will compare to standing before an audience and making men think your thoughts after you. It will give you a sense of strength, a feeling of power. It will appeal to your pride of personal accomplishment. It will set you off from and raise you above your fellowmen. There is magic in it and a never-to-be-forgotten thrill. 'Two minutes before I begin,' a speaker confessed, 'I would rather be whipped than start; but two minutes before I finish, I would rather be shot than stop.'

When Julius Caesar sailed over the channel from Gaul and landed with his legions on what is now England, what did he do to insure the success of his arms? A very clever thing: He halted his soldiers on the chalk cliffs of Dover, and, looking down over the waves two hundred feet below, they saw red tongues of fire consume every ship in which they had crossed. In the enemy's country, with the last link with the Continent gone, the last means of retreating burned, there was but one thing left for them to do: to advance, to conquer. That is precisely what they did.

Such was the spirit of the immortal Caesar. Why not make it yours, too, in this war to exterminate your foolish fear of audiences.

SECOND: ACT CONFIDENTLY

To develop courage when you are facing an audience, act as if you already have it. Of course, unless you are prepared, all the acting in the world will avail but little. But granted that ycu know what you are going to talk about, step out briskly and take a deep breath. In fact, breathe deeply for thirty seconds before you ever face your audience. The increased supply of oxygen will buoy you up and give you courage.

When a youth of the Peuhl tribe in Central Africa attains manhood and wishes to take unto himself a wife, he is compelled to undergo the ceremony of flagellation. The women of the tribe foregather, singing and clapping their hands to the rhythm of tom-toms. The candidate strides forth stripped naked to the waist. Suddenly a man armed with a cruel whip sets upon the lad, beating his bare skin, lashing him, flogging him like a fiend. Welts appear; often the skin is cut, blood flows; scars are made that last a lifetime. During this scourging, a venerable judge of the tribe crouches at the feet of the victim to see if he moves or exhibits the slightest evidence of pain. To pass the test successfully the tortured aspirant must not only endure the ordeal, but, as he endures it, he must sing a paean of praise.

In every age, in every clime, men have always admired courage; so, no matter how your heart may be pounding inside, stride forth bravely, stop, stand still like the scourged youth of Central Africa, and like him, act as if you loved it.

Draw yourself up to your full height and look your audience straight in the eyes, and begin to talk as confidently as if every one of them owed you money. Imagine that they do. Imagine that they have assembled there to bet you for an extension of credit. The psychological effect on you will be beneficial.

Do not nervously button and unbutton your coat, and fumble with your hands. If you must make nervous movements, place your hands behind your back and twist your fingers there where no one can see the performance—or wiggle your toes.

So take the offensive against your fears. Go out to meet them, battle them, conquer them by sheer boldness at every opportunity.

Have a message, and then think of yourself as a courier boy instructed to deliver it. We pay slight attention to the boy. It is the courier that we want. The message—that is the thing. Keep your mind on it. Keep your heart in it. Know it like the back of your hand. Believe it feelingly. Then talk as if you were determined to say it. Do that, and the chances are ten to one that you will soon be master of the occasion and master of yourself.

THIRD: KNOW THOROUGHLY WHAT YOU ARE GOING TO TALK ABOUT

Unless a man has thought out and planned his talk and knows what he is going to say, he can't feel very comfortable when he faces his auditors. He is like the blind leading the blind. Under such circumstances, your speaker ought to be self-conscious, ought to feel repentant, ought to be ashamed of his negligence.

'I was elected to the Legislature in the autumn of 1881,' Theodore Roosevelt wrote in his autobiography, 'and found myself the youngest man in that body. Like all young men and inexperienced members, I had considerable difficulty in teaching myself to speak. I profited much by the advice of a hard-headed old countryman—who was unconsciously paraphrasing the Duke of Wellington, who was himself doubtless paraphrasing somebody else. The advice ran: "Don't speak until you are sure you have something to say, and know just what it is; then say it, and sit down".'

This 'hard-headed old countryman' ought to have told Roosevelt of another aid in overcoming nervousness. He ought to have added: 'It will help you to throw off your embarrassment if you can find something to do before an audience—if you can exhibit something, write a word on the blackboard or point out a spot on the map, or move a table or throw open a window, or shift some books and papers—any physical action with a purpose behind it may help you to feel more at home.'

True, it is not always easy to find an excuse for doing such things, but there is the suggestion. Use it if you can, but use it the first few times only. A baby does not cling to chairs after it learns to walk.

FOURTH: PRACTISE! PRACTISE! PRACTISE!

The last point we have to make here is emphatically the most important. Even though you forget everything you have read so far, do remember this: the first way, The last way, the never-failing way to develop self-confidence in speaking is—to speak. Really the whole matter finally simmers down to but one essential: practise, practise, practise.

'Any beginner,' warned Roosevelt, 'is apt to have "buck fever".' "Buck fever" means a state of intense nervous excitement which may be entirely divorced from timidity. It may affect a man the first time he has to speak to a large audience just as it may affect him the first time he sees a buck-deer or goes into battle. What such a man needs is not courage, but nerve control and cool-headedness. This he can get only by actual practice. He must, by custom and repeated exercise of self-mastery, get his nerves thoroughly under control. This is largely a matter of habit; in the sense of repeated effort and repeated exercise of willpower. If the man has the right stuff in him, he will grow stronger and stronger with each exercise of it.'

So, persevere. Don't remain away from any session of the course because the business duties of the week have rendered it impossible for you to prepare something. Prepared or unprepared, come. Let the instructor, the class, suggest a topic for you after you have come before them.

You want to get rid of your audience fear? Let us see what causes it. Fear is the result of a lack of confidence and what causes that? It is the result of not knowing what you can really do. And not knowing what you can do is caused by a lack of experience. When you get a record of successful experience behind you, your fears will vanish; they will melt like night mists under the glare of a July sun.

One thing is certain: the accepted way to learn to swim is to plunge into the water. You have been reading this book long enough. Let us toss it aside now, and get busy with the real work in hand.

Choose your subject, preferably one on which you have some knowledge, and construct a three-minute talk. Practise the talk by yourself a number of times. Then give it, if possible, to the group for whom it is intended, or before your class, putting into the effort all your force and power.

It is never easy to keep reaching for dreams. Strength and courage can sometimes be lonely friends. but those who reach, walk in stardust.
—Anonymous

Healing takes courage, and we all have courage,
even if we have to dig a little to find it.
—Tori Amos

2

HOW TO OPEN A TALK

You have to care. And that care has to come from your soul.
Public speaking is the art of having everybody thinking
you are talking to them.
—Dennis Van Gerven

I once asked Dr Lynn Harold Hough, formerly president of Northwestern University, what was the most important fact that his long experience as a speaker had taught him. After pondering for a minute, he replied, 'To get an arresting opening, something that will seize the attention immediately.' He plans in advance almost the precise words of both his opening and closing. John Bright did the same thing. Gladstone did it. Webster did it. Lincoln did it. Practically every speaker with common sense and experience does it.

Foresee how you are going to begin when the mind is fresh to grasp every word you utter. Foresee what impression you are going to leave last—when nothing else follows to obliterate it.

Ever since the days of Aristotle, books on this subject have divided the speech into three sections: the introduction, the body, the conclusion. Until comparatively recently, the introduction often was, and could really afford to be, as leisurely as a cart ride. The speaker then was both a bringer of news and an entertainer. A hundred years ago he often filled the niche in the community that is usurped today by the newspaper, the radio, the telephone, the movie theatre.

But conditions have altered amazingly. The world has been made over. Inventions have speeded up life more in the last hundred years than they had formerly in all the ages. And the speaker must fall in line with the impatient tempo of the times. If you are going to use an introduction, believe me, it ought to be short as a billboard advertisement. This is about the temper of the average modern audience: 'Got anything to say? All right, let's have it quickly and with very little trimmings. No oratory! Give us the facts quickly and sit down.'

When Woodrow Wilson addressed Congress on such a momentous question as an ultimatum on submarine warfare, he announced his topic and centred the audience's attention on the subject with just twenty-three words:

A situation has arisen in the foreign relations of the country of which it is my plain duty to inform you very frankly.

But do inexperienced speakers usually achieve such commendable swiftness and succinctness in their openings? Strict veracity compels us to record that they do not. The majority of untrained and unskilled speakers will begin in one of two ways—both of which are bad. Let us discuss them forthwith.

THE PITFALLS OF OPENING WITH A SO-CALLED HUMOROUS STORY

For some lamentable reason, the novice often feels that he ought to be funny as a speaker. He may, by nature, mind you, be as solemn as the encyclopaedia, utterly devoid of the lighter touch, yet the moment he stands up to talk he imagines he feels, or ought to feel, the spirit of Mark Twain descending upon him. So he is inclined to open with a humorous story, especially if the occasion is an after-dinner affair. What happens?

If an entertainer were to misfire a few times before a vaudeville audience that had paid for their seats, they would 'boo' and shout 'give him the bird'. But the average group listening to a speaker is very sympathetic; so, out of sheer charity, they will do their best to manufacture a few chuckles while, deep in their hearts, they pity the would-be humorous speaker for his failure! They themselves feel uncomfortable. Haven't you, my dear reader, witnessed this kind of fiasco time after time? The writer has. In all the difficult realm of speech-making, what is more difficult, more rare, than the ability to make an audience laugh? Humour is a hair-trigger affair; it is so much a matter of individuality, of personality. You are either born with the predilection for being humorous or you are not—much as you are born with or without brown eyes. Not much can be done about either.

You may be one of those fortunately endowed individuals who has the rare gift of humour. If so, by all means, cultivate it. You will be thrice welcome wherever you speak. But if your talent lies in other directions, it is folly—and it ought to be high treason—for you to attempt to wear the mantle of Chauncey M. Depew.

Were you to study his speeches, and Lincoln's, and Job Hedges', you would probably be surprised at the few stories they told, especially in their openings. Edwin James Cattell confided to me that he had never told a funny story for the mere sake of humour. It had to be relevant, had to illustrate a point. Humour ought to be merely the frosting on the cake, merely the chocolate between the layers, not the cake itself.

Must the opening then be heavy-footed, elephantine and excessively solemn? Not at all. Tickle our risibilities, if you can, by some local reference, something anent the occasion or the remarks of some other speaker. Observe some incongruity. Exaggerate it. That brand of humour is forty times more likely to succeed than stale jokes about Pat and Mike, or a mother-in-law, or a goat.

Perhaps the easiest way to create merriment is to tell a joke on yourself. Depict yourself in some ridiculous and embarrassing situation. That gets down to the very essence of much humour.

Note how cleverly Rudyard Kipling raised laughs in this opening to one of his talks in England. He is retailing here, not manufactured anecdotes, but some of his own experiences and playfully stressing their incongruities:

> My Lords, Ladies and Gentlemen: When I was a young man
> in India I used to report criminal cases for the newspaper that

employed me. It was interesting work because it introduced me to forgers and embezzlers and murderers and enterprising sportsmen of that kind. (Laughter.) Sometimes, after I had reported their trials, I used to visit my friends in jail when they were doing their sentences. (Laughter.) I remember one man who got off with a life sentence for murder. He was a clever, smooth-speaking chap, and he told me what he called the story of his life. He said: 'Take it from me that when a man gets crooked, one thing leads to another until he finds himself in such a position that he has to put somebody out of the way to get straight again.' (Laughter.) Well, that exactly describes the present position of the cabinet. (Laughter and cheers.)

Don't be apologetic

The second egregious blunder that the beginner is wont to make in his opening, is this: He apologizes. 'I am no speaker... I am not prepared to talk.... I have nothing to say...'

Don't! Don't! The opening words of a poem by Kipling are: 'There's no use in going further.' That is precisely the way an audience feels when a speaker opens in that fashion.

Anyway, if you are not prepared, some of us will discover it without your assistance. Others will not. Why call their attention to it? Why insult your audience by suggesting that you did not think them worth preparing for, that just any old thing you happened to have on the fire would be good enough to serve them? No. No. We don't want to hear your apologies. We are there to be informed and interested, to be interested, remember that.

The moment you come before the audience, you have our attention naturally, inevitably. It is not difficult to get it for the first five seconds, but it is difficult to hold it for the next five minutes. If you once lose it, it will be doubly difficult to win it back. So begin with something interesting in your very first sentence. Not the second. Not the third. The first! F-I-R-S-T. First!

'How?' you ask. Rather a large order, I admit. And in attempting to harvest the material to fill it, we must tread our way down devious and dubious paths, for so much depends upon you, upon your audience, your subject, your material, the occasion, and so on. However, we hope that the tentative suggestions discussed and illustrated in the remainder of this chapter will yield something usable and of value.

Curiosity wins over the cat

Here is an opening used by Mr Howell Healy in a talk given before a session of this course. Do you like it? Does it get your interest immediately?

Eighty-two years ago, and just about this time of year, there was published in London a little volume, a story, which was destined to become immortal. Many people have called it 'the greatest little book in the world'. When it first appeared, friends meeting one another in the Strand or Pall Mall, asked the question, 'Have you read it?' The answer invariably was: 'Yes, God bless him, I have.'

The day it was published a thousand copies were sold. Within a fortnight, the demand had consumed fifteen thousand. Since then it has run into countless editions, and has been translated into every language under heaven. A few years ago, J.P. Morgan purchased the original manuscript for a fabulous sum; it now reposes among his other priceless treasures in that magnificent art gallery which he called his library.

What is this world-famous book? Dickens' *A Christmas Carol*....

Do you consider that a successful opening? Did it hold your attention, heighten your interest as it progressed? Why? Was it not because it aroused your curiosity, held you in suspense?

Curiosity! Who is not susceptible to it?

So arouse your audience's curiosity with your first sentence, and you have their interested attention.

One can often arouse curiosity by beginning with an effect, and making people anxious to hear the cause. For example, one student began with this striking statement: 'A member of one of our state legislatures recently stood up in his legislative assembly and proposed the passage of a law prohibiting tadpoles from becoming frogs within two miles of any school house.'

You smile. Is the speaker joking? How absurd. Was that actually done? Yes. The speaker went on to explain:

> Every man who aspires to speak in public ought to study the technique that magazine writers employ to hook the reader's interest immediately. You can learn far more from them about how to open a speech than you can by studying collections of printed speeches.

Why not begin with a story

Harold Bell Wright has admitted in an interview that his novels have brought him more than a hundred thousand dollars a year. Booth Tarkington and Robert W. Chambers earned similar amounts. For seventeen years Doubleday Page and Company had one large press, which did nothing in all that time but turn out a ceaseless flood of the novels by the late Gene Stratton Porter. Over seventeen million copies of her books were sold, and they brought her more than three million dollars in royalties. Do people like to hear stories? Those figures sound like it, don't they?

We especially like to hear a man relate narratives from his own experience.

Note that openings should have action. They must start something. They must arouse your curiosity. You want to read on, you want to know more, you want to find out what it is all about.

Begin with a specific illustration

It is difficult, it is arduous, for the average audience to follow abstract statements very long. Illustrations are easier to listen to, far easier. Then why not start with one? It is hard to get men to do that. I know. I have tried. They feel somehow that they must first make a few general statements. Not at all. Open with your illustration, arouse the interest, then follow with your general remarks.

Use an exhibit

Perhaps the easiest way in the world to gain attention is to hold up something for people to look at. Even savages and halfwits, and babes in the cradle and monkeys in a zoo and dogs on the street will give heed to that kind of stimulus. It can be used sometimes with effectiveness before the most dignified audience. For example, Mr S.S. Ellis opened one of his talks by holding a coin between his thumb and forefinger, and high above his shoulder. Naturally everyone looked. Then he inquired: 'Has anyone here ever found a coin like this on the pavement? It announces that the fortunate finder will be given a lot free in such and such an estate development. He has but to call and present this coin...' Mr Ellis then proceeded to reveal the coloured man in the cordwood and to condemn the misleading and unethical practices involved.

Ask a question

Mr Ellis' opening has another commendable feature. It begins by asking a question, by getting the audience thinking with the speaker, cooperating with him. Note that the *Saturday Evening Post* article on gangsters opens with two questions in the first three sentences: 'Are gangsters really organized?... How?' The use of this question-key is really one of the simplest, surest ways to unlock the minds of your audience and let yourself in. When other tools prove useless, you can always fall back on it.

Why not open with a question from some tie your topic up to the vital interests of your hearers

Begin on some note that goes straight to the selfish interests of the audience. That is one of the best of all possible ways to start. It is sure to get attention. We are mightily interested in the things that touch us significantly, momentously.

Take an example: During the last season, I heard a student begin a talk on the prime urgency of conserving our forests. He opened like this: 'We ought to be proud of our national resources...' From that sentence, he went on to show that we were wasting our timber at a shameless and indefensible pace. But the opening was bad, too general, too vague. He did not make his subject seem vital to us. There was a printer in that audience. The destruction of our forests will mean something very real to his business. There was a banker; it is going to affect him for it will affect our general prosperity...and so on. Why not begin, then, by saying: 'The subject I am going to speak about affects your business, Mr Appleby; and yours, Mr Saul. In fact, it will, in some measure, affect the price of the food we eat and the rent that we pay. It touches the welfare and prosperity of us all.'

Is that exaggerating the importance of conserving our forests? No, I think not. It is only obeying Elbert Hubbard's injunction to 'paint the picture large and put the matter in a way that compels attention'.

The attention power of shocking facts

'A good magazine article,' said S.S. McClure, the founder of the periodical bearing his name, 'is a series of shocks.'

They jar us out of our daydreams; they seize, they demand attention. Here are some illustrations: Mr N.D. Ballantine began his address on The Marvels of Radio with this statement: 'Do you realize that the sound of a fly walking across a pane of glass here can be broadcasted by radio and made to roar away off in Central Africa like the falls of Niagara?'

The opening is successful if you can put the requisite power and earnestness behind your words. They live. They breathe.

THE VALUE OF THE SEEMINGLY CASUAL OPENING

How do you like the following opening, and why? Mary E. Richmond is addressing the annual meeting of the League of Women Voters in the days before legislation against child marriages: Yesterday, as the train passed through a city not far away from here, I was reminded of a marriage that took place there a few years ago. Because many other marriages in this state have been just as hasty and disastrous as this one, I am going to begin what I have to say today with some of the details of this individual instance.

It was on December 12th that a high school girl of fifteen in that city met for the first time a junior in a nearby college who had just attained his majority. On December 15th, only three days later, they procured a marriage licence by swearing that the girl was eighteen and was therefore free from the necessity of procuring parental consent. Leaving the city clerk's office with their licence, they applied at once to a priest (the girl was a Catholic), but very properly he refused to marry them. In some way, perhaps through this priest, the child's mother received news of the attempted marriage. Before she could find her daughter, however, a justice of the peace had united the pair. The bridegroom then took his bride to a hotel where they spent two days and two nights, at the end of which time he abandoned her and never lived with her again.

Personally, I like that opening very much. The very first sentence is good. It forecasts an interesting reminiscence. We want to hear the details. We settle down to listen to a human interest story. In addition to that, it seems very natural. It does not smack of the study, it is not formal, it does not smell of the lamp... 'Yesterday, as the train passed through a city not far from here, I was reminded of a marriage that took place there a few years ago.' Sounds natural, spontaneous, human. Sounds like one person relating an interesting story to another. An audience likes that. But it is very liable to shy at something too elaborate, something that reeks of preparation with malice aforethought. We want the art that conceals art.

I've always been good at public speaking, but I never really enjoyed it. Then I started to really enjoy it, and that's made all the difference.
—Mimi Kennedy

Before anything else, preparation is the key to success.
—Alexander Graham Bell

3

HOW TO CLOSE A TALK

Good speech: A beginning and a conclusion placed not too far apart.
—Anonymous

Would you like to know in what parts of your speech you are most likely to reveal your inexperience or your expertness, your inaptitude or your finesse? I'll tell you: In the opening and the closing. They are the hardest things in almost any activity to manage adroitly. For example, at a social function aren't the most trying feats the graceful entrance and the graceful leave-taking? In a business interview, aren't the most difficult tasks the winning approach and the successful close?

The close is really the most strategic point in a speech; what one says last, the final words left ringing in the ears when one ceases—these are likely to be remembered longest.

What are the most common errors? Let us discuss a few and search for remedies.

First, there is the man who finishes with: 'That is about all I have to say on the matter; so I guess I shall stop.' That is not an ending. That is a mistake. That reeks of the amateur.

That is almost unpardonable. If that is all you have to say, why not round off your talk, and promptly take your seat and stop without talking about stopping. Do that, and the inference that that is all you have to say may, with safety and good taste, be left to the discernment of the audience.

Then there is the speaker who says all he has to say, but he does not know how to stop. The remedy? An ending has to be planned some time, doesn't it? Is it the part of wisdom to try to do it after you are facing an audience, while you are under the strain and stress of talking, while your mind must be intent on what you are saying? Or does common sense suggest the advisability of doing it quietly, calmly, beforehand?

Some speakers never get to the end at all. Along in the middle of their journey, they begin to sputter and misfire like an engine when the petrol supply is about exhausted; after a few desperate lunges, they come to a complete standstill, a breakdown. They need, of course, better preparation, more practice—more petrol in the tank.

Many novices stop too abruptly. Their method of closing lacks smoothness, lacks finish. Properly speaking, they have no close; they merely cease suddenly, jerkily. The effect is unpleasant, amateurish. It is as if a friend in a social conversation were to break off brusquely and dart out of the room without a graceful leave-taking.

How can a beginner develop the proper feeling for the close of an address? By mechanical rules?

No. Like culture, it is too delicate for that. It must be a matter of sensing, almost of intuition. Unless a speaker can feel when it is done harmoniously, adroitly, how can he himself hope to do it?

However, this feeling can be cultivated; this expertness can be developed somewhat, by studying the ways in which accomplished speakers have achieved it.

But you are not going to deliver immortal pronouncements as President in Washington or as Prime Minister in Ottawa or Melbourne. Your problem, perhaps, will be how to close a simple talk before a group of businessmen. How shall you set about it? Let us search a bit. Let us see if we cannot uncover some fertile suggestions.

Summarize your points

Even in a short talk of three to five minutes, a speaker is very apt to cover so much ground that at the close the listeners are a little hazy about all his main points. However, few speakers realize that. They are misled into assuming that because these points are crystal clear in their own minds, they must be equally lucid to their hearers. Not at all. The speaker has been pondering over his ideas for some time. But his points are all new to the audience; they are flung at the audience like a handful of shot. Some may stick, but the most are liable to roll off in confusion.

Some anonymous Irish politician is reported to have given this recipe for making a speech: 'First, tell them that you are going to tell them, then tell them, then tell them that you have told them.' Not bad, you know. In fact, it is often highly advisable to 'tell them that you have told them'. Briefly, of course, speedily—a mere outline, a summary.

Here is a good example. The speaker is a student of Mr Bills' class in Public Speaking. He is also a traffic manager for railways:

In short, gentlemen, our own backdoor yard experience with this block device, the experience in its use in the East, in the West, in the North—the sound operating principles underlying its operation, the actual demonstration in the money saved in one year in wreck prevention, move me most earnestly and unequivocally to recommend its immediate installation on our Southern branch.

You see what he has done? You can see it and feel it without having heard the rest of the talk. He has summed up in a few sentences, in sixty-two words, practically all the points he has made in the entire talk.

Don't you feel that a summary like that helps? If so, make that technique your own.

A terse, sincere compliment

The great state of Pennsylvania should lead the way in hastening the coming of the new day. Pennsylvania, the great producer of iron and steel, mother of the greatest railroad company in the world, third among our agricultural states—Pennsylvania is the keystone of our business arch. Never was the prospect before her greater, never was her opportunity for leadership more brilliant.

With these words, Charles Schwab closed his address before the

Pennsylvania Society of New York. He left his hearers pleased, happy, optimistic. That is an admirable way to finish; but, in order to be effective, it must be sincere. No gross flattery. No extravagances. This kind of closing, if it does not ring true, will ring false, very false. And like a false coin, people will have none of it.

A humorous close

'Always leave them laughing,' said George Cohan, 'when you say goodbye.' If you have the ability to do it, and the material, fine! But how? Each man must do it in his own individual way.

The climax

The climax is a popular way of ending. It is often difficult to manage and is not an ending for all speakers nor for all subjects. But when well done, it is excellent. It works up to a crest, a peak, getting stronger sentence by sentence.

Lincoln used the climax in preparing his notes for a lecture on Niagara Falls. Note how each comparison is stronger than the preceding, how he gets a cumulative effect by comparing its age to Columbus, Christ, Moses, Adam, and so on:

It calls up the indefinite past. When Columbus first sought this continent—when Christ suffered on the cross—when Moses led Israel through the Red Sea—nay, even when Adam first came from the hands of his Maker; then, as now, Niagara was roaring here. The eyes of that species of extinct giants whose bones fill the mounds of America have gazed on Niagara, as ours do now. Contemporary with the first race of men, and older than the first man, Niagara is as strong and fresh today as ten thousand years ago. The Mammoth and Mastodon, so long dead that fragments of their monstrous bones alone testify that they ever lived, have gazed on Niagara—in that long, long time never still for a moment, never dried, never frozen, never slept, never rested.

4

SELF-CONFIDENCE THROUGH PREPARATION

*One important key to success is self-confidence. An important key to
self-confidence is preparation.*
—Arthur Ashe

It has been my professional duty as well as pleasure to listen to and
criticize approximately six thousand speeches a year each season
since 1912. These were made, not by college students, but by mature
business and professional men. If that experience has engraved on
my mind any one thing more deeply than another, surely it is this:
The urgent necessity of preparing a talk before one starts to make
it and of having something clear and definite to say, something that
has impressed one, something that won't stay unsaid. Aren't you
unconsciously drawn to the speaker who, you feel, has a real message
in his head and heart that he zealously desires to communicate to
your head and heart? That is half the secret of speaking.

When a speaker is in that kind of mental and emotional state he
will discover a significant fact: Namely, that his talk will almost make
itself. Its yoke will be easy, its burden will be light. A well-prepared
speech is already nine-tenths delivered.

The primary reason why most men take this course, is to acquire
confidence and courage and self-reliance. And the one fatal mistake
many make is neglecting to prepare their talks. How can they even
hope to subdue the cohorts of fear, the cavalry of nervousness, when
they go into the battle with wet powder and blank shells, or with no
ammunition at all? Under the circumstances, small wonder that they
are not exactly at home before an audience. 'I believe,' said Lincoln in

the White House, 'that I shall never be old enough to speak without embarrassment when I have nothing to say.'

If you want confidence, why not do the things necessary to bring it about?

Why don't those enrolled in this course prepare their talks more carefully? Why? Some don't clearly understand what preparation is or how to go about it wisely; others plead a lack of time. So we shall discuss these problems rather fully—and we trust lucidly and profitably—in this chapter.

THE RIGHT WAY TO PREPARE

What is preparation? Reading a book? That is one kind, but not the best. Reading may help; but if one attempts to lift a lot of 'canned' thoughts out of a book and to give them out immediately as his own, the whole performance will be lacking in something. The audience may not know precisely what is lacking, but they will not warm to the speaker.

Let us cite an illustration of how to do it and how not to do it. A gentleman, whom we shall call Mr Flynn, was a student of this course. One afternoon he devoted his talk to eulogizing his home tour. He had hastily and superficially gleaned his facts from a tourist booklet. They sounded like it—dry, disconnected, undigested. He had not thought over his subject adequately. It had not elicited his enthusiasm. He did not feel what he was saying deeply enough to make it worthwhile expressing. The whole affair was flat and flavourless and unprofitable.

A fortnight later something happened that touched Mr Flynn to the core: A thief stole his motorcar out of a public garage. He rushed to the police and offered rewards, but it was all in vain. The police admitted that it was well-nigh impossible for them to cope with the crime situation; yet, only a week previously, they had found time to walk about the street, chalk in hand, and fine Mr Flynn because he had parked his car fifteen minutes at a kerb. These 'chalk cops', who were so busy annoying respectable citizens that they could not catch criminals, aroused his ire. He was indignant. He had something now to say, not something that he had got out of a book, but something that was leaping hot out of his own life and experience. Here was something that was part and parcel of the real man—something that had aroused his feelings and convictions. In his speech eulogizing the city, he had laboriously pulled out sentence by sentence; but now he had but to stand on his feet and open his mouth, and his condemnation of the police welled up and boiled forth like Vesuvius in action. A speech like that is almost foolproof. It can hardly fail. It was experience plus reflection.

HOW TO PREPARE YOUR TALK

What topics ought you to speak on during the sessions of this course? Anything that interests you. If possible, choose your own topics; you will be more fortunate still if your topic chooses you. However, you will often have topics suggested for you by your instructor.

Don't make the almost universal mistake of trying to cover too much ground in a brief talk. Just take one or two angles of a subject and attempt to cover them adequately. You will be fortunate if you can do that in the short speeches that are necessitated by the time schedule of this course.

Determine your subject a week in advance so that you will have time to think it over in odd moments. Think it over for seven days; dream over it for seven nights. Think of it the last thing when you retire. Think of it the next morning while you are shaving, while you are bathing, while you are riding downtown, while you are waiting for lifts, for lunch, for appointments. Discuss it with your friends. Make it a topic of conversation.

Ask yourself all possible questions concerning it. If, for example, you are to speak on divorce, ask yourself what causes divorce, what are the effects economically, socially. How can the evil be remedied? Should divorce be made impossible? More difficult? Easier?

Suppose you were going to talk on why you enrolled for this

course. You ought then to ask yourself such questions as these: What are my troubles? What do I hope to get out of this instruction? Have I ever made a public talk? If so, when? Where? What happened? Why do I think this training is valuable for a businessman? Do I know men who are forging ahead commercially largely because of their self-confidence, their presence, their ability to talk convincingly? Do I know others who will probably never achieve a gratifying measure of success because they lack these positive assets? Be specific. Tell the stories of these men without mentioning their names.

If you stand up and think clearly and keep going for two or three minutes, that is all that will be expected of you during your first few talks. A topic, such as why you enrolled for this course, is very easy; that is obvious. If you will spend a little time selecting and arranging your material on that topic, you will be almost sure to remember it, for you will be speaking of your own observations, your own desires, your own experiences.

On the other hand, let us suppose that you have decided to speak on your business or profession. How shall you set about preparing such a talk? You already have a wealth of material on that subject. Your problem, then, will be to select and arrange it. Do not attempt to tell us all about it in three minutes. It can't be done. The attempt will be too sketchy, too fragmentary. Take one and only one phase of your topic: Expand and enlarge that. For example, why not tell us how you came to be in your particular business or profession? Was it a result of accident or choice? Relate your early struggles, your defeats, your hopes, your triumphs. Give us a human interest narrative, a real-life picture based on first-hand experiences. The truthful, inside story of almost any man's life—if told modestly and without offending egotism—is most entertaining. It is almost sure-fire speech material.

Or take another angle of your business: What are its troubles? What advice would you give to a young man entering it?

Or tell us about the people with whom you come in contact—the honest and dishonest ones. Tell us of your problems with labour, your problems with your customers. What has your business taught you about the most interesting topic in the world: Human nature? If you speak about the technical side of your business, about things, your talk may very easily prove uninteresting to others. But people, personalities—one can hardly go wrong with that kind of material.

Above all else, don't make your talk an abstract preachment. That will bore us. Make your talk a regular layer cake of illustrations and general statements. Think of concrete cases you have observed, and of the fundamental truths which you believe those specific instances illustrate. You will also discover that these concrete cases are far easier to remember than abstractions; they are far easier to talk about. They will also aid and brighten your delivery.

Some men, in speaking of their businesses, commit the unforgivable error of talking only of the features that interest them. Shouldn't the speaker try to ascertain what will entertain not himself but his hearers? Shouldn't he try to appeal to their selfish interests? If, for example, he sells fire insurance, shouldn't he tell them how to prevent fires on their own property? If he is a banker, shouldn't he give them advice on finance or investments?

While preparing, study your audience. Think of their wants, their wishes. That is sometimes half the battle.

In preparing some topics, it is very advisable—if time permits—to do some reading, to discover what others have thought, what others have said on the same subject. But don't read until you have first thought yourself dry.

5

HOW FAMOUS SPEAKERS PREPARED
THEIR ADDRESSES

Luck is what happens when preparation meets opportunity.
—Seneca

I was present once at a luncheon of a Rotary Club when the principal speaker was a prominent government official. The high position that he occupied gave him prestige, and we were looking forward with pleasure to hearing him. He had promised to tell us about the activities of his own department, and it was one in which almost every businessman was interested.

He knew his subject thoroughly, knew far more about it than he could possibly use, but he had not planned his speech. He had not selected his material. He had not arranged it in orderly fashion. Nevertheless, with a courage born of inexperience, he plunged heedlessly, blindly, into his speech. He did not know where he was going, but he was on his way.

His mind was, in short, a mere hodgepodge, and so was the mental feast he served us. He brought on the ice cream first, and then placed the soup before us. Fish and nuts came next. And, on top of that, there was something that seemed to be a mixture of soup and ice cream and good red herring. I have never, anywhere or at any time, seen a speaker more utterly confused.

He had been trying to talk impromptu, but, in desperation now, he drew a bundle of notes out of his pocket, confessing that his secretary had compiled them for him—and no one questioned the veracity of his assertion. The notes themselves evidently had no more order than a van full of scrap iron. He fumbled through them nervously, glancing from one page to another, trying to orient himself, trying to find a way out of the wilderness, and he attempted to talk as he did so. It was impossible. He apologized and, calling for water, took a drink with a trembling hand, uttered a few more scattering sentences, repeated himself, dug into his notes again.... Minute by minute he grew more helpless, more lost, more bewildered, more embarrassed. Nervous perspiration stood out on his forehead, and his handkerchief shook as he wiped it away. We in the audience sat watching the fiasco, our sympathies stirred, our feelings harrowed. We suffered positive and vicarious embarrassment. But with more doggedness than discretion, the speaker continued, floundering, studying his notes, apologizing and drinking. Everyone except him felt that the spectacle was rapidly approaching total disaster, and it was a relief to us all when he sat down and ceased his death struggles. It was one of the most uncomfortable audiences I have ever been in, and he was the most ashamed and humiliated speaker I have ever seen. He had made his talk as Rousseau said a love letter should be written: He had begun without knowing what he was going to say, and he had finished without knowing what he had uttered.

The moral of the tale is just this: 'When a man's knowledge is not in order,' said Herbert Spencer, 'the more of it he has, the greater will be his confusion of thought.'

No sane man would start to build a house without some sort of plan, but why will he begin to deliver a speech without the vaguest kind of outline or programme?

A speech is a voyage with a purpose, and it must be charted. The man who starts nowhere, generally gets there.

I wish that I could paint this saying of Napoleon's in flaming letters of red a foot high over every doorway on the globe where students of public speaking foregather: 'The art of war is a science in which nothing succeeds which has not been calculated and thought out.'

What is the best and most effective arrangement for a given set of ideas? No one can say until he has studied them. It is always a new problem, an eternal question that every speaker must ask and answer himself again and again. No infallible rules can be given, but we can, at any rate, illustrate briefly here with a concrete case just what we mean by orderly arrangements.

THE WAY DOCTOR CONWELL PLANNED HIS SPEECHES

There are not, as I have already said, any infallible rules that will solve the question of the best arrangement. There are no designs or schemes or charts that will fit all or even a majority of speeches; yet here are a few speech plans that will prove usable in some instances. The late Dr Russell H. Conwell, the author of the famous Acres of Diamonds— once informed me that he had built many of his innumerable speeches on this outline:

State your facts.
Argue from them.
Appeal for action.
Many students of this course have found this plan very helpful and stimulating.
Show something that is wrong.
Show how to remedy it.
Ask for cooperation.
Or to put it in another way:
Here is a situation that ought to be remedied.
We ought to do so and so about the matter.
You ought to help for these reasons.
Yet another speech plan could be:
Secure interested attention.
Win confidence.
State your facts; educate people regarding the merits of your proposition.
Appeal to the motives that make men act.

PLAY PATIENCE WITH YOUR NOTES

Make notes. Having got your various ideas and illustrations down on scraps of paper, play patience with them—toss them into series of related piles. These main piles ought to represent, approximately, the main points of your talk. Subdivide them into smaller lots. Throw out the chaff until there is nothing but number one wheat left—and even some of the wheat will probably have to be put aside and not used. No man, if he works right, is ever able to use but a percentage of the material he gathers.

TO USE OR NOT TO USE NOTES

Although he was an excellent impromptu speaker, Lincoln, after he reached the White House, never made any address, not even an informal talk to his cabinet, until he had carefully put it all down in writing beforehand. Of course, he was obliged to read his inaugural addresses. The exact phraseology of historical state papers of that character is too important to be left to extemporizing. But, before in Illinois, Lincoln never used even notes in his speaking. 'They always tend to tire and confuse the listener,' he said.

And who of us, pray, would contradict him? Don't notes destroy about 50 per cent of your interest in a talk? Don't they prevent, or at least render difficult, a very precious contact and intimacy that ought to exist between the speaker and the audience? Don't they create an air of artificiality? Don't they restrain an audience from feeling that the speaker has the confidence and reserve power that he ought to have?

Make notes, I repeat, during the preparation—elaborate ones, profuse ones. You may wish to refer to them when you are practising your talk alone. You may possibly feel more comfortable if you have them stored away in your pocket when you are facing an audience; but, like the hammer and saw and axe in a train, they should be emergency tools, only for use in the case of a smash-up, a total wreck, and threatening death and disaster.

If you must use notes, make them extremely brief and write them in large letters on an ample sheet of paper. Then arrive early at the place where you are to speak and hide your notes behind some books on a table. Glance at them when you must, but endeavour to screen your weakness from the audience. John Bright used to secrete his notes in his big hat lying on the table before him.

DO NOT MEMORIZE WORD FOR WORD

Don't read, and don't attempt to memorize your talk word for word. That consumes time, and courts disaster. Yet, in spite of this warning, some of the men reading these lines will try it; if they do, when they stand up to speak they will be thinking of what? Of their messages? No, they will be attempting to recall their exact phraseology. They will be thinking backwards, not forwards, reversing the usual processes of the human mind. The whole exhibition will be stiff and cold and colourless and inhuman. Do not, I beg of you, waste hours and energy in such futility.

When you have an important business interview, do you sit down and memorize verbatim what you are going to say? Do you? Of course not. You reflect until you get your main ideas clearly in mind. You may make a few notes and consult some records. You say to yourself, 'I shall bring out this point and that. I am going to say that a certain thing ought to be done for these reasons...' Then you enumerate the reasons to yourself and illustrate them with concrete cases. Isn't that the way you prepare for a business interview? Why not use the same common sense method in preparing a talk?

REHEARSE

After you have your ideas firmly in mind, then rehearse your talk from beginning to end. Do it silently, mentally, as you walk the street, as you wait for cars and lifts. Get off in a room by yourself and go over it aloud, gesturing, saying it with life and energy. As you practise, imagine there is a real audience before you. Imagine it so strongly that when there is one, it will seem like an old experience. That is the reason why so many criminals are able to go to the scaffold with such bravado; they have already done it so many thousand times in their imagination that they have lost fear of it. When the actual execution does take place, it seems like something that they have gone through very often before.

Luck is what happens when preparation meets opportunity.

—Seneca

ESSENTIAL ELEMENTS OF SUCCESSFUL SPEAKING

Years ago, when I first engaged in educational work, I was astounded to learn how large a percentage of students who enrolled in night schools of all sorts grew weary and fainted by the wayside before their goals were attained. The number is both lamentable and amazing. It is a sad commentary on human nature.

This is the sixth lesson of this course, and I know from experience that some of the men who are reading these lines are already growing disheartened because they have not, in six short weeks, conquered their fear of audiences, and gained self-confidence. What a pity, for 'how poor are they that have not patience. What wound did ever heal but by degrees?'

THE NECESSITY OF PERSISTENCE

When we start to learn any new thing, like French, or golf, or public speaking, we never advance steadily. We do not improve gradually. We do it by sudden jerks, by abrupt starts. Then we remain stationary a time, or we may even slip back and lose some of the ground we have previously gained. These periods of stagnation, or retrogression, are well known by all psychologists; and they have been named 'plateaus in the curve of learning'. Students of public speaking will sometimes be stalled for weeks on one of these plateaus. Work as hard as they may, they cannot get off it. The weak ones give up in despair. Those with grit persist, and they find that suddenly, overnight, without their knowing how or why it has happened, they have made great progress. They have lifted from the plateau like an aeroplane. Abruptly they have found the knack of the thing. Abruptly they have acquired naturalness and force and confidence in their speaking.

If you will but persevere, you will soon eradicate everything but this initial fear; and that will be initial fear, and nothing more. After the first few sentences, you will have control of yourself. You will be speaking with positive pleasure.

DON'T GIVE UP

One time a young man who aspired to study law, wrote to Lincoln for advice, and Lincoln replied: 'If you are resolutely determined to make a lawyer of yourself, the thing is more than half done already... Always bear in mind that your own resolution to succeed is more important than any other one thing.'

Lincoln knew. He had gone through it all. He had never, in his entire life, had more than a total of one year's schooling. And books? Lincoln once said he had walked and borrowed every book within fifty miles of his home. A log fire was usually kept going all night in the cabin. Sometimes he read by the light of that fire. There were cracks between the logs, and Lincoln often kept a book sticking in a crack. As soon as it was light enough to read in the morning, he rolled over on his bed of leaves, rubbed his eyes, pulled out the book and began devouring it.

He walked twenty and thirty miles to hear a speaker and, returning home, he practised his talks everywhere—in the fields, in the woods, before the crowds gathered at Jones' grocery at Gentryville. He joined literary and debating societies in New Salem and Springfield, and practised speaking on the topics of the day much as you are doing now as a member of this course.

A sense of inferiority always troubled him. In the presence of women he was shy and dumb. When he courted Mary Todd he used to sit in the parlour, bashful and silent, unable to find words, listening while she did the talking. Yet that was the man who, by practise and home study, made himself into the speaker who debated with the accomplished orator, Senator Douglas. That was the man who, at Gettysburg, and again in his second inaugural address, rose to heights of eloquence that have rarely been attained in all the annals of mankind.

There is an excellent picture of Abraham Lincoln in the President's office. 'Often when I had some matter to decide,' said Theodore Roosevelt, 'something involved and difficult to dispose of, something where there were conflicting rights and interests, I would look up at Lincoln, try to imagine him in my place, try to figure out what he would do in the same circumstances. It may sound odd to you, but, frankly, it seemed to make my troubles easier of solution.'

Why not try Roosevelt's plan? Why not, if you are discouraged and feeling like giving up the fight to make a speaker of yourself, why not pull out of your pocket one of the five dollar notes that bear a likeness of Lincoln, and ask yourself what he would do under the circumstances. You know what he would do. You know what he did do. After he had been beaten by Stephen A. Douglas in the race for the US Senate, he admonished his followers not to 'give up after one nor one hundred defeats'.

THE CERTAINTY OF REWARD

How I wish I could get you to prop this book open on your breakfast table every morning for a week until you had memorized these words from Professor William James, the famous psychologist:

> Let no youth have any anxiety about the upshot of his education, whatever the line of it may be. If he keeps faithfully busy each hour of the working day, he may safely leave the final result to itself. He can, with perfect certainty, count on waking up some fine morning to find himself one of the competent ones of his generation, in whatever pursuit he may have singled out.

The entire question of your success as a speaker hinges upon only two things—your native ability, and the depth and strength of your desires.

I have known and carefully watched literally thousands of men trying to gain self-confidence and the ability to talk in public. Those that succeeded were, in only a few instances, men of unusual brilliancy. For the most part, they were the ordinary run of businessmen that you will find in your own hometown. But they kept on. Smarter men sometimes got discouraged or too deeply immersed in money making, and they did not get very far, but the ordinary individual with grit and singleness of purpose—at the end of the chapter, he was at the top.

That is only human and natural. Don't you see the same thing occurring all the time in commerce and the professions? Rockefeller said some time ago that the first essential for success in business was patience. It is likewise one of the first essentials for success in this course.

CLIMBING THE 'WILDER KAISER'

A few summers ago, I started out to scale a peak in the Austrian Alps called the Wilder Kaiser. Baedeker said that the ascent was difficult, and a guide was essential for amateur climbers. We, a friend and I, had none, and we were certainly amateurs, so a third party asked us if we thought we were going to succeed. 'Of course,' we replied.

'What makes you think so?' he inquired.

'Others have done it without guides,' I said, 'so I know it is within reason, and I never undertake anything thinking defeat.'

As an Alpinist, I am the merest, bungling novice, but that is the proper psychology for anything from essaying public speaking to an assault on Mount Everest.

Think success in this course. See yourself in your imagination talking in public with perfect self-control.

It is easily in your power to do this. Believe that you will succeed. Believe it firmly and you will then do what is necessary to bring success about.

The most valuable thing that most members acquire from a course in public speaking is an increased confidence in themselves, an additional faith in their ability to achieve. And than that, what is more important for one's success in almost any undertaking?

THE WILL TO WIN

Here is a bit of sage advice from Elbert Hubbard that I cannot refrain from quoting. If the average man would only apply and live the wisdom contained in it, he would be happier, more prosperous:

> Whenever you go out of doors, draw the chin in, carry the crown of the head high and fill the lungs to the utmost; drink in the sunshine, greet your friends with a smile and put soul into every handclasp. Do not fear being misunderstood and do not waste a minute thinking about your enemies. Try to fix firmly in your mind what you would like to do, and then, without veering off direction, you will move straight to the goal. Keep your mind on the great and splendid things you would like to do, and then, as the days go gliding by, you will find yourself unconsciously seizing upon the opportunities that are required for the fulfilment of your desire, just as the coral insect takes from the running tide the elements it needs. Picture in your mind the able, earnest, useful person you desire to be, and the thought you hold is hourly transforming you into that particular individual.... Thought is supreme. Preserve a right mental attitude—the attitude of courage, frankness and good cheer. To think rightly is to create. All things come through desire and every sincere prayer is answered. We become like that on which our hearts are fixed. Carry your chin in and the crown of your head high. We are gods in the chrysalis.

> *Permanence, perseverance and persistence in spite of all obstacles, discouragement, and impossibilities: It is this, that in all things distinguishes the strong soul from the weak.*
> —Thomas Carlyle

THE IMPROVEMENT OF MEMORY

Memory...is the diary that we all carry about with us.
—Oscar Wilde

'The average man,' says the noted psychologist, Professor Carl Seashore, 'does not use above 10 per cent of his actual inherited capacity for memory. He wastes the 90 per cent by violating the natural laws of remembering.'

Are you one of these average men? If so, you are struggling under a handicap both socially and commercially; consequently, you will be interested in, and profit by, reading and rereading this chapter. It describes and explains these natural laws of remembering and shows how to use them in business as well as in speaking.

These 'natural laws of remembering' are very simple. There are only three. Every so-called 'memory system' has been founded upon them. Briefly, they are impression, repetition, and association.

The first mandate of memory is: Get a deep, vivid and lasting impression of the thing you wish to retain. And to do that, you must concentrate. Five minutes of vivid, energetic concentration will produce greater results than days of mooning about in a mental haze.

This is one of the secrets of power, especially memory power.

POWER OF OBSERVATION

Thomas Edison found that twenty-seven of his assistants had used, every day for six months, a certain path which led from his lamp factory to the main works at Menlo Park, New Jersey. A cherry tree grew along that path, and yet not one of these twenty-seven men had, when questioned, ever been conscious of that tree's existence.

'The average person's brain,' observes Mr Edison with heat and energy, 'does not observe a thousandth part of what the eye observes. It is almost incredible how poor our powers of observation—genuine observation—are.'

Introduce the average man to two or three of your friends and, the chances are that two minutes afterwards he cannot recall the name of a single one of them. And why? Because he never paid sufficient attention to them in the first place; he never accurately observed them. He will likely tell you he has a poor memory. No, he has a poor observation.

The late Mr Pulitzer, who made the *New York World*, had three words placed over the desk of every man in his editorial offices: Accuracy

ACCURACY, ACCURACY

That is what we want. Hear the man's name precisely. Insist on it. Ask him to repeat it. Inquire how it is spelled. He will be flattered by your interest and you will be able to remember his name because you have concentrated on it. You have got a clear accurate impression.

MEMORIZING A BOOK AS LONG AS THE NEW TESTAMENT

One of the largest universities in the world is the El Hazar at Cairo. It is a Mohammedan institution with twenty-one thousand students. The entrance examination requires every applicant to repeat the Koran from memory. The Koran is about as long as the New Testament, and three days are required to recite it!

The Chinese students, or 'study boys' as they are called, have to memorize some of the religious and classical books of China.

How are these Arab and Chinese students—many of them men of mediocre ability—able to perform these apparently prodigious feats of memory?

By repetition, the second 'natural law of remembering'. You can memorize an almost endless amount of material if you will repeat it often enough. Go over the knowledge you want to remember. Use it. Apply it. Employ the new word in your conversation. Call the stranger by his name if you want to remember it. Talk over in conversation the points you want to make in your public address. The knowledge that is used tends to stick.

THE KIND OF REPETITION THAT COUNTS

But the mere blind, mechanical going over a thing by rote is not enough. Intelligent repetition, repetition done in accordance with certain well-established traits of the mind—that is what we must have. For example, Professor Ebbinghaus gave his students a long list of nonsense syllables to memorize, such as 'deyux', 'qoli', and so on. He found that these students memorized as many of these syllables by thirty-eight repetitions, distributed over a period of three days, as they did by sixty-eight repetitions done at a single sitting. Other psychological tests have repeatedly shown similar results.

This is a very significant discovery about the working of our memories. It means that we know now that the man who sits down and repeats a thing over and over until he finally fastens it in his memory, is using twice as much time and energy as is necessary to achieve the same results when the repeating process is done at judicious intervals.

This peculiarity of the mind—if we can call it such—can be explained by two factors:

First, during the intervals between repetitions, our subconscious minds are busy making the associations more secure. As Professor William James sagely remarks: 'We learn to swim during the winter and to skate during the summer.'

Second, the mind, coming to the task at intervals, is not fatigued by the strain of an unbroken application. Sir Richard Burton, the translator of the Arabian Nights, spoke twenty-seven languages like a native: Yet he confessed that he never studied or practised any language for more than fifteen minutes at a time, 'for, after that, the brain lost its freshness.'

Surely, now, in the face of these facts, no man who prides himself on his common sense, will delay the preparation of a talk until the night before it is to be given. If he does, his memory will, of necessity, be working at only one-half its possible efficiency.

Here is a very helpful discovery about the way in which we forget. Psychological experiments have repeatedly shown that of the new material we have learned, we forget more during the first eight hours than during the next thirty days. An amazing ratio! So, immediately before you go into a business conference, immediately before you make a speech, look over your data, think over your facts, refresh your memory.

PROFESSOR WILLIAM JAMES EXPLAINS THE SECRET OF A GOOD MEMORY

So much for the first two laws of remembering. The third one, association, however, is the indispensable element in recalling. In fact, it is the explanation of memory itself. 'Our mind is,' as Professor James has sagely observed, essentially an associating machine.... Suppose I am silent for a moment, and then say in commanding accents: 'Remember! Recollect!' Does your faculty of memory obey the order, and reproduce any definite image from your past? Certainly not. It stands staring into vacancy, and asking, 'What kind of thing do you wish me to remember?' It needs, in short, a cue. But, if I say, remember the date of your birth, or remember what you had for breakfast, or remember the succession of notes in the musical scale; then your faculty of memory immediately produces the required result: The cue determines its vast set of potentialities toward a particular point. And if you now look to see how this happens, you immediately perceive that the cue is something contiguously associated with the thing recalled. The words, 'date of my birth,' have an ingrained association with a particular number, month, and year; the words, 'breakfast this morning,' cut off all other lines of recall except those which lead to coffee and bacon and eggs; the words, 'musical scale,' are inveterate mental neighbours of do, re, mi, fa, sol, la, etc. The laws of association govern, in fact, all the trains of our thinking which are not interrupted by sensations breaking on us from without. Whatever appears in the mind must be introduced; and, when introduced, it is as the associate of something already there. This is as true of what you are recollecting as it is of everything else you think of.... An educated memory depends upon an organized system of associations, and its goodness depends on two of their peculiarities: First, on the persistency of the associations; and, second, on their number.... The 'secret of a good memory' is thus the secret of forming diverse and multiple associations with every fact we care to retain. But this forming of associations with a fact—what is it but thinking about the fact as much as possible? Briefly, then, of two men with the same outward experiences, the one who thinks over his experiences most, and weaves them into the most systematic relations with each other, will be the one with the best memory.

HOW TO LINK YOUR FACTS TOGETHER

Very good, but how are we to set about weaving our facts into systematic relations with each other? The answer is: By finding their meaning, by thinking them over. For example, if you will ask and answer these questions about any new fact, that process will help to weave it into a systematic relation with other facts.

    (a) Why is this so?
    (b) How is this so?
    (c) When is it so?
    (d) Where is it so?
    (e) Who said it is so?

If it is a stranger's name, for example, and it is a common one, we can perhaps tie it to some business friend who bears the same name. On the other hand, if it is unusual, we can take occasion to say so. This often leads the stranger to talk about his name. For example: While writing this chapter, I was introduced to a Mrs Soter. I requested her to spell the name and remarked upon its unusualness. 'Yes,' she replied, 'it is very uncommon. It is a Greek word meaning "the Saviour".' Then she told me about her husband's people who had come from Athens and of the high positions they had held in the government there. I have found it quite easy to get people to talk about their names, and it always helps me to remember them.

Observe the stranger's looks sharply. Note the colour of his eyes and his hair, and look closely at his features. Note how he is dressed. Listen to his manner of talking. Get a clear, keen, vivid impression of his looks and personality, and associate these with his name. The next time these sharp impressions return to your mind, they will help bring the name with them.

Haven't you had the experience, when meeting a man for the second or third time, to discover that although you could remember his business or profession, you could not recall his name? The reason is this: A man's business is something definite and concrete. It has a meaning. It will adhere like a court plaster while his meaningless name will roll away like hail falling on a steep roof. Consequently, to make sure of your ability to recall a man's name, fashion a phrase about it that will tie it up to his business. There can be no doubt whatever about the efficacy of this method.

HOW TO REMEMBER DATES

Dates can best be retained by connecting them with important dates already firmly established in the mind. Isn't it far more difficult, for example, for an American to remember that the Suez Canal was opened in 1869 than to remember that the first ship passed through it four years after the close of the Civil War? If an American tried to remember that the first settlement in Australia was made in 1788, the date is likely to drop out of his mind like a loose bolt out of a car; it is far more likely to stick if he thinks of it in connection with July 4, 1776, and remembers that it occurred twelve years after the Declaration of Independence. That is like screwing a nut on the loose bolt. It holds.

It is well to bear this principle in mind when you are selecting a telephone number. For example, they might forget that your phone number was 1492, if you gave them the information in a colourless fashion; but would it slip their minds if you said, 'You can easily remember my phone number; 1492, the year Columbus discovered America.'

HOW TO REMEMBER THE POINTS OF YOUR TALK

There are only two ways by which we can possibly think of a thing: First, by means of an outside stimulus; second, by association with something already in the mind. Applied to speeches, that means just this: First, you can recall your points by the aid of some outside stimulus such as notes—but who likes to see a speaker use notes? Second, you can remember your points by associating them with something already in the mind. They should be arranged in such a logical order that the first one leads inevitably to the second, and the second to the third as naturally as the door of one room leads into another.

That sounds simple, but it may not prove so for the beginner whose thinking powers are rendered hors de combat with fear. There is, however, a method of tying your points together that is easy, rapid, and all but foolproof. I refer to the use of a nonsense sentence. To illustrate: Suppose you wish to discuss a veritable jumble of ideas, unassociated and hence hard to remember, such as, for example, cow, cigar, Napoleon, house, religion. Let us see if we cannot weld those ideas like the links of a chain by means of this absurd sentence: 'The cow smoked a cigar and hooked Napoleon, and the house burned down with religion.'

Now, will you please cover the above sentence with your hand while you answer these questions? What is the third point in that talk, the fifth, fourth, second, first?

Does the method work? It does! And the members of this course are urged to use it.

Any group of ideas can be linked together in some such fashion, and the more ridiculous the sentence used for the linking, the easier it will be to recall.

WHAT TO DO IN CASE OF A COMPLETE BREAKDOWN

Let us suppose that, in spite of all his preparation and precaution, a speaker, in the middle of his talk, suddenly finds his mind a blank—suddenly finds himself staring at his hearers completely balked, unable to go on—a terrifying situation. He feels that he might be able to think of his next point, of some point, if he had only ten, fifteen seconds of grace; but even fifteen seconds of frantic silence before an audience would be little less than disastrous. What is to be done? When a certain well-known US Senator recently found himself in this situation he asked his audience if he were speaking loudly enough, if he could be heard distinctly in the back of the room. He knew that he was. He was not seeking information. He was seeking time. And in that momentary pause, he grasped his thought and proceeded.

But perhaps the best life-saver in such a mental hurricane is this: Use the last word, or phrase, or idea in your last sentence for the beginning of a new sentence. This will make an endless chain that, like Tennyson's brook and, I regret to say, with as little purpose as Tennyson's brook, will run on forever. Let us see how it works in practise. Let us imagine that a speaker, talking on Business Success, finds himself in a blind mental alley after having said: 'The average employee does not get ahead because he takes so little real interest in his work, displays so little initiative.'

'Initiative'. Start a sentence with 'initiative'. You will probably have no idea of what you are going to say or how you are going to end the sentence, but, nevertheless, begin. Even a poor showing is more to be desired than utter defeat.

'Initiative means originality, doing a thing on your own, without eternally waiting to be told.'

That is not a scintillating observation. It won't make speech history. But isn't it better than an agonizing silence? Our last phrase was what?—'waiting to be told.' All right, let us start a new sentence with that idea.

'The constant telling and guiding and driving of employees who refuse to do any original thinking is one of the most exasperating things imaginable.'

Well, we got through that one. Let us plunge again. This time we must say something about imagination:

'Imagination—that is what is needed. Vision. "Where there is no vision," Solomon said, "the people perish".'

We did two that time without a hitch. Let us take heart and continue:

'The number of employees who perish each year in the battle of business is really lamentable. I say lamentable, because with just a little more loyalty, a little more ambition, a little more enthusiasm, these same men and women might have lifted themselves over the line of demarcation between success and failure. Yet the failure in business never admits that this is the case.'

And so on.... While the speaker is saying these platitudes off the top of his mind, he should, at the same time, be thinking hard of the next point in his planned speech, of the thing he had originally intended to say.

This endless chain method of talking will, if continued very long, trap the speaker into discussing plum pudding or the price of canary birds. However, it is a splendid first aid to the injured mind broken down temporarily through forgetfulness: And, as such, it has been the means of resuscitating many a gasping and dying speech.

WE CANNOT IMPROVE OUR MEMORIES FOR ALL CLASSES OF THINGS

I have pointed out in this chapter how we may improve our methods of getting vivid impressions, of repeating and of tying our facts together. But memory is so essentially a matter of association that 'there can be', as Professor James points out, 'no improvement of the general or elementary faculty of memory; there can only be improvement of our memory for special systems of associated things.'

By memorizing, for instance, a quotation a day from Shakespeare, we may improve our memory for literary quotations to a surprising degree. Each additional quotation will find many friends in the mind to tie to. But the memorizing of everything from Hamlet to Romeo will not necessarily aid one in retaining facts about the cotton market or the Bessemer process for desiliconizing pig iron.

Let us repeat: If we apply and use the principles discussed in this chapter, we will improve our manner and efficiency for memorizing anything, but, if we do not apply these principles, then the memorizing of ten million facts about football will not help us in the slightest in memorizing facts about the stock market. Such unrelated data cannot be tied together. 'Our mind is essentially an associating machine.'

It is safe to say that the businessman's most
immediate need is a serviceable memory.
—E.B. Gowin

8

THE SECRET OF GOOD DELIVERY

Instructions for making a speech:
Be sincere, be brief, be seated.
—Franklin D. Roosevelt

Shortly after the close of the last war, I met two brothers in London, Sir Ross and Sir Keith Smith. They had just made the first aeroplane flight from London to Australia, had won the fifty thousand dollar prize offered by the Australian government, had created a sensation throughout the British Empire, and had been knighted by the King.

Captain Hurley, a well-known scenic photographer, had flown with them over a part of their trip, taking motion pictures; so I helped them prepare an illustrated travel talk of their flight and trained them in the delivery of it. They gave it twice daily for four months in Philharmonic Hall, London, one speaking in the afternoon and the other at night.

They had had identically the same experience, had sat side by side as they flew halfway around the world, and they delivered the same talk almost word for word. Yet, somehow it didn't sound like the same talk at all.

There is something besides the mere words in a talk which counts. It is the flavour with which they are delivered. 'It is not so much what you say as how you say it.'

I have often noticed in college contests that it is not always the speaker with the best material who wins. Rather, it is the speaker who can talk so well that his material sounds best.

'Three things matter in a speech,' Lord Morley once observed with gay cynicism, 'who says it, how he says it, and what he says—and, of the three, the last matters the least.' An exaggeration? Yes, but scratch the surface of it and you will find the truth shining through. Look well, therefore, to your delivery.

THE ART OF DELIVERY

What does a department store do when it 'delivers' the article you have bought? Does the driver just toss the package into the backyard and let it go at that? Is merely getting a thing out of one's own hands the same as getting it delivered?

Let me give you an illustration that is typical of the fashion in which thousands of men talk. I happened on one occasion to be stopping in Murren, a summer resort in the Swiss Alps. I was living at a hotel operated by a London company, and they usually sent out from England a couple of lecturers each week to talk to the guests. One of them was a well-known English novelist. Her topic was 'The Future of the Novel'. She admitted that she had not selected the subject herself; and the long and short of it was that she had nothing to say about it that she really cared enough about saying to make it worthwhile expressing. She had hurriedly made some rambling notes, and she stood before the audience ignoring her hearers, not even looking at them, staring sometimes over their heads, sometimes at her notes, sometimes at the floor. She called off her words into the primeval void with a faraway look in her eyes and a faraway ring in her voice.

That kind of performance isn't delivering a talk at all. It is a soliloquy. It has no sense of communication. And that is the first essential of good talking: A sense of communication. The audience must feel that there is a message being delivered straight from the mind and heart of the speaker to their minds and their hearts. The kind of talk I have just described might just as well have been spoken out in the sandy, waterless wastes of the Gobi desert. In fact, it sounded as if it were being delivered in some such spot rather than to a group of living human beings.

This matter of delivering a talk is, at the same time, a very simple and a very intricate process. It is also a very much misunderstood and abused one.

THE SECRET OF GOOD DELIVERY

An enormous amount of nonsense and twaddle has been written about delivery. It has been shrouded in rules and rites and made mysterious. Old-fashioned 'elocution', that abomination in the sight of God and man, has often made it ridiculous.

A modern audience, regardless of whether it is fifteen people at a business conference or a thousand people under a tent, wants the speaker to talk just as directly as he would in a chat, and in the same general manner that he would employ in speaking to one of them in conversation.

In the same manner, but not with the same amount of force. If he tries that, he will hardly be heard. In order to appear natural he has to use much more energy in talking to forty people than he does in talking to one; just as a statue on top of a building has to be of heroic size in order to make it appear of lifelike proportions to an observer on the ground.

I have just described the delivery of a certain novelist. In the same ballroom in which she had spoken, I had the pleasure, a few nights later, of hearing Sir Oliver Lodge. His subject was 'Atoms and Worlds'. He had devoted to it more than half a century of thought and study and experiment and investigation. He had something that was essentially a part of his heart and mind and life, something that he wanted very much to say. He forgot—and I, for one, thanked God that he did forget—that he was trying to make a speech. That was the least of his worries. He was concerned only with telling the audience about atoms, telling us accurately and lucidly and feelingly. He was earnestly trying to get us to see what he saw and to feel what he felt.

And what was the result? He delivered a remarkable talk. It had both charm and power. It made a deep impression. He was a speaker of unusual ability. Yet I am sure he didn't regard himself in that light.

I am sure that few people who heard him ever think of him as a public speaker at all.

If you, my dear reader, speak in public so that people hearing you will suspect that you have had training in public speaking, you will not be a credit to your instructor. He desires you to speak with such intensified and exalted naturalness that your auditors will never dream that you have been trained. A good window does not call attention to itself. It merely lets in the light. A good speaker is like that. He is so natural that his hearers never notice his manner of speaking; they are conscious only of his matter.

The problem of teaching or of training men in delivery is not one of superimposing additional characteristics; it is largely one of removing impediments, of freeing men, of getting them to speak with the same naturalness that they would display if someone were to knock them down.

Hundreds of times I have stopped speakers in the midst of their talks and implored them to 'talk like a human being'. Hundreds of nights I have come home mentally fatigued and nervously exhausted from trying to drill and force men to talk naturally. No, believe me, it is not so easy as it sounds.

And the only way under high Heaven by which you can get the knack of this enlarged naturalness is by practise. And, as you practise, if you find yourself talking in a stilted manner, pause and say sharply to yourself mentally: 'Here! What is wrong? Wake up. Be human.' Then pick out some man in the audience, some man in the back, the dullest looking chap you can find, and talk to him. Forget there is anyone else present at all. Converse with him. Imagine that he has asked you a question and that you are answering it. If he were to stand up and talk to you, and you were to talk back to him, that process would immediately and inevitably make your talking more conversational, more natural, more direct. So, imagine that that is precisely what is taking place.

Sincerity and enthusiasm and high earnestness will help you too. When a man is under the influence of his feelings, his real self comes to the surface. The bars are down. The heat of his emotions has burned all barriers away. He acts spontaneously. He talks spontaneously. He is natural.

So, in the end, even this matter of delivery comes back to the thing which has already been emphasized repeatedly in these pages: Namely, put your heart in your talks.

FEATURES OF NATURAL SPEAKING

We are going to discuss here some of the features of natural speaking in order to make them more clear, more vivid. I have hesitated about doing it, for someone is almost sure to say: 'Ah, I see, just force myself to do these things and I'll be all right.' No, you won't. Force yourself to do them and you will be all wooden and all mechanical.

You used most of these principles yesterday in your conversation, used them as unconsciously as you digested your dinner last night. That is the way to use them. It is the only way. And it will come, as far as public speaking is concerned, as we have already said, only by practice.

First: Stress important words, subordinate unimportant ones

In conversation, we hit one syllable in a word, and hit it hard, and hurry over the others like a pay car passing a string of hoboes. For example, MassaCHUsetts, afFLICtion, atTRACtiveness, enVIRonment. We do almost the same thing with a sentence. We make one or two important words tower up like a skyscraper.

This is not a strange or unusual process I am describing. Listen. You can hear it going on about you all the time. You yourself did it a hundred, maybe a thousand, times yesterday. You will doubtless do it a hundred times tomorrow.

Here is an example. Read the following quotation, striking the works in big type hard. Run over the others quickly. What is the effect?

I have SUCCEEDED in whatever I have undertaken, because I have WILLED it. I have NEVER HESITATED which has given me an ADVANTAGE over the rest of mankind.'—Napoleon.

This is not the only way to read these lines. Another speaker would do it differently perhaps. There are no ironclad rules for emphasis. It all depends.

Second: Change your pitch

The pitch of our voices in conversation flows up and down the scale from high to low and back again, never resting, but always shifting like the face of the sea. Why? No one knows, and no one cares. The effect is pleasing, and it is the way of nature. We never had to learn to do this: It came to us as children, unsought and unaware, but let us stand up and face an audience, and the chances are our voices will become as dull and flat and monotonous as the alkali deserts.

When you find yourself talking in a monotonous pitch—and usually it will be a high one—just pause for a second and say to yourself: 'I am speaking like a wooden Indian. Talk to these people. Be human. Be natural.'

Will that kind of lecture to yourself help you any? A little, perhaps. The pause itself will help you. You have to work out your own salvation by practice.

You can make any phrase or word that you choose stand out like a green bay-tree by either suddenly lowering or raising your pitch on it.

Third: Vary your rate of speaking

When a little child talks, or when we talk in ordinary conversation, we constantly change our rate of speaking. It is pleasing. It is natural. It is unconscious. It is emphatic. It is, in fact, one of the very best of all possible ways to make an idea stand out prominently.

Walter B. Stevens, in his Reporter's Lincoln, issued by the Missouri Historical Society, tells us that this was one of Lincoln's favourite methods of driving a point home:

He would speak several words, with great rapidity, come to the word or phrase he wished to emphasize, and let his voice linger and bear hard on that, and then he would rush to the end of his sentence like lightning... He would devote as much time to the word or two he wished to emphasize as he did to half a dozen less important words following it.

Try this: Say 'thirty million dollars' quickly and with an air of triviality so that it sounds like a very small sum. Now, say 'thirty thousand dollars': Say it slowly, say it feelingly, say it as if you were tremendously impressed with the hugeness of the amount. Haven't you now made the thirty thousand sound larger than the thirty million?

Fourth: Pause before and after important ideas

Lincoln often paused in his speaking. When he had come to a big idea that he wished to impress deeply on the minds of his hearers, he bent forward, looked directly into their eyes for a moment and said nothing at all. This sudden silence had the same effect as a sudden noise: It attracted notice. It made everyone attentive, alert, awake to what was coming next. For example, when his famous debates with Douglas were drawing to a close, when all the indications pointed to his defeat, he became depressed, his old habitual melancholy stealing over him at times, and imparting to his words a touching pathos. In one of his concluding speeches, he suddenly 'stopped and stood silent for a moment, looking round upon the throng of half-indifferent, half-friendly faces before him, with those deep-sunken weary eyes that always seemed full of unshed tears. Folding his hands, as if they too were tired of the helpless fight, he said, in his peculiar monotone: "My friends, it makes little difference, very little difference, whether Judge Douglas or myself is elected to the United States Senate, but the great issue which we have submitted to you today is far above and beyond any personal interests or the political fortunes of any man. And my friends," here he paused again, and the audience were intent on every word, "that issue will live and breathe and burn when the poor, feeble, stammering tongues of Judge Douglas and myself are silent in the grave'".

'These simple words,' relates one of his biographers, 'and the manner in which they were spoken, touched every heart to the core.'

Lincoln also paused after the phrase he wanted to emphasize.

He added to their force by keeping silent while the meaning sank in and effected its mission.

Read this selection aloud without pausing; then read it again, making the pauses I have indicated. What is the effect of the pauses?

'Selling goods is a battle,' (pause and let the idea of battle soak in) 'and only fighters can win in it.' (Pause and let that point soak in.) 'We may not like these conditions, but we didn't have the making of them and we can't alter them.' (Pause.) 'Take your courage with you when you enter the selling game.' (Pause.) 'If you don't,' (pause and lengthen out suspense for a second) 'you'll strike out every time you come to bat, and score nothing higher than a string of goose eggs.' (Pause). 'The fellow who knocks the cover off the ball or lifts it over the fence is always the chap who steps up to the plate' (pause and increase the suspense as to what you are going to say about this extraordinary player) 'with grim determination in his heart.'

A speaker may follow the directions I have set down in this lesson and still have a hundred faults. He may talk in public just as he does in conversation and consequently, he may speak with an unpleasant voice and make grammatical errors and be awkward and offensive and do a score of unpleasant things. A man's natural method of every day talking may need a vast number of improvements. Perfect your natural method of talking in conversation, and then carry that method to the platform.

> *The mastery of forceful speech is one of the noblest*
> *purposes to which a man can address himself.*
> —Newell Dwight Hillis

> *Perhaps there is no more important component of character than*
> *steadfast resolution. The boy who is going to make a great man, or*
> *is going to count in any way in after-life, must make up his mind*
> *not merely to overcome a thousand obstacles, but to win in spite of a*
> *thousand repulses and defeats.*
> —Theodore Roosevelt

9

PLATFORM PRESENCE AND PERSONALITY

Let the counsel of thine own heart stand, for no man is more faithful
unto thee than it. It is sometimes wont to show thee more than seven
watchmen who sit above in a high tower.

—Rudyard Kipling

The Carnegie Institute of Technology at one time gave intelligence tests to one hundred prominent businessmen. The tests were similar to those used in the army during the war, and the results led the institute to declare that personality contributes more to business success than does superior intelligence.

That is a very significant pronouncement: Very significant for the businessman, very significant for the educator, very significant for the professional man, very significant for the speaker.

Personality—with the exception of preparation—is probably the most important factor in public address. 'In eloquent speaking,' declared Elbert Hubbard, 'it is manner that wins, not words.' Rather it is manner plus ideas. But personality is a vague and elusive thing, defying analysis like the perfume of the violet. It is the whole combination of the man, the physical, the spiritual, the mental; his traits, his predilections, his tendencies, his temperament, his cast of mind, his vigour, his experience, his training, his life. It is as complex as Einstein's theory of relativity, almost as little understood.

If you wish to make the most of your individuality, go before your audience rested. A tired man is not magnetic nor attractive. Don't make the all-too-common error of putting off your preparation and your planning until the very last moment, and then working at a furious pace, trying to make up for lost time. If you do, you are bound to store up bodily poisons and brain fatigues that will prove terrific drags, holding you down, sapping your vitality, weakening both your brain and your nerves.

When you have to make an important talk, beware of your hunger. Eat as sparingly as a saint. On Sunday afternoons, Henry Ward Beecher used to have biscuits and milk at five, and nothing after that.

'When I am singing in the evening,' said Madame Melba, 'I do not dine but have a very light repast at five o'clock, consisting of either fish, chicken, or sweetbread, with a baked apple and a glass of water. I always find myself very hungry for supper when I get home from the opera or concert.'

How wisely Melba and Beecher acted, I never realized until after I became a professional speaker myself and tried to deliver a two-hour talk each evening having consumed a hearty meal.

WHAT MAKES A GOOD SPEAKER

Do nothing to dull your energy. It is magnetic. Vitality, aliveness, enthusiasm: They are among the first qualities I have always sought for in employing speakers and instructors of speaking. People cluster around the energetic speaker, the human dynamo of energy, like wild geese around a field of autumn wheat.

THE IMPORTANCE OF GROOMING

An inquiry was sent to a large group of people by a psychologist and university president, asking them the impression clothes made on them. All but unanimously, they testified that when they were well groomed and faultlessly and immaculately attired, the knowledge of it, the feeling of it, had an effect which, while it was difficult to explain, was still very definite, very real. It gave them more confidence, brought them increased faith in themselves, and heightened their self-respect. They declared that when they had the look of success they found it easier to think success, to achieve success. Such is the effect of clothes on the wearer himself.

What effect do they have on an audience? I have noticed time and again that if a speaker has baggy trousers, shapeless coat and footwear, fountain pen and pencils peeping out of his breast pocket, a newspaper or a pipe and tin of tobacco bulging out the sides of his garment—I have noticed that an audience has as little respect for that man as he has for his own appearance. Aren't they very likely to assume that his mind is as sloppy as his unkempt hair and unpolished shoes?

BEING IN THE SPOTLIGHT

A number of years ago, I was writing the life story of a certain banker for a magazine. I asked one of his friends to explain the reason for his success. No small amount of it, he said, was due to the man's winning smile. At first thought, that may sound like exaggeration but I believe it is really true. Other men, scores of them, hundreds of them, may have had more experience and as good financial judgment, but he had an additional asset they didn't possess—he had a most agreeable personality. And a warm, welcoming smile was one of the striking features of it. It gained one's confidence immediately. It secured one's goodwill instantly. We all want to see a man like that succeed, and it is a real pleasure to give him our patronage.

'He who cannot smile,' says a Chinese proverb, 'ought not to keep a shop.' And isn't a smile just as welcome before an audience as behind a counter? I am thinking now of a particular student who attended a course in public speaking conducted by a Chamber of Commerce. He always came out before the audience with an air that said he liked to be there, that he loved the job that was before him. He always smiled and acted as if he were glad to see us, and so immediately and inevitably his hearers warmed towards him and welcomed him.

But I have seen speakers—students of this course, I regret

to admit—who walked out before the other members in a cold, perfunctory manner as if they had a disagreeable task to perform, and that, when it was over, they would thank God. We in the audience were soon feeling the same way. These attitudes are contagious.

SEAT YOUR AUDIENCE TOGETHER

As a public lecturer, I have frequently spoken to a small audience scattered through a large hall in the afternoon, and to a large audience packed into the same hall at night. The evening audience has laughed heartily at the same things that brought only a smile to the faces of the afternoon group; the evening crowd has applauded generously at the very places where the afternoon gathering was utterly unresponsive. Why?

For one thing, the elderly women and the children that are likely to come in the afternoon cannot be expected to be as demonstrative as the more vigorous and discriminating evening crowd; but that is only a partial explanation.

The fact is that no audience will be easily moved when it is scattered. Nothing so dampens enthusiasm as wide, open spaces and empty chairs between the listeners.

If you are going to talk to a small group, you should choose a small room. Better to pack the aisles of a small place than to have people scattered through the lonely, deadening spaces of a large hall.

If your hearers are scattered, ask them to move down front and be seated near you. Insist on this, before you start speaking.

Unless the audience is a fairly large one, and there is a real reason, a necessity, for the speaker standing on a platform, don't do so. Get down on the same level with them. Stand near them. Break up all formality. Get an intimate contact. Make the thing conversational.

OPEN THE WINDOWS

Keep the air fresh. In the well-known process of public speaking, oxygen is just as essential as the larynx, pharynx and human epiglottis. All the eloquence of Cicero, and all the feminine pulchritude in Ziegfeld's Follies, could hardly keep an audience awake in a room poisoned with bad air. So, when I am one of a number of speakers, before beginning, I almost always ask the audience to stand up and rest for two minutes while the windows are thrown open.

For fourteen years Major James B. Pond travelled all over the United States and Canada as manager for Henry Ward Beecher when that famous preacher was at his flood tide as a popular lecturer. Before the audience assembled, Pond always visited the hall or church or theatre where Beecher was to appear, and rigorously inspected the lighting, seating, temperature and ventilation. Pond had been a blustering, roaring old army officer and he loved to exercise authority; so if the place was too warm or the air was dead and he could not get the windows open, he hurled books through them, smashing and shattering the glass. He believed with Spurgeon that 'the next best thing to the Grace of God for a preacher is oxygen'.

LET LIGHT SHINE ON YOUR FACE

Unless you are demonstrating spiritualism before a group of people, flood the room, if possible, with lights. It is as easy to domesticate a quail as to develop enthusiasm in a half-lighted room gloomy as the inside of a thermos bottle.

Read David Belasco's articles on stage production, and you will discover that the average speaker does not have the foggiest shadow of the ghost of an idea of the tremendous importance of proper lighting.

Let the light strike your face. People want to see you. The subtle changes that ought to play across your features are a part, and a very real part, of the process of self-expression. Sometimes they mean more than your words. If you stand directly under a light, your face may be dimmed by a shadow; if you stand directly in front of a light, it is sure to be. Would it not, then, be the part of wisdom to select, before you arise to speak, the spot that will give you the most advantageous illumination?

NO TRUMPERY ON THE PLATFORM

And do not hide behind a table. People want to look at the whole man. They will even lean out in the aisles to see all of him.

Some well-meaning soul is pretty sure to give you a table and a water pitcher and a glass; but if your throat becomes dry, a pinch of salt or a taste of lemon will start the saliva again better than Niagara.

You do not want the water nor the pitcher. Neither do you want all the other useless and ugly impedimenta that clutter up the average platform.

The sales rooms of the various automobile makers are beautiful, orderly, pleasing to the eye. The Paris offices of the large perfumers and jewellers are artistically and luxuriously appointed. Why? It is good business. One has more respect, more confidence, more admiration for a concern housed like that.

For the same reason, a speaker ought to have a pleasing background. The ideal arrangement, to my way of thinking, would be no furniture at all. Nothing behind the speaker to attract attention or at either side of him—nothing but a curtain of dark blue velvet.

But what does he usually have behind him? Maps and signs and tables, perhaps a lot of dusty chairs, some piled on top of the others. And what is the result? A cheap, slovenly, disorderly atmosphere. So clear all the trumpery away.

'The most important thing in public speaking,' said Henry Ward Beecher, 'is the man.'

So let the man stand out like the snow clad top of the Jungfrau towering against the blue skies of Switzerland.

NO GUESTS ON THE PLATFORM

I was once in London, Ontario, when the Prime Minister of Canada was speaking. Presently the janitor, armed with a long pole, started to ventilate the room, moving about from window to window. What happened? The audience, almost to a man, ignored the speaker for a little while and stared at the janitor as intently as if he had been performing some miracle.

An audience cannot resist—or, what comes to the same thing, it will not resist—the temptation to look at moving objects. If a speaker will only remember that truth, he can save himself some trouble and needless annoyance.

First, he can refrain from twiddling his thumbs, playing with his clothes and making little nervous movements that detract from him.

Second, the speaker should arrange, if possible, to have the audience seated so they won't have their attention distracted by seeing the latecomers enter.

Third, he should have no guests on the platform. A few years ago Raymond Robins delivered a series of talks. I, along with a number of others, was invited to sit on the platform with him. I declined on the ground that it was unfair to the speaker. I noted the first night how many of these guests shifted about and put one leg over the other and back again, and so on; and every time one of them moved, the audience looked away from the speaker to the guest. I called Mr Robins' attention to this the next day; and during the remainder of his evenings with us, he very wisely occupied the platform alone.

THE ART OF SITTING DOWN

Isn't it well for the speaker himself not to sit facing the audience before he begins? Isn't it better to arrive as a fresh exhibit than an old one?

But, if we must sit, let us be careful of how we sit. You have seen men look round to find a chair with the modified movements of a foxhound lying down for the night. They turned round and when they did locate a chair, they doubled up and flopped down into it with all the self-control of a sack of sand.

A man who knows how to sit feels the chair strike the back of his legs, and, with his body easily erect from head to hips, he sinks into it with his body under perfect control.

POISE

We just said, a few pages previously, not to play with your clothes because it attracted attention. There is another reason also. It gives an impression of weakness, a lack of self-control. Every movement that does not add to your presence detracts from it. There are no neutral movements. None. So stand still and control yourself physically and that will give you an impression of mental control, of poise.

After you have risen to address your audience, do not be in a hurry to begin. That is the hallmark of the amateur. Take a deep breath. Look over your audience for a moment; and, if there is a noise or disturbance, pause until it quiets down.

Hold your chest high. But why wait until you get before an audience to do this? Why not do it daily in private? Then you will do it unconsciously in public.

And what shall you do with your hands? Forget them. If they fall naturally to your sides, that is ideal. If they feel like a bunch of bananas to you, do not be deluded into imagining that anyone else is paying the slightest attention to them or has the slightest interest in them.

They will look best hanging relaxed at your sides. They will attract the minimum of attention there. Not even the hypercritical can criticize that position. Besides, they will be unhampered and free to flow naturally into gestures when the urge makes itself felt.

But suppose that you are very nervous and that you find putting them behind your back or shoving them into your pockets helps to relieve your self-consciousness—what should you do? Use your common sense. I have heard a number of celebrated speakers of this generation. Many, if not most, put their hands into their pockets occasionally while speaking. If a man has something to say worthwhile, and says it with contagious conviction, surely it will matter little what he does with his hands and feet. If his head is full and heart stirred, these secondary details will very largely take care of themselves.

There is often as much eloquence in the tone of the voice, in the eyes, and in the air of a speaker as in his choice of words.
—La Rochefoucauld

10

HOW TO MAKE YOUR MEANING CLEAR

Be brief, be pointed, let your matter stand lucid in order, solid and at hand; spend not your words on trifles but condense; strike with the mass of thought, not drops of sense; press to the close with vigor, once begun, and leave—how hard the task.
—Joseph Story

What do we mean by the purpose of an address? Just this: Every talk, regardless of whether the speaker realizes it or not, has one of four major goals. What are they?

1. To make something clear.
2. To impress and convince.
3. To get action.
4. To entertain.

Let us illustrate these by a concrete example.

Lincoln, who was always more or less interested in mechanics, once invented and patented a device for lifting stranded boats off sand bars and other obstructions. He worked in a mechanic's shop near his law office, making a model of his apparatus. Although the device finally came to naught, he was decidedly enthusiastic over its possibilities. When friends came to his office to view the model, he took no end of pains to explain it. The main purpose of those explanations was clearness.

When he delivered his immortal oration at Gettysburg, when he gave his first and second inaugural addresses, when Henry Clay died and Lincoln delivered an eulogy on his life—on all these occasions,

Lincoln's main purpose was impressiveness and conviction. He had to be clear, of course, because he could be convincing; but, in these instances, clearness was not his major consideration.

In his talks to juries, he tried to win favourable decisions. In his political talks, he tried to win votes. His purpose, then, was action. Two years before he was elected President, Lincoln prepared a lecture on Inventions. His purpose was entertainment. At least, that should have been his goal, but he was evidently not very successful in attaining it. His career as a popular lecturer was, in fact, a distinct disappointment. In one town, not a person came to hear him.

But he did succeed and he succeeded famously in the other speeches of his that I have referred to. And why? Because, in those instances, he knew his goal, and he knew how to achieve it. He knew where he wanted to go and how to get there. And because so many speakers don't know just that, they often flounder and come to grief.

Profit by his example. Know your goal. Choose it wisely before you set out to prepare your talk. Know how to reach it. Then set about it, doing it skilfully and with science.

All this requires knowledge, special and technical instruction. The remainder of this chapter will show you how to make your talks clear.

USE COMPARISONS TO PROMOTE CLEARNESS

As to clearness: Do not underestimate the importance of it or the difficulty. I recently heard a certain Irish poet give an evening of readings from his own poems. Not 10 per cent of the audience, half the time, knew what he was talking about. Many talkers, both in public and private, are a lot like that.

When I discussed the essentials of public speaking with Sir Oliver Lodge, a man who has been lecturing to university classes and to the public for forty years, he emphasized most of all the importance, first, of knowledge and preparation, and second, of 'taking good pains to be clear'.

And when you talk on a subject strange to your hearer or hearers, can you hope that they will understand you any more readily than people understood the Master?

Hardly. So what can we do about it? What did He do when confronted by a similar situation? Solved it in the most simple and natural manner imaginable: Described the things people did not know by likening them to things they did know.

Here is a rather striking and half-amusing example of the use of this principle: Some missionaries were translating the Bible into the dialect of a tribe near equatorial Africa. They progressed to the verse: 'Though your sins be as scarlet, they shall be white as snow.' How were they to translate that? Literally? Meaningless. Absurd. The natives had never scooped snow off the pathway on a February morning. They did not even have a word for snow. They could not have told the difference between snow and coal tar, but they had climbed coconut trees many times and shaken down a few nuts for lunch; so the missionaries likened the unknown to the known, and changed the verse to read: 'Though your sins be as scarlet, they shall be as white as the meat of a coconut.'

Under the circumstances, it would be hard to improve on that, wouldn't it?

Sir Oliver Lodge happily uses this method when explaining the size and nature of atoms to a popular audience. I heard him tell a European audience that there were as many atoms in a drop of water as there were drops of water in the Mediterranean Sea; and many of his hearers had spent over a week sailing from Gibraltar to the Suez Canal. To bring the matter still closer home, he said there were as many atoms in one drop of water as there were blades of grass on all the earth.

Use this principle henceforth in your talks. If you are describing the great pyramid, first tell your hearers it is 451 feet, then tell them how high that is in terms of some building they see every day. Tell how many city blocks the base would cover. Don't speak about so many thousand gallons of this or so many hundred thousand barrels of that without also telling how many rooms the size of the one you are speaking in could be filled with that much liquid. Instead of saying twenty feet high, why not say one and a half times as high as this ceiling? Instead of talking about distance in terms of rods or miles, is it not clearer to say as far as from here to some station, or to such and such a street?

AVOID TECHNICAL TERMS

If you belong to a profession the work of which is technical—if you are a lawyer, a physician, an engineer, or are in a highly specialized line of business—be doubly careful when you talk to outsiders, to express yourself in plain terms and to give necessary details.

I say be doubly careful for, as a part of my professional duties, I have listened to hundreds of speeches that failed right at this point and failed woefully. The speakers appeared totally unconscious of the general public's widespread and profound ignorance regarding their particular specialties. So what happened? They rambled on and on, uttering thoughts, using phrases that fitted into their experience and were instantly and continuously meaningful to them; but to the uninitiated, they were about as clear as a river after the rains have fallen on the newly-ploughed cornfields along its banks.

What should such a speaker do? He ought to read and heed the following advice from the facile pen of ex-Senator Beveridge:

It is a good practice to pick out the least intelligent looking person in the audience and strive to make that person interested in your argument. This can be done only by lucid statement of fact and clear reasoning. An even better method is to centre your talk on some small boy or girl present with parents.

Say to yourself—say out loud to your audience, if you like—that you will try to be so plain that the child will understand and remember your explanation of the question discussed, and after the meeting be able to tell what you have said.

APPEAL TO THE SENSE OF SIGHT

'One seeing,' says an old Japanese proverb, 'is better than a hundred times telling about.'

So, if you wish to be clear, picture your points, visualize your ideas.

Mr Rockefeller talks about how he appealed to the sense of sight to make clear the financial situation of the Colorado Fuel and Iron Company:

> I found that they (the employees of the Colorado Fuel and Iron Co.) imagined the Rockefellers had been drawing immense profits from their interests in Colorado; no end of people had told them so. I explained the exact situation to them. I showed them that during the fourteen years in which we had been connected with the Colorado Fuel and Iron Co., it had never paid one cent in dividends upon the common stock.
>
> At one of our meetings, I gave a practical illustration of the finances of the company. I put a number of coins on the table. I swept off a portion which represented their wages—for the first claim upon the company is the payroll. Then I took away more coins to represent the salaries of the officers, and then the remaining coins to represent the fees of the directors. There were no coins left for the stockholders. And when I asked: 'Men, is it fair, in this corporation where we are all partners, that three of the partners should get all the earnings, be they large or small—all of them—and the fourth nothing?'
>
> After the illustration, one of the men made a speech for higher wages. I asked him, 'Is it fair for you to want more wages when one of the partners gets nothing?' He admitted that it did not look like a square deal; I heard no more about increasing the wages.

Make your eye appeals definite and specific. Paint mental pictures that stand out as sharp and clear as a stag's horn silhouetted against the setting sun. For example, the word 'dog' calls up a more or less definite picture of such an animal—perhaps a cocker spaniel, a Scotch terrier, a St. Bernard, or a Pomeranian. Notice how much more distinct an image springs into your mind when I say 'bulldog'—the term is less inclusive.

RESTATE YOUR IMPORTANT IDEAS IN DIFFERENT WORDS

Napoleon declared repetition to be the only serious principle of rhetoric. He knew that because an idea which was clear to him was not always proof that it was instantly grasped by others. He knew that it takes time to comprehend new ideas, that the mind must be kept focused on them. In short, he knew they must be repeated. Not in exactly the same language. People will rebel at that, and rightly so. But if the repetition is couched in fresh phraseology, if it is varied, your hearers will never regard it as repetition at all.

Let us take a specific example. The late Mr Bryan said: 'You cannot make people understand a subject, unless you understand that subject yourself. The more clearly you have a subject in mind, the more clearly can you present that subject to the minds of others.'

The last sentence here is merely a restatement of the idea contained in the first, but when these sentences are spoken, the mind does not have time to see that it is repetition. It only feels that the subject has been made more clear.

I seldom teach a single session of this course without hearing one or perhaps half a dozen talks that would have been more clear, more impressive, had the speaker but employed this principle of restatement. It is almost entirely ignored by the beginner. And what a pity!

USE GENERAL ILLUSTRATIONS AND SPECIFIC INSTANCES

One of the surest and easiest ways to make your points clear is to follow them with general illustrations and concrete cases. What is the difference between the two? One, as the term implies, is general; the other, specific.

Let us illustrate the difference between them and the uses of each with a concrete example. Suppose we take the statement: 'There are professional men and women who earn astonishingly large incomes.' Is that statement very clear? Have you a clear-cut idea of what the speaker really means? No, and the speaker himself cannot be sure of what such an assertion will call up in the minds of others. It may cause the country doctor to think of a family doctor in a small city with an income of five thousand. It may cause a successful mining engineer to think in terms of the men in his profession who make a hundred thousand a year. The statement, as it stands, is entirely too vague and loose. It needs to be tightened. A few illuminating details ought to be given to indicate what professions the speaker refers to and what he means by 'astonishingly large'.

'There are lawyers, prize-fighters, song-writers, novelists, playwrights, painters, actors and singers who make more than the President of the United States.'

Be concrete. Be definite. Be specific. This quality of definiteness not only makes for clearness but for impressiveness and conviction and interest also.

11

IMPROVING YOUR DICTION

Be impeccable with your word. Speak with integrity. Say only what you mean. Avoid using the word to speak against yourself or to gossip about others. Use the power of your word in the direction of truth and love.
—Don Miguel Ruiz

A short time ago an Englishman, without employment and without financial reserves, was walking the streets seeking a position. He entered the office of Mr Paul Gibbons, a well-known businessman, and asked for an interview. Mr Gibbons looked at the stranger distrustfully. His appearance was emphatically against him. His clothes were shabby and threadbare, and over all of him were written large the unmistakable signs of financial distress. Half out of curiosity, half out of pity, Mr Gibbons granted the interview. At first, he had intended to listen for only a moment, but the moments grew into minutes, and the minutes mounted into an hour; and the conversation still continued. It ended by Mr Gibbons telephoning Mr Roland Taylor, the manager of a well-known firm of stockbrokers; and Mr Taylor, one of the leading financiers of that city, invited this stranger to lunch and secured for him a desirable position. How was this man, with the air and outward appearance of failure, able to effect such a prized connection within so short a time?

The secret can be divulged in a single phrase: His command of the English language. He was, in reality, an Oxford man who had come to town on a business mission which had ended in disaster, leaving him stranded, without funds and without friends. But he spoke his mother tongue with such precision and beauty that his listeners soon forgot his rusty shoes, his frayed coat, his unshaven face. His diction became an immediate passport into the best business circles.

This man's story is somewhat extraordinary, but it illustrates a broad and fundamental truth, namely, that we are judged each day by our speech. Our words reveal our refinements; they tell the discerning listener of the company we have kept; they are the hallmarks of education and culture.

We have only four contacts with the world, you and I. We are evaluated and classified by four things: By what we do, by how we look, by what we say, and by how we say it. Yet many a man blunders through a long life time, after he leaves school, without any conscious effort to enrich his stock of words, to master their shades of meaning, to speak with precision and distinction. He comes habitually to use the overworked and exhausted phrases of the office and street. Small wonder that his talk lacks distinction and individuality. Small wonder that he often violates the accepted traditions of pronunciation, and that he sometimes transgresses the very canons of English grammar itself. I have heard even college graduates say 'ain't', and 'he don't', and 'between you and I'. And if men with academic degrees gracing their names commit such errors, what can we expect of those whose education has been cut short by the pressure of economic necessity?

Years ago, I stood one afternoon daydreaming in the Colosseum at Rome. A stranger approached me, an English colonial. He introduced himself, and began talking of his experiences in the Eternal City. He had not spoken three minutes until he had said 'you was', and 'I done'. That morning, when he arose, he had polished his shoes and put on spotless linen in order to maintain his own self-respect and to win the respect of those with whom he came in contact, but he had made no attempt whatever to polish his phrases and to speak spotless sentences. He would have been ashamed, for example, of not raising his hat to a woman when he spoke, but he was not ashamed—no, he was not even conscious—of violating the usages of grammar, of offending the ears of discriminating auditors. By his own words, he stood revealed and placed and classified. His woeful use of the English language proclaimed to the world continually and unmistakably that he was not a person of culture.

Dr Charles W. Eliot, after he had been President of Harvard for a third of a century, declared: 'I recognize but one mental acquisition as a necessary part of the education of a lady or gentleman, namely, an accurate and refined use of the mother tongue.' This is a significant pronouncement. Ponder over it.

But how, you ask, are we to become intimate with words, to speak them with beauty and accuracy? Fortunately, there is no mystery about the means to be employed, no legerdemain. The method is an open secret.

'This self-educated man,' writes Robinson in his book Lincoln as a Man of Letters, 'clothed his mind with the materials of genuine culture. Call it genius or talent, the process of his attainment was that described by Professor Emerton in speaking of the education of Erasmus: "He was no longer at school, but was simply educating himself by the only pedagogical method which ever yet produced any results anywhere, namely, by the method of his own tireless energy in continuous study and practice".'

How little there is that is new! How much even the great speakers owe to their reading and to their association with books!

Books! There is the secret! He who would enrich and enlarge his stock of words must soak and tan his mind constantly in the vats of literature. 'The only lamentation that I always feel in the presence of a library', said John Bright, 'is that life is too short and I have no hope of a full enjoyment of the ample repast spread before me'. Bright left school at fifteen, and went to work in a cotton mill, and he never had the chance of schooling again. Yet he became one of the most brilliant speakers of the generation, famous for his superb command of the English language.

Charles James Fox read Shakespeare aloud to improve his style. Gladstone called his study a 'Temple of Peace', and in it he kept 15,000 books. He was helped most, he confessed, by reading the works of St. Augustine, Bishop Butler, Dante, Aristotle, and Homer. The Iliad and The Odyssey enthralled him. He wrote six books on Homeric poetry and Homeric times.

Tennyson studied the Bible daily. Tolstoy read and re-read the Gospels until he knew long passages by memory. Ruskin's mother forced him by steady, daily toil to memorize long chapters of the Bible and to read the entire Book through aloud each year, 'every syllable, hard names and all, from Genesis to the Apocalypse.' To that discipline and study Ruskin attributed his taste and style in literature.

Whenever I read a book or a passage that particularly pleased me, in which a thing was said or an effect rendered with propriety, in which there was either some conspicuous force or some happy distinction in the style, I must sit down at once and set myself to ape that quality. I was unsuccessful, and I knew it; and tried again, and was again unsuccessful, and always unsuccessful; but at least in these vain bouts I got some practice in rhythm, in harmony, in construction, and coordination of parts.

That, like it or not, is the way to learn to write; whether I have profited or not, that is the way.

Enough of names and specific stories. The secret is out. Lincoln wrote it to a young man eager to become a successful lawyer: 'It is only to get the books and to read and study them carefully. Work, work, work is the main thing.'

If you begin reading, what will be your reward? Gradually, unconsciously but inevitably, your diction will begin to take on added beauty and refinement. Gradually, you will begin to reflect somewhat the glory and beauty and majesty of your companions.

THE SECRET OF MARK TWAIN'S WAY WITH WORDS

How did Mark Twain develop his delightful facility with words? As a young man, he travelled all the way from Missouri to Nevada by the ponderously slow and really painful stage coach. Food—and sometimes even water—had to be carried for both passengers and horses. Extra weight might have meant the difference between safety and disaster; baggage was charged for by the ounce, and yet Mark Twain carried with him a Webster's Unabridged Dictionary over mountain passes, across scorched deserts, and through a land infested with bandits and Indians. He wanted to make himself master of words, and with his characteristic courage and common sense, he set about doing the things necessary to bring that mastery about.

My father never allowed any member of his household to use an incorrect expression. Any slip on the part of one of the children was at once corrected; any unfamiliar word was immediately explained; each of us was encouraged to find a use for it in our conversation so as to fix it in our memories.

A speaker who is often complimented upon the firm texture of his sentences and the simple beauty of his language, during the course of a conversation recently, lifted the embargo on the secret of his power to choose true and incisive words. Each time he discovers an unfamiliar word in conversation or reading matter, he notes it in his memorandum book. Then, just prior to retiring at night, he consults his dictionary and makes the word his own. If he has gathered no material in this fashion during the day, he studies a page or two of Fernald's Synonyms, Antonyms and Prepositions, noting the exact meaning of the words which he would ordinarily interchange as perfect synonyms. A new word a day—that is his motto. This means in the course of a year three hundred and sixty-five additional tools for expression. These new words are stored away in a small pocket notebook, and their meanings reviewed at odd moments during the day. He has found that a word becomes a permanent acquisition to his vocabulary when he has used it three times.

ROMANTIC STORIES BEHIND THE WORDS YOU USE

Use a dictionary not only to ascertain the meaning of the word, but also to find its derivation. Its history, its origin is usually set down in brackets after the definition. Do not imagine for a moment that the words you speak each day are only dull, listless sounds. They are reeking with colour, they are alive with romance. You cannot, for example, say so prosaic a thing as, 'Telephone the grocer for sugar', without using words that we have borrowed from many different languages and civilizations. Telephone is made from two Greek words, tele, meaning far, and phone, meaning sound. Grocer comes from an old French word, grossier, and the French came from the Latin, grossarius; it literally means one who sells by the wholesale or gross. We got our word sugar from the French; the French borrowed it from the Spanish; the Spanish lifted it from the Arabic; the Arabic took it from the Persian; and the Persian word shaker was derived from the Sanskrit carkara, meaning candy.

The seventh month, July, was named after Julius Caesar; so the Emperor Augustus, not to be outdone, called the next month August. But the eighth month had only thirty days at that time, and Augustus did not propose to have the month named after him any shorter than a month named after Julius; so he took one day away from February and added it to August, and the marks of this vain-glorious theft are evident on the calendar hanging in your home today. Truly, you will find the history of words fascinating.

Please look up in a large dictionary the derivation of these words: atlas, boycott, cereal, colossal, concord, curfew, education, finance, lunatic, panic, palace, pecuniary, sandwich, tantalize. Get the stories behind them. It will make them doubly colourful, doubly interesting. You will use them, then, with added zest and pleasure.

REWRITING ONE SENTENCE A HUNDRED AND FOUR TIMES

Strive to say precisely what you mean, to express the most delicate nuances of thought. That is not always easy—not even for experienced writers. Fanny Hurst told me that she sometimes rewrote her sentences from fifty to a hundred times. Only a few days prior to the conversation she said she had rewritten one sentence one hundred and four times by actual count. Yet she was so accomplished a writer that the magazines were paying her four hundred pounds a story. Mabel

Herbert Urner confided to me that she sometimes spent an entire afternoon eliminating only one or two sentences from a short story that was to be syndicated through the newspapers.

Milton is reported to have employed eight thousand words, and Shakespeare fifteen thousand. A standard dictionary contains fifty thousand less than half a million; but the average man, according to popular estimates, gets along with approximately two thousand. He has some verbs, enough connectives to stick them together, a handful of nouns, and a few overworked adjectives. He is too lazy, mentally, or too absorbed in business, to train for precision and exactness. The result? Let me give you an illustration. I once spent a few unforgettable days on the rim of the Grand Canyon of Colorado. In the course of an afternoon, I heard a lady apply the same adjective to a Chow dog, an orchestral selection, a man's disposition, and the Grand Canyon itself. They were all 'beautiful'.

What should she have said? Here are the synonyms that Roget lists for beautiful. Which adjectives do you think she should have employed?

Adjective: beautiful, beauteous, handsome, pretty, lovely, graceful, elegant, exquisite, delicate, dainty.

comely, fair, goodly, bonny good-looking, well-favoured, well-informed, well-proportioned, shapely, symmetrical, harmonious.

bright, bright-eyed, rosy-cheeked, rosy, ruddy, blooming, in full bloom.

trim, trig, tidy, neat, spruce, smart, jaunty, dapper.

brilliant, shining, sparkling, radiant, splendid, resplendent, dazzling, glowing, glossy, sleek, rich, gorgeous, superb, magnificent, grand, fine.

artistic, aesthetic, picturesque, pictorial, enchanting, attractive, becoming, ornamental.

perfect, unspotted, spotless, immaculate, undeformed, undefaced.

passable, presentable, tolerable, not amiss

The synonyms just quoted have been taken from Roget's Treasury of Words. It is an abridged edition of Roget's Thesaurus. What a help this book is! Personally, I never write without having it at my elbow. I find occasion to use it ten times as often as I use the dictionary.

What years of toil Roget consecrated to its making; yet it will come and sit on your desk and serve you a lifetime for the price of an inexpensive necktie. It is not a book to be stored away on a library shelf. It is a tool to be used constantly. Use it when writing out and polishing the diction of your talks. Use it in dictating your letters and your business reports. Use it daily, and it will double and treble your power with words.

Soak yourself full of the world's best literature so that you will have words, strong words, clear words, for your speaking.

—Dr Lynn Harold Hough

12

HOW TO INTEREST YOUR AUDIENCE

*I believe in anything that will engage the audience and
make the story more effective.*
—J.J. Abrams

If you were invited to dine at the home of a rich man in certain
sections of China, it would be proper to toss chicken bones and
olive seeds over your shoulder on to the floor. You pay your host
a compliment when you do that. You show that you realize that he
is wealthy, that he has plenty of servants to tidy up after the meal.
And he likes it.

You can be reckless with the remains of your sumptuous meal
in a rich man's home, but in some parts of China the poorer people
must save even the water they bathe in. To heat water costs so much
that they must buy it at a hot-water shop. After they have bathed in it,
they can take it back and sell it secondhand to the shopkeeper from
whom they purchased it. When the second customer has soiled it, the
water still retains a market value, although the price has softened a bit.

Have you found these facts about Chinese life interesting? If so,
do you know why? Because those are very unusual aspects of very
usual things. They are strange truths about such commonplace events
as dining out and bathing.

That is what interests us—something new about the old.

There lies one of the secrets of interesting people. That is a
significant truth, one that we ought to profit by in our everyday
intercourse. The entirely new is not interesting; the entirely old has
no attractiveness for us. We want to be told something new about

the old. You cannot, for example, interest a farmer with a description of the Cathedral at Bourges, or the Mona Lisa. They are too new to him. There is no tie-up to his old interests. But you can interest him by relating the fact that farmers in Holland till land below the level of the sea and dig ditches to act as fences and build bridges to serve as gates. Your farmer will listen open-mouthed while you tell him that Dutch farmers keep the cows, during the winter, under the same roof that houses the family, and sometimes the cows look out through lace curtains at driving snows. He knows about cows and fences—new slants, you see, on old things. 'Lace curtains! For a cow!' he'll exclaim. 'I'll be jiggered!' And he will retail that story to his friends.

THE THREE MOST INTERESTING THINGS IN THE WORLD

What would you say they are—the three most interesting subjects in the world? Sex, property and religion. By the first we can create life, by the second we maintain it, by the third we hope to continue it in the world to come.

But it is our sex, our property, our religion that interests us. Our interests swarm about our own egos.

We are not interested in a talk on How to Make Wills in Peru; but we may be interested in a talk entitled 'How to Make Our Wills'. We are not interested—except, perhaps, out of curiosity—in the religion of the Hindoo; but we are vitally interested in a religion that insures us unending happiness in the world to come.

Do you want to know what kind of person you are? Ah, now we are on an interesting topic. We are talking about you. Here is a way for you to hold the mirror up to your real self, and see you as you really are. Watch your reveries. What do we mean by reveries? Let Professor James Harvey Robinson answer. We are quoting from The Mind in the Making:

We all appear to ourselves to be thinking all the time during our waking hours, and most of us are aware that we go on thinking while we are asleep, even more foolishly than when awake. When uninterrupted by some practical issue we are engaged in what is known as a reverie. This is our spontaneous and favourite kind of thinking. We allow our ideas to take their own course and this course is determined by our hopes and fears, our spontaneous desires, their fulfilment or frustration, by our likes and dislikes, our loves and hates and resentments. There is nothing else anything like so interesting to ourselves as ourselves. All thought that is not more or less laboriously controlled and directed will inevitably circle about the beloved ego. It is amusing and pathetic to observe this tendency in ourselves and in others. We learn politely and generously to overlook this truth, but if we dare to think of it, it blazes forth like the noontide sun.

Our reveries form the chief index of our fundamental character. They are a reflection of our nature as modified by often hidden and forgotten experiences...The reverie doubtless influences all our speculations in its persistent tendency to self-magnification and self-justification, which are its chief preoccupations.

So remember that the people you are to talk to spend most of their time when they are not concerned with the problems of business, in thinking about and justifying and glorifying themselves. Remember that the average man will be more concerned about the cook leaving than about Italy paying her debts. He will be more wrought up over a dull razor blade than over a revolution in South America. His own toothache will distress him more than an earthquake in Asia destroying half a million lives. He would rather listen to you say some nice thing about him than hear you discuss the ten greatest men in history.

HOW TO BE A GOOD CONVERSATIONALIST

The reason so many people are poor conversationalists is because they talk about only the things that interests them. That may be deadly boring to others. Reverse the process. Lead the other person into talking about his interests, his business, his golf score, his success—

or, if it is a mother, her children. Do that and listen intently and you will give pleasure; consequently you will be considered a good conversationalist—even though you have done very little of the talking.

Mr Harold Dwight recently made an extraordinarily successful speech at a banquet which marked the final session of a public speaking course. He talked about each man in turn around the entire table, told how he had talked when the course started, how he had improved; recalled the talks various members had made, the subjects they had discussed; he mimicked some of them, exaggerated their peculiarities, had everyone laughing, had everyone pleased. With such material, he could not possibly have failed. It was absolutely ideal. No other topic under the blue dome of Heaven would have so interested that group. Mr Dwight knew how to handle human nature.

AN IDEA THAT WON TWO MILLION READERS

A few years ago, the American Magazine enjoyed an amazing growth. Its sudden leap in circulation became one of the sensations of the publishing world. The secret? The secret was the late John M. Siddall and his ideas. When I first met Siddall he had charge of the Interesting People Department of that periodical. I had written a few articles for him; and one day he sat down and talked to me for a long time.

'People are selfish,' he said. 'They are interested chiefly in themselves. They are not very much concerned about whether the government should own the railroads; but they do want to know how to get ahead, how to draw more salary, how to keep healthy. If I were editor of this magazine,' he went on,

I would tell them how to take care of their teeth, how to take baths, how to keep cool in summer, how to get a position, how to handle employees, how to buy homes, how to remember, how to avoid grammatical errors, and so on. People are always interested in human stories, so I would have some rich man tell how he made a million. I would get prominent bankers and presidents of various corporations to tell the stories of how they battled their ways up from the ranks to power and wealth. Shortly after that, Siddall was made editor. The magazine then had a small circulation, and was comparatively a failure. Siddall did just what he said he would do. The response? It was overwhelming. The circulation figures climbed up to two hundred thousand, three, four, half a million.... Here was something the public wanted. Soon a million people a month were buying it, then a million and a half, finally two millions. It did not stop there, but continued to grow for many years. Siddall appealed to the selfish interests of his readers.

THE KIND OF SPEECH MATERIAL THAT ALWAYS HOLDS ATTENTION

You may possibly bore people if you talk about things and ideas, but you can hardly fail to hold their attention when you talk about people. Tomorrow there will be millions of conversations floating over fences in the backyards, over tea tables and dinner tables—and what will be the predominating note in most of them? Personalities. He said this. Mrs So-and-so did that. I saw her doing this, that and the other. He is making a fortune, and so on.

I have addressed many gatherings of schoolchildren, and I soon learned by experience that in order to keep them interested I had to tell them stories about people. As soon as I became general and dealt with abstract ideas, Johnny became restless and wriggled in his seat, Tommy made a face at someone, Billy threw something across the aisle.

True, these were audiences of children; but the intelligence tests used in the army during the last war revealed the startling fact that 49 per cent of the people in the United States have a mental age of about thirteen. So one can hardly go wrong in making a generous use of human interest stories. Our magazines that are read by millions are filled with them.

I once asked a group of businessmen in Paris to talk on How

to Succeed. Most of them praised the homely virtues, preached at, lectured to, and bored their hearers. (Incidentally, I recently heard one of the most prominent businessmen make this identical mistake in a radio talk on this identical topic.)

So I halted this class, and said something like this:

We don't want to be lectured to. No one enjoys that. Remember you must be entertaining or we will pay no attention whatever to what you are saying. Also remember that one of the most interesting things in the world is sublimated, glorified gossip. So tell us the stories of two men you have known. Tell why one succeeded and why the other failed. We will gladly listen to that, remember it and possibly profit by it. It will also, by the way, be far easier for you to deliver than are these wordy, abstract preachments.

There was a certain member of that course who invariably found it difficult to interest either himself or his audience. This night, however, he seized the human story suggestion, and told us of two of his classmates in college. He made his talk interesting and illuminating with a score of amusing and human details... He talked on and on—this man who could not ordinarily find material for a three minute speech—and he was surprised beyond words to learn when he stopped that he had held the floor on this occasion for half an hour. The speech had been so interesting that it seemed short to everyone. It was this student's first real triumph.

Almost every student can profit by this incident. The average speech would be far more appealing if it were rich and replete with human interest stories. The speaker ought to attempt to make only a few points and to illustrate them with concrete cases. Such a method of speech building can hardly fail to get and hold attention.

If possible, these stories ought to tell of struggles, of things fought for and victories won. All of us are tremendously interested in fights and combats. There is an old saying that all the world loves a lover. It doesn't. What all the world loves is a scrap. It wants to see two lovers struggling for the hand of one woman. As an illustration of this fact, read almost any novel, magazine story, or go to see almost any film drama. When all the obstacles are removed and the reputed hero takes the so-called heroine in his arms, the audience begins reaching for their hats and coats. Five minutes later the sweeping women are gossiping over their broom handles.

The story of how a man battled in business or profession against discouraging odds and won is always inspiring, always interesting. A magazine editor once told me that the real, inside story of any person's life is entertaining. If one has struggled and fought—and who hasn't—his story, if correctly told, will appeal. There can be no doubt of that.

PICTURE-BUILDING WORDS

In this process of interest-getting, there is one aid, one technique, that is of the highest importance; yet it is all but ignored. The average speaker does not seem to be aware of its existence. He has probably never consciously thought about it at all. I refer to the process of using words that create pictures. The speaker who is easy to listen to is the one who sets images floating before your eyes. The one who employs foggy, commonplace, colourless symbols sets the audience to nodding.

Pictures. Pictures. Pictures. They are as free as the air you breathe. Sprinkle them through your talks, your conversation, and you will be more entertaining, more influential.

Picture-building phrases swarm through the pages of the Bible and through Shakespeare like bees around a cider mill. For example, a commonplace writer would have said that a certain thing would be superfluous, like trying to improve the perfect. How did Shakespeare express the same thought? With a picture phrase that is immortal: 'To gild refined gold, to paint the lily, to throw perfume on the violet.'

Did you ever pause to observe that the proverbs that are passed on from generation to generation are almost all visual sayings? 'A bird in the hand is worth two in the bush.' 'It never rains but it pours.' 'You can lead a horse to water but you can't make him drink.' And you will find the same picture element in almost all the similes that have lived for centuries and grown hoary with too much use: 'Sly as a fox.' 'Dead as a door nail.' 'Flat as a pancake.' 'Hard as a rock.'

INTEREST IS CONTAGIOUS

We have been discussing so far the kind of material that interests an audience. However, one might mechanically follow all the suggestions made here and speak according to Cocker, and yet be vapid and dull. Catching and holding the interest of people is a delicate thing, a matter of feeling and spirit. It is not like operating a steam engine. No book of precise rules can be given for it.

Interest, be it remembered, is contagious. Your hearers are almost sure to catch it if you have a bad case of it yourself. A short time ago, a gentleman rose during a session of this course and warned his audience that if the present methods of catching rock fish were continued, the species would become extinct. And in a very few years! He felt his subject. It was important. He was in real earnest about it. Everything about his matter and manner showed that. When he arose to speak, I did not know that there was such an animal as a rock fish. I imagine that most of the audience shared my lack of knowledge and lack of interest. But before the speaker finished, all of us had caught something of his concern. All of us would probably have been willing to have signed a petition to the legislature to protect the rock fish by law.

I once asked Richard Washburn Child, then American Ambassador to Italy, the secret of his success as an interesting writer. He replied: 'I am so excited about life that I cannot keep still. I just have to tell people about it.' One cannot keep from being enthralled with a speaker or writer like that.

13

CAPTURING YOUR AUDIENCE AT ONCE

A good teacher, like a good entertainer, first must hold his audience's attention, then he can teach his lesson.
—John Henrik Clarke

Several years ago a fuel and iron company was suffering from labour troubles. Shooting had taken place; there had been bloodshed. The air was electric with bitter hatreds. The very name of Rockefeller was anathema. Yet John D. Rockefeller Jr. wanted to talk to the employees of that concern. He wanted to explain, to persuade them to his way of thinking, to get them to accept his beliefs. He realized that in the very opening of his speech he must eradicate all ill-feeling, all antagonism. At the very outset, he did it beautifully and sincerely. Most public speakers can study his method with profit:

> This is a red-letter day in my life. It is the first time I have ever had the good fortune to meet the representatives of the employees of this great company, its officers and superintendents, together, and I can assure you that I am proud to be here, and that I shall remember this gathering for as long as I live. Had this meeting been held two weeks ago, I should have stood here a stranger to most of you, recognizing few faces. Having had the opportunity last week of visiting all the camps in the southern coalfields and of talking individually with practically all of the representatives, except those who were away; having visited in your homes, met many of your wives and children, we meet here not as strangers but as friends, and it is in this spirit of

mutual friendship that I am glad to have this opportunity to discuss with you our common interests.

Since this is a meeting of the officers of the company and the representatives of the employees, it is only by your courtesy that I am here, for I am not so fortunate as to be either one or the other; and yet I feel that I am intimately associated with you men, for, in a sense, I represent both the stockholders and the directors.

That is tact—supreme tact. And the speech, in spite of the bitter hatred that had existed, was successful. The men who had been striking and fighting for higher wages never said anything more about it after Rockefeller had explained all the facts in the situation.

A DROP OF HONEY AND TWO-GUN MEN

'It is an old and true maxim, "That a drop of honey catches more flies than a gallon of gall." So with men. If you would win a man to your cause, first convince him that you are his sincere friend. Therein is a drop of honey that catches his heart; which, say what he will, is the great high road to his reason, and when once gained, you will find but little trouble in convincing his judgment of the justice of your cause, if indeed that cause really be a just one.'

For example, I have heard hundreds of speeches on the hotly contested subject of prohibition. In almost every instance, the speaker, with all the tact of a bull in a china shop, opened with some positive and perhaps belligerent statement. He showed once and for all which direction he faced and under which flag he fought. He showed that his mind was made up so firmly that there was not the slightest chance of it being changed; yet he was expecting others to abandon their cherished beliefs and to accept his. The effect? About the same that results from all arguments: No one was convinced. Instantly, he lost by his blunt, aggressive opening the sympathetic attention of all who differed with him; instantly, they discounted all he said and would say; instantly, they challenged his statements; instantly, they held his opinions in contempt. His talk served but to entrench them more strongly behind the bulwark of their own beliefs.

You see, he made, at the very outset, the fatal mistake of prodding his listeners, of getting them bending backwards and saying through their shut teeth: 'No! No! No!'

Is not that a very serious situation if one wishes to win converts to his way of thinking? A most illuminating statement on this point is the following quotation from Professor Overstreet's lectures before the School for Social Research.

'A "No" response is a most difficult handicap to overcome. When a person has said "No", all his pride of personality demands that he remain consistent with himself. He may later feel that the "No" was ill advised; nevertheless, there is his precious pride to consider! Once having said a thing, he must stick to it. Hence it is of the very greatest importance that we start a person in the affirmative direction...' The skillful speaker gets at the outset a number of 'yes-responses'. He has thereby set the psychological processes of his listeners moving in the affirmative direction. It is like the movement of a billiard ball. Propel it in one direction, and it takes some force to deflect it; far more force to send it back in the opposite direction.

The psychological patterns here are quite clear. When a person says 'No' and really means it, he is doing far more than saying a word of two letters. His entire organism—glandular, nervous, muscular— gathers itself together into a condition of rejection. There is, usually in minute but sometimes in observable degree, a physical withdrawal, or readiness for withdrawal. The whole neuro-muscular system, in short, sets itself on guard against acceptance. Where, on the contrary, a person says 'Yes', none of the withdrawing activities take place. The organism is in a forward-moving, accepting, open attitude. Hence the more 'Yeses' we can, at the very outset, induce, the more likely we are to succeed in capturing the attention for our ultimate proposal.

It is a very simple technique—this yes-response. And yet how much neglected! It often seems as if people get a sense of their own importance by antagonizing at the outset. The radical comes into a conference with his conservative brethren; and immediately he must make them furious! What, as a matter of fact, is the good of it? If he simply does it in order to get some pleasure out of it for himself, he may be pardoned. But if he expects to achieve something, he is only psychologically stupid.

Get a student to say 'No' at the beginning, or a customer, child, husband, or wife, and it takes the wisdom and the patience of angels to transform that bristling negative into an affirmative.

How is one going to get these desirable 'yes-responses' at the very outset? Fairly simple. 'My way of opening and winning an argument,' confided Lincoln, 'is to first find a common ground of agreement.' Lincoln found it even when he was discussing the highly inflammable subject of slavery. 'For the first half-hour,' declared *The Mirror*, a neutral paper reporting one of his talks, 'his opponents would agree with every word he uttered. From that point he began to lead them off, little by little, until it seemed as if he had got them all into his fold.'

THE BEST ARGUMENT IS AN EXPLANATION

Is it not quite evident that the speaker who argues with his audience is merely arousing their stubbornness, putting them on the defensive, making it well-nigh impossible for them to change their minds? Is it wise to start by saying, 'I am going to prove so and so?' Aren't your hearers liable to accept that as a challenge and remark silently, 'Let's see you do it.'

Is it not much more advantageous to begin by stressing something that you and all of your hearers believe, and then to raise some pertinent question that everyone would like to have answered? Then take your audience with you in an earnest search for the answer. While on that search, present the facts as you see them so clearly that they will unconsciously be led to accept your conclusions as their own. They will have much more faith in some truth that they believe they have discovered for themselves. 'The best argument is that which seems merely an explanation.'

In every controversy, no matter how wide and bitter the differences, there is always some common ground of agreement on which the speaker can invite everyone to assemble for the search after facts that he is going to conduct.

THE BEST SPEECH SHAKESPEARE WROTE

The most famous speech that Shakespeare put into the mouth of any of his characters—Mark Antony's funeral oration over the body of Julius Caesar—is a classic example of supreme tact.

This was the situation. Caesar had become dictator. Naturally, inevitably, a score of his political enemies were envious, and were eager to tear him down, to destroy him, to make his power their own. Twenty-three of them banded together under the leadership of Brutus and Cassius and thrust their daggers into his body... Mark Antony had been Caesar's Secretary of State. He was a handsome chap, this Antony, a ready writer, a powerful speaker. He could represent the government well at public affairs. Small wonder Caesar had chosen him as his right hand man. Now, with Caesar out of the way, what should the conspirators do with Antony? Remove him? Kill him? There had been enough bloodshed already; there was enough to justify as it was. Why not win this Antony to their side, why not use his undeniable influence, his moving eloquence, to shield them and further their own ends? Sounded safe and reasonable, so they tried it. They saw him and went so far as to permit him to 'say a few words' over the corpse of the man who had all but ruled the world...

Antony mounts the rostrum in the Roman Forum. Before him lies the murdered Caesar. A mob surges noisily and threateningly about Antony, a rabble friendly to Brutus, Cassius and the other assassins. Antony's purpose is to turn this popular enthusiasm into intense hatred, to stir the plebeians to rise in mutiny and slay those that had struck Caesar down. He raises his hands, the tumult ceases, he starts to speak. Note how ingeniously, how adroitly he begins, praising Brutus and the other conspirators:

> For Brutus is an honorable man;
> So are they all, all honorable men.

Observe that he does not argue. Gradually, unobtrusively, he presents certain facts about Caesar; tells how the ransom from his captives filled the general coffers, how he wept when the poor cried, how he refused a crown, how he willed his estates to the public. He presents the facts, asks the mob questions, and lets them draw their own conclusions. The evidence is presented, not as something new, but as something they had for the moment forgotten:

> I tell you that which you yourselves do know.

And with a magic tongue through it all, he whipped up their feelings, stirred their emotions, aroused their pity, heated their anger. Antony's masterpiece of tact and eloquence is given here in its entirety. Search where you will, range through all the broad fields of literature and oratory, and I doubt if you will find half a dozen speeches to equal this. It merits the serious study of every man who aspires to excel in the fine art of influencing human nature. But there is another reason, entirely aside from the one we are considering now, why Shakespeare ought to be read and reread by businessmen; he possessed a larger vocabulary than did any other writer who ever lived; he used words more magically, more beautifully. No one can study *Macbeth* and *Hamlet* and *Julius Caesar* without unconsciously brightening and widening and refining his own diction. Here is an excerpt of the speech.

> Ant. Friends, Romans, countrymen, lend me your ears:
> I come to bury Caesar, not to praise him.
> The evil that men do lives after them;
> The good is oft interred with their bones:
> So let it be with Caesar. The noble Brutus Hath told you

Caesar was ambitious:
If it were so, it was a grievous fault;
And grievously hath Caesar answer'd it.
Here, under leave of Brutus and the rest—
For Brutus is an honourable man;
So are they all, all honourable men—
Come I to speak in Caesar's funeral.
He was my friend, faithful and just to me:
But Brutus says he was ambitious;
And Brutus is an honourable man.
He hath brought many captives home to Rome,
Whose ransoms did the general coffers fill:
Did this in Caesar seem ambitious?
When that the poor have cried, Caesar hath wept:
Ambition should be made of sterner stuff:
Yet Brutus says he was ambitious;
And Brutus is an honourable man.

You have to respect your audience. Without them, you're essentially standing alone, singing to yourself.
—K.D. Lang

If the audience knew what they wanted then they wouldn't be the audience, they would be the artist.
—Alan Moore

THE QUICK & EASY WAY TO EFFECTIVE SPEAKING

PART 1
Basic Principles of Effective Speaking

1

ACQUIRING THE BASIC SKILLS

I started teaching classes in public speaking in 1912, the year the Titanic went down in the icy waters of the North Atlantic.

Over the years, at these classes, people are given the opportunity of sharing what they hope to gain from this training. Naturally, the phraseology varies; but the central desire, the basic want in the vast majority of cases, remains surprisingly the same: 'When I am called upon to stand up and speak, I become so self-conscious, so frightened, that I can't think clearly, can't concentrate, can't remember what I intended to say. I want to gain self-confidence, poise, and the ability to think on my feet. I want to get my thoughts together in logical order, and I want to be able to talk clearly and convincingly before a business or social group.'

Does this sound familiar? Have you experienced these same feelings of inadequacy? Would you give a small fortune to have the ability to speak convincingly and persuasively in public? The very fact that you have begun reading the pages of this book is proof of your interest in acquiring the ability to speak effectively.

I know what you are going to say, what you would say if you could talk to me: 'But Mr Carnegie, do you really think I could develop the confidence to get up and face a group of people and address them in a coherent, fluent manner?'

I have spent nearly all my life helping people get rid of their fears and develop courage and confidence. I could fill many books with the stories of the miracles that have taken place in my classes. It is not, therefore, a question of my thinking. I know you can, if you practice the directions and suggestions that you will find in this book.

Is there the faintest shadow of a reason why you should not be able to think as well in a perpendicular position before an audience as you can sitting down? Is there any reason why you should play host to butterflies in your stomach and become a victim of the 'trembles' when you get up to address an audience? Surely, you realize that this condition can be remedied, that training and practice will wear away your audience—fright and give you self-confidence.

This book will help you to achieve that goal. It is not an ordinary textbook. It is not filled with rules concerning the mechanics of speaking. It does not dwell on the physiological aspects of vocal production and articulation. It is the distillation of a lifetime spent in training adults in effective speaking. It starts with you as you are, and from that premise works naturally to the conclusion of what you want to be. All you have to do is co-operate—follow the suggestions in this book, apply them in every speaking situation, and persevere.

In order to get the most out of this book, and to get it with rapidity and dispatch, you will find these four guideposts useful:

FIRST: TAKE HEART FROM OTHERS' EXPERIENCE

There is no such animal, in or out of captivity, as a born public speaker. In those periods of history when public speaking was a refined art that demanded close attention to the laws of rhetoric and the niceties of delivery, it was even more difficult to be born a public speaker. Now we think of public speaking as a kind of enlarged conversation. Gone forever is the old grandiloquent style and the stentorian voice. What we like to hear at our dinner meetings, in our church services, on our TV sets and radios, is straightforward speech, conceived in common sense and dedicated to the proposition that we like speakers to talk with, and not at, us.

Despite what many school texts would lead us to believe, public speaking is not a closed art, to be mastered only after years of perfecting the voice and struggling with the mysteries of rhetoric. I have spent almost all of my teaching career proving to people that it is easy to speak in public, provided they follow a few simple, but important, rules. When I started to teach at the 125th Street YMCA in New York City back in 1912, I didn't know this any more than my first students knew it. I taught those first classes pretty much the way I had been taught in my college years in Warrensburg, Missouri. But I soon discovered that I was on the wrong track; I was trying to teach adults in the business world as though they were college freshmen. I saw the futility of using Webster, Burke, Pitt, and O'Connell as examples to imitate. What the members of my classes wanted was enough courage to stand on their hind legs and make a clear, coherent report at their next business meeting. It wasn't long before I threw the textbooks out the window, got right up there on the podium and, with a few simple ideas, worked with those fellows until they could give their reports in a convincing manner. It worked, because they kept coming back for more.

Of the thousands of people I have taught, one example comes to mind as I write because of the dramatic impact it had on me at the time. Some years ago, shortly after he joined my course, D.W. Ghent, a successful businessman in Philadelphia, invited me to lunch. He leaned across the table and said: 'I have sidestepped every opportunity to speak to various gatherings, Mr Carnegie, and there have been many. But now I am chairman of a board of college trustees.

'I must preside at their meetings. Do you think it will be possible for me to learn to speak at this late date in life?'

I assured him, on the basis of my experience with men in similar positions who had been members of my classes, that there was no doubt in my mind that he would succeed.

About three years later we lunched together again at the Manufacturers' Club. We ate in the same dining room and at the very same table we had occupied at our first meeting. Reminding him of our former conversation, I asked him whether my prediction had come true. He smiled, took a little red-backed notebook out of his pocket, and showed me a list of speaking engagements for the next several months. 'The ability to make these talks,' he confessed, 'the pleasure I get in giving them, the additional service I can render in the community—these are among the most gratifying things in my life.'

But that was not all. With a feeling of justifiable pride, Mr Ghent then played his ace card. His church group had invited the prime minister of England to address a convocation in Philadelphia. And the Philadelphian selected to make the introduction of the distinguished statesman, on one of his rare trips to America, was none other than Mr D.W. Ghent.

This was the man who had leaned across that same table less than three years before and asked me whether I thought he would ever be able to talk in public!

Sounds like a miracle, doesn't it? It is a miracle—a twentieth-century miracle of conquering fear.

SECOND: KEEP SIGHT OF YOUR GOAL

When Mr Ghent spoke of the pleasure his newly acquired skill in public speaking gave him, he touched upon what I believe (more than any other one factor) contributed to his success. It's true he followed the directions and faithfully did the assignments. But I'm sure he did these things because he wanted to do them, and he wanted to do them because he saw himself as a successful speaker. He projected himself into the future and then worked toward bringing that projection into reality. That is exactly what you must do.

Concentrate your attention on what self-confidence and the ability to talk more effectively will mean to you. Think of what it may mean to you socially, of the friends it will bring, of your increased capacity to be of service in your civic, social, or church group, of the influence you will be able to exert in your business. In short, it will prepare you for leadership.

There is no predicting how far the ability to speak on your feet will take you. Think of the satisfaction and pleasure that will be yours when you stand up and confidently share your thoughts and feelings with your audience. I have traveled around the world several times, but I know of few things that give greater delight than holding an audience by the power of the spoken word. You get a sense of strength, a feeling of power. 'Two minutes before I begin,' said one of my graduates, 'I would rather be whipped than start; but two minutes before I finish, I would rather be shot than stop.'

Begin now to picture yourself before an audience you might be called upon to address. See yourself stepping forward with confidence, listen to the hush fall upon the room as you begin, feel the attentive absorption of the audience as you drive home point after point, feel the warmth of the applause as you leave the platform, and hear the words of appreciation with which individual members of the audience greet you when the meeting is over. Believe me, there is a magic in it and a never-to-be-forgotten thrill.

William James, Harvard's most distinguished professor of psychology, wrote six sentences that could have a profound effect on your life, six sentences that are the open sesame to Ali Baba's treasure cave of courage: 'In almost any subject, your passion for the subject will save you. If you care enough for a result, you will most certainly attain it. If you wish to be good, you will be good. If you wish to be rich, you will be rich. If you wish to be learned, you will be learned. Only then you must really wish these things and wish them with exclusiveness and not wish one hundred other incompatible things just as strongly.'

THIRD: PREDETERMINE YOUR MIND TO SUCCESS

I was asked once, on a radio program, to tell in three sentences the most important lesson I have ever learned. This is what I said: 'The biggest lesson I have ever learned is the stupendous importance of what we think. If I knew what you think, I would know what you are, for your thoughts make you what you are. By changing our thoughts, we can change our lives.'

You have set your sights on the goal of increased confidence and more effective communication. From now on, you must think positively, not negatively, about your chances to succeed in this endeavor. You must develop a buoyant optimism about the outcome of your efforts to speak before groups. You must set the seal of determination upon every word and action that you devote toward the development of this ability.

In one of my classes in the Middle West, a man stood up the first night and unabashedly said that as a builder of homes he wouldn't be content until he became a spokesman for the American Home Builders' Association. He wanted nothing more than to go up and down this country and tell everybody he met the problems and achievements of his industry. Joe Haverstick meant what he said. He was the kind of class member that delights an instructor: he was in dead earnest. He wanted to be able to talk, not on local issues only, but on national ones, and there was no half-heartedness about his desires. He prepared his talks thoroughly, practiced them carefully, and never missed a single session, though it was the busy season of the year for men in his business. He did precisely what such a class member always does—he progressed at a rate that surprised him. In two months he had become one of the outstanding members of the class. He was voted its president.

The instructor handling that class was in Norfolk, Virginia, about a year later, and this is what he wrote: 'I had forgotten all about Joe Haverstick back in Ohio when, one morning while I was having breakfast, I opened the Virginia Pilot. There was a picture of Joe and a write-up about him. The night before, he had addressed a large meeting of area builders, and I saw that Joe was not just a spokesman for the National Home Builders' Association; he was its president.'

So, to succeed in this work, you need the qualities that are essential in any worthwhile endeavor: desire amounting to enthusiasm, persistence to wear away mountains, and the self-assurance to believe you will succeed.

FOURTH: SEIZE EVERY OPPORTUNITY TO PRACTICE

The course I gave in the 125th Street YMCA before World War I has been changed almost beyond recognition. Every year new ideas have been woven into the sessions and old ones cast away. But one feature of the course remains unchanged. Every member of every class must get up once, and in the majority of cases, twice, and give a talk before his fellow members. Why? Because no one can learn to speak in public without speaking in public any more than a person can learn to swim without getting in the water. You could read every volume ever written about public speaking—including this one—and still not be able to speak. This book is a thorough guide. But you must put its suggestions into practice.

When George Bernard Shaw was asked how he learned to speak so compellingly in public, he replied: 'I did it the same way I learned to skate—by doggedly making a fool of myself until I got used to it.' As a youth, Shaw was one of the most timid persons in London. He often walked up and down the Embankment for twenty minutes or more before venturing to knock at a door. 'Few men,' he confessed, 'have suffered more from simple cowardice or have been more horribly ashamed of it.'

Finally, he hit upon the best and quickest and surest method ever yet devised to conquer timidity, cowardice, and fear. He determined to make his weak point his strongest asset. He joined a debating society. He attended every meeting in London where there was to be a public discussion, and he always arose and took part in the debate. By throwing his heart into the cause of socialism, and by going out and speaking for that cause, George Bernard Shaw transformed himself into one of the most confident and brilliant speakers of the first half of the twentieth century.

Opportunities to speak are on all sides. Join organizations and volunteer for offices that will require you to speak. Stand up and assert yourself at public meetings, if only to second a motion. Don't take a back seat at departmental meetings. Speak up! Teach a Sunday School class. Become a Scout leader. Join any group where you will have an opportunity to participate actively in the meetings. You have but to look around you to see that there is scarcely a single business, community, political, professional, or even neighborhood activity that does not challenge you to step forward and speak up. You will never know what progress you can make unless you speak, and speak, and speak again.

As you read on in this book, and as you put its principles into practice, you will be heading into adventure. You will find it is an adventure in which your power of self-direction and your vision will sustain you. You will find it is an adventure that can change you, inside and out.

> *Don't wait for a huge platform before you give of your best performance.*
> —Bernard Kelvin Clive

> *Act enthusiastic and you will be enthusiastic.*
> —Dale Carnegie

2

DEVELOP CONFIDENCE

'Five years ago, Mr Carnegie, I came to the hotel where you were conducting one of your demonstrations. I walked up to the door of the meeting room and then stopped. I knew if I entered that room and joined a class, sooner or later I'd have to make a speech. My hand froze on the doorknob. I couldn't go in. I turned my back and walked out of the hotel.

'If I had only known then how you make it easy to conquer fear, the paralysing fear of an audience, I wouldn't have lost these past five years.'

The man who spoke these revealing words wasn't talking across a table or a desk. He was directing his remarks to an audience of some two hundred people. It was the graduation session of one of my courses in New York City. As he gave his talk, I was particularly impressed by his poise and self-assurance. Here was a man, I thought, whose executive skills will be tremendously increased by his newly acquired expressiveness and confidence. As his instructor, I was delighted to see that he had dealt a death blow to fear, and I couldn't help thinking how much more successful, and what is more, how much happier this man would have been if his victory over fear had come five or ten years before.

In years of training men and women to speak in public, I have picked up some ideas to help you quickly overcome stage fright and develop confidence in a few short weeks of practice.

FIRST: GET THE FACTS ABOUT FEAR OF SPEAKING IN PUBLIC

You are not unique in your fear of speaking in public. Surveys in colleges indicate that eighty to ninety per cent of all students enrolled in speech classes suffer from stage fright at the beginning of the course. I am inclined to believe that the figure is higher among adults at the start of my course, almost one hundred per cent.

A certain amount of stage fright is useful! It is nature's way of preparing us to meet unusual challenges in our environment. So, when you notice your pulse beating faster and your respiration speeding up, don't become alarmed. Your body, ever alert to external stimuli, is getting ready to go into action. If these physiological preparations are held within limits, you will be capable of thinking faster, talking more fluently, and generally speaking with greater intensity than under normal circumstances.

Many professional speakers have assured me that they never completely lose all stage fright. It is almost always present just before they speak, and it may persist through the first few sentences of their talk. This is the price these men and women pay for being like race horses and not like draft horses.

The chief cause of your fear of public speaking is simply that you are unaccustomed to speak in public. For most people, public speaking is an unknown quantity, and consequently one fraught with anxiety and fear factors. For the beginner, it is a complex series of strange situations, more involved than, say, learning to play tennis or drive a car. To make this fearful situation simple and easy: practice, practice, practice. You will find, as thousands upon thousands have, that public speaking can be made a joy instead of an agony merely by getting a record of successful speaking experiences behind you.

If stage fright gets out of hand and seriously curtails your effectiveness by causing mental blocks, lack of fluency, uncontrollable tics, and excessive muscular spasm, you should not despair. These symptoms are not unusual in beginners. If you make the effort, you will find the degree of stage fright soon reduced to the point where it will prove a help and not a hindrance.

SECOND: PREPARE IN THE PROPER WAY

The principal speaker at a New York Rotary Club luncheon several years ago was a prominent government official. We were looking forward to hearing him describe the activities of his department. It was obvious almost at once that he had not planned his speech. At first he tried to talk impromptu. Failing in that attempt, he pulled out of his pocket a sheaf of notes which evidently had no more order than a flatcar full of scrap iron. He fumbled awhile with these, all the time becoming more embarrassed and inept in his delivery. Minute by minute he became more helpless, more bewildered. But he kept on floundering, apologizing, trying to make some semblance of sense out of his notes and raising a glass of water with a trembling hand to his parched lips. He was a sad picture of a man completely overcome by fright, due to almost total lack of preparation. He finally sat down, one of the most humiliated speakers I have ever seen. He made his talk as Rousseau says a love letter should be written: he began without knowing what he was going to say, and finished without knowing what he had said.

Since 1912, it has been my professional duty to evaluate over five thousand talks a year. From that experience, one great lesson stands out like Mount Everest, towering above all the others: only the prepared speaker deserves to be confident. How can anyone ever hope to storm the fortress of fear if he goes into battle with defective weapons, or with no ammunition at all? 'I believe,' said Lincoln, 'that I shall never be old enough to speak without embarrassment when I have nothing to say.'

Never memorize word for word: By 'perfect preparation' do I mean that you should memorize your talk? To this question I give back a thunderous NO. In their attempts to protect their egos from the dangers of drawing a mental blank before an audience, many speakers fall headlong into the trap of memorization.

When H.V. Kaltenborn, the dean of American news commentators, was a student at Harvard University, he took part in a speech contest. He selected a short story entitled 'Gentlemen, the King.' He memorized it word for word and rehearsed it hundreds of times. The day of the contest he announced the title, 'Gentlemen, the King.' Then his mind went blank. It not only went blank; it went black. He was terrified. In desperation he started telling the story in his own words. He was the most surprised boy in the hall when the judges gave him first prize. From that day to this, H.V. Kaltenborn has never read nor memorized a speech. That has been the secret of success in his broadcasting career. He makes a few notes and talks naturally to his listeners without a script.

The man who writes out and memorizes his talks is wasting his time and energy, and courting disaster. All our lives we have been speaking spontaneously. We haven't been thinking of words. We have been thinking of ideas. If our ideas are clear, the words come as naturally and unconsciously as the air we breathe.

I have heard countless scores of men and women try to deliver memorized talks, but I don't remember even one speaker who wouldn't have been more alive, more effective, more human, if he had tossed his memorized talk into the waste basket. If he had done that, he might have forgotten some of his points. He might have rambled, but at least he would have been human.

Abe Lincoln once said: 'I don't like to hear a cut-and-dried sermon. When I hear a man preach, I like to see him act as if he were fighting bees.' Lincoln said he wanted to hear a speaker cut loose and get excited. No speaker ever acts as if he were fighting bees when he is trying to recall memorized words.

Assemble and Arrange Your Ideas Beforehand: What, then, is the proper method of preparing a talk? Simply this: search your background for significant experiences that have taught you something about life, and assemble your thoughts, your ideas, your convictions, that have welled up from these experiences. True preparation means brooding over your topics.

Rehearse Your Talk: Should you rehearse your talk after you have it in some kind of order? By all means. Here is a sure-fire method that is easy and effective. Use the ideas you have selected for your talk in everyday conversation with your friends and business associates. Instead of going over the ball scores, just lean across the luncheon table and say something like this: 'You know, Joe, I had an unusual experience one day. I'd like to tell you about it.' Joe will probably be happy to listen to your story. Watch him for his reactions. Listen to his response. He may have an interesting idea that may be valuable. He won't know that you are rehearsing your talk, and it really doesn't matter. But he probably will say that he enjoyed the conversation.

Allan Nevins, the distinguished historian, gives similar advice to writers: 'Catch a friend who is interested in the subject and talk out what you have learned at length. In this way you discover facts of interpretation that you might have missed, points of arguments that had been unrealized, and the form most suitable for the story you have to tell.'

THIRD: PREDETERMINE YOUR MIND TO SUCCESS

In the first chapter, you remember, this sentence was used in reference to building the right attitude toward public speaking training in general. The same rule applies to the specific task now facing you, that of making each opportunity to speak a successful experience. There are three ways to accomplish this:

Lose Yourself in Your Subject: After you have selected your subject, arranged it according to plan, and rehearsed it by 'talking it out' with your friends, your preparation is not ended. You must sell yourself on the importance of your subject. You must have the attitude that has inspired all the truly great personages of history—a belief in your cause. How do you fan the fires of faith in your message? By exploring all phases of your subject, grasping its deeper meanings, and asking yourself how your talk will help the audience to be better people for having listened to you.

Keep Your Attention Off Negative Stimuli: For instance, thinking of yourself making errors of grammar or suddenly coming to an end of your talk somewhere in the middle of it is certainly a negative projection that could cancel confidence before you started. It is especially important to keep your attention off yourself just before your turn to speak. Concentrate on what the other speakers are saying, give them your wholehearted attention and you will not be able to work up excessive stage fright.

Give Yourself a Pep Talk: Unless he is consumed by some great cause to which he has dedicated his life, every speaker will experience moments of doubt about his subject matter. He will ask himself whether the topic is the right one for him, whether the audience will be interested in it. He will be sorely tempted to change his subject. At times like these, when negativism is most likely to tear down self-confidence completely, you should give yourself a pep talk. In clear, straightforward terms tell yourself that your talk is the right one for you, because it comes out of your experience, out of your thinking about life. Say to yourself that you are more qualified than any member of the audience to give this particular talk and, by George, you are going to do your best to put it across. Is this old-fashioned Coué teaching? It may be, but modern experimental psychologists now agree that motivation based on autosuggestion is one of the strongest incentives to rapid learning, even when simulated. How much more powerful, then, will be the effect of a sincere pep talk based on the truth?

FOURTH: ACT CONFIDENT

The most famous psychologist that America has produced, Professor William James, wrote as follows:

To develop courage when you are facing an audience, act as if you already had it. Of course, unless you are prepared, all the acting in the world will avail but little. But granted that you know what you are going to talk about, step out briskly and take a deep breath. In fact, breathe deeply for thirty seconds before you ever face your audience. The increased supply of oxygen will buoy you up and give you courage. The great tenor, Jean de Reszke, used to say that when you had your breath so you 'could sit on it', nervousness vanished.

Draw yourself up to your full height and look your audience straight in the eyes, and begin to talk as confidently as if every one of them owed you money. Imagine that they do. Imagine that they have assembled there to beg you for an extension of credit. The psychological effect on you will be beneficial.

If you doubt that this philosophy makes sense, take the word of an American who will always be a symbol of courage. Once he was the most timorous of men; by practicing self-assurance, he became one of the boldest; he was the trust-busting, audience-swaying, Big-Stick-wielding President of the United States, Theodore Roosevelt.

'Having been a rather sickly and awkward boy,' he confesses in his autobiography, 'I was, as a young man, at the first both nervous and distrustful of my powers. I had to train myself painfully and laboriously not merely as regards my body but as regards my soul and spirit.'

Fortunately, he has disclosed how he achieved the transformation. 'When a boy,' he wrote, 'I read a passage in one of Marryat's books which always impressed me. In this passage, the captain of some small British man-of-war is explaining to the hero how to acquire the quality of fearlessness. He says that at the outset almost every man is frightened when he goes into action, but that the course to follow is for the man to keep such a grip on himself that he can act just as if he were not frightened. After this is kept up long enough, it changes from pretense to reality, and the man does in very fact become fearless by sheer dint of practicing fearlessness when he does not feel it.

'This was the theory upon which I went. There were all kinds of things of which I was afraid at first, ranging from grizzly bears to 'mean' horses and gunfighters; but by acting as if I were not afraid I gradually ceased to be afraid. Most men can have the same experience if they choose.'

To be yourself in a world that is constantly trying to make you
something else is the greatest accomplishment.
—Ralph Waldo Emerson

3

SPEAK EFFECTIVELY, THE QUICK AND EASY WAY

I seldom watch television in the daytime. But a friend recently asked me to listen to an afternoon show that was directed primarily to housewives. It enjoyed a very high rating, and my friend wanted me to listen because he thought the audience participation part of the show would interest me. It certainly did. I watched it several times, fascinated by the way the master of ceremonies succeeded in getting people in the audience to make talks in a way that caught and held my attention. These people were obviously not professional speakers. They had never been trained in the art of communication. Some of them used poor grammar and mispronounced words. But all of them were interesting. When they started to talk they seemed to lose all fear of being on camera and they held the attention of the audience.

Why was this? I know the answer because I have been employing the techniques used in this program for many years. These people, plain, ordinary men and women, were holding the attention of viewers all over the country; they were talking about themselves, about their most embarrassing moments, their most pleasant memory, or how they met their wives or husbands. They were not thinking of introduction, body, and conclusion. They were not concerned with their diction or their sentence structure. Yet they were getting the final seal of approval from the audience—complete attention in what they had to say. This is dramatic proof of what to me is the first of three cardinal rules for a quick and easy way to learn to speak in public:

FIRST: SPEAK ABOUT SOMETHING YOU HAVE EARNED THE RIGHT TO TALK ABOUT THROUGH EXPERIENCE OR STUDY

The men and women whose live flesh-and-blood stories made that television program interesting were talking from their own personal experience. They were talking about something they knew. Consider what a dull program would have resulted if they had been asked to define communism or to describe the organizational structure of the United Nations. Yet that is precisely the mistake that countless speakers make at countless meetings and banquets. They decide they must talk about subjects of which they have little or no personal knowledge and to which they have devoted little or no attention. They pick a subject like Patriotism, or Democracy, or Justice, and then, after a few hours of frantic searching through a book of quotations or a speaker's handbook for all occasions, they hurriedly throw together some generalizations vaguely remembered from a political science course they once took in college, and proceed to give a talk distinguished for nothing other than its length. It never occurs to these speakers that the audience might be interested in factual material bringing these high-flown concepts down to earth.

At an area meeting of Dale Carnegie instructors in the Conrad Hilton Hotel in Chicago some years ago, a student speaker started like this: 'Liberty, Equality, Fraternity. These are the mightiest ideas in the dictionary of mankind. Without liberty, life is not worth living. Imagine what existence would be like if your freedom of action would be restricted on all sides.'

That is as far as he got, because he was wisely stopped by the instructor, who then asked him why he believed what he was saying. He was asked whether he had any proof or personal experience to back up what he had just told us. Then he gave us an amazing story.

He had been a French underground fighter. He told us of the indignities he and his family suffered under Nazi rule. He described in vivid language how he escaped from the secret police and how he finally made his way to America. He ended by saying: 'When I walked down Michigan Avenue to this hotel today, I was free to come or go, as I wished. I passed a policeman and he took no notice of me. I walked into this hotel without having to present an identification card, and when this meeting is over I can go anywhere in Chicago I choose to go. Believe me, freedom is worth fighting for.' He received a standing ovation from that audience.

Tell us what life has taught you

Speakers who talk about what life has taught them never fail to keep the attention of their listeners. I know from experience that speakers are not easily persuaded to accept this point of view—they avoid using personal experiences as too trivial and too restrictive. They would rather soar into the realms of general ideas and philosophical principles, where unfortunately the air is too rarefied for ordinary mortals to breathe. They give us editorials when we are hungry for the news. None of us is averse to listening to editorials, when they are given by a man who has earned the right to editorialize—an editor or publisher of a newspaper. The point, though, is this: Speak on what life has taught you and I will be your devoted listener. It was said of Emerson that he was always willing to listen to any man, no matter how humble his station, because he felt he could learn something from every man he met. I have listened to more adult talks, perhaps, than any other man west of the Iron Curtain, and I can truthfully say that I have never heard a boring talk when the speaker related what life had taught him, no matter how slight or trivial the lesson may have been.

Look for topics in your background

Once a group of our instructors were asked to write on a slip of paper what they considered was the biggest problem they had with beginning speakers. When the slips were tallied, it was found that 'getting beginners to talk on the right topic' was the problem most frequently encountered in early sessions of my course.

What is the right topic? You can be sure you have the right

topic for you if you have lived with it, made it your own through experience and reflection. How do you find topics? By dipping into your memory and searching your background for those significant aspects of your life that made a vivid impression on you. Several years ago, we made a survey of topics that held the attention of listeners in our classes. We found that the topics most approved by the audience were concerned with certain fairly defined areas of one's background:

Early Years and Upbringing. Topics that deal with the family, childhood memories, schooldays, invariably get attention, because most of us are interested in the way other people met and overcame obstacles in the environment in which they were reared.

Whenever possible, work into your talks illustrations and examples from your early years. The popularity of plays, movies, and stories that deal with the subject of meeting the challenges of the world in one's early years attests to the value of this area for subject matter of talks. But how can you be sure anyone will be interested in what happened to you when you were young? There's one test. If something stands out vividly in your memory after many years have gone by, that almost guarantees that it will be of interest to an audience.

Early Struggles to Get Ahead. This is an area rich in human interest. Here again the attention of a group can be held by recounting your first attempts to make your mark on the world. How did you get into a particular job or profession? What twist of circumstances accounted for your career? Tell us about your setbacks, your hopes, your triumphs when you were establishing yourself in the competitive world. A real-life picture of almost anyone's life—if told modestly—is almost surefire material.

Hobbies and Recreation. Topics in this area are based on personal choice and, as such, are subjects that command attention. You can't go wrong talking about something you do out of sheer enjoyment. Your natural enthusiasm for your particular hobby will help get this topic across to any audience.

Special Areas of Knowledge. Many years of working in the same field have made you an expert in your line of endeavor. You can be certain of respectful attention if you discuss aspects of your job or profession based on years of experience or study.

Unusual Experiences. Have you ever met a great man? Were you under fire during the war? Have you gone through a spiritual crisis in your life? These are experiences that make the best kind of speech material.

Beliefs and Convictions. Perhaps you have given a great deal of time and effort to thinking about your position on vital subjects confronting the world today. If you have devoted many hours to the study of issues of importance, you have earned the right to talk about them. But when you do, be certain that you give specific instances for your convictions. Audiences do not relish a talk filled with generalizations. Please don't consider the casual reading of a few newspaper articles sufficient preparation to talk on these topics. If you know little more about a subject than the people in your audience, it is best to avoid it. On the other hand, if you have devoted years of study to some subject, it is undoubtedly a topic that is made to order for you. By all means, use it

Only by talking about something you have earned the right to talk about will you be able to fulfill the second requirement for learning to speak in public quickly and easily. Here it is:

SECOND: BE SURE YOU ARE EXCITED ABOUT YOUR SUBJECT

Not all topics that you and I have earned the right to talk about make us excited. For instance, as a do-it yourself devotee, I certainly am qualified to talk about washing dishes. But somehow or other I can't get excited about this topic. As a matter of fact, I would rather forget about it altogether. Yet I have heard housewives—household executives, that is—give superb talks about this same subject. They have somehow aroused within themselves such a fury of indignation about the eternal task of washing dishes, or they have developed such ingenious methods of getting around this disagreeable chore, that they have become really excited about it. As a consequence, they have been able to talk effectively about this subject of washing dishes. Here is a question that will help you determine the suitability of topics you feel qualified to discuss in public: if someone stood up and directly opposed your point of view, would you be impelled to speak with conviction and earnestness in defense of your position? If you would, you have the right subject for you.

When a member of one of our classes says, 'I don't get excited about anything, I lead a humdrum sort of life,' our instructors are trained to ask him what he does in his spare time. One goes to the movies, another bowls, and another cultivates roses. One man told his instructor that he collected books of matches. As the instructor continued to question him about this unusual hobby, he gradually became animated. Soon he was using gestures as he described the cabinets in which he stored his collection. He told his instructor that he had match books from almost every country in the world. When he became excited about his favorite topic, the instructor stopped him. 'Why don't you tell us about this subject? It sounds fascinating to me.' He said that he didn't think anyone would be interested! Here was a man who had spent years in pursuit of a hobby that was almost a passion with him; yet he was negative about its value as a topic to speak about. This instructor assured this man that the only way to gauge the interest value of a subject was to ask yourself how interested you are in it. He talked that night with all the fervor of the true collector, and I heard later that he gained a certain amount of local recognition by going to various luncheon clubs and talking about match book collecting.

This illustration leads directly to the third guiding principle for those who want a quick and easy way to learn to speak in public.

THIRD: BE EAGER TO SHARE YOUR TALK WITH YOUR LISTENERS

There are three factors in every speaking situation: the speaker, the speech or the message, and the audience. The first two rules in this chapter dealt with the interrelationships of the speaker to a speech. Up to this point there is no speaking situation. Only when the speaker relates his talk to a living audience will the speaking situation come to life. The talk may be well prepared; it may concern a topic which the speaker is excited about; but for complete success, another factor must enter into his delivery of the talk. He must make his listeners feel that what he has to say is important to them. He must not only be excited about his topic, but he must be eager to transfer this excitement to his listeners. In every public speaker of note in the history of eloquence, there has been this unmistakable quality of salesmanship, evangelism, call it what you will. The effective speaker earnestly desires his listeners to feel what he feels, to agree with his point of view, to do what he thinks is right for them to do, and to enjoy and relive his experience with him. He is audience-centered and not self-centered. He knows that the success or failure of his talk is not for him to decide—it will be decided in the minds and hearts of his hearers.

I trained a number of men in the New York City Chapter of the American Institute of Banking to speak during a thrift campaign. One of the men in particular wasn't getting across to his audience. The first step in helping that man was to fire up his mind and heart with zeal for his subject. I told him to go off by himself and to think over this subject until he became enthusiastic about it. I asked him to remember that the Probate Court Records in New York show that more than 85 per cent of the people leave nothing at all at death; that only 3.3 per cent leave $10,000 or over. He was to keep constantly in mind that he was not asking people to do him a favor or something that they could not afford to do. He was to say to himself: 'I am preparing these people to have meat and bread and clothes and comfort in their old age, and to leave their wives and children secure.' He had to remember he was going out to perform a great social service. In short, he had to be a crusader.

He thought over these facts. He burned them into his mind. He aroused his own interest, stirred his own enthusiasm, and came to feel that he, indeed, had a mission. Then, when he went out to talk, there was a ring to his words that carried conviction. He sold his listeners on the benefits of thrift because he had an eager desire to help people. He was no longer just a speaker armed with facts; he was a missionary seeking converts to a worthwhile cause.

A speaker should approach his preparation not by what he wants to say, but by what he wants to learn.
—Todd Stocker

For better or worse, you must play your own instrument in the orchestra of life.
—Dale Carnegie

PART 2
Techniques of Effective Speaking

4

INTRODUCING SPEAKERS, PRESENTING AND ACCEPTING AWARDS

When you are called upon to speak in public, you may introduce another speaker or make a longer talk to inform, entertain, convince, or persuade. John Mason Brown, the writer and lecturer, whose lively talks have won audiences everywhere in the country, was speaking one night with the man who was to introduce him to his audience.

'Stop worrying about what you are going to say,' the man told Mr Brown. 'Relax. I don't believe in preparing a speech. Nope, preparation's no good. Spoils the charm of the thing; kills gaiety. I just wait for the inspiration to come to me when I'm on my feet— and it never fails.'

These reassuring words let Mr Brown look forward to a fine introduction, he recalls in his book, *Accustomed As I Am*. But when the man arose to make it, it came out this way:

Gentlemen, may I have your attention, please? We have bad news for you tonight. We wanted to have Isaac F. Marcosson speak to you, but he couldn't come. He's sick. (Applause.) Next we asked Senator Bledridge to address you...but he was busy. (Applause.) Finally we tried in vain to get Doctor Lloyd Grogan of Kansas City to come down to speak to you. (Applause.) So, instead, we have—John Mason Brown. (Silence.)

Mr Brown, recalling this disaster, said only: 'At least my friend, that inspirationalist, got my name correctly.'

Of course you can see that this man, who was so sure his inspiration would carry him through, couldn't have done much worse if he had tried to do so. His introduction violated every obligation he had both to the speaker whom he was introducing and to the audience which was to hear the speaker. There aren't many of these obligations, but they are important, and it is astonishing how many program chairmen fail to realize this.

The speech of introduction serves the same purpose as a social introduction. It brings the speaker and the audience together, establishes a friendly atmosphere, and creates a bond of interest between them. The man who says, "You don't have to make a speech, all you have to do is introduce the speaker," is guilty of understatement. No speech is more mangled than the speech of introduction, probably because it is looked upon as unimportant by many chairmen who are entrusted with the duty of preparing and delivering it.

An introduction—that term was fashioned from two Latin words, intro, to the inside, and ducere, to lead—ought to lead us to the inside of the topic sufficiently to make us want to hear it discussed. It ought to lead us to the inside facts regarding the speaker, facts that demonstrate his fitness for discussing this particular topic. In other words, an introduction ought to 'sell' the topic to the audience and it ought to 'sell' the speaker. And it ought to do these things in the briefest amount of time possible.

Here are some suggestions to help you make a well-organized speech of introduction.

FIRST: THOROUGHLY PREPARE WHAT YOU ARE GOING TO SAY

Even though the introductory talk is short, hardly ever exceeding one minute, it demands careful preparation. First, you must gather your facts. These will center around three items: the subject of the speaker's talk, his qualifications to speak on that subject, and his name. Often a fourth item will become apparent—why the subject chosen by the speaker is of special interest to the audience.

Be certain that you know the correct title of the talk and something about the speaker's development of the subject matter. There is nothing more embarrassing than for the speaker to take exception to the introduction by disclaiming part of it as untrue of his stand on the subject. This can be obviated by making sure you know what the speaker's subject is and refraining from trying to predict what he will say. But your duty as introducer demands that you give the title of the speaker's talk correctly and point out its relevancy to the audience's interests. If at all possible, try to get this information directly from the speaker. If you have to rely on a third party, a program chairman, for instance, try to get the information in writing and check with the speaker just before the meeting.

But perhaps most of your preparation will involve getting the facts on the speaker's qualifications. In some cases you will be able to get an accurate listing from Who's Who or a comparable work, if your speaker is nationally or regionally well known. On the local level you can appeal to the public relations or personnel office of the concern where he works, or in some cases verify your facts by calling a close friend or a member of his family. The main idea is to get your biographical facts correct. People close to your speaker will be glad to furnish you with material.

Of course, too many facts will become boring, especially when one degree implies the speaker's acquisition of lesser degrees. To say that a man received a B.S. and an M.A. degree is superfluous when you indicate that he is a Doctor of Philosophy. Likewise, it is best to indicate the highest and most recent offices a man has held rather than to string out a catalogue of the positions he has held since leaving college. Above all, do not pass over the most distinguished achievements of a man's career instead of the less important

For example, I heard a well-known speaker—a man who ought to have known better—introduce the Irish poet W. B. Yeats. Yeats was to read his own poetry. Three years prior to that he had been awarded the Nobel Prize in literature, the highest distinction that can be bestowed upon a man of letters. I am confident that not ten per cent of that particular audience knew of the award or its significance. Both ought, by all means, to have been mentioned. They ought to have been announced even if nothing else were said. But what did the chairman do? He utterly ignored these facts, and wandered off into talking about mythology and Greek poetry.

Above all, be certain of the speaker's name and begin at once to familiarize yourself with its pronunciation. In his delightful essay, 'We Have with Us Tonight,' Stephen Leacock, the distinguished Canadian humorist, tells of one introduction he received in which the introducer said:

> There are many of us who have awaited Mr Learoyd's coming with the most pleasant anticipations. We seemed from his books to know him already as an old friend. In fact I do not think I exaggerate when I tell Mr Learoyd that his name in our city has long been a household word. I have very, very great pleasure in introducing to you—Mr Learoyd.

The main purpose of your research is to be specific, for only by being specific will the introduction achieve its purpose—to heighten the audience's attention and make it receptive to the speaker's talk. The chairman who comes to a meeting poorly prepared usually comes up with something as vague and soporific as this:

Our speaker is recognized everywhere as an authority on his subject. We are interested in hearing what he has to say on this subject, because he comes from a great distance. It gives me great pleasure to present, let's see now, oh, here it is, Mr Blank.

By taking a little time to prepare we can avoid the sad impression such an introduction makes upon both speaker and audience.

SECOND: FOLLOW THE T-I-S FORMULA

For most introductions, the T-I-S formula serves as a handy guide in organizing the facts you have collected in your research:

1. T stands for Topic. Start your introduction by giving the exact title of the speaker's talk.
2. I stands for Importance. In this step you bridge over the area between the topic and the particular interests of the group.
3. S stands for Speaker. Here you list the speaker's outstanding qualifications, particularly those that relate to his topic. Finally, you give his name, distinctly and clearly.

THIRD: BE ENTHUSIASTIC

In making an introduction of a speaker, manner is quite as important as matter. You should try to be friendly and instead of saying how happy you are, be genuinely pleasant making your talk. If you give the introduction with a sense of building to a climax at the end when you announce the speaker's name, the sense of anticipation will be increased and the audience will applaud the speaker more enthusiastically. This display of the audience's good feeling will in turn help to stimulate the speaker to do his best.

FOURTH: BE WARMLY SINCERE

Be sure to be sincere. Do not indulge in deprecatory remarks or snide humor. A tongue-in-cheek type of introduction is often misinterpreted by some members of the audience. Be warmly sincere, because you are in a social situation that demands the highest kind of finesse and tact. You may be on familiar terms with the speaker, but the audience isn't, and some of your remarks, innocent though they be, may be misconstrued.

FIFTH: THOROUGHLY PREPARE THE TALK OF PRESENTATION

'It has been proved that the deepest yearning of the human heart is for recognition—for honour!'

When Margery Wilson, the author, wrote this she expressed a universal feeling. We all want to get along well in life. We want to be appreciated. Someone else's commendation, if it is only a word—let alone a gift presented at a formal affair—lifts the spirit magically.

When we make a speech of presentation, we reassure the recipient that he really is somebody. He has succeeded in a certain effort. He is deserving of honor. We have come together to pay him this honor. What we have to say should be brief but we should give it careful thought. It may not mean much to those who are used to receiving honors, but to others less fortunate it may be something to be remembered brightly all the rest of a lifetime.

We, therefore, should give serious consideration to our choice of words in presenting the honor. Here is a time-tested formula:

1. Tell why the award is made. Perhaps it is for long service, or for winning a contest, or for a single notable achievement. Explain this simply.
2. Tell something of the group's interest in the life and activities of the person to be honored.
3. Tell how much the award is deserved and how cordially the group feels toward the recipient.
4. Congratulate the recipient and convey everyone's good wishes for the future.

Nothing is so essential to this little talk as sincerity. Everyone realizes this, perhaps without saying so. So if you have been chosen to make a speech of presentation, you as well as the recipient have been honored. Your associates know you can be trusted with the task that demands a heart as well as a head. This must not tempt you to make certain mistakes that some speakers make. They are mistakes concerned with exaggeration.

At a time such as this, it is easy to exaggerate someone's virtues far beyond their real measure. If the award is deserved, we must say so, but we should not add words of over-praise. Exaggerated praise makes the recipient uncomfortable and it doesn't convince an audience which knows better.

We also should avoid exaggerating the importance of the gift itself. Instead of stressing its intrinsic value, we should emphasize the friendly sentiments of those who are giving it.

SIXTH: EXPRESS YOUR SINCERE FEELINGS IN THE TALK OF ACCEPTANCE

This should be even shorter than the speech of presentation. It certainly shouldn't be anything we have memorized: yet being ready to make it will be an advantage. If we know we are to be given a present, with a speech of presentation, we shouldn't be at a loss for words of acknowledgment that will be a credit to us.

Just to mumble, 'thank you' and 'greatest day in my life' and 'most wonderful thing that ever happened to me,' is not very good. Here, as in the speech of presentation, a danger of exaggeration lurks. 'Greatest day' and 'most wonderful thing' take in too much territory. You can express heartfelt gratitude better in more moderate terms. Here is a suggested format:

1. Give a warmly sincere 'thank you' to the group.
2. Give credit to others who have helped you, your associates, employers, friends, or family.
3. Tell what the gift or award means to you. If it is wrapped, open it and display it. Tell the audience how useful or decorative it is and how you intend to use it.
4. End with another sincere expression of your gratitude.

Fear doesn't exist anywhere except in the mind.
—Dale Carnegie

5

ORGANIZING THE LONGER TALK

No sane man would start to build a house without some sort of plan; but why will he begin to deliver a talk without the vaguest notion of what he wishes to accomplish?

What is the best and most effective arrangement for a given set of ideas? No one can say until he has studied them. It is always a new problem, an eternal question that every speaker must ask and answer himself again and again. No infallible rules can be given; but we can, at any rate, indicate the three major phases of the longer talk to get action: the attention step, the body, and conclusion. For each, there are some time-tested methods of developing each phase.

FIRST: GET ATTENTION IMMEDIATELY

I once asked Dr Lynn Harold Hough, formerly president of Northwestern University, what was the most important fact his long experience as a speaker has taught him. After pondering a moment, he replied, 'To get an arresting opening, something that will seize favorable attention immediately.' Dr Hough struck at the heart of the matter of all persuasive speaking: how to get the audience 'tuned in' right from the speaker's first words. Here are some methods which, if applied, will give high attention value to your opening phrases.

Begin your talk with an incident

Lowell Thomas, who has made a world-wide reputation as a news analyst, lecturer, and motion picture producer, began a talk on Lawrence of Arabia with this statement:

I was going down Christian Street in Jerusalem one day when I met a man clad in the gorgeous robes of an oriental potentate. At his side hung the curved gold sword worn only by the descendants of the prophet Mohammed...

And he was off—off with a story from his experience. That is what hooks attention. That kind of opening is almost foolproof. It can hardly fail. It moves, it marches. We follow because we identify ourselves as part of a situation and we want to know what is going to happen. I know of no more compelling method of opening a talk than by the use of a story. One of my own talks which I have given many times begins with these words:

A speaker who begins a talk with a story from his experience is on safe ground, for there is no groping for words, no loss of ideas. The experience he is relating is his, a re-creation, as it were, of part of his life, the very fiber of his being. The result? A self-assured, relaxed manner which will help a speaker establish himself on a friendly basis with an audience.

Arouse suspense

Here is the way Mr Powell Healy began a talk at the Penn Athletic Club in Philadelphia:

Eighty-two years ago, there was published in London a little volume, a story, which was destined to become immortal. Many people have called it 'the greatest little book in the world' When it first appeared, friends meeting one another on the Strand or Pall Mall asked the question, 'Have you read it?' The answer invariably was: 'Yes, God bless him, I have.'

The day it was published a thousand copies were sold. Within a fortnight the demand had consumed fifteen thousand. Since then it has run into countless thousands of editions and has been translated into every language under heaven. A few years ago, J.P. Morgan purchased the original manuscript for a fabulous sum and it now reposes among the priceless treasures in his magnificent art gallery. What is this world famous book? It is...

Are you interested? Are you eager to know more? Has the speaker captured the favorable attention of his listeners? Do you feel this opening has held your attention, heightened your interest as it progressed? Why? Because it aroused your curiosity and held you in suspense.

Curiosity! Who is not susceptible to it?

Perhaps you, too! You are asking just who is the author and what is the book mentioned above? To satisfy your curiosity, here is the answer: The author: Charles Dickens, the book: *A Christmas Carol.*

State an arresting fact

Clifford R. Adams, director of the Marriage Counseling Service of the Pennsylvania State College, began an article in *The Reader's Digest*, entitled 'How to Pick a Mate', with these startling facts—facts that make you gasp, facts that make an arresting opener:

Today the chances that our young people will find happiness through marriage are slim indeed. The rise of our divorce rate is frightening. One marriage in five or six landed on the rocks in 1940. By 1946, it is expected to be one in four. And if long-range trends continue, the rate in fifty years will be one in two.

This method of making startling statements at the beginning of a talk is effective in establishing contact with the listener because it jars the mind. It is a kind of "shock technique" that enlists attention by using the unexpected to focus attention upon the subject matter of the talk.

One of our class members in Washington, D.C., used this method, arousal of curiosity, as effectively as anyone I have ever heard. Her name, Meg Sheil. Here is her opening:

'I was a prisoner for ten years. Not in an ordinary prison, but in one whose walls were worry about my inferiority and whose bars were the fear of criticism.' Don't you want to know more about this true-life episode?

A danger of the startling opener must be avoided, that is, the tendency to be over-dramatic or too sensational. I remember one speaker who started his talk by shooting a pistol into the air. He got attention all right, but he also blasted the eardrums of his listeners. Make your opening conversational in manner. An efficient way to discover whether you have an opener that is conversational is to try it out across the dinner table. If the way you open your talk isn't conversational enough to be spoken across the dinner table, it probably won't be conversational enough for an audience either.

If you want to interest your listeners, don't begin with an introduction. Begin by leaping right into the heart of your story.

That is what Frank Bettger does. He is the author of How I Raised Myself From Failure to Success in Selling. He is an artist when it comes to creating suspense in his first sentence. I know, because he and I traveled together all over the United States giving talks on selling under the auspices of the United States Junior Chamber of Commerce. I always admired the superb way he opened his talk on enthusiasm. No preaching. No lecturing. No sermonizing. No general statements. Frank Bettger leaped right into the heart of his subject in his first sentence. He began his talk on enthusiasm like this:

'Shortly after I started out as a professional baseball player, I got one of the biggest shocks of my life.'

What effect did this opening have on his audience? I know, I was there. I saw the reaction. He had everyone's attention instantly. Everyone was eager to hear why and how he was shocked, and what he did about it.

Ask for a show of hands

A splendid way to get interested attention is to ask the audience to raise their hands in answer to a question. For example, I have opened my talk on 'How to Prevent Fatigue' with this question:

'Let's see your hands. How many of you get tired more quickly than you feel you ought to?'

Note this point: When you ask for a show of hands, usually give the audience some warning that you are going to do so. Do not open a talk with: 'How many people here believe the income tax should be lowered? Let's see your hands.' Give the audience a chance to be ready for the vote by saying, for instance: 'I am going to ask for a show of hands on a question of importance to you. This is the question: "How many of you believe that trading stamps benefit the consumer?"'

The technique of asking for a show of hands gets a priceless reaction known as 'audience participation.' When you use it, your talk is no longer a one-sided affair. The audience is participating in it now. When you ask, 'How many of you get tired more quickly than you feel you ought to?' everyone starts thinking of his favorite topic: himself, his aches, his fatigue. He lifts his hand and possibly looks around to see who else has his hand up. He forgets that he is listening to a talk. He smiles. He nods to a friend sitting next to him. The ice is broken. You, the speaker, are at ease, and so is the audience.

Promise to tell the audience how they can get something they want

An almost unfailing way to get alert attention is to promise to tell your listeners how they can get what they want by doing what you suggest. Following are some illustrations of what I mean:

'I am going to tell you how to prevent fatigue. I am going to tell you how to add one hour a day to your waking life.'

'I'm going to tell you how you can materially increase your income.'

'I promise that, if you will listen to me for ten minutes, I'll tell you one sure way to make yourself more popular.'

The 'promise' type of opener is sure to get attention because it goes straight to the self-interests of the audience. All too often speakers neglect to tie their topics to the vital interests of their hearers. Instead of opening the door to attention, they slam it shut with dull openings that trace the history of the subject matter or laboriously dwell upon the background necessary to an understanding of the topic.

Use an exhibit

Perhaps the easiest way in the world to gain attention is to hold up something for people to look at. Almost any creature, from the simplest to the most complex, will give heed to that kind of stimulus. It can be used sometimes with effectiveness before the most dignified audience. For example, Mr S.S. Ellis, of Philadelphia, opened one of his talks in one of our classes by holding a coin between his thumb and forefinger, and high above his shoulder. Naturally everyone looked. Then he inquired: 'Has anyone here ever found a coin like this on the sidewalk? It announces that the fortunate finder will be given a lot free in such and such a real estate development. He has but to call and present this coin...' Mr Ellis then proceeded to condemn the misleading and unethical practices involved.

All of the foregoing methods are commendable. They may be used separately or they may be combined. Recognize that how you open a talk largely determines whether the audience is going to accept you and your message.

SECOND: AVOID GETTING UNFAVORABLE ATTENTION

Please, please, I urge you, remember that you must not only capture the attention of your audience, but you must capture their favorable attention. Please note that I said favorable attention. No rational person would begin a talk by insulting his audience or by making any obnoxious or disagreeable statement that would turn them against him and his message. Yet how frequently speakers begin talks by attracting attention through the use of-one of the following devices.

Do not open with an apology

To begin a talk with an apology does not get you off to a good start either. How often we all have heard speakers begin by calling the attention of the audience to their lack of preparation or their lack of ability. If you are not prepared, the audience will probably discover it without your assistance. Why insult your audience by suggesting that you did not think them worth preparing for, that just any old thing you had on the fire was good enough to serve them? No, we don't want to hear apologies; we want to be informed and interested—to be interested: remember that. Let your opening sentence capture the interest of your audience. Not the second sentence. Not the third sentence. The first!

Avoid the 'funny' story opening

You may have noticed that there is one method of opening a talk, and one much favored by speakers, that is not recommended here: the so-called 'funny' story opening. For some lamentable reason, the novice feels that he ought to 'lighten up' his talk by telling a joke; he assumes that the mantel of Mark Twain has descended upon his shoulders. Do not fall into this trap; you will discover to your embarrassment the painful truth that the 'funny' story is more often pathetic than funny—and the story may be known to persons in your audience.

A sense of humor, though, is a prized asset for any speaker. A talk need not begin, nor be, heavy-footed, elephantine, and excessively solemn. Not at all. If you have the ability to tickle the risibilities of your audience by some witty reference to a local situation or to something arising out of the occasion or the remarks of a previous speaker, then by all means do so. Observe some incongruity. Exaggerate it. That type of humor is more likely to succeed than stale jokes about Pat and Mike, or mothers-in-law, or shaggy dogs, because it is relevant and because it is original.

Perhaps the easiest way to create merriment is to tell a story on yourself. Depict yourself in some ridiculous and embarrassing situation. That gets down to the very essence of humor. Jack Benny has used this device for years. He was one of the first major radio comedians to 'poke fun' at himself. By making himself the butt of jokes concerning his ability to play the violin, his miserliness, and his age, Jack Benny works a rich vein of humor that keeps his ratings high from year to year.

Audiences open their hearts, as well as their minds, to speakers who deliberately deflate themselves by calling attention to some deficiency or failing on their part, in a humorous sense, of course. On the other hand, creating the image of the "stuffed shirt" or the visiting expert with all the answers leaves an audience cold and unreceptive.

THIRD: SUPPORT YOUR MAIN IDEAS

In the longer talk to get action you will have several points; the fewer the better, but all of them will require support material. A method of supporting the point of a talk is what you want the audience to do, by illustrating it with a story, an experience out of your life. This type of example is popular because it appeals to a basic drive in people, summed up by the slogan, 'Everybody Loves a Story'. An incident or happening is the kind of example most often used by the average speaker, but it is by no means the only way your point can be supported. You might also use statistics, which are nothing more than illustrations scientifically grouped, expert testimony, analogies, exhibits, or demonstrations.

Use statistics

Statistics are used to show the proportion of instances of a certain kind. They can be impressive and convincing, especially as evidence where an isolated example might not do as well. The effectiveness of the Salk anti-poliomyelitis vaccine program was measured by statistics gathered in all parts of the country. Isolated cases of ineffectiveness were the exceptions that proved the rule. A talk based on one of these exceptions would not, therefore, convince a parent that the Salk vaccine program would not protect his child.

Statistics, of themselves, can be boring. They should be judiciously used, and when used they should be clothed in a language that makes them vivid and graphic.

Here is an example of how statistics can be impressive by comparing them with things familiar to us. In backing up his point that a vast amount of time is lost by New Yorkers' neglecting to answer telephones promptly an executive said:

Out of each one hundred telephone connections made, seven show a delay of more than a minute before the person called answers.

Every day 2,80,000 minutes are lost in this way. In the course of six months, this minute delay in New York is about equal to all the business days that have elapsed since Columbus discovered America.

Mere numbers and amounts, taken by themselves, are never very impressive. They have to be illustrated; they ought, if possible, to be put in terms of our experiences.

Use the testimony of experts

Frequently you can effectively back up the points you want to make in the body of your talk by the use of the testimony of an expert. Before using testimony it should be tested by answering these questions:

1. Is the quotation I am about to use accurate?
2. Is it taken from the area of the man's expert knowledge? To quote Joe Louis on economics would obviously be exploiting his name but not his forte.
3. Is the quotation from a man who is known and respected by the audience?
4. Are you sure that the statement is based on firsthand knowledge, not personal interest or prejudice?

Use analogies

An analogy, according to Webster, is a 'relation of likeness between two things...consisting in the resemblance not of the things themselves but of two or more attributes, circumstances, or effects.'

The use of an analogy is a fine technique for supporting a main idea.

Here is, perhaps one of the most outstanding analogies in the history of eloquence; it was used by Lincoln in answer to his critics during a crucial period of the Civil War:

Gentlemen, I want you to suppose a case for a moment. Suppose that all the property you were worth was in gold, and you had put it in the hands of Blondin, the famous rope-walker, to carry across the Niagara Falls on a tightrope. Would you shake the rope while he was passing over it, or keep shouting to him, 'Blondin, stoop a little more! Go a little faster!' No, I am sure you would not. You would hold your breath as well as your tongue, and keep your hands off until he was safely over. Now the government is in the same situation. It is carrying an immense weight across a stormy ocean. Untold treasures are in its hands. It is doing the best it can. Don't badger it! Just keep still, and it will get you safely over.

Use a demonstration with or without an exhibit

Some years ago, Henry Morton Robinson wrote an interesting article on 'How Lawyers Win Cases' for Your Life magazine. In it, he describes how a lawyer named Abe Hummer is credited with a telling dramatic demonstration of showmanship while representing an insurance company in a damage suit. The plaintiff, a Mr Postlethwaite, stated that as a result of falling down an elevator shaft his shoulder had been so severely injured that he was unable to raise his right arm.

Hummer appeared to be gravely concerned. 'Now Mr Postlethwaite,' he said confidently, 'show the jury how high you can raise your arm.' Gingerly, Postlethwaite brought his arm up to ear level. 'Now show us how high you could raise it before you were injured,' urged Hummer. 'As high as this,' said the plaintiff, shooting his arm at full length over his head.

You may draw your own conclusion regarding the reaction of the jury to this demonstration.

In the longer talk to secure action you might make three, or at most, four points. They could be uttered in less than a minute. To recite them to an audience would be dull and boring. What makes these points come alive? It is the support material you use. This is what gives sparkle and interest to your talk. By the use of incidents, comparisons and demonstrations, you make your main ideas clear and vivid; by the use of statistics and testimony you substantiate the truth and emphasize the importance of your main points.

FOURTH: APPEAL FOR ACTION

I dropped in to talk a few minutes one day with George F. Johnson, the industrialist and humanitarian. He was President of the great Endicott-Johnson Corporation at the time. More interesting to me, though, was the knowledge that he was a speaker who could make his hearers laugh, and sometimes cry, and often remember for a long time what he said.

He didn't have a private office. He had a corner of a big, busy factory, and his manner was as unpretentious as his old wooden desk.

'You've come at a good time,' he said as he stood up to greet me. 'I've just got a job out of the way. I've jotted down what I want to say at the end of a talk I'm going to give to the workers tonight.'

'It's always a relief to get a talk ship-shape in your mind from beginning to end,' I told him.

'Oh, I haven't got it all in mind yet,' he said. 'Just the general idea and the specific way I want to finish it.'

He was not a professional speaker. He never went in for ringing words or fine phrases. From experience, however, he had learned one of the secrets of successful communication. He knew that if a talk is to go over well, it has to have a good ending. He realized that the conclusion of a talk is the part toward which all that precedes it must reasonably move if an audience is to be impressed.

The close is really the most strategic point in a talk, what one says last, the final words left ringing in the ears when one ceases—these are likely to be remembered longest. Unlike Mr Johnson, beginners seldom appreciate the importance of this; their endings often leave much to be desired.

What are their most common errors? Let us discuss a few and search for remedies.

First, there is the man who finishes with: 'That is about all I have to say on the matter, so I guess I shall stop.' This speaker usually throws a smoke screen over his inability to end a talk satisfactorily by lamely saying 'thank you'. That is not an ending. That is a mistake.

It reeks of the amateur. That is almost unpardonable. If that is all you have to say, why not round off your talk, and promptly take your seat and stop without talking about stopping. Do that, and the inference that that is all you have to say may, with safety and good taste, be left to the discernment of the audience.

Then, there is the speaker who says all he has to say, but he does not know how to stop. I believe it was Josh Billings who advised people to take the bull by the tail instead of the horns, since it would be easier to let go. This speaker has the bull by the frontal extremities, and wants to part company with him, but try as hard as he will, he can't get near a friendly fence or tree. So he finally thrashes about in a circle, covering the same ground, repeating himself, leaving a bad impression...

The remedy? An ending has to be planned sometime, doesn't it? Is it the part of wisdom to try to do it after you are facing an audience, while you are under the strain and stress of talking, while your mind must be intent on what you are saying? Or does common sense suggest the advisability of doing it quietly, calmly, beforehand?

How do you go about bringing your talk to a climactic close? Here are a few suggestions:

Summarize

In the longer talk a speaker is very apt to cover so much ground that at the close the listeners are a little hazy about all his main points. However, few speakers realize that. They are misled into assuming that because these points are crystal clear in their own minds, they must be equally lucid to their hearers. Not at all. The speaker has been pondering over his ideas for some time. But his points are all new to the audience; they are flung at the audience like a handful of shot. Some may stick, but most are liable to roll off in confusion. The hearers are liable, in the words of Shakespeare, to 'remember a mass of things but nothing distinctly'.

Here is a good example. The speaker, a traffic manager for one of Chicago's railways, ends his talk with this summary:

In short, gentlemen, our own back-door yard experience with this block device; the experience in its use in the East, in the West, in the North; the sound operating principles underlying its operation; the actual demonstration in the money saved in one year in wreck prevention—move me most earnestly and unequivocally to recommend its immediate installation on our Southern branch.

You see what he has done? You can see it and feel it without having heard the rest of the talk. He has summed up in a few sentences, in sixty-two words, practically all the points he had made in the entire talk.

Don't you feel that a summary like that helps? If so, make that technique your own.

Ask for action

The closing just quoted is also an excellent illustration of the ask-for-action ending. The speaker wanted something done: a block device installed on the Southern branch of his road. He based his request for action on the money it would save, on the wrecks it would prevent. The speaker wanted action, and he got it. This was not a mere practice talk. It was delivered before the board of directors of a railway, and it secured the installation of the block device for which it asked.

In your final words of a talk to secure action the time has come to ask for the order. So ask for it! Tell your audience to join, contribute, vote, write, telephone, buy, boycott, enlist, investigate, acquit, or whatever it is you want them to do. Be sure to obey these caution signs, however:

Ask them to do something specific. Don't say, 'Help the Red Cross'. That's too general. Say, instead, 'Send your enrollment fee of one dollar tonight to the American Red Cross, 125 Smith Street in this city.'

Ask the audience for some response that is within their power to give. Make it as easy as you can for your audience to act on your appeal. Don't say, 'Write your congressman to vote against this bill.' Ninety-nine per cent of your listeners won't do it. They are not vitally interested; or it is too much trouble; or they will forget. So make it easy and pleasant to act. How? By writing a letter yourself to your congressman, saying, 'We, the undersigned, urge you to vote against Bill No. 74321.' Pass the letter around with a fountain pen, and you will probably get a lot of signers—and perhaps lose your fountain pen.

90 per cent of how well the talk will go is determined before the speaker steps on the platform.
—Somers White

Only the prepared speaker deserves to be confident.
—Dale Carnegie

6

APPLYING WHAT YOU HAVE LEARNED

A t the fourteenth session of my course I have often heard with pleasure students tell how they used the techniques in this book in their everyday lives. Salesmen point to increased sales, managers to promotions, executives to a widened span of control, all due to the increased skill with which they gave instructions and solved problems using the tools of effective speech.

Perhaps you are wondering when to begin applying what you have learned in the previous thirteen chapters of this book. You may be surprised if I answer that query by one word: Immediately.

Even though you are not planning to make a speech in public for some time, if at all, I am certain you will find that the principles and techniques in this book are applicable every day. When I say start using these techniques now, I mean in the very next speaking situation in which you find yourself.

If you analyse the speaking that you do every day, you will be amazed by the similarity of purpose between your daily speaking and the type of formal communication discussed in these pages. By applying the techniques described in this book to everyday conversation we can make ourselves more effective, get our ideas across more efficiently, and motivate others with skill and fact.

FIRST: USE SPECIFIC DETAIL IN EVERYDAY CONVERSATION

Take just one of these techniques, for instance. Remember in Chapter Four I appealed to you to put detail in your talk. In that way you make your ideas come alive, in a vivid and graphic way. Of course I was thinking mainly of speaking before groups. But isn't the use of detail just as important in everyday conversation? Just think for a moment of the really interesting conversationalists of your acquaintance. Aren't they the ones who fill their talk with colorful, dramatic details, who have the ability to use picturesque speech?

Before you can begin to develop your conversational skills you must have confidence. So almost all that was said in the first three chapters of this book will be useful in giving you the security to mix with others and to voice your opinions in an informal social group. Once you are eager to express your ideas even on a limited scale, you will begin to search your experience for material that can be converted to conversation. Here a wonderful thing happens—your horizons begin to expand and you see your life take on new meaning.

Though few of us are professional teachers, all of us use speech to inform others on many occasions during the day. As parents instructing our children, as neighbors explaining a new method of pruning roses, as tourists exchanging ideas on the best route to follow, we constantly find ourselves in conversational situations that require clarity and coherence of thought, vitality and vigor of expression. What was said in Chapter Eight in relation to the talk to inform is applicable in these situations as well.

SECOND: USE EFFECTIVE SPEAKING TECHNIQUES IN YOUR JOB

Now we enter the area of the communicative process as it affects our jobs. As salesmen, managers, clerks, department heads, group leaders, teachers, ministers, nurses, executives, doctors, lawyers, accountants, and engineers. We are all charged with the responsibility of explaining specialized areas of knowledge and giving professional instructions. Our ability to make these instructions in clear, concise language may often be the yardstick used by our superiors in judging our competence. How to think quickly and verbalize adroitly is a skill acquired in presenting speeches of information, but this skill is by no means limited to formal speaking—it can be used every day by every one of us. The need for clarity in business and professional speech today is highlighted by the recent spate of oral communications courses in industry, government, and professional organizations.

THIRD: SEEK OPPORTUNITIES TO SPEAK IN PUBLIC

In addition to using the principles of this book in everyday speech, where incidentally you will reap the greatest rewards, you should seek every opportunity to speak in public. How do you do this? By joining a club where public speaking of some sort goes on. Don't just be an inactive member, a mere looker-on. Pitch in and help by doing committee work. Most of these jobs go begging. Get to be program chairman. That will give you an opportunity to interview good speakers in your community, and you certainly will be called upon to make speeches of introduction.

As soon as possible, develop a twenty to thirty minute talk. Use the suggestions in this book as a guide. Let your club or organization know that you are prepared to address them. Offer your services to a speaker's bureau in your town. Fund-raising campaigns are looking for volunteers to speak for them. They provide you with a speaker's kit which will be of great help in preparing your talk. Many speakers of consequence have begun in this way. Some of them have risen to great prominence. Take Sam Levenson, for example, the radio and TV star and a speaker whose services are sought all over the country. He was a high school teacher in New York. Just as a sideline he began making short talks about what he knew best, his family, relatives, his students, and the unusual aspects of his job. These talks took fire, and he was soon asked to address so many groups it began to interfere with his teaching chores. But, by this time he was a guest on network programs and it wasn't long before Sam Levenson transferred his talents entirely to the entertainment world.

FOURTH: YOU MUST PERSIST

When we learn any new thing, like French or golf or speaking in public, we never advance steadily. We do not improve gradually. We do it by waves, by abrupt starts and sudden stops. Then we remain stationary a time, or we may even slip back and lose some of the ground we have previously gained. These periods of stagnation, or retrogression, are well known by all psychologists; they have been named 'plateaus in the curve of learning'. Students of effective speaking will sometimes be stalled, perhaps for weeks, on one of these plateaus. Work as hard as they may, they cannot seem to get off it. The weak ones give up in despair. Those with grit persist, and they find that suddenly, almost overnight, without knowing how or why it has happened, they have made great progress. They have lifted from the plateau like an airplane. Abruptly they have acquired naturalness, force, and confidence in their speaking.

You may always, as has been stated elsewhere in these pages, experience some fleeting fear, some shock, some nervous anxiety, the first few moments you face an audience. Even the greatest musicians have felt it in spite of their innumerable public appearances. Paderewski always fidgeted nervously with his cuffs immediately before he sat down at the piano. But as soon as he began to play, all of his audience-fear vanished quickly like a mist in August sunshine.

His experience will be yours. If you will but persevere, you will soon eradicate everything, including this initial fear; and that will be initial fear, and nothing more. After the first few sentences, you will have control of yourself. You will be speaking with positive pleasure.

FIFTH: KEEP THE CERTAINTY OF REWARD BEFORE YOU

How I wish I could get you to prop this book open on your breakfast table every morning until you had memorized these words from Professor William James:

Let no youth have any anxiety about the upshot of his education, whatever the line of it may be. If he keeps faithfully busy each hour of the working day, he may safely leave the final result to itself. He can, with perfect certainty, count on waking up some fine morning to find himself one of the competent ones of his generation, in whatever pursuit he may have singled out.

And now, with the renowned Professor James to fall back upon, I shall go so far as to say that if you keep right on practicing intelligently, you may confidently hope to wake up one fine morning and find yourself one of the competent speakers of your city or community.

Regardless of how fantastic that may sound to you now, it is true as a general principle. Exceptions, of course, there are. A man with an inferior mentality and personality, and with nothing to talk about, is not going to develop into a local Daniel Webster; but, within reason, the assertion is correct.

I have known and carefully watched literally thousands of persons trying to gain self-confidence and the ability to talk in public. Those that succeeded were, in only a few instances, persons of unusual brilliancy. For the most part, they were the ordinary run of businessmen you will find in your own home town. But they kept on. More exceptional men sometimes got discouraged or too deeply immersed in money-making, and they did not get very far; but the ordinary individual with grit and singleness of purpose, at the end of the road, was at the top.

That is only human and natural. Don't you see the same tiling occurring all the time in commerce and the professions? John D. Rockefeller, Sr., said that the first essential for success in business was patience and the knowledge that reward is ultimately certain. It is likewise one of the first essentials for success in effective speaking.

A few summers ago, I started out to scale a peak in the Austrian Alps called the Wilder Kaiser. Baedaker said that the ascent was difficult, and a guide was essential for amateur climbers. A friend and I had none, and we were certainly amateurs; so a third party asked us if we thought we were going to succeed. 'Of course,' we replied. 'What makes you think so?' he inquired.

'Others have done it without guides,' I said, 'so I know it is within reason, and I never undertake anything thinking defeat.'

That is the proper psychology for anything from speaking to an assault on Mt. Everest.

How well you succeed is largely determined by thoughts you have prior to speaking. See yourself in your imagination talking to others with perfect self-control.

It is easily in your power to do this. Believe that you will succeed. Believe it firmly, and you will then do what is necessary to bring success about.

The most valuable thing that most members acquire from training in our classes is an increased confidence in themselves, an additional faith in their ability to achieve. What is more important for one's success in almost any undertaking?

Emerson wrote, 'Nothing great was ever achieved without enthusiasm.' That is more than a well-turned literary phrase; it is the road map to success.

William Lyon Phelps was probably the most beloved and the most popular professor ever to teach at Yale University. In his book The Excitement of Teaching, he states, 'With me, teaching is more than an art or an occupation. It is a passion. I love to teach, as a painter loves to paint, as a singer loves to sing, as a poet loves to write. Before I get out of bed in the morning, I think with ardent delight of my group of students.'

Is there any wonder a teacher so filled with enthusiasm for his job, so excited about the work ahead of him, achieved success?

If you put enthusiasm into learning how to speak more effectively you will find that the obstacles in your path will disappear. This is a challenge to focus all your talent and power on the goal of effective communication with your fellow men. Think of the self-reliance, the assurance, the poise that will be yours, the sense of mastery that comes from being able to hold the attention, stir the emotions, and convince a group to act. You will find that competence in self-expression will lead to competence in other ways as well, for training in effective speaking is the royal road to self-confidence in all the areas of working and living.

Speakers who talk about what life has taught them never fail to keep the attention of their listeners.

—Dale Carnegie

PART 3
The Three Aspects of Every Speech

7

EARNING THE RIGHT TO TALK

Many years ago, a Doctor of Philosophy and a rough-and-ready fellow who had spent his youth in the British Navy were enrolled in one of our classes in New York. The man with the degree was a college professor; the ex-tar was the proprietor of a small side-street trucking business. His talks were far better received by the class than those given by the professor. Why? The college man used beautiful English. He was urbane, cultured, refined. His talks were always logical and clear. But they lacked one essential—concreteness. They were vague and general. Not once did he illustrate a point with anything approaching a personal experience. His talks were usually nothing more than a series of abstract ideas held together by a thin string of logic.

On the other hand, the trucking firm proprietor's language was definite, concrete, and picturesque. He talked in terms of everyday facts. He gave us one point and then backed it up by telling us what happened to him in the course of his business. He described the people he had to deal with and the headaches of keeping up with regulations. The virility and freshness of his phraseology made his talks highly instructive and entertaining.

I cite this instance, not because it is typical of college professors or of men in the trucking business, but because it illustrates the attention-compelling power of rich, colorful details in a talk.

There are four ways to develop speech material that guarantees audience attention. If you follow these four steps in your preparation you will be well on the way to commanding the eager attention of your listeners.

FIRST: LIMIT YOUR SUBJECT

Once you have selected your topic, the first step is to stake out the area you want to cover and stay strictly within those limits. Don't make the mistake of trying to cover the open range. One young man attempted to speak for two minutes on the subject of 'Athens from 500 B.C. to the Korean War'. How utterly futile! He barely had gone beyond the founding of the city before he had to sit down, another victim of the compulsion to cover too much in one talk. This is an extreme example, I know; I have heard thousands of talks, less encompassing in scope, that failed to hold attention for the same reason—they covered far too many points. Why? Because it is impossible for the mind to attend to a monotonous series of factual points. If your talk sounds like the World Almanac you will not be able to hold attention very long. Take a simple subject, like a trip to Yellowstone Park. In their eagerness to leave nothing out, most people have something to say about every scenic view in the Park. The audience is whisked from one point to another with dizzying speed. At the end, all that remains in the mind is a blur of waterfalls, mountains, and geysers. How much more memorable such a talk would be if the speaker limited himself to one aspect of the Park, the wildlife or the hot springs, for example. Then there would be time to develop the kind of pictorial detail that would make Yellowstone Park come alive in all its vivid color and variety.

This is true of any subject, whether it be salesmanship, baking cakes, tax exemptions, or ballistic missiles. You must limit and select before you begin, narrow your subject down to an area that will fit the time at your disposal.

In a short talk, less than five minutes in duration, all you can expect is to get one or two main points across. In a longer talk, up to thirty minutes, few speakers ever succeed if they try to cover more than four or five main ideas.

SECOND: DEVELOP RESERVE POWER

It is far easier to give a talk that skims over the surface than to dig down for facts. But when you take the easy way you make little or no impression on the audience. After you have narrowed your subject, then the next step is to ask yourself questions that will deepen your understanding and prepare you to talk with authority on the topic you have chosen: 'Why do I believe this? When did I ever see this point exemplified in real life? What precisely am I trying to prove? Exactly how did it happen?'

Questions like these call for answers that will give you reserve power, the power that makes people sit up and take notice. It was said of Luther Burbank, the botanical wizard, that he produced a million plant specimens to find one or two superlative ones. It is the same with a talk. Assemble a hundred thoughts around your theme, then discard ninety.

'I always try to get ten times as much information as I use, sometimes a hundred times as much,' said John Gunther not long ago. The author of the bestselling 'Inside' books was speaking of the way he prepared to write a book or give a talk.

On one occasion in particular, his actions bore out his words. In 1956, he was working on a series of articles on mental hospitals. He visited institutions, talked to supervisors, attendants, and patients. A friend of mine was with him, giving some small assistance in the research, and he told me they must have walked countless miles upstairs and down, along corridors, building to building, day after day. Mr Gunther filled notebooks. Back in his office, he stacked up government and state reports, private hospital reports, and reams of committees' statistics.

'In the end,' my friend told me, 'he wrote four short articles, simple enough and anecdotal enough to make good speeches. The paper on which they were typed weighed, perhaps, a few ounces. The filled notebooks, and everything else he used as the basis for the few ounces of product, must have weighed twenty pounds.'

A surgeon friend of mine said: 'I can teach you in ten minutes how to take out an appendix. But it will take me four years to teach you what to do if something goes wrong.' So it is with speaking: Always prepare so that you are ready for any emergency, such as a change of emphasis because of a previous speaker's remarks, or a well-aimed question from the audience in the discussion period following your talk.

THIRD: FILL YOUR TALK WITH ILLUSTRATIONS AND EXAMPLES

In the Art of Readable Writing, Rudolf Flesch begins one of his chapters with this sentence: 'Only stories are really readable.' He then shows how this principle is used by Time and Reader's Digest. Almost every article in these top-circulation magazines either is written as pure narrative or is generously sprinkled with anecdotes. There is no denying the power of a story to hold attention in talking before groups as well as writing for magazines.

Norman Vincent Peale, whose sermons have been heard by millions on radio and television, says that his favorite form of supporting material in a talk is the illustration or example. He once told an interviewer from the Quarterly Journal of Speech that 'the true example is the finest method I know of to make an idea clear, interesting, and persuasive. Usually, I use several examples to support each major point.'

Readers of my books are soon aware of my use of the anecdote as a means of developing the main points of my message. How can we acquire this most important technique of using illustrative material? There are five ways of doing this: Humanize, Personalize, Specify, Dramatize, and Visualize.

Humanize your talk

I once asked a group of American businessmen in Paris to talk on "How to Succeed." Most of them merely listed a lot of abstract qualities and gave preachments on the value of hard work, persistence, and ambition.

So I halted this class, and said something like this: 'We don't want to be lectured to. No one enjoys that. Remember, you must be entertaining or we will pay no attention whatever to what you are saying. Also remember that one of the most interesting things in the world is sublimated, glorified gossip. So tell us the stories of two men you have known. Tell why one succeeded and why the other failed. We will gladly listen to that, remember it, and possibly profit by it.'

There was a certain member of that course who invariably found it difficult to interest either himself or his audience. This night, however, he seized the human interest suggestion and told us of two of his classmates in college. One of them had been so conservative that he had bought shirts at the different stores in town, and made charts showing which ones laundered best, wore longest, and gave the most service per dollar invested. His mind was always on pennies; yet, when he was graduated—it was an engineering college—he had such a high opinion of his own importance that he was not willing to begin at the bottom and work his way up, as the other graduates were doing. Even when the third annual reunion of the class came, he was still making laundry charts of his shirts, while waiting for some extraordinarily good thing to come his way. It never came. A quarter of a century has passed since then, and this man, dissatisfied and soured on life, still holds a minor position.

The speaker then contrasted with this failure the story of one of his classmates who had surpassed all expectations. This particular chap was a good mixer. Everyone liked him. Although he was ambitious to do big things later, he started as a draftsman. But he was always on the lookout for opportunity. Plans were then being made for the New York World's Fair. He knew engineering talent would be needed there, so he resigned from his position in Philadelphia and moved to New York. There he formed a partnership and engaged immediately in the contracting business. They did considerable work for the telephone company, and this man was finally taken over by that concern at a large salary.

I have recorded here only the bare outline of what the speaker told. He made his talk interesting and illuminating with a score of amusing and human interest details. He talked on and on—this man who could not ordinarily find material for a three-minute speech. Almost everyone can profit by this incident. The average speech would be far more appealing if it were rich with human interest stories. The speaker should attempt to make only a few points and to illustrate them with concrete cases. Such a method of speech building can hardly fail to get and hold attention.

Of course, the richest source of such human interest material is your own background. Don't hesitate to tell us about your experiences because of some feeling that you should not talk about yourself. The only time an audience objects to hearing a person talk about himself is when he does it in an offensive, egotistical way. Otherwise, audiences are tremendously interested in the personal stories speakers tell. They are the surest means of holding attention; don't neglect them.

Personalize your talk by using names

By all means, when you tell stories involving others, use their names, or, if you want to protect their identity, use fictitious names. Even impersonal names like 'Mr Smith' or 'Joe Brown' are far more descriptive than 'this man' or 'a person'. The label identifies and individualizes. As Rudolf Flesch points out, 'Nothing adds more realism to a story than names; nothing is as unrealistic as anonymity. Imagine a story whose hero has no name.'

If your talk is full of names and personal pronouns you can be sure of high listenability, for you will have the priceless ingredient of human interest in your speech.

Be specific, fill your talk with detail

You might say at this point, 'this is all very fine, but how can I be sure of getting enough detail into my talk?' There is one test. Use the 5-W formula every reporter follows when he writes a news story: answer the questions When? Where? Who? What? and Why? If you follow this formula your examples will have life and color.

Of course, too much detail is worse than none. All of us have been bored by lengthy recitals of superficial, irrelevant details. If you clutter your talk with too much detail, your audience will blue-pencil your remarks by refusing to give you their complete attention. There is no blue pencil more severe than inattentiveness.

Dramatize your talk by using dialogue

Suppose you want to give an illustration of how you succeeded in calming down an irate customer by using one of the rules of human relations. You could begin like this:

'The other day a man came into my office. He was pretty mad because the appliance we had sent out to his house only the week before was not working properly. I told him that we would do all we could to remedy the situation. After a while he calmed down and seemed satisfied that we had every intention to make things right.' This anecdote has one virtue—it is fairly specific—but it lacks names, specific details, and, above all, the actual dialogue which would make this incident come alive. Here it is with these added qualities:

'Last Tuesday, the door of my office slammed and I looked up to see the angry features of Charles Blexam, one of my regular customers. I didn't have time to ask him to take a seat. "Ed, this is the last straw," he said, "you can send a truck right out and cart that wash machine out of my basement."

'I asked him what was up. He was too willing to reply.

'"It won't work," he shouted, the clothes get all tangled, and my wife's sick and tired of it."

'I asked him to sit down and explain it in more detail.

"'I haven't got time to sit down. I'm late for work and I wish I'd never come in here to buy an appliance in the first place. Believe me, I'll never do it again.' Here he hit the desk with his hand and knocked over my wife's picture.

"'Look, Charley,' I said, 'if you will just sit down and tell me all about it, I promise to do whatever you want me to do.'' With that, he sat down, and we calmly talked it over.'

It isn't always possible to work dialogue into your talk, but you can see how the direct quotation of the conversation in the excerpt above helps to dramatize the incident for the listener. If the speaker has some imitative skill and can get the original tone of voice into the words, dialogue can become more effective. Also, dialogue gives your speech the authentic ring of everyday conversation. It makes you sound like a real person talking across a dinner table, not like a pedant delivering a paper before a learned society or an orator ranting into a microphone.

Visualize by demonstrating what you are talking about

Psychologists tell us that more than eighty-five per cent of our knowledge comes to us through visual impressions. No doubt this accounts for the enormous effectiveness of television as an advertising as well as entertainment medium. Public speaking, too, is a visual as well as auditory art.

One of the best ways to enrich a talk with detail is to incorporate visual demonstration into it. You might spend hours just telling me how to swing a golf club, and I might be bored by it. But get up and show me what you do when you drive a ball down the fairway and I am all eyes and ears. Likewise, if you describe the erratic maneuvers of an airplane with your arms and shoulders, I am more intent on the outcome of your brush with death.

It is a good idea to ask yourself, 'How can I put some visual detail into my talk?' Then proceed to demonstrate, for, as the ancient Chinese observed, one picture is worth ten thousand words.

FOURTH: USE CONCRETE, FAMILIAR WORDS THAT CREATE PICTURES

In the process of getting and holding attention, which is the first purpose of every speaker, there is one aid, one technique, that is of the highest importance. Yet, it is all but ignored. The average speaker does not seem to be aware of its existence. He has probably never consciously thought about it at all. I refer to the process of using words that create pictures. The speaker who is easy to listen to is the one who sets images floating before your eyes. The one who employs foggy, commonplace, colorless symbols sets the audience to nodding.

Pictures, Pictures. Pictures. They are as free as the air you breathe. Sprinkle them through your talks, your conversation, and you will be more entertaining, more influential.

Lincoln continually talked in visual terminology. When he became annoyed with the long, complicated, red-tape reports that came to his desk in the White House, he objected to them, not with colorless phraseology, but with a picture phrase that it is almost impossible to forget. 'When I send a man to buy a horse,' he said, 'I don't want to be told how many hairs the horse has in his tail. I wish only to know his points.'

Make your eye appeals definite and specific. Paint mental pictures that stand out as sharp and clear as a stag's antlers silhouetted against the setting sun. For example, the word 'dog' calls up a more or less definite picture of such an animal—perhaps a cocker spaniel, a Scottish terrier, a St. Bernard, or a Pomeranian. Notice how much more distinct an image springs into your mind when a speaker says 'bulldog'—the term is less inclusive. Doesn't 'a brindle bulldog' call up a still more explicit picture? Is it not more vivid to say 'a black Shetland pony' than to talk of 'a horse'?

It is detail that makes conversation sparkle. Anyone who is intent upon making himself a more effective conversationalist may profit by following the advice contained in this chapter. Salesmen, too, will discover the magic of detail when applied to their sales presentations. Those in executive positions, housewives, and teachers will find that giving instructions and dispensing information will be greatly improved by the use of concrete, factual detail.

> *If you can't write your message in a sentence,*
> *you can't say it in an hour.*
> —Dianna Booher

> *Tell the audience what you're going to say, say it;*
> *then tell them what you've said.*
> —Dale Carnegie

8

VITALIZING THE TALK

Right after the First World War, I was in London working with Lowell Thomas, who was giving a series of brilliant lectures on Allenby and Lawrence of Arabia to packed houses. One Sunday I wandered into Hyde Park to the spot near Marble Arch entrance where speakers of every creed, color, and political and religious persuasion are allowed to air their views without interference from the law. For a while I listened to a Catholic explaining the doctrine of the infallibility of the Pope, then I moved to the fringes of another crowd, intent upon what a Socialist had to say about Karl Marx. I strolled over to a third speaker, who was explaining why it was right and proper for a man to have four wives! Then I moved away and looked back at the three groups.

Would you believe it? The man who was talking about polygamy had the fewest number of people listening to him! There was only a handful. The crowds around the other two speakers were growing larger by the minute. I asked myself why? Was it the disparity of topics? I don't think so. The explanation, I saw as I watched, was to be found in the speakers themselves. The fellow who was talking about the advantages of having four wives didn't seem to be interested in having four wives himself. But the other two speakers, talking from almost diametrically opposed points of view, were wrapped up in their subjects. They talked with life and spirit. Their arms moved in impassioned gestures. Their voices rang with conviction. They radiated earnestness and animation.

Vitality, aliveness, enthusiasm—these are the first qualities I have always considered essential in a speaker. People cluster around the energetic speaker like wild turkeys around a field of autumn wheat.

How do you acquire this vital delivery that will keep the attention of your audience? In the course of this chapter I will give you three sovereign ways to help you put enthusiasm and excitement into your speaking.

FIRST: CHOOSE SUBJECTS YOU ARE EARNEST ABOUT

In Chapter Three was stressed the importance of feeling deeply about your subject. Unless you are emotionally involved in the subject matter you have chosen to talk about, you cannot expect to make your audience believe in your message. Obviously, if you select a topic that is exciting to you because of long experience with it, such as a hobby or recreational pursuit, or because of deep reflection or personal concern about it (as, for instance, the need for better schools in your community), you will have no difficulty in talking with excitement. The persuasive power of earnestness was never more vividly demonstrated to me than in a talk made before one of my classes in New York City more than two decades ago. I have heard many persuasive talks, but this one, which I call the Case of Blue Grass vs. Hickory Wood Ashes, stands out as a kind of triumph of sincerity over common sense.

A top-flight salesman of one of the best-known selling organizations in the city made the preposterous statement that he had been able to make blue grass grow without the aid of seeds or roots. He had, according to his story, scattered hickory wood ashes over newly plowed ground. Presto! Blue grass had appeared! He firmly believed that the hickory wood ashes, and the hickory wood ashes alone, were responsible for the blue grass.

Commenting on his talk, I gently pointed out to him that his phenomenal discovery would, if true, make him a millionaire, for blue grass seed was worth several dollars a bushel. I also told him that it would make him the outstanding scientist of all history. I informed him that no man, living or dead, had ever been able to perform the miracle he claimed to have performed: no man had ever been able to produce life from inert matter.

I told him that very quietly, for I felt that his mistake was so palpable, so absurd, as to require no emphasis in the refutation. When I had finished, every other member of the course saw the folly of his assertion; but he did not see it, not for a second. He was in earnest about his contention, deadly in earnest. He leaped to his feet and informed me that he was not wrong. He had not been relating theory, he protested, but personal experience. He knew whereof he spoke. He continued to talk, enlarging on his first remarks, giving additional information, piling up additional evidence, sincerity and honesty ringing in his voice.

Again I informed him that there was not the remotest hope in the world of his being right or even approximately right or within a thousand miles of the truth. In a second he was on his feet once more, offering to bet me five dollars and to let the U.S. Department of Agriculture settle the matter.

And do you know what happened? Several members in the class were won over to his side. Many others were beginning to be doubtful. If I had taken a vote I am certain that more than half of the businessmen in that class would not have sided with me. I asked them what had shaken them from their original position. One after another said it was the speaker's earnestness, his belief, so energetically stated, that made them begin to doubt the common sense viewpoint.

Well, in the face of that display of credulity I had to write the Department of Agriculture. I was ashamed, I told them, to ask such an absurd question. They replied, of course, that it was impossible to get blue grass or any other living thing from hickory wood ashes, and they added that they had received another letter from New York asking the same question. That salesman was so sure of his position that he sat down and wrote a letter, too!

This incident taught me a lesson I'll never forget. If a speaker believes a thing earnestly enough and says it earnestly enough, he will get adherents to his cause, even though he claims he can produce blue grass from dust and ashes. How much more compelling will our convictions be if they are arrayed on the side of common sense and truth!

Not long ago, a legislative hearing on capital punishment was presented on television. Many witnesses were called to give their viewpoints on both sides of this controversial subject. One of them was a member of the police department of the city of Los Angeles, who had evidently given much thought to this topic. He had strong convictions based on the fact that eleven of his fellow police officers had been killed in gun battles with criminals. He spoke with the deep sincerity of one who believed to his heart's core in the righteousness of his cause. The greatest appeals in the history of eloquence have all been made out of the depths of someone's deep convictions and feelings. Sincerity rests upon belief, and belief is as much a matter of the heart and of warmly feeling what you are saying as it is of the mind and coldly thinking of what to say.

You may say, as one man once did, that you have no strong convictions or interests. I am always a little surprised at this, but I told this man to get busy and get interested in something. 'What, for instance?' he asked. In desperation I said, 'Pigeons.' 'Pigeons?' he asked in a bewildered tone. 'Yes,' I told him, 'pigeons. Go out on the square and look at them, feed them, go to the library and read about them, then come back here and talk about them.' He did. When he came back there was no holding him down. He started to talk about pigeons with all the fervor of a fancier. When I tried to stop him he was saying something about forty books on pigeons and he had read them all. He gave one of the most interesting talks I have ever heard.

Here is another suggestion: Learn more and more about what you now consider a pretty good topic. The more you know about something the more earnest and excitedly enthusiastic you will become. Percy H. Whiting, the author of the *Five Great Rules of Selling*, tells salesmen never to stop learning about the product they are selling. As Mr Whiting says, 'The more you know about a good product, the more enthusiastic you become about it.' The same thing is true about your topics—the more you know about them, the more earnest and enthusiastic you will be about them.

SECOND: RELIVE THE FEELINGS YOU HAVE ABOUT YOUR TOPIC

Suppose you are telling your audience about the policeman who stopped you for going one mile over the speed limit. You can tell us that with all the cool disinterestedness of an onlooker, but it happened to you and you had certain feelings which you expressed in quite definite language. The third-person approach will not make much of an impression on your audience. They want to know exactly how you felt when that policeman wrote out that ticket. So, the more you relive the scene you are describing, or recreate the emotions you felt originally, the more vividly you will express yourself.

One of the reasons why we go to plays and movies is that we want to hear and see emotions expressed. We have become so fearful of giving vent to our feelings in public that we have to go to a play to satisfy this need for emotional expression.

When you speak in public, therefore, you will generate excitement and interest in your talk in proportion to the amount of excitement you put into it. Don't repress your honest feelings; don't put a damper on your authentic enthusiasms. Show your listeners how eager you are to talk about your subject, and you will hold their attention.

THIRD: ACT IN EARNEST

When you walk before your audience to speak, do so with an air of anticipation, not like a man who is ascending the gallows. The spring in your walk may be largely put on, but it will do wonders for you and it gives the audience the feeling that you have something you are eager to talk about. Just before you begin, take a deep breath. Keep away from furniture or from the speaker's stand. Keep your head high and your chin up. You are about to tell your listeners

266 • THE VERY BEST OF DALE CARNEGIE

something worthwhile, and every part of you should inform them of that clearly and unmistakably.

Above all, remember this: acting in earnest will make you feel earnest.

> *If you don't know what you want to achieve in*
> *your presentation your audience never will.*
> —Harvey Diamond

> *There are always three speeches, for every one you actually gave. The*
> *one you practiced, the one you gave, and the one you wish you gave.*
> —Dale Carnegie

9

DELIVERING THE TALK

Would you believe it? There are four ways, and only four ways, in which we have contact with the world. We are evaluated and classified by these four contacts: what we do, how we look, what we say, and how we say it. This chapter will deal with the last of these—how we say it.

When I first started to teach public speaking classes, I spent a great deal of time on the use of vocal exercises to develop resonance, increase the range of voice, and enhance inflectional agility. In time, I realized that my students would have to settle for the vocal equipment they were born with. I found that if I expended the time and energy I formerly devoted to helping class members to "breathe diaphragmatically" and worked on the far more important objectives of freeing them from their inhibitions and general reluctance to let themselves go, I would achieve quick and lasting results that were truly amazing. I thank God I had the sense to do this.

FIRST: CRASH THROUGH YOUR SHELL OF SELF-CONSCIOUSNESS

In my course there are several sessions that have as their purpose the freeing of tightly bound and tense adults. I got down on my knees, literally, to implore my class members to come out of their shells and find out for themselves that the world would treat them with cordiality and welcome when they would do so. It took some doing, I admit, but it was worth it. As Marshal Foch says of the art of war, 'it is simple enough in its conception, but unfortunately complicated in its execution.' The biggest stumbling block, of course, is stiffness, not only of the physical, but of the mental as well, a kind of hardening of the categories that comes with growing up.

It is not easy to be natural before an audience. Actors know that. When you were a child, say, four years old, you probably could have mounted a platform and talked naturally to an audience. But when you are twenty-and-four, or forty-and-four, what happens when you mount a platform and start to speak? Do you retain that unconscious naturalness that you possessed at four?

The problem of teaching or of training adults in delivery is not one of superimposing additional characteristics; it is largely one of removing impediments, of getting them to speak with the same naturalness that they would display if someone were to knock them down.

Hundreds of times I have stopped speakers in the midst of their talks and implored them to "talk like a human being." Hundreds of nights I have come home mentally fatigued and nervously exhausted from trying to drill members of my classes to talk naturally. No, believe me, it is not so easy as it sounds.

In one of the sessions of my course I ask the class to act out portions of dialogue, some of which is in dialect. I ask them to throw themselves into these dramatic episodes with abandon. When they do, they discover to their amazement that, though they may have acted like a fool, they didn't feel badly when they were doing it. The class too is amazed at the dramatic ability some of the class members display. My point is that once you let your hair down before a group you are not likely to hold yourself back when it comes to the normal, everyday expression of your opinions whether to individuals or before groups.

The sudden freedom you feel is like a bird taking wing after being imprisoned in a cage. You see why it is that people flock to the theater and the movies—because there they see their fellow human beings act with little or no inhibition, there they see people wearing their emotions prominently displayed on their sleeves.

SECOND: DON'T TRY TO IMITATE OTHERS—BE YOURSELF

We all admire speakers who can put showmanship into their speaking, who are not afraid to express themselves, not afraid to use the unique, individual, imaginative way of saying what they have to say to the audience.

Shortly after the close of the First World War, I met two brothers in London, Sir Ross and Sir Keith Smith. They had just made the first aeroplane flight from London to Australia to win a fifty-thousand-dollar prize offered by the Australian government. They had created a sensation throughout the British Empire and had been knighted by the King.

Captain Hurley, a well-known scenic photographer, had flown with them over a part of their trip, taking motion pictures; so I helped them prepare an illustrated travel talk of their flight and trained them in the delivery of it. They gave it twice daily for four months in Philharmonic Hall, London, one speaking in the afternoon, the other at night.

They had had identically the same experience, they had sat side by side as they flew halfway around the world, and they delivered the same talk, almost word for word. Yet, somehow it didn't sound like the same talk at all.

There is something besides the mere words in a talk which counts. It is the flavor with which they are delivered. It is not so much just what you say as how you say it.

Brulloff, the great Russian painter, once corrected a pupil's study. The pupil looked in amazement at the altered drawing, exclaiming: 'Why, you have touched it only a tiny bit, but it is quite another thing.' Brulloff replied, 'Art begins where the tiny bit begins.' That is as true of speaking as it is of painting and of Paderewski's playing.

There is no other human being in the world like you. Hundreds of millions of people have two eyes and a nose and a mouth; but none of them looks precisely like you; and none of them has exactly your traits and methods and cast of mind. Few of them will talk and express themselves just as you do when you are speaking naturally. In other words, you have an individuality. As a speaker, it is your most precious possession. Cling to it. Cherish it. Develop it. It is the spark that will put force and sincerity into your speaking. 'It is your only real claim to importance.' Please, I beg you, do not attempt to force yourself in a mold and thereby lose your distinctiveness.

THIRD: CONVERSE WITH YOUR AUDIENCE

Let me give you an illustration that is typical of the fashion in which thousands of persons talk. I happened on one occasion to be stopping in Murren, a summer resort in the Swiss Alps. I was living at a hotel operated by a London company; and they usually sent out from England a couple of lecturers each week to talk to the guests. One of them was a well-known English novelist. Her topic was 'The Future of the Novel'. She admitted that she had not selected the subject herself; and the long and short of it was that she had nothing she cared to say about it to make it worthwhile expressing. She had hurriedly made some rambling notes; and she stood before the audience, ignoring her hearers, not even looking at them, staring sometimes over their heads, sometimes at her notes, sometimes at the floor. She unreeled words into the primeval void with a far-away look in her eyes and a far-away ring in her voice.

That isn't delivering a talk at all. It is a soliloquy. It has no sense of communication. And that is the first essential of good talking: a sense of communication. The audience must feel that there is a message being delivered straight from the mind and heart of the speaker to their minds and their hearts. The kind of talk I have just described might as well have been spoken out in the sandy, waterless wastes of the Gobi desert. In fact, it sounded as if it were being delivered in some such spot rather than to a group of living human beings.

A modern audience, regardless of whether it is fifteen people at a business conference or a thousand people under a tent, wants the speaker to talk just as directly as he would in a chat, and in the same general manner he would employ in speaking to one of them in conversation, in the same manner, but with greater force or energy. In order to appear natural, he has to use much more energy in talking to forty people than he does in talking to one, just as a statue on top of a building has to be of heroic size in order to make it appear of lifelike proportions to an observer on the ground. At the close of one of Mark Twain's lectures in a Nevada mining camp, an old prospector approached him and inquired: 'Be them your natural tones of eloquence?'

That is what the audience wants: 'your natural tones of eloquence,' enlarged a bit. The only way to acquire the knack of this enlarged naturalness is by practice. And, as you practice, if you find yourself talking in a stilted manner, pause and say sharply to yourself mentally: 'Here! What is wrong? Wake up! Be human.' Then mentally pick out a person in the audience, someone in the back or the least attentive person you can find, and talk to this person. Forget there is anyone else present at all. Converse with this person. Imagine that he has asked you a question and that you are answering it, and that you are the only one who can answer it. If he were to stand up and talk to you, and you were to talk back to him, that process would immediately and inevitably make your speaking more conversational, more natural, more direct. So, imagine that is precisely what is taking place.

Earlier in this chapter was described the delivery of a certain novelist. In the same ballroom in which she had spoken, we had the pleasure, a few nights later, of hearing Sir Oliver Lodge. His subject was 'Atoms and Worlds'. He had devoted to this subject more than half a century of thought and study and experiment and investigation. He had something that was essentially a part of his heart and mind and life, something that he wanted very much to say. He forgot that he was trying to make a 'speech'. That was the least of his worries. He was concerned only with telling the audience about atoms, telling us accurately, lucidly, and feelingly. He was earnestly trying to get us to see what he saw and to feel what he felt.

And what was the result? He delivered a remarkable talk. It had both charm and power. It made a deep impression. He was a speaker of unusual ability. Yet I am sure he didn't regard himself in that light. I am sure that few people who heard him ever thought of him as a 'public speaker' at all.

If you speak in public so that people hearing you will suspect that you have had training in public speaking, you will not be a credit to your instructor, especially an instructor in one of my courses. He desires you to speak with such intensified naturalness that your audience will never dream that you have been 'formally' trained. A good window does not call attention to itself. It merely lets in the light. A good speaker is like that. He is so disarmingly natural that his hearers never notice his manner of speaking: they are conscious only of his matter.

FOURTH: PUT YOUR HEART INTO YOUR SPEAKING

Sincerity and enthusiasm and high earnestness will help you, too. When a man is under the influence of his feelings, his real self comes to the surface. The bars are down. The heat of his emotions has burned all barriers away. He acts spontaneously. He talks spontaneously. He is natural.

So, in the end, even this matter of delivery comes back to the thing which has already been emphasized repeatedly in these pages: namely, put your heart into your talks.

Edmund Burke wrote speeches so superb in logic and reasoning and composition that they are today studied as classic models of oratory in the colleges of the land; yet Burke, as a speaker, was a notorious failure. He didn't have the ability to deliver his gems, to make them interesting and forceful; so he was called "the dinner bell" of the House of Commons. When he arose to talk, the other members coughed and shuffled and either went to sleep or went out in droves.

You can throw a steel-jacketed bullet at a man with all your might, and you cannot make even a dent in his clothing. But put powder behind a tallow candle and you can shoot it through a pine board. Many a tallow candle speech with powder makes, I regret to say, more of an impression than a steel-jacketed talk with no force, no excitement, behind it.

FIFTH: PRACTICE MAKING YOUR VOICE STRONG AND FLEXIBLE

When we are really communicating our ideas to our listeners we are making use of many elements of vocal and physical variety. We shrug our shoulders, move our arms, wrinkle our brows, increase our volume, change pitch and inflection, and talk fast or slow as the occasion and the material may dictate. It is well to remember that all these are effects and not causes. That is why it is so important that we have a topic we know and a topic we are excited about when we go before an audience. That is why we must be so eager to share that topic with our listeners. Since most of us lose the spontaneity and naturalness of youth as we grow older, we tend to slip into a definite mold of physical and vocal communication. We find ourselves less ready to use gestures and animation; we rarely raise or lower our voices from one pitch to another. In short, we lose the freshness and spontaneity of true conversation. We may get into the habit of talking too slowly or too rapidly, and our diction, unless carefully watched, tends to become ragged and careless. In this book you have been repeatedly told to act natural, and you may suppose that I therefore condone poor diction or monotonous delivery provided it is natural. On the contrary, I say that we should be natural in the sense that we express our ideas and express them with spirit. On the other hand, every good speaker will not accept himself as incapable of improvement in breadth of vocabulary, richness of imagery and diction, and variety and force of expression. These are areas in which everyone interested in self-improvement will seek to improve.

It is an excellent idea to evaluate oneself in terms of volume, pitch variation, and pace. This can be done with the aid of a tape recorder. On the other hand, it would be useful to have friends help you make this evaluation. If it is possible to secure expert advice, so much the better. It should be remembered, however, that these are areas for practice away from the audience. To concern yourself with technique when you are before an audience will prove fatal to effectiveness. Once there, pour yourself into your talk, concentrate your whole being on making a mental and emotional impact on your audience, and nine chances out of ten you will speak with more emphasis and force than you could ever get from books.

Best way to conquer stage fright is to
know what you're talking about.
—Michael H. Mescon

There are four ways, and only four ways, in which we have contact with
the world. We are evaluated and classified by these four contacts: what
we do, how we look, what we say, and how we say it.
—Dale Carnegie

10

SHARING THE TALK WITH THE AUDIENCE

R ussell Conwell's famous lecture, 'Acres of Diamonds', was given nearly six thousand times. You would think that a talk repeated so often would become set in the speaker's mind, that no word or intonation would vary in delivery. That was not the case. Dr Conwell knew that audiences differ. He recognized that he had to make each successive audience feel that his talk was a personal, living thing created for it, and it alone. How did he succeed in keeping this interrelationship between speaker, speech, and audience alive from one speaking engagement to the next? 'I visit a town or city,' he wrote, 'and try to arrive there early enough to see the postmaster, the barber, the hotel manager, the principal of the schools, some of the ministers, and then go into the stores and talk with people, and see what has been their history and what opportunities they had. Then I give my lecture and talk to those people about the subjects that apply to them locally.'

Dr Conwell was thoroughly aware that successful communication depends upon how well the speaker can make his talk a part of the listeners and the listeners a part of the talk. That is why we have no true copy of 'Acres of Diamonds', one of the most popular talks ever given from a lecture platform. With his clever insight into human nature and his painstaking industry, Dr Conwell did not give the same lecture twice, although he addressed almost six thousand different audiences on the same subject. You can profit from his example by making certain that your talks are always prepared with a specific audience in mind. Here are some simple rules that will help you to build up a strong feeling of rapport with your listeners.

FIRST: TALK IN TERMS OF YOUR LISTENERS' INTERESTS

That is exactly what Dr Conwell did. He made a point of working into his lecture plenty of local allusions and examples. His audiences were interested because his talk concerned them, their interests, their problems. This linkage with what your hearers are most interested in, namely, themselves, will insure attention and guarantee that the lines of communication will remain open.

Ask yourself how knowledge of your subject will help the members of your audience solve their problems and achieve their goals. Then proceed to show them that, and you will have their complete attention. If you are an accountant and you start your talk by saying something like this, 'I am going to show you how to save from fifty to a hundred dollars on your tax return,' or you are a lawyer and you tell your listeners how to go about making a will, you will be certain to have an interested audience. Surely, there is some topic in your special fund of knowledge that can be of real help to members of your audience.

When asked what interests people, Lord Northcliffe, the William Randolph Hearst of British journalism, replied, 'themselves.' He built a newspaper empire on that single truth.

Harold Dwight, of Philadelphia, made an extraordinarily successful talk at a banquet which marked the final session of our course. He talked about each person in turn around the entire table, how he had spoken when the course started, how he had improved; he recalled the talks various members had made, the subjects they had discussed; he mimicked some of them, exaggerated their peculiarities, had everyone laughing, had everyone pleased. With such material, he could not possibly have failed. It was absolutely ideal. No other topic under the blue dome of heaven would have so interested that group. Mr Dwight knew how to handle human nature.

The next time you face an audience, visualize them as eager to hear what you have to say—as long as it applies to them. Speakers who fail to take this essential egocentricity of their listeners into account are apt to find themselves facing a restless audience, one squirming in boredom, glancing at wristwatches, and looking hopefully toward the exit doors.

SECOND: GIVE HONEST, SINCERE APPRECIATION

Audiences are composed of individuals, and they react like individuals. Openly criticize an audience and they resent it. Show your appreciation for something they have done that is worthy of praise, and you win a passport into their hearts. This often requires some research on your part. Such fulsome phrases as 'this is the most intelligent audience I have ever addressed,' are resented as hollow flattery by most audiences.

In the words of a great speaker, Chauncey M. Depew, you have to 'tell them something about themselves that they didn't think you could possibly know.' For example, a man who spoke before the Baltimore Kiwanis Club recently could find nothing unusual about that club except that it had in its membership a past international president and an international trustee. This was no news to the members of the club. So he tried to give it a new twist. He started his talk with this sentence: 'The Baltimore Kiwanis Club is one club in 101,898!' The members listened. This speaker was certainly wrong—because there were only 2,897 Kiwanis Clubs in the world. The speaker then went on:

Yes, even if you don't believe it, it is still a fact that your club, mathematically at least, is one in 101,898. Not one club in 100,000 or one in 200,000, but just exactly one in 101,898.

How do I figure that out? Kiwanis International has only 2,897 member clubs. Well, the Baltimore club has a past president of Kiwanis International and an international trustee. Mathematically, the chances that any Kiwanis club will have both a past president and an international trustee at the same time are one in 101,898—and the reason I know it's right is that I got a Johns Hopkins Ph.D. in mathematics to figure it out for me.

Be exactly one hundred per cent sincere. An insincere statement may occasionally fool an individual, but it never fools an audience. 'This highly intelligent audience... This exceptional gathering of the beauty and chivalry of HoHokus, New Jersey... I'm glad to be here because I love each one of you.' No, no, no! If you can't show sincere appreciation, don't show any!

THIRD: IDENTIFY YOURSELF WITH THE AUDIENCE

As soon as possible, preferably in the first words you utter, indicate some direct relationship with the group you are addressing. If you are honored by being asked to speak, say so. When Harold Macmillan spoke to the graduating class at De Pauw University in Greencastle, Indiana, he opened up the lines of communication in his first sentence.

'I am very grateful for your kind words of welcome,' he said, 'for a Prime Minister of Great Britain to be invited to your great university is an unusual occasion. But I feel that my present office was not the only nor, indeed, perhaps the main reason for your invitation.'

Then he mentioned that his mother was an American, born in Indiana, and that her father had been one of De Pauw's first graduates.

'I can assure you that I am proud to be associated with De Pauw University,' he said, 'and to renew an old family tradition.'

You may be sure that Macmillan's reference to an American school and to the American way of life which his mother and her pioneer father knew made friends for him at once.

Another way to open the lines of communication is to use the names of people in the audience. I once sat next to the main speaker at a banquet and I was amazed at his curiosity concerning various people in the hall. All through the meal he kept asking the master of ceremonies who the person in the blue suit at one table was, or what was the name of the lady in the flowered hat. When he arose to speak, it became evident at once why he was curious. He very cleverly wove some of the names he had learned into his talk, and I could see the evident pleasure on the faces of the persons whose names were used and I sensed the warm friendliness of the audience that this simple technique won for the speaker.

One word of caution: If you are going to work strange names into your talk, having learned them through inquiries made for the occasion, be sure you have them exactly right; be sure you understand fully the reason for your use of the names; be sure you mention them only in a favorable way; and use them in moderation.

Another method of keeping the audience at peak attentiveness is to use the pronoun 'you' rather than the third-person 'they.' In this way you keep the audience in a state of self-awareness, which I have pointed out earlier cannot be overlooked by the speaker if he is to hold the interest and attention of his listeners.

FOURTH: MAKE YOUR AUDIENCE A PARTNER IN YOUR TALK

Did it ever occur to you that you can keep an audience hanging on every word by using a little showmanship? The moment you choose some member of the audience to help you demonstrate a point or dramatize an idea, you will be rewarded by a noticeable rise in attention. Being aware of themselves as an audience, the members of it are keenly conscious of what happens when one of its own is brought into 'the act' by the speaker. If there is a wall between the man on the platform and the people out there, as many speakers say, the use of audience participation will break that wall down. I remember a speaker who was explaining the distance it takes to stop a car after the brakes have been applied. He asked one of his listeners in the front row to stand and help demonstrate how this distance varied with the speed of the car. The man in the audience took the end of a steel tape measure and carried it forty-five feet down the aisle, where he stopped on a signal from the speaker. As I watched this procedure I couldn't help but notice how the whole audience became engrossed in the talk. I said to myself that the tape measure, in addition to being a graphic illustration of the speaker's point, was certainly a line of communication between that speaker and this audience. Without that touch of showmanship the audience might still be concerned with what it was going to have for dinner or what programs would be on TV that evening.

One of my favorite methods of getting audience participation is simply to ask questions and to get responses, I like to get the audience on its feet, repeating a sentence after me, or answering my questions by raising their hands. If you use audience participation you confer the rights of partnership on your listeners.

FIFTH: PLAY YOURSELF DOWN

Of course, nothing will take the place of sincerity in this speaker-audience relationship. Norman Vincent Peale once gave some very useful advice to a fellow minister who was having great difficulty keeping the audience intent upon his sermons. He asked this minister to question his feelings about the congregation he addressed each Sunday morning—did he like them, did he want to help them, did he consider them his intellectual inferiors? Dr Peale said that he never ascended the pulpit without feeling a strong sense of affection for the men and women he was about to face. An audience is quick in taking the measure of a speaker who assumes that he is superior in mental accomplishment or in social standing. Indeed, one of the best ways for a speaker to endear himself to an audience is to play himself down.

Edmund S. Muskie, then U.S. Senator from Maine, demonstrated this when he spoke to the American Forensic Association in Boston.

'I approach my assignment this morning with many doubts,' he said. 'In the first place, I am conscious of the professional qualifications of this audience, and question the wisdom of exposing my poor talents to your critical view. In the second place, this is a breakfast meeting—an almost impossible time of day for a man to be on guard effectively; and failure in this respect can be fatal to a politician. And thirdly, there is my subject—the influence which debating has had on my career as a public servant. As long as I am active politically, there is likely to be a sharp division of opinion among my constituents as to whether that influence has been good or bad.

'Facing these doubts, I feel very much like the mosquito who found himself unexpectedly in a nudist colony. I don't know where to begin.'

Senator Muskie went on, from there, to make a fine address.

You can make more friends in two months by becoming interested in other people than you can in two years by trying to get other people interested in you.

—Dale Carnegie

PART 4
The Two Methods of Delivering A Talk

11

THE SHORT TALK TO GET ACTION

What do we mean by the purpose of a talk? Just this: every talk, regardless of whether the speaker realizes it or not, has one of four major goals. What are they?

1. To persuade or get action.
2. To inform.
3. To impress and convince.
4. To entertain.

Let us illustrate these by a series of concrete examples from Abraham Lincoln's speaking career.

Few people know that Lincoln once invented and patented a device for lifting stranded boats off sand bars and other obstructions. He worked in a mechanic's shop near his law office making a model of his apparatus. When friends came to his office to view the model, he took no end of pains to explain it. The main purpose of those explanations was to inform.

When he delivered his immortal oration at Gettysburg, when he gave his first and second inaugural addresses, when Henry Clay died and Lincoln delivered a eulogy on his life—on all these occasions, Lincoln's main purpose was to impress and convince.

In his talks to juries, he tried to win favorable decisions. In his political talks, he tried to win votes. His purpose, then, was action. Two years before he was elected president, Lincoln prepared a lecture on inventions. His purpose was to entertain. At least, that should have been his goal; but he was evidently not very successful in attaining it. His career as a popular lecturer was, in fact, a distinct disappointment. In one town, not a person came to hear him.

But he succeeded notably in his other speeches, some of which have become classics of human utterance. Why? Largely because in those instances he knew his goal, and he knew how to achieve it.

Because so many speakers fail to line up their purpose with the purpose of the meeting at which they are speaking, they often flounder and come to grief.

For example: A United States congressman was once hooted and hissed and forced to leave the stage of the old New York Hippodrome, because he had—unconsciously, no doubt, but nevertheless, unwisely— chosen to make an informative talk. The crowd did not want to be instructed. They wanted to be entertained. They listened to him patiently, politely, for ten minutes, a quarter of an hour, hoping the performance would come to a rapid end. But it didn't. He rambled on and on; patience snapped; the audience would not stand for more. Someone began to cheer ironically. Others took it up. In a moment, a thousand people were whistling and shouting. The speaker, obtuse and incapable as he was of sensing the temper of his audience, had the bad taste to continue. That aroused them. A battle was on. Their impatience mounted to ire. They determined to silence him. Louder and louder grew their storm of protest. Finally, the roar of it, the anger of it, drowned his words—he could not have been heard twenty feet away. So he was forced to give up, acknowledge defeat, and retire in humiliation.

Profit by his example. Fit the purpose of your talk to the audience and the occasion. If the congressman had decided in advance whether his goal of informing the audience would fit the goal of the audience in coming to the political rally, he would not have met with disaster. Choose one of the four purposes only after you have analysed the audience and the occasion which brings them together.

To give you guidance in the important area of speech construction, this entire chapter is devoted to the short talk to get action. The next three chapters will be devoted to the other major speech purposes: to inform, to impress and convince, and to entertain. Each purpose demands a different organizational pattern of treatment, each has its own stumbling blocks that must be hurdled. First, let's get down to the brass tacks of organizing our talks to get the audience to act.

Is there some method of marshaling our material so that we will have the best chance for successful follow- through on what we ask the audience to do? Or is it just a matter of hit-and-miss tactics?

I remember discussing this subject with my associates back in the thirties when my classes were beginning to catch on all over the country. Because of the size of our groups we were using a two-minute limit on the talks given by class members. This limitation did not affect the talk when the purpose of the speaker was merely to entertain or inform. But when we came to the talk to actuate, that was something else. The talk to get action just didn't get off the ground when we used the old system of introduction, body, and conclusion—the organizational pattern followed by speakers since Aristotle. Something new and different was obviously needed to provide us with a sure-fire method of obtaining results in a two-minute talk designed to get action from the listeners.

We held meetings in Chicago, Los Angeles, and New York. We appealed to all our instructors, many of them on the faculties of speech departments in some of our most respected universities. Others were men who held key posts in business administration. Some were from the rapidly expanding field of advertising and promotion. From this amalgam of background and brains, we hoped to get a new approach to speech organization, one that would be streamlined, and one that would reflect our age's need for a psychological as well as a logical method for influencing the listener to act.

We were not disappointed. From those discussions came the Magic Formula of speech construction. We began using it in our classes and we have been using it ever since. What is the Magic Formula? Simply this: Start your talk by giving us the details of your Example, an incident that graphically illustrates the main idea you wish to get across. Second, in specific clear-cut terms give your Point, tell exactly what you want your audience to do; and third, give your Reason, that is, highlight the advantage or benefit to be gained by the listener when he does what you ask him to do.

This is a formula highly suited to our swift-paced way of life. Speakers can no longer afford to indulge in long, leisurely introductions. Audiences are composed of busy people who want whatever the speaker has to say in straightforward language. They are accustomed to the digested, boiled-down type of journalism that presents the facts straight from the shoulder. They are exposed to hard-driving Madison Avenue advertising that shoots the message in forceful, clear terms from signboard, television screen, magazine, and newspaper. Every word is measured and nothing is wasted. By using the Magic Formula you can be certain of gaining attention and focusing it upon the main point of your message. It cautions against indulgence in vapid opening remarks, such as: 'I didn't have time to prepare this talk very well,' or 'When your chairman asked me to talk on this subject, I wondered why he selected me.' Audiences are not interested in apologies or excuses, real or simulated. They want action. In the Magic Formula you give them action from the opening word.

The formula is ideal for short talks, because it is based upon a certain amount of suspense. The listener is caught up in the story you are relating but he is not aware of what the point of your talk is until near the end of the two- or three-minute period. In cases where demands are made upon the audience, this is almost necessary for success. No speaker who wants his audience to dig deep in their pocketbooks for a cause, no matter how worthy, will get very far by starting like this: 'Ladies and gentlemen. I'm here to collect five dollars from each of you.' There would be a scramble for the exits. But if the speaker describes his visit to the Children's Hospital, where he saw a particularly poignant case of need, a little child who lacked financial help for an operation in a distant hospital, and then asks for contributions, the chances of getting support from his audience would be immeasurably enhanced. It is the story, the Example, that prepares the way for the desired action.

The Magic Formula can be used also in writing business letters and giving instructions to fellow employees and subordinates. Mothers can use it when motivating their children, and children will find it useful when appealing to their parents for a favor or privilege. You will find it a psychological tool that can be used to get your ideas across to others every day of your life.

Even in advertising, the Magic Formula is used every day. Eveready Batteries recently ran a series of radio and television commercials built upon this Formula. In the Example step, the announcer told of someone's experience of being trapped, for instance, in an overturned car late at night. After giving the graphic details of the accident, he then called upon the victim to finish the story by telling how the beams of the flashlight, powered by Eveready Batteries, brought help in time. Then the announcer went on to the Point and Reason: "Buy Eveready Batteries and you may survive a similar emergency." These stories were all true experiences out of the Eveready Battery Company's files. I don't know how many Eveready Batteries this particular advertising series sold, but I do know that the Magic Formula is an effective method of presenting what you want an audience to do, or to avoid. Let us take up the steps, one at a time.

FIRST: GIVE YOUR EXAMPLE, AN INCIDENT FROM YOUR LIFE

This is the part of your talk that will take up the major portion of your time. In it you describe an experience that taught you a lesson. Psychologists say we learn in two ways: one, by the Law of Exercise, in which a series of similar incidents leads to a change of our behavioral patterns; and two, by the Law of Effect, in which a single event may be so startling as to cause a change in our conduct. All of us have had this type of unusual experience. We do not have to search long for these incidents because they lie close to the surface of our memories. Our conduct is guided to a large extent by these experiences. By vividly reconstructing these incidents we can make them the basis of influencing the conduct of others. We can do this because people respond to words in much the same way that they respond to real happenings. In the Example part of your talk, then, you must recreate a segment of your experience in such a way that it tends to have the same effect upon your audience as it originally had upon you. This places upon you the obligation to clarify, intensify, and dramatize your experiences in a way that will make them interesting and compelling to your listeners. Below are a number of suggestions which will help to make the Example step of your action talk clear, intense, and meaningful.

Build your example upon a single personal experience

The incident type of example is particularly powerful when it is based upon a single event that had a dramatic impact upon your life. It may not have taken more than a few seconds, but in that short span of time you learned an unforgettable lesson. Not long ago a man in one of our classes told of a terrifying experience when he tried to swim to shore from his overturned boat. I am sure that everyone in his audience made up his mind that, faced with a similar situation, he would follow this speaker's advice and stay with the capsized boat until help came. I remember another example of a speaker's harrowing experience involving a child and an overturned power mower. That incident was so graphically etched in my mind that I will always be on guard when children are hovering near my power mower. Many of our instructors have been so impressed by what they have heard in their classes that they have acted promptly to prevent similar accidents around their homes. One keeps a fire extinguisher handy in his kitchen, for instance, because of a talk he heard which vividly recreated a tragic fire that started from a cooking accident. Another has labeled all bottles containing poison, and has seen to it that they are out of the reach of his children. This action was prompted by a talk detailing the experience of a distraught parent when she discovered her child unconscious in the bathroom with a bottle of poison clutched in her hand.

A single personal experience that taught you a lesson you will never forget is the first requisite of a persuasive action talk. With this kind of incident you can move audiences to act—if it happened to you, your listeners reason, it can happen to them, and they had better take your advice by doing what you ask them to do.

Start your talk with a detail of your example

One of the reasons for starting your talk with the Example step is to catch attention at once. Some speakers fail to get attention with their opening words because all too often these words consist only of repetitious remarks, clichés, or fragmentary apologies that are of no interest to the audience. 'Unaccustomed as I am to public speaking,' is particularly offensive, but many other commonplace methods of beginning a talk are just as weak in attention-getting value. Going into the details of how you came to choose the subject, revealing to the audience that you are not too well prepared (they will discover that fact soon enough), or announcing the topic or theme of your talk like a preacher giving the text of the sermon are all methods to avoid in the short talk to get action.

Take a tip from top-flight magazine and newspaper writers: begin right in your example and you will capture the attention of your audience immediately.

Here are some opening sentences that drew my attention like a magnet: 'In 1942, I found myself on a cot in a hospital'; 'Yesterday at breakfast my wife was pouring the coffee and...'; 'Last July I was driving at a fast clip down Highway 42...'; 'The door of my office opened and Charlie Vann, our foreman, burst in'; 'I was fishing in the middle of the lake; I looked up and saw a motor boat speeding toward me.'

If you start your talk with phrases that answer one of the questions, Who? When? Where? What? How? or Why?, you will be using one of the oldest communication devices in the world to get attention—the story. 'Once upon a time' are the magic words that open the floodgates of a child's imagination. With this same human interest approach you can captivate the minds of your listeners with your first words.

Fill your example with relevant detail

Detail, of itself, is not interesting. A room cluttered with furniture and bric-a-brac is not attractive. A picture filled with too many unrelated details does not compel the eyes to linger upon it. In the same way, too many details—unimportant details—make conversation and public speaking a boring test of endurance. The secret is to select only those details that will serve to emphasize the point and reason of the talk. If you want to get across the idea that your listeners should have their cars checked before going on a long trip, then all the details of your Example step should be concerned with what happened to you when you failed to have your car checked before taking a trip. If you tell about how you enjoyed the scenery or where you stayed when you arrived at your destination, you will only succeed in clouding the point and dissipating attention.

But relevant detail, couched in concrete, colorful language, is the best way to recreate the incident as it happened and to picturize it for the audience. To say merely that you once had an accident because of negligence is bald, uninteresting, and hardly likely to move anyone to be more careful behind the wheel of a car. But to paint a word picture of your frightening experience, using the full range of multisensory phraseology, will etch the event upon the consciousness of the listeners.

The abundance of detail makes it easy for the audience to project themselves into the picture. After all, your purpose is to make your audience see what you saw, hear what you heard, feel what you felt. The only way you can possibly achieve this effect is to use an abundance of concrete details. As was pointed out in Chapter Four, the task of preparation of a talk is a task of reconstructing the answers to the questions Who? When? Where? How? and Why? You must stimulate the visual imagination of your listeners by painting word pictures.

Relive your experience as you relate it

In addition to using picturesque details, the speaker should relive the experience he is describing. All great speakers have a sense of the dramatic, but this is not a rare quality, to be found only in the eloquent. Most children have a plentiful supply of it. Many persons of our acquaintance are gifted with a sense of timing, facial expression, mimicry, or pantomime that is a part, at least, of this priceless ability to dramatize. Most of us have some skill along these lines, and with a little effort and practice we can develop more of it.

The more action and excitement you can put into the retelling of your incident, the more it will make an impression on your listeners. No matter how rich in detail a talk may be, it will lack punch if the speaker does not give it with all the fervor of re-creation. Are you describing a fire? Give us the feeling of excitement that ran through the crowd as the firemen battled the blaze. Are you telling us about an argument with your neighbor? Relive it; dramatize it. Are you relating your final struggles in the water as panic swept over you? Make your audience feel the desperation of those awful moments in your life. For one of the purposes of the example is to make your talk memorable. Your listener will remember your talk and what you want them to do only if the example sticks in their minds.

In addition to making your talk more easily remembered, the incident-example makes your talk more interesting, more convincing, and easier to understand. Your experience of what life has taught you is freshly perceived by the audience: they are in a sense, predetermined to respond to what you want them to do. This brings us right to the doorstep of the second phase of the Magic Formula.

SECOND: STATE YOUR POINT, WHAT YOU WANT THE AUDIENCE TO DO

The Example step of your talk to get action has consumed more than three-quarters of your time. Assume you are talking for two minutes. You have about twenty seconds in which to hammer home the desired action you wish the audience to take and the benefit they can expect as a result of doing what you ask. The need for detail is over. The time for forthright, direct assertion has come. It is the reverse of the newspaper technique. Instead of giving the headline first, you give the news story and then you headline it with your Point or appeal for action. This step is governed by three rules:

Make the point brief and specific

Be precise in telling the audience exactly what you want them to do. People will do only what they clearly understand. It is essential to ask yourself just exactly what it is you want the audience to do now that they have been disposed to action by your example. It is a good idea to write the point out as you would a telegram, trying to reduce the number of words and to make your language as clear and explicit as possible. Don't say: 'Help the patients in our local orphanage.' That's too general. Say instead: 'Sign up tonight to meet next Sunday to take twenty-five children on a picnic.' It is important to ask for an overt action, one that can be seen, rather than mental actions, which are too vague. For instance, 'Think of your grandparents now and then,' is too general to be acted upon. Say instead: 'Make a point of visiting your grandparents this weekend.' A statement such as, 'Be patriotic,' should be converted into 'Cast your vote next Tuesday.'

Make the point easy for listeners to do

No matter what the issue is, controversial or otherwise, it is the speaker's responsibility to word his point, the request for action, in such a way that it will be easy for his listeners to understand and to do. One of the best ways to do this is to be specific. If you want your listeners to improve their ability to remember names, don't say: 'Start now to improve your memory of names.' That is so general it is difficult to do. Say instead, 'Repeat the name of the next stranger you meet five times within five minutes after you meet him.'

State the point with force and conviction

The Point is the entire theme of your talk. You should give it, therefore, with forcefulness and conviction. As a headline stands out in block letters, your request for action should be emphasized by vocal animation and directness. You are about to make your last impression on the audience. Make it in such a way that the audience feels the sincerity of your appeal for action. There should be no uncertainty or diffidence about the way you ask for the order. This persuasiveness of manner should carry over to your last words, in which you give the third step of the Magic Formula.

THIRD: GIVE THE REASON OR BENEFIT THE AUDIENCE MAY EXPECT

Here again, brevity and economy are necessary. In the reason step you hold out the incentive or reward the listeners may expect if they do what you have asked in the Point.

Be sure the reason is relevant to the example

Much has been written about motivation in public speaking. It is a vast subject and a useful one for anyone engaged in persuading others to act. In the short talk to get action, on which we are centering our attention in this chapter, all you can hope to do is highlight the benefit in a sentence or two and then sit down. It is most important, however, that you focus upon the benefit that was brought out in the Example step. If you tell of your experience in saving money by buying a used car, and urge your listeners to buy a secondhand car, you must emphasize in your reason that they, too, may enjoy the economical advantages of buying secondhand. You should not deviate from the example by giving as your reason the fact that some used cars have better styling than the latest models.

Be sure to stress one reason—and one only

Most salesmen can give half-dozen reasons why you should buy their product, and it is quite possible that you can give several reasons to back up your Point and all of them may be relevant to the Example you used. But again it is best to choose one outstanding reason or benefit and rest your case on it Your final words to the audience should be as clear-cut as the message on an advertisement in a national magazine. If you study these ads upon which so much talent has been expended, you will develop skill in handling the point and reason of your talk. No ad attempts to sell more than one product or one idea at a time. Very few ads in the big circulation magazines use more than one reason why you should buy. The same company may change its motivational appeal from one medium to another, from television to newspapers, for instance, but rarely will the same company make different appeals in one ad, whether vocal or visual.

If you study the ads you see in magazines and newspapers and on television and analyse their content you will be amazed at how often the Magic Formula is used to persuade people to buy. You will become aware of the ribbon of relevancy which binds the whole ad or commercial together into a unified package.

There are other ways of building up an example, for instance, by using exhibits, giving a demonstration, quoting authorities, making comparisons, and citing statistics.

Remember, no one ever complains about a speech being too short!
—Ira Hayes

Your purpose is to make your audience see what you saw, hear what you heard, feel what you felt. Relevant detail, couched in concrete, colorful language, is the best way to recreate the incident as it happened and to picture it for the audience.
—Dale Carnegie

12

THE TALK TO INFORM

Probably you often have heard speakers like one who once made a United States Senate investigating committee squirm with annoyance. He was a high-ranking government official, but he did not know any better than to talk on and on, vaguely, without ever making his meaning clear. He was pointless and obscure, and the committee's confusion mounted by the moment. Finally one of its members, Samuel James Ervin, Jr., speaking as the senior Senator from North Carolina, got a chance to say a few words—and they were telling ones.

He said the official reminded him of a husband he knew back home. The husband notified his lawyer he wanted to divorce his wife, although he conceded she was beautiful, a fine cook, and a model mother.

'They why do you want to divorce her?' his lawyer asked.

'Because she talks all the time,' the husband replied.

'What does she talk about?'

'That's the trouble,' the husband answered, 'she never says!'

This is the trouble, too, with many speakers, both women and men. Their hearers don't know what such speakers are talking about. They never say. They never make their meaning clear.

I am going to give you methods to help make your meaning clear when you set out to inform, and not motivate, your listeners.

We make informative talks many times every day: giving directions or instructions, making explanations and reports. Of all the types of talks given every week to audiences everywhere, the talk to inform is second only to the talk to persuade or get action. The ability to speak clearly precedes the ability to move others to action. Owen D. Young, one of America's top industrialists, emphasizes the need for clear expression in today's world:

As one enlarges his ability to get others to understand him, he opens up to that extent his opportunity for usefulness. Certainly in our society, where it is necessary for men even in the simplest matters to co-operate with each other, it is necessary for them first of all to understand each other. Language is the principal conveyor of understanding, and so we must learn to use it, not crudely but discriminatingly.

13

THE TALK TO CONVINCE

There was once a small group of men and women who found themselves in the path of a hurricane. Not a real hurricane, but the next thing to it. In short, a hurricane of a man named Maurice Goldblatt. Here is how one of that group described it:

> We were sitting around a luncheon table in Chicago. We knew this man was reputed to be a powerful speaker. We watched him intently as he stood up to speak.
>
> He began quietly—a spruce, pleasant man of middle age—thanking us for inviting him. He wanted to talk about something serious, he said, and he hoped we would forgive him if he disturbed us.
>
> Then, like a whirlwind, he struck. He leaned forward and his eyes transfixed us. He didn't raise his voice, but it seemed to me that it crashed like a gong.
>
> 'Look around you,' he said. 'Look at one another. Do you know how many of you sitting now in this room are going to die of cancer? One in four of all of you who are over forty-five. One in four!'
>
> He paused, and his face lightened. 'That's a plain, harsh fact, but it needn't be for long,' he said. 'Something can be done about it. This something is progress in the treatment of cancer and in the search for its cause.'
>
> He looked at us gravely, his gaze moving around the table. 'Do you want to help toward this progress?' he asked.

Could there have been an answer except 'Yes!' in the minds of any of us then? 'Yes!' I thought, and I found later that so did the others. In less than a minute, Maurice Goldblatt had won us. He had drawn us personally into his subject. He had us on his side, in the campaign he was waging for a humanitarian cause.

Getting a favorable reaction is every speaker's objective anytime, anywhere. As it happened, Mr Goldblatt had a dramatically good reason for wanting to get one from us. He and his brother, Nathan, starting with little more than nothing, had built up a department store chain doing a business of more than $100,000,000 a year. Fabulous success had come to them after long, hard years, and then Nathan, ill only a short time, had died of cancer. After that, Maurice Goldblatt saw to it that the Goldblatt Foundation gave the first million dollars to the University of Chicago's cancer research program, and he gave his own time—retiring from business—to the work of interesting the public in the fight against cancer.

These facts, together with Maurice Goldblatt's personality, won us. Sincerity, earnestness, enthusiasm—a blazing determination to give himself to us for a few minutes, just as he was giving himself year in and out to a great cause—all of these factors swept us up into a feeling of agreement with the speaker, a friendliness for him, a willingness to be interested and moved.

FIRST: WIN CONFIDENCE BY DESERVING IT

Quintilian described the orator as 'a good man skilled in speaking.' He was talking about sincerity and character. Nothing said in this book, nor anything which will be said, can take the place of this essential attribute of speaking effectiveness. Pierpont Morgan said that character was the best way to obtain credit; it is also the best way to win the confidence of the audience.

'The sincerity with which a man speaks,' said Alexander Woolcott, "imparts to his voice a color of truth no perjurer can feign."

Especially when the purpose of our talk is to convince, it is necessary to set forth our own ideas with the inner glow that comes from sincere conviction. We must first be convinced before we attempt to convince others.

SECOND: GET A YES-RESPONSE

Walter Dill Scott, former president of Northwestern University, said that 'every idea, concept, or conclusion which enters the mind is held as true unless hindered by some contradictory idea.' That boils down to keeping the audience yes-minded. My good friend Professor Harry Overstreet brilliantly examined the psychological background of this concept in a lecture at the New School for Social Research in New York City:

The skillful speaker gets at the outset a number of yes-responses. He has thereby set the psychological processes of his listeners moving in the affirmative direction. It is like the movement of a billiard ball. Propel it in one direction, and it takes some force to deflect it, far more force to send it back in the opposite direction.

The psychological patterns here are quite clear.

When a person says 'No' and really means it, he is doing far more than saying a word of two letters. His entire organism— glandular, nervous, muscular—gathers itself together into a condition of rejection. There is, usually in minute but sometimes in observable degree, a physical withdrawal, or readiness for withdrawal. The whole neuromuscular system, in short, sets itself on guard against acceptance. Where, on the contrary, a person says 'Yes,' none of the withdrawing activities takes place. The organism is in a forward-moving, accepting, open attitude. Hence the more 'Yesses' we can, at the very outset, induce, the more likely we are to succeed in capturing the attention for our ultimate proposal.

It is a very simple technique—this yes-response. And yet how much neglected! It often seems as if people get a sense of their own importance by antagonizing at the outset. The radical comes into a conference with his conservative brethren; and immediately he must make them furious! What, as a matter of fact, is the good of it? If he simply does it in order to get some pleasure out of it for himself, he may be pardoned. But if he expects to achieve something, he is only psychologically stupid.

Get a student to say 'No' at the beginning, or a customer, child, husband, or wife, and it takes the wisdom and patience of angels to transform that bristling negative into an affirmative.

How is one going to get these desirable 'yes-responses' at the very outset? Fairly simple. 'My way of opening and winning an argument,' confided Lincoln, 'is to first find a common ground of agreement.' Lincoln found it even when he was discussing the highly inflammable subject of slavery. 'For the first half hour,' declared *The Mirror*, a neutral paper reporting one of his talks, 'his opponents would agree with every word he uttered. From that point he began to lead them off, little by little, until it seemed as if he had got them all into his fold.'

Is it not evident that the speaker who argues with his audience is merely arousing their stubbornness, putting them on the defensive, making it well-nigh impossible for them to change their minds? Is it wise to start by saying, 'I am going to prove so and so'? Aren't your hearers liable to accept that as a challenge and remark silently, 'Let's see you do it'?

Is it not much more advantageous to begin by stressing something that you and all of your hearers believe, and then to raise some pertinent question that everyone would like to have answered? Then take your audience with you in an earnest search for the answer. While on that search, present the facts as you see them so clearly that they will be led to accept your conclusions as their own. They will have much more faith in some truth that they have discovered for themselves. 'The best argument is that which seems merely an explanation.'

In every controversy, no matter how wide and bitter the differences, there is always some common ground of agreement on which a speaker can invite everyone to meet. To illustrate: On February 3, 1960, the prime minister of Great Britain, Harold Macmillan, addressed both houses of the Parliament of the Union of South Africa. He had to present the United Kingdom's non-racial viewpoint before the legislature body at a time when apartheid was the prevailing policy. Did he begin his talk with this essential difference in outlook? No. He began by stressing the great economic progress made by South Africa, the significant contributions made by South Africa to the world. Then, with skill and tact he brought up the questions of differing viewpoints. Even here, he indicated that he was well aware that these differences were based on sincere conviction. His whole talk was a masterly statement reminding one of Lincoln's gentle but firm utterances in the years before Fort Sumter. 'As a fellow member of the Commonwealth,' said the Prime Minister, 'it is our earnest desire to give South Africa our support and encouragement, but I hope you won't mind my saying frankly that there are some aspects of your policies which make it impossible for us to do this without being false to our deep convictions about the political destinies of free men to which in our own territories we are trying to give effect. I think we ought as friends to face together, without seeking to apportion credit or blame, the fact that in the world of today this difference of outlook lies between us.'

No matter how determined one was to differ with a speaker, a statement like that would tend to convince you of the speaker's fair-mindedness.

What would have been the result had Prime Minister Macmillan set out immediately to emphasize the difference in policy rather than the common ground of agreement? Professor James Harvey Robinson's enlightening book, The Mind in the Making, gives the psychological answer to that question:

We sometimes find ourselves changing our minds without any resistance or heavy emotion, but if we are told we are wrong we resent the imputation and harden our hearts. We are incredibly heedless in the formation of our beliefs, but find ourselves filled with an illicit passion for them when anyone proposes to rob us of their companionship. It is obviously not the ideas themselves that are dear to us, but our self-esteem which is threatened... The little word my is the most important one in human affairs, and properly to reckon with it is the beginning of wisdom. It has the same force whether it is my dinner, my dog, and my house, or my faith, my country and my God. We not only resent the imputation that our watch is wrong, or our car shabby, but that our conception of the canals of Mars, of the pronunciation of "Epictetus," of the medicinal value of salicine, or of the date of Sargon I, are subject to revision... We like to continue to believe what we have been accustomed to accept as true, and the resentment aroused when doubt is cast upon any of our assumptions leads us to seek every manner of excuse for clinging to it. The result is that most of our so-called reasoning consists in finding arguments for going on believing as we already do.

THIRD: SPEAK WITH CONTAGIOUS ENTHUSIASM

Contradicting ideas are much less likely to arise in the listener's mind when the speaker presents his ideas with feeling and contagious enthusiasm. I say 'contagious', for enthusiasm is just that. It thrusts aside all negative and opposing ideas. When your aim is to convince, remember it is more productive to stir emotions than to arouse thoughts. Feelings are more powerful than cold ideas. To arouse feelings one must be intensely in earnest. Regardless of the petty phrases a man may concoct, regardless of the illustrations he may assemble, regardless of the harmony of his voice and the grace of his gestures, if he does not speak sincerely, these are hollow and glittering trappings. If you would impress an audience, be impressed yourself. Your spirit, shining through your eyes, radiating through your voice, and proclaiming itself through your manner, will communicate itself to your audience.

Every time you speak, and especially when your avowed purpose is to convince, what you do determines the attitude of your listeners. If you are lukewarm, so will they be; if you are flippant and antagonistic, so will they be. 'When the congregation falls asleep,' wrote Henry Ward Beecher, 'there is only one thing to do; provide the usher with a sharp stick and have him prod the preacher.'

I was once one of three judges called on to award the Curtis medal at Columbia University. There were half a dozen undergraduates, all of them elaborately trained, all of them eager to acquit themselves well. But—with only a single exception—what they were striving for was to win the medal. They had little or no desire to convince.

They had chosen their topics because these topics permitted oratorical development. They had no deep personal interest in the arguments they were making. And their successive talks were merely exercises in the art of delivery.

The exception was a Zulu Prince. He had selected as his theme 'The Contribution of Africa to Modern Civilization'. He put intense feeling into every word he uttered. His talk was no mere exercise; it was a living thing, born of conviction and enthusiasm. He spoke as the representative of his people, of his continent; with wisdom, high character, and good will, he brought us a message of his people's hopes and a plea for our understanding.

We gave him the medal although he was possibly no more accomplished in addressing a large group than two or three of his competitors. What we judges recognized was that his talk had the true fire of sincerity; it was ablaze with truth. Beside it, the other talks were only flickering gas-logs.

The Prince had learned in his own way in a distant land that you can't project your personality in a talk to others by using reason alone: you have to reveal to them how deeply you yourself believe in what you say.

FOURTH: SHOW RESPECT AND AFFECTION FOR YOUR AUDIENCE

'The human personality demands love and it also demands respect,' Dr Norman Vincent Peale said as a prelude to speaking of a professional comedian. 'Every human being has an inner sense of worth, of importance, of dignity. Wound that and you have lost that person forever. So when you love and respect a person you build him up and, accordingly, he loves and esteems you.

'At one time I was on a program with an entertainer. I did not know the man well, but since that meeting I read that he was having difficulty, and I think I know why.

'I had been sitting beside him quietly for I was about to speak. "You aren't nervous, are you?" he asked.

'"Why, yes," I replied. "I always get a little nervous before I stand up before an audience. I have a profound respect for an audience and the responsibility makes me a bit nervous. Don't you get nervous?"

'"No," he said, "Why should I? Audiences fall for anything. They are a lot of dopes."

'I don't agree with you,' I said. They are your sovereign judges. I have great respect for audiences.'

When he read about this man's waning popularity Dr Peale was sure the reason lay in an attitude that antagonized others instead of winning them.

What an object lesson for all of us who want to impart something to other people!

FIFTH: BEGIN IN A FRIENDLY WAY

An atheist once challenged William Paley to disprove his contention that there was no Supreme Being. Very quietly Paley took out his watch, opened the case, and said: 'If I were to tell you that those levers and wheels and springs made themselves and fitted themselves together and started running on their own account, wouldn't you question my intelligence? Of course, you would. But look up at the stars. Every one of them has its perfect appointed course and motion— the earth and planets around the sun, and the whole group pitching along at more than a million miles a day. Each star is another sun with its own group of worlds, rushing on through space like our own solar system. Yet there are no collisions, no disturbance, no confusion. All quiet, efficient, and controlled. Is it easier to believe that they just happened or that someone made them so?'

Suppose he had retorted to his antagonist at the outset: 'No God? Don't be a silly ass. You don't know what you are talking about.' What would have happened? Doubtlessly a verbal joust—a wordy war would have ensued, as futile as it was fiery. The atheist would have risen with an unholy zeal upon him to fight for his opinions with all the fury of a wildcat. Why? Because, as Professor Overstreet has pointed out, they were his opinions, and his precious, indispensable self-esteem would have been threatened; his pride would have been at stake.

Since pride is such a fundamentally explosive characteristic of human nature, wouldn't it be the part of wisdom to get a man's pride working for us, instead of against us? How? By showing, as Paley did, that the thing we propose is very similar to something that our opponent already believes. That renders it easier for him to accept than to reject your proposal. That prevents contradictory and opposing ideas from arising in the mind to vitiate what we have said.

Paley showed delicate appreciation of how the human mind functions. Most men, however, lack this subtle ability to enter the citadel of a man's beliefs arm in arm with the owner. They erroneously imagine that in order to take the citadel, they must storm it, batter it down by a frontal attack. What happens? The moment hostilities commence, the drawbridge is lifted, the great gates are slammed and bolted, the mailed archers draw their long bows—the battle of words and wounds is on. Such frays always end in a draw; neither has convinced the other of anything.

Our problem in making a talk to convince or impress others is just this: to plant the idea in their minds and to keep contradicting and opposing ideas from arising. He who is skilled in doing that has power in speaking and influencing others. Here is precisely where the rules in my book *How to Win Friends and Influence People* will be helpful.

Almost every day of your life you are talking to people who differ from you on some subject under discussion. Aren't you constantly trying to win people to your way of thinking, at home, in the office, in social situations of all kinds? Is there room for improvement in your methods? How do you begin?

The success of your presentation will be judged not by the knowledge you send but by what the listener receives.

—Lilly Walters

You have it easily in your power to increase the sum total of this world's happiness now. How? By giving a few words of sincere appreciation to someone who is lonely or discouraged. Perhaps you will forget tomorrow the kind words you say today,
but the recipient may cherish them over a lifetime.

—Dale Carnegie

14

IMPROMPTU TALKS

Not long ago a group of business leaders and government officials met at the dedication of a pharmaceutical corporation's new laboratory. One after another, half a dozen subordinates to the research director arose and told of the fascinating work being done by chemists and biologists. They were developing new vaccines against communicable diseases, new antibiotics to fight viruses, new tranquilizers to ease tension. Their results, first with animals and then with human beings, were dramatic.

'This is marvelous,' an official said to the research director. 'Your men are really magicians. But why aren't you up there, speaking, too?'

'I can talk to my feet—not to an audience,' the research director said gloomily.

A little later, the chairman took him by surprise.

'We haven't heard from our director of research,' he said. 'He doesn't like to give a formal speech. But I'm going to ask him to say a few words to us.'

It was pitiful. The director stood up and managed no more than a couple of sentences. He apologized for not speaking at length, and that was the gist of his contribution.

There he was, a brilliant man in his field, and he seemed as awkward and confused as a man could be. This was not necessary. He could have learned to speak impromptu on his feet. I have never seen a serious and determined member of our classes who couldn't learn this. At the start, it takes what this research director hadn't given it—a resolute and brave rejection of one's defeatist attitude. Then, perhaps for quite a while, it takes an unwavering will to do the job no matter how hard it may be.

'I get along all right if I've prepared my talk and practiced it,' you may say. 'But I'm at a loss for words if I'm asked to talk when I don't expect it.'

The ability to assemble one's thoughts and to speak on the spur of the moment is even more important, in some ways, than the ability to speak only after lengthy and laborious preparation. The demands of modern business and the current casualness with which modern oral communication is carried on make it imperative to be able to mobilize our thoughts quickly and verbalize fluently. Many of the decisions that affect industry and government today are made, not by one man, but around the conference table. The individual still has his say, but what he has to say has to be forcefully stated in the forum of group opinion. This is where the ability to speak impromptu comes alive and produces results.

FIRST: PRACTISE IMPROMPTU SPEAKING

Anyone of normal intelligence who possesses a fair portion of self-control can make an acceptable, often a brilliant, impromptu talk—which simply means 'talking off the cuff'. There are several ways you can improve your ability to express yourself fluently when called upon suddenly to say a few words. One method is to use a device that some famous movie actors used.

Years ago Douglas Fairbanks wrote an article for *American Magazine* in which he described a game of wits he, Charlie Chaplin, and Mary Pickford played almost every night for two years. It was more than a game. It was practice in that most difficult of all speaking arts— thinking on one's feet. As Fairbanks wrote, the 'game' went like this:

Each of us would write a subject on a slip of paper. Then we folded the slips and shook them up. One would draw. Immediately he would have to stand and talk for sixty seconds on that subject. We never used the same subject twice. One night I had to talk on 'lampshades'. Just try it if you think it is easy. I got through somehow.

But the point is all three of us have sharpened up since we began the game. We know a lot more about a variety of miscellaneous subjects. But, far better than that, we are learning to assemble our knowledge and thoughts on any topic at a moment's notice. We are learning how to think on our feet.

Several times during my course the class members are asked to talk impromptu. Long experience has taught me that this kind of practice does two things: (1) it proves to the people in the class that they can think on their feet, and (2) this experience makes them much more secure and confident when they are giving their prepared talks. They realize that, if the worst should happen and they experience a blackout while giving their prepared material, they still can talk intelligently on an impromptu basis until they get back on the track again.

So, at one time or another, the class member hears, 'Tonight each of you will be given a different subject on which to talk. You won't know what it is until you stand up to speak. Good luck!'

What happens? An accountant finds he is called on to speak about advertising. An advertising salesman has to talk on kindergartens. A schoolteacher's topic may be banking, and a banker's topic may be school teaching. A clerk may be assigned to talk on production, and a production expert may be asked to discuss transportation.

Do they hang their heads, and give up? Never! They don't pretend to be authorities. They work the subjects around to fit their knowledge of something familiar to them. In their first efforts, they may not give a fine talk. But they do get up; they do talk. For some it is easy; for some it is hard, but they don't give up; they all find that they can do far better than they'd thought they would. This is thrilling to them. They see that they can develop an ability which they didn't believe they had.

I believe that if they can do this, anybody can do it—with will power and confidence—and that the more often one tries to do it, the easier it will be.

SECOND: BE MENTALLY READY TO SPEAK IMPROMPTU

When you are called on to speak without preparation usually you are expected to make some remarks about a subject upon which you can speak with authority. The problem here is to face up to the situation of talking and to decide what exactly you want to cover in the short time at your disposal. One of the best ways to become adept at this is to prepare yourself mentally for these situations. When you are at a meeting keep asking yourself what you would say now if you were called upon. What aspect of your subject would be most appropriate to cover at this time? How would you phrase your approval or rejection of the proposals now being put forth on the floor?

So the first bit of advice I offer is this: condition yourself mentally to speak impromptu on all occasions.

This requires thinking on your part, and thinking is the hardest thing in the world to do. But I am certain that no man ever made a reputation as an impromptu speaker who did not prepare himself by devoting hours of analysis to every public situation in which he was a participant. Just as an airline pilot readies himself to act with cool precision in an emergency by continually posing to himself problems that could arise at any moment, the man who shines as an impromptu speaker prepares himself by making countless talks that are never given. Such talks really are not 'impromptu'; they are talks with general preparation.

Because your subject is known, your problem is one of organization to fit the time and the occasion. As an impromptu speaker you will naturally speak for only a short time. Decide what aspect of your topic would fit the situation. Don't apologize because you are unprepared. This is the expected thing. Launch into your topic as soon as possible, if not immediately, and please, I beg you, follow this advice.

THIRD: GET INTO AN EXAMPLE IMMEDIATELY

Why? For three reasons: (1) You will free yourself at once of the necessity to think hard about your next sentence, for experiences are easily recounted even in an impromptu situation. (2) You will get into the swing of speaking, and your first-moment jitters will fly away, giving you the opportunity to warm up to your subject matter.

(3) You will enlist the attention of your audience at once. As pointed out in Chapter Seven, the incident-example is a sure-fire method of capturing attention immediately.

An audience absorbed in the human interest aspect of your example will give you reassurance when you need it most—during the first few moments of speaking. Communication is a two-way process; the speaker who captures attention is immediately aware of it. As he notes the receptive forces and feels the glow of expectancy, like an electric current, play over the heads of his audience, he is challenged to go on, to do his best, to respond. The rapport thus established between speaker and audience is the key to all successful speaking—without it true communication is impossible. That is why I urge you to begin with an example, especially when you are called on to say a few words.

FOURTH: SPEAK WITH ANIMATION AND FORCE

As has been said several times before in this book, if you speak with energy and forcefulness, your external animation will have a beneficial effect upon your mental processes. Have you ever watched a man in a conversational group who suddenly begins to gesture as he speaks? Soon he is talking fluently, sometimes brilliantly, and he begins to attract a group of eager listeners. The relation of physical activity to the mind is a close one. We use the same words to describe manual and mental operations; for instance, we say 'we grasp an idea', or 'we clutch at a thought'. Once we get the body charged up and animated, as William James pointed out, we very soon will get the mind functioning at a rapid pace. So my advice to you is to throw yourself with abandon into your talk and you will help to insure your success as an impromptu speaker.

FIFTH: USE THE PRINCIPLE OF THE HERE AND NOW

The time will come when someone will tap you on the shoulder and say 'How about a few words?' Or it might come without warning at all. You are relaxed and enjoying the remarks of the master of ceremonies when suddenly you realize he is talking about you. Everybody turns in your direction and before you know it you are introduced as the next speaker.

In this kind of situation your mind is apt to shoot off, like Stephen Leacock's famous but befuddled horseman, who got on his horse 'and made off in all directions'. Now, if ever, is the time to remain calm. You can get a breather as you address the chairman. Then it is best to stay close to the meeting in the remarks you make. Audiences are interested in themselves and what they are doing. There are three sources therefore from which you can draw ideas for an impromptu speech.

First is the audience itself. Remember this, I pray you, for easy speaking. Talk about your listeners, who they are and what they are doing, especially what specific good they perform to the community or for humanity. Use a specific example.

The second is the occasion. Surely you can dwell on the circumstances that brought the meeting about. Is it an anniversary, a testimonial, an annual meeting, a political or patriotic occasion?

Lastly, if you have been an attentive listener, you might indicate your pleasure in something specific another speaker said before you and amplify that. The most successful impromptu talks are those that are really impromptu. They express things that the speaker feels in his heart about the audience and the occasion. They fit the situation like hand in glove. They are tailor-made for this occasion, and this occasion alone. Therein lies their success: they flower out of the moment and then, like rare-blossoming roses, they fade from the scene. But the pleasure enjoyed by your audience lives on, and sooner than you think you begin to be looked upon as an impromptu speaker.

SIXTH: DON'T TALK IMPROMPTU—GIVE AN IMPROMPTU TALK

There is a difference as implied in the statement above. It is not enough just to ramble on and string together a series of disconnected nothings on a flimsy thread of inconsequence. You must keep your ideas logically grouped around a central thought which might well be the point you want to get across. Your examples will cohere to this central idea. And again, if you speak with enthusiasm, you will find that what you say off the cuff has a vitality and punch that your prepared talks do not have.

You can become a competent impromptu speaker if you take to heart some of the suggestions made in this chapter. You can practice along lines of the classroom techniques explained in the early part of this chapter.

At a meeting you can do a little preliminary planning and you can keep yourself aware of the possibility of being called upon at any moment If you think you may be asked to contribute your comments or suggestions, pay careful attention to the other speakers. Try to be ready to condense your ideas into a few words. When the time comes, say what you have in mind as plainly as you can. Your views have been sought. Give them briefly, and sit down.

Norman Bel-Geddes, the architect and industrial designer, used to say that he couldn't put his thoughts into words unless he was on his feet. Pacing up and down his office, as he talked to associates about complex plans for building or exhibit, he was at his best. He had to learn how to speak when sitting down, and of course he did.

With most of us, it's the other way around; we have to learn to speak standing up, and of course we can. The chief secret lies in making a start—giving one short talk—and then making another start, and another, and another.

We will find that each successive talk comes more easily. Each talk will be better than its predecessors. We will realize in the end speaking impromptu to a group is merely an extension of the same thing we do when we speak impromptu to friends in our living room.

> *It usually takes me more than three weeks to*
> *prepare a good impromptu speech.*
> —Mark Twain

> *When dealing with people, remember you are not dealing with creatures*
> *of logic, but creatures of emotion.*
> —Dale Carnegie

HOW TO STOP WORRYING AND
START LIVING

1

HOW TO ANALYSE AND SOLVE WORRY PROBLEMS

Will any magic formula solve all worry problems? No, of course not.

Then what is the answer? The answer is that we must equip ourselves to deal with different kinds of worries by learning the three basic steps of problem analysis. The three steps are:

1. Get the facts.
2. Analyse the facts.
3. Arrive at a decision—and then act on that decision.

Obvious stuff? Yes, Aristotle taught it—and used it. And you and I must use it too if we are going to solve the problems that are harassing us and turning our days and nights into veritable hells.

Let's take the first rule: Get the facts. Why is it so important to get the facts? Because unless we have the facts we can't possibly even attempt to solve our problem intelligently. Without the facts, all we can do is stew around in confusion. My idea? No, that was the idea of late Herbert E. Hawkes, Dean of Columbia College, Columbia University, for twenty-two years. He had helped two hundred thousand students solve their worry problems; and he told me that 'confusion is the chief cause of worry.' He put it this way—he said: 'Half the worry in the world is caused by people trying to make decisions before they have sufficient knowledge on which to base a decision. For example,' he said, 'if I have a problem which has to be faced at three o'clock next Tuesday, I refuse to even try to make a decision about it until next Tuesday arrives. In the meantime, I concentrate on getting all the facts that bear on the problem. I don't worry,' he said. 'I don't agonize over my problem. I don't lose any sleep. I simply concentrate on getting the facts. And by the time Tuesday rolls around, if I've got all the facts, the problem usually solves itself!'

I asked Dean Hawkes if this meant he had licked worry entirely. 'Yes,' he said, 'I think I can honestly say that my life is now almost totally devoid of worry. I have found,' he went on, 'that if a man will devote his time to securing facts in an impartial, objective way, his worries will usually evaporate in the light of knowledge.'

Let me repeat that: 'If a man will devote his time to securing facts in an impartial, objective way, his worries will usually evaporate in the light of knowledge.'

But what do most of us do? If we bother with facts at all—and Thomas Edison said in all seriousness, 'There is no expedient to which a man will not resort to avoid the labour of thinking'—if we bother with facts at all, we hunt like bird dogs after the facts that bolster up what we already think—and ignore all the others! We want only the facts that justify our acts—the facts that fit in conveniently with our wishful thinking and justify our preconceived prejudices!

Is it any wonder, then, that we find it so hard to get at the answers to our problems? Wouldn't we have the same trouble trying to solve a second-grade arithmetic problem, if we went ahead on the assumption that two plus two equals five? Yet there are a lot of people in this world who make life a hell for themselves and others by insisting that two plus two equals five—or maybe five hundred!

What can we do about it? We have to keep our emotions out of our thinking; and, as Dean Hawkes put it, we must secure the facts in 'an impartial, objective' manner.

When we are worried, our emotions are riding high. But here are two ideas that I have found helpful when trying to step aside from my problems, in order to see the facts in a clear, objective manner.

When trying to get the facts, I pretend that I am collecting this information not for myself, but for some other person. This helps me to take a cold, impartial view of the evidence. This helps me eliminate my emotions.

While trying to collect the facts about the problem that is worrying me, I sometimes pretend that I am a lawyer preparing to argue the other side of the issue. In other words, I try to get all the facts against myself—all the facts that are damaging to my wishes, all the facts I don't like to face.

Then I write down both my side of the case and the other side of the case—and I generally find that the truth lies somewhere in between these two extremities.

Here is the point I am trying to make. Neither you nor I nor Einstein nor the Supreme Court of the United States is brilliant enough to reach an intelligent decision on any problem without first getting the facts. Thomas Edison knew that. At the time of his death, he had two thousand five hundred notebooks filled with facts about the problems he was facing.

So Rule 1 for solving our problems is: Get the facts. Let's do what Dean Hawkes did—let's not even attempt to solve our problems without first collecting all the facts in an impartial manner.

However, getting all the facts in the world won't do us any good until we analyse them and interpret them.

I have found from costly experience that it is much easier to analyse the facts after writing them down. In fact, merely writing the facts on a piece of paper and stating our problem clearly goes a long way towards helping us reach a sensible decision.

Let me show you all this as it works out in practice. Since the Chinese say one picture is worth ten thousand words, suppose I show you a picture of how one man put exactly what we are talking about into concrete action.

Let's take the case of Galen Litchfield—a man I have known for several years; one of the most successful American businessmen in the Far East. Mr Litchfield was in China in 1942, when the Japanese invaded Shanghai. And here is his story as he told it to me while a guest in my home:

Shortly after the Japs took Pearl Harbor, they came swarming into Shanghai. I was the manager of the Asia Life Insurance Company in Shanghai. They sent us an 'army liquidator'— he was really an admiral—and gave me orders to assist this man in liquidating our assets. I didn't have any choice in the matter. I could co-operate—or else. And the 'or else' was certain death.

I went through the motions of doing what I was told, because I had no alternative. But there was one block of securities, worth $7,50,000, which I left off the list I gave to the admiral. I left that block of securities off the list because they belonged to our Hong Kong organization and had nothing to do with the Shanghai assets. All the same, I feared I might be in hot water if the Japs found out what I had done. And they soon found out.

I wasn't in the office when the discovery was made, but my head accountant was there. He told me that the Jap admiral flew into a rage, and stamped and swore, and called me a thief and a traitor! I had defied the Japanese army! I knew what that meant. I would be thrown into the Bridgehouse!

The Bridgehouse! The torture chamber of the Japanese Gestapo! I had had personal friends who had killed themselves rather than be taken to that prison. I had had other friends who had died in that place after ten days of questioning and torture. Now I was slated for the Bridgehouse myself!

What did I do? I heard the news on Sunday afternoon. I suppose I should have been terrified. And I would have been terrified if I hadn't had a definite technique for solving my problems. For years, whenever I was worried I had always gone to my typewriter and written down two questions—and the answers to these questions:

1. What am I worrying about?
2. What can I do about it?

I used to try to answer those questions without writing them down. But I stopped that years ago. I found that writing down both the questions and the answers clarifies my thinking. So, that Sunday afternoon, I went directly to my room at the Shanghai YMCA, and got out my typewriter. I wrote:

1. What am I worrying about?

I am afraid I will be thrown into the Bridgehouse tomorrow morning.

Then I typed out the second question:

2. What can I do about it?

I spent hours thinking out and writing down the four courses of action I could take—and what the probable consequence of each action would be.

I can try to explain to the Japanese admiral. But he 'no speak English.' If I try to explain to him through an interpreter, I may stir him up again. That might mean death, for he is cruel, would rather dump me in the Bridgehouse than bother talking about it.

I can try to escape. Impossible. They keep track of me all the time. I have to check in and out of my room at the YMCA. If I try to escape, I'll probably be captured and shot.

I can stay here in my room and not go near the office again. If I do, the Japanese admiral will be suspicious, will probably send soldiers to get me and throw me into the Bridgehouse without giving me a chance to say a word.

I can go down to the office as usual on Monday morning. If I do, there is a chance that the Japanese admiral may be so busy that he will not think of what I did. Even if he does think of it, he may have cooled off and may not bother me. If this happens, I am all right. Even if he does bother me, I'll still have a chance to try to explain to him. So, going down to the office as usual on Monday morning, and acting as if nothing had gone wrong, gives me two chances to escape the Bridgehouse.

As soon as I thought it all out and decided to accept the fourth plan—to go down to the office as usual on Monday morning—I felt immensely relieved.

When I entered the office the next morning, the Japanese admiral sat there with a cigarette dangling from his mouth. He glared at me as he always did; and said nothing. Six weeks later—thank God—he went back to Tokyo and my worries were ended.

As I have already said, I probably saved my life by sitting down that Sunday afternoon and writing out all the various steps I could take and then writing down the probable consequence of each step and calmly coming to a decision. If I hadn't done that, I might have floundered and hesitated and done the wrong thing on the spur of the moment. If I hadn't thought out my problem and come to a decision, I would have been frantic with worry all Sunday afternoon. I wouldn't have slept that night. I would have gone down to the office Monday morning with a harassed and worried look; and that alone might have aroused the suspicion of the Japanese admiral and spurred him to act.

Experience has proved to me, time after time, the enormous value of arriving at a decision. It is the failure to arrive at a fixed purpose, the inability to stop going round and round in maddening circles, that drives men to nervous breakdowns and living hells. I find that fifty per cent of my worries vanishes once I arrive at a clear, definite decision; and another forty per cent usually vanishes once I start to carry out that decision.

So I banish about ninety per cent of my worries by taking these four steps:

1. Writing down precisely what I am worrying about.
2. Writing down what I can do about it.
3. Deciding what to do.
4. Starting immediately to carry out that decision.

Galen Litchfield is now the Far Eastern Director for Starr, Park and

Freeman, Inc., 111 John Street, New York, representing large insurance and financial interests.

In fact, as I said before, Galen Litchfield today is one of the most important American businessmen in Asia; and he confessed to me that he owes a large part of his success to this method of analyzing worry and meeting it head-on.

Why is his method so superb? Because it is efficient, concrete and goes directly to the heart of the problem. On top of all that, it is climaxed by the third and indispensable rule: Do something about it. Unless we carry out our action, all our fact-finding and analysis is whistling upwind—it's a sheer waste of energy.

William James said this: 'When once a decision is reached and execution is the order of the day, dismiss absolutely all responsibility and care about the outcome.' (In this case, William James undoubtedly used the word 'care' as a synonym for 'anxiety'.) He meant—once you have made a careful decision based on facts, go into action. Don't stop to reconsider. Don't begin to hesitate, worry and retrace your steps. Don't lose yourself in self-doubting which begets other doubts. Don't keep looking back over your shoulder.

Why don't you employ Galen Litchfield's technique to one of your worries right now?

Here is question No. 1—What am I worrying about?

Question No. 2—What can I do about It?

Question No. 3—What am I going to do about it.

Question No. 4—When am I going to start doing it?

It's not stress that kills us, it is our reaction to it.
—Hans Selye

Worry is the stomach's worst poison.
—Alfred Nobel

HOW TO ELIMINATE FIFTY PER CENT
OF YOUR BUSINESS WORRIES

If you are a businessman, you are probably saying to yourself right now: 'The title of this chapter is ridiculous. I have been running my business for nineteen years; and I certainly know the answers if anybody does. The idea of anybody trying to tell me how I can eliminate fifty per cent of my business worries—it's absurd!'

Fair enough—I would have felt exactly the same way myself a few years ago if I had seen this title on a chapter. It promises a lot—and promises are cheap.

Let's be very frank about it: maybe I won't be able to help you eliminate fifty per cent of your business worries. In the last analysis, no one can do that, except yourself. But what I can do is to show you how other people have done it—and leave the rest up to you!

Since worry is that serious, wouldn't you be satisfied if I could help you eliminate even ten per cent of your worries? ...Yes? ...Good! Well, I am going to show you how one business executive eliminated not fifty per cent of his worries, but seventy-five per cent of all the time he formerly spent in conferences, trying to solve business problems.

Furthermore, I am not going to tell you this story about a 'Mr Jones' or a 'Mr X' or 'a man I know in Ohio'—vague stories that you can't check up on. It concerns a very real person—Leon Shimkin, a partner and general manager of one of the foremost publishing houses in these United States: Simon and Schuster, Rockefeller Center, New York 20, New York.

Here is Leon Shimkin's experience in his own words:

For fifteen years, I spent almost half of every business day holding conferences, discussing problems. Should we do this or that—do nothing at all? We would get tense; twist in our chairs; walk the floor; argue and go around in circles. When night came, I would be utterly exhausted. I fully expected to go on doing this sort of thing for the rest of my life. I had been doing it for fifteen years, and it never occurred to me that there was a better way of doing it. If anyone had told me that I could eliminate three fourths of all the time I spent in those worried conferences, and three fourths of my nervous strain—I would have thought he was a wild-eyed, slap-happy, armchair optimist. Yet I devised a plan that did just that. I have been using this plan for eight years. It has performed wonders for my efficiency, my health and my happiness.

It sounds like magic—but like all magic tricks, it is extremely simple when you see how it is done.

Here is the secret: First, I immediately stopped the procedure I had been using in my conferences for fifteen years—a procedure that began with my troubled associates reciting all the details of what had gone wrong, and ending up by asking: 'What shall we do?' Second, I made a new rule—a rule that everyone who wishes to present a problem to me must first prepare and submit a memorandum answering these four questions:

Question 1: What is the problem?

(In the old days we used to spend an hour or two in a worried conference without anyone knowing specifically and concretely what the real problem was. We used to work ourselves into a lather discussing our troubles without ever troubling to write out specifically what our problem was.)

Question 2: What is the cause of the problem?

(As I look back over my career, I am appalled at the wasted hours I have spent in worried conferences without ever trying to find out clearly the conditions which lay at the root of the problem.)

Question 3: What are all possible solutions of the problem?

(In the old days, one man in the conference would suggest one solution. Someone else would argue with him. Tempers would flare. We would often get clear off the subject, and at the end of the conference no one would have written down all the various things we could do to attack the problem.)

Question 4: What solution do you suggest?

(I used to go into a conference with a man who had spent hours worrying about a situation and going around in circles without ever once thinking through all possible solutions and then writing down: 'This is the solution I recommend.')

My associates rarely come to me now with their problems. Why? Because they have discovered that in order to answer those four questions they have to get all the facts and think their problems through. And after they have done that they find, in three fourths of the cases, they don't have to consult me at all, because the proper solution has popped out like a piece of bread popping out from an electric toaster. Even in those cases where consultation is necessary, the discussion takes about one third the time formerly required, because it proceeds along an orderly, logical path to a reasoned conclusion.

Much less time is now consumed in the house of Simon and Schuster in worrying and talking about what is wrong; and a lot more action is obtained towards making those things right.

My friend Frank Bettger, one of the top insurance men in America, tells me he not only reduced his business worries, but nearly doubled his income, by a similar method. Frank says:

Years ago, when I first started to sell insurance, I was filled with a boundless enthusiasm and love for my work. Then something happened. I became so discouraged that I despised my work and thought of giving it up. I think I would have quit—if I hadn't got the idea, one Saturday morning, of sitting down and trying to get at the root of my worries.

1. I asked myself first, 'What is the problem?' The problem was that I was not getting high enough returns for the staggering amount of calls I was making. I seemed to do pretty well at selling a prospect, until the moment came for closing a sale. Then the customer would say, 'Well, I'll think it over, Mr Bettger. Come and see me again.' It was the time I wasted on these follow-up calls that was causing my depression.

2. I asked myself, 'What are the possible solutions?' But to get the answer to that one, I had to study the facts. I got out my record book for the last twelve months and studied the figures.

I made an astounding discovery! Right there in black and white, I discovered that seventy per cent of my sales had been closed on the very first interview! Twenty-three per cent of my sales had been closed on the second interview! And only seven per cent of my sales had been closed on those third, fourth, fifth, etc., interviews, which were running me ragged and taking up time. In other words, I was wasting fully one half of my working day on a part of my business which was responsible for only seven per cent of my sales!

3. 'What is the answer?' The answer was obvious. I immediately cut out all visits beyond the second interview, and spent the extra time building up new prospects. The results were unbelievable. In a very short time, I had raised the cash value of every visit I made from $2.80 to $4.27 a call!

As I said, Frank Bettger is now one of the best-known life-insurance salesmen in the country. He is with Fidelity Mutual of Philadelphia, and writes a million dollars worth of policies a year. But he was on the point of giving up. He was on the point of admitting failure—

until analyzing the problem gave him a boost on the road to success. Can you apply these questions to your business problems? To repeat my challenge—they can reduce your worries by fifty per cent. Here they are again:

What is the problem?

What is the CAUSE of the problem?

What are all possible solutions to the problem?

What solution do you suggest?

Nothing is permanent in this wicked world—not even our troubles.
—Charlie Chaplin

Forget the past—the future will give you plenty to worry about.
—George Allen, Sr.

3

'SEVENTY PER CENT OF ALL OUR WORRIES…'

If I knew how to solve everybody's financial worries, I wouldn't be writing this book, I would be sitting in the White House—right beside the President. But here is one thing I can do: I can quote some authorities on this subject and make some highly practical suggestions, and point out where you can obtain books and pamphlets that will give you additional guidance.

Seventy per cent of all our worries are about money. Most people believe that they would have no more financial worries if they could increase their income by only ten per cent. That is true in many cases, but in a surprisingly large number of cases it is not true. For example, while writing this chapter, I interviewed an expert on budgets: Mrs Elsie Stapleton—a woman who spent years as financial adviser to the customers of Wanamaker's Department Store in New York and of Gimbels. She has spent additional years as an individual consultant, trying to help people who were frantic with worry about money. She has helped people in all kinds of income brackets, all the way from a porter who earned less than a thousand dollars a year to an executive earning one hundred thousand a year. And this is what she told me: 'More money is not the answer to most people's financial worries. In fact, I have often seen it happen that an increase in income accomplished nothing but an increase in spending—and an increase in headaches. What causes most people to worry,' she said, 'is not that they haven't enough money, but that they don't know how to spend the money they have!' …You snorted at that last sentence, didn't you? Well, before you snort again, please remember that Mrs Stapleton did not say that was true of all people. She said, 'most people'. She didn't mean you. She meant your sisters and your cousins, whom you reckon by the dozens.

Here's something to consider—where your money is concerned, you're in business for yourself! And it is literally 'your business' what you do with your money.

But what are the principles of managing our money? How do we begin to make a budget and a plan? Here are eleven rules.

Rule 1: Get the facts down on paper!

When Arnold Bennett started out in London fifty years ago to be a novelist, he was poor and hard-pressed. So he kept a record of what he did with every sixpence. Did he wonder where his money was going? No. He knew. He liked the idea so much that he continued to keep such a record even after he became rich, world-famous, and had a private yacht.

You and I, too, will have to get notebooks and start keeping records. For the rest of our lives? No, not necessarily. Experts on budgets recommend that we keep an accurate account of every nickel we spend for at least the first month—and, if possible, for three months. This is to give us an accurate record of where our money goes, so we can draw up a budget.

Oh, you know where your money goes? Well, maybe so; but if you do, you are one in a thousand! Mrs Stapleton tells me it is a common occurrence for men and women to spend hours giving her facts and figures, so she can get them down on paper—then, when they see the result on paper, they exclaim, 'Is that the way my money goes?' They can hardly believe it. Are you like that? Could be.

Rule 2: Get a tailor-made budget that really fits your needs!

Mrs Stapleton tells me that two families may live side by side in identical houses, in the very same suburb, have the same number of children in the family, and receive the same income—yet their budgeting needs will be radically different. Why? Because people are different. She says a budget has to be a personal, custom-made job. The idea of a budget is not to wring all the joy out of life. The idea is to give us a sense of material security—which in many cases means emotional security and freedom from worry. 'People who live on budgets,' Mrs Stapleton told me, 'are happier people.'

But how do you go about it? First, as I said, you must list all expenses. Then get advice.

Rule 3: Learn how to spend wisely.

By this I mean: learn how to get the best value for your money. All large corporations have professional buyers and purchasing agents who do nothing but get the very best buys for their firms. As steward and manager of your personal estate, why shouldn't you do likewise?

Rule 4: Don't increase your headaches with your income.

Mrs Stapleton told me that the budgets she dreads most to be called into consultation on are family incomes of five thousand a year. I asked her why. 'Because,' she said, 'five thousand a year seems to be a goal to most American families. They may go along sensibly and sanely for years—then, when their income rises to five thousand a year, they think they have "arrived". They start branching out. Buy a house in the suburbs 'that doesn't cost any more than renting an apartment.' Buy a car, a lot of new furniture, and a lot of new clothes—and the first thing you know, they are running into the red. They are actually less happy than they were before—because they have bitten off too much with their increase in income.'

That is only natural. We all want to get more out of life. But in the long run, which is going to bring us more happiness—forcing ourselves to live within a tight budget, or having dunning letters in the mail and creditors pounding on the front door?

Rule 5: Try to build credit, in the event you must borrow.

Be sure your insurance policies have a savings aspect, if you want to borrow on them, for this means a cash value. Certain types of insurance, called 'term insurance,' are merely for your protection over a given period of time and do not build up reserves. These policies are obviously of no use to you for borrowing purposes. Therefore, the rule is: Ask questions! Before you sign for a policy, find out if it has a cash value in case you have to raise money.

Now, suppose you don't have insurance you can borrow on, and you don't have any bonds, but you do own a house, or a car, or some other kind of collateral. Where do you go to borrow? By all means, to a bank! Banks have a reputation to maintain in the community; and they will usually deal with you fairly. Frequently, if you are in a financial jam, the bank will go so far as to discuss your problems with you, make a plan, and help you work your way out of your worry and indebtedness. I repeat, if you have collateral, go to a bank!

However, suppose you are one of the thousands who don't have collateral, don't own any property, and have nothing to offer as guarantee except your wages or salary?

Rule 6: Protect yourself against illness, fire and emergency expenses.

Insurance is available, for relatively small sums, on all kinds of accidents, misfortunes and conceivable emergencies. I am not suggesting that you cover yourself for everything from slipping in the bathtub to catching German measles—but I do suggest that you protect yourself against the major misfortunes that you know could cost you money and therefore do cost you worry. It's cheap at the price.

For example, I know a woman who had to spend ten days in a hospital last year and, when she came out, was presented a bill—for exactly eight dollars! The answer? She had hospital insurance.

Rule 7: Teach your children a responsible attitude towards money.

I shall never forget an idea I once read in Your Life magazine. The author, Stella Weston Tuttle, described how she was teaching her little girl a sense of responsibility about money. She got an extra checkbook from the bank and gave it to her nine-year-old daughter. When the daughter was given her weekly allowance, she 'deposited' the money with her mother, who served as a bank for the child's funds. Then, throughout the week, whenever she wanted a nickel or a dime, she 'drew a check' for that amount and kept track of her balance. The little girl not only found that fun, but began to learn real responsibility in handling her money.

An excellent method!

Rule 8: If you are a housewife, maybe you can make a little extra money off your kitchen stove.

If after you budget your expenses wisely you still find that you don't have enough to make ends meet, you can then do one of two things: you can either scold, fret, worry and complain, or you can plan to make a little additional money on the side. How? Well, all you have to do to make money is to fill an urgent need that isn't being adequately filled now. That is what Mrs Nellie Speer,

37-09 83rd Street, Jackson Heights, New York, did. In 1932, she found herself living alone in a three-room apartment. Her husband had died, and both of her children were married. One day, while having some ice cream at a drugstore soda fountain, she noticed that the fountain was also selling bakery pies that looked sad and dreary. She asked the proprietor if he would buy some real home-made pies from her. He ordered two. 'Although I was a good cook,' Mrs Speer said, as she told me the story, 'I had always had servants when we lived in Georgia, and I had never baked more than a dozen pies in my life. After getting that order for two pies, I asked a neighbour woman how to cook an apple pie. The soda-fountain customers were delighted with my first two home-baked pies—one apple, one lemon. The drugstore ordered five the next day. Then orders gradually came in from other fountains and luncheonettes. Within two years, I was baking five thousand pies a year—I was doing all the work myself in my own tiny kitchen, and I was making a thousand dollars a year clear, without a penny's expense except the ingredients that went into the pies.'

The demand for Mrs Speer's home-baked pastry became so great that she had to move out of her kitchen into a shop and hire two girls to bake for her: pies, cakes, bread, and rolls. During the war, people stood in line for an hour at a time to buy her home-baked foods.

'I have never been happier in my life,' Mrs Speer said. 'I work in the shop twelve to fourteen hours a day, but I don't get tired because it isn't work to me. It is an adventure in living. I am doing my part to make people a little happier. I am too busy to be lonesome or worried. My work has filled a gap in my life left vacant by the passing of my mother and husband and my home.'

When I asked Mrs Speer if she felt that other women who were good cooks could make money in their spare time in a similar way, in towns of ten thousand and up, she replied, 'Yes—of course they can!'

Here is the point I am trying to make. Nellie Speer, in Jackson Heights, New York, instead of worrying about finances, did something positive. She started in an extremely small way to make money off the kitchen stove—no overhead, no rent, no advertising, no salaries. Under these conditions, it is almost impossible for a woman to be defeated by financial worries.

Look around you. You will find many needs that are not filled. For example, if you train yourself to be a good cook, you can probably make money by starting cooking classes for young girls right in your own kitchen. You can get your students by ringing door-bells.

There are many opportunities for both men and women. But one word of warning: unless you have a natural gift for selling, don't attempt door-to-door selling. Most people hate it and fail at it.

Rule 9: Don't gamble—ever.

I am always astounded by the people who hope to make money by betting on the ponies or playing slot machines, I know a man who makes his living by owning a string of these 'one-armed bandits,' and he has nothing but contempt for the foolish people who are so naïve as to imagine that they can beat a machine that is already rigged against them.

I also know one of the best-known bookmakers in America. He was a student in my adult-education classes. He told me that with all his knowledge of horse racing, he couldn't make money betting on the ponies. Yet the facts are that foolish people bet six billion dollars a year on the races—six times as much as our total national debt back in 1910. This bookmaker also told me that if he had an enemy that he despised, he could think of no better way of ruining him than by getting him to bet on the races. When I asked him what would happen to the man who played the races according to the tipster sheets, he replied: 'You could lose the United States Mint by betting that way.'

Rule 10: If we can't possibly improve our financial situation, let's be good to ourselves and stop resenting what can't be changed.

If we can't possibly improve our financial situation, maybe we can improve our mental attitude towards it. Let's remember that other people have their financial worries, too. We may be worried because we can't keep up with the Joneses; but the Joneses are probably worried because they can't keep up with the Ritzes; and the Ritzes are worried because they can't keep up with the Vanderbilts.

Some of the most famous men in American history have had their financial troubles. Both Lincoln and Washington had to borrow money to make the trip to be inaugurated as President.

If we can't have all we want, let's not poison our days with worry and resentment. Let's be good to ourselves. And let's remember that even if we owned the world with a hog-tight fence around it, we could eat only three meals a day and sleep in one bed at a time—even a ditch digger can do that; and he will probably eat with more gusto and sleep more peacefully than Rockefeller.

To lessen financial worries, let's try to follow these eleven rules:

Get the facts down on paper!

Get a tailor-made budget that really fits your needs!

Learn how to spend wisely.

Don't increase your headaches with your income.

Try to build credit, in the event you must borrow.

Protect yourself against illness, fire and emergency expenses.

Do not have your life-insurance proceeds paid to your widow in cash.

Teach your children a responsible attitude towards money.

If you are a housewife, maybe you can make a little extra money off your kitchen stove.

Don't gamble—ever.

If we can't possibly improve our financial situation, let's be good to ourselves and stop resenting what can't be changed.

> *Worry is a cycle of inefficient thoughts*
> *whirling around a center of fear.*
> —Corrie Ten Boom

> *Our fatigue is often caused not by work,*
> *but by worry, frustration and resentment.*
> —Dale Carnegie

PART 2

4

LIVE IN 'DAY-TIGHT COMPARTMENTS'

In the spring of 1871, a young man picked up a book and read twenty-one words that had a profound effect on his future. A medical student at the Montreal General Hospital, he was worried about passing the final examination, worried about what to do, where to go, how to build up a practice, how to make a living.

The twenty-one words that this young medical student read in 1871 helped him to become the most famous physician of his generation. He organized the world-famous Johns Hopkins School of Medicine. He became Regius Professor of Medicine at Oxford—the highest honour that can be bestowed upon any medical man in the British Empire. He was knighted by the King of England. When he died, two huge volumes containing 1,466 pages were required to tell the story of his life.

His name was Sir William Osler. Here are the twenty-one words that he read in the spring of 1871—twenty-one words from Thomas Carlyle that helped him lead a life free from worry: 'Our main business is not to see what lies dimly at a distance, but to do what lies clearly at hand.'

Forty-two years later, on a soft spring night when the tulips were blooming on the campus, this man, Sir William Osler, addressed the students of Yale University. He told those Yale students that a man like himself who had been a professor in four universities and had written a popular book was supposed to have 'brains of a special quality.' He declared that that was untrue. He said that his intimate friends knew that his brains were 'of the most mediocre character.'

What, then, was the secret of his success? He stated that it was owing to what he called living in 'day-tight compartments.' What did he mean by that? A few months before he spoke at Yale, Sir William Osler had crossed the Atlantic on a great ocean liner where the captain, standing on the bridge, could press a button and—presto!—there was a clanging of machinery and various parts of the ship were immediately shut off from one another—shut off into watertight compartments. 'Now each one of you,' Dr Osler said to those Yale students, 'is a much more marvellous organization than the great liner, and bound on a longer voyage. What I urge is that you so learn to control the machinery as to live with 'day-tight compartments' as the most certain way to ensure safety on the voyage. Get on the bridge, and see that at least the great bulkheads are in working order. Touch a button and hear, at every level of your life, the iron doors shutting out the Past—the dead yesterdays. Touch another and shut off, with a metal curtain, the Future—the unborn tomorrows. Then you are safe—safe for today! The future is today.... There is no tomorrow. The day of man's salvation is now. Waste of energy, mental distress, nervous worries dog the steps of a man who is anxious about the future.... Shut close, then, the great fore and aft bulkheads, and prepare to cultivate the habit of a life of 'day-tight compartments.''

Did Dr Osler mean to say that we should not make any effort to prepare for tomorrow? No. Not at all. But he did go on in that address to say that the best possible way to prepare for tomorrow is to concentrate with all your intelligence, all your enthusiasm, on doing today's work superbly today. That is the only possible way you can prepare for the future.

During the war, our military leaders planned for the morrow, but they could not afford to have any anxiety. 'I have supplied the best men with the best equipment we have,' said Admiral Ernest J. King, who directed the United States Navy, 'and have given them what seems to be the wisest mission. That is all I can do.'

'If a ship has been sunk,' Admiral King went on, 'I can't bring it up. If it is going to be sunk, I can't stop it. I can use my time much better working on tomorrow's problem than by fretting about yesterday's. Besides, if I let those things get me, I wouldn't last long.'

Whether in war or peace, the chief difference between good thinking and bad thinking is this: good thinking deals with causes and effects and leads to logical, constructive planning; bad thinking frequently leads to tension and nervous breakdowns.

One of the most appalling comments on our present way of life is that half of all the beds in our hospitals are reserved for patients with nervous and mental troubles, patients who have collapsed under the crushing burden of accumulated yesterdays and fearful tomorrows. Yet a vast majority of those people would be walking the streets today, leading happy, useful lives, if they had only heeded the words of Sir William Osler: 'Live in day-tight compartments.'

One of the most tragic things I know about human nature is that all of us tend to put off living. We are all dreaming of some magical rose garden over the horizon—instead of enjoying the roses that are blooming outside our windows today.

Why are we such fools—such tragic fools?

'How strange it is, our little procession of life!' wrote Stephen Leacock. 'The child says, "When I am a big boy." But what is that? The big boy says, "When I grow up." And then, grown up, he says, "When I get married." But to be married, what is that after all? The thought changes to "When I'm able to retire." And then, when retirement comes, he looks back over the landscape traversed; a cold wind seems to sweep over it; somehow he has missed it all, and it is gone. Life, we learn too late, is in the living, in the tissue of every day and hour.'

The late Edward S. Evans of Detroit almost killed himself with worry before he learned that life 'is in the living, in the tissue of every day and hour.' Brought up in poverty, Edward Evans made his first money by selling newspapers, then worked as a grocer's clerk. Later, with seven people dependent upon him for bread and butter, he got a job as an assistant librarian. Small as the pay was, he was afraid to quit. Eight years passed before he could summon up the courage to start out on his own. But once he started, he built up an original investment of fifty-five borrowed dollars into a business of his own that made him twenty thousand dollars a year. Then came a frost, a killing frost. He endorsed a big note for a friend—and the friend went bankrupt. Quickly on top of that disaster came another: the bank in which he had all his money collapsed. He not only lost every cent he had, but was plunged into debt for sixteen thousand dollars. His nerves couldn't take it. 'I couldn't sleep or eat,' he told me. 'I became strangely ill. Worry and nothing but worry,' he said, 'brought on this illness. One day as I was walking down the street, I fainted and fell on the sidewalk. I was no longer able to walk. I was put to bed and my body broke out in boils. These boils turned inward until just lying in bed was agony. I grew weaker every day. Finally my doctor told me that I had only two more weeks to live. I was shocked. I drew up my will, and then lay back in bed to await my end. No use now to struggle or worry. I gave up, relaxed and went to sleep. I hadn't slept two hours in succession for weeks; but now with my earthly problems drawing to an end, I slept like a baby. My exhausting weariness began to disappear. My appetite returned. I gained weight.

'A few weeks later, I was able to walk with crutches. Six weeks later, I was able to go back to work. I had been making twenty thousand dollars a year; but I was glad now to get a job for thirty dollars a week. I got a job selling blocks to put behind the wheels of automobiles when they are shipped by freight. I had learned my lesson now. No more worry for me—no more regret about what had happened in the past—no more dread of the future. I concentrated all my time, energy and enthusiasm into selling those blocks.' Edward S. Evans shot up fast now. In a few years, he was president of the company—the Evans Products Company. It has been listed on the New York Stock Exchange for years. If you ever fly over Greenland you may land on Evans Field—a flying field named in his honour.

Yet Edward S. Evans never would have achieved these victories if he hadn't learned to live in day-tight compartments.

Every day brings a choice: to practice stress or to practice peace.
—Joan Borysenko

Life is too short to worry about anything. You had better enjoy it because the next day promises nothing.
—Eric Davis

5

WHAT WORRY MAY DO TO YOU

Some time ago, a neighbour rang my doorbell one evening and urged me and my family to be vaccinated against smallpox. He was only one of thousands of volunteers who were ringing doorbells all over New York City. Frightened people stood in lines for hours at a time to be vaccinated. Vaccination stations were opened not only in all hospitals, but also in firehouses, police precincts, and in large industrial plants. More than two thousand doctors and nurses worked feverishly day and night, vaccinating crowds. The cause of all this excitement? Eight people in New York City had smallpox—and two had died. Two deaths out of a population of almost eight million.

Now, I have lived in New York for over thirty-seven years; and no one has ever yet rung my doorbell to warn me against the emotional sickness of worry—an illness that, during the last thirty-seven years, has caused ten thousand times more damage than smallpox.

No doorbell ringer has ever warned me that one person out of ten now living in these United States will have a nervous breakdown—induced in the vast majority of cases by worry and emotional conflicts. So I am writing this chapter to ring your doorbell and warn you.

I recently had some correspondence with Dr Harold C. Habein of the Mayo Clinic. He read a paper at the annual meeting of the American Association of Industrial Physicians and Surgeons, saying that he had made a study of 176 business executives whose average age was 44.3 years. He reported that slightly more than a third of these executives suffered from one of three ailments peculiar to high-tension living—heart disease, digestive-tract ulcers and high blood pressure. Think of it—a third of our business executives are wrecking their bodies with heart disease, ulcers and high blood pressure before they even reach forty-five. Can any man possibly be a success who is paying for business advancement with stomach ulcers and heart trouble? What shall it profit a man if he gains the whole world—and loses his health? Even if he owned the whole world, he could sleep in only one bed at a time and eat only three meals a day. Even a ditchdigger can do that—and probably sleep more soundly and enjoy his food more than a high-powered executive. Frankly, I would rather be a sharecropper down in Alabama with a banjo on my knee than wreck my health at forty-five by trying to run a railroad or a cigarette company.

Doctors figure that one American in every twenty now alive will spend a part of his life in an institution for the mentally ill. One out of every six of our young men called up by the draft in the Second World War was rejected as mentally diseased or defective.

What causes insanity? No one knows all the answers. But it is highly probable that in many cases fear and worry are contributing factors. The anxious and harassed individual who is unable to cope with the harsh world of reality breaks off all contact with his environment and retreats into a private dream world of his own making, and this solves his worry problems.

Worry can put you into a wheel chair with rheumatism and arthritis. Dr Russell L. Cecil, of the Cornell University Medical School, is a world-recognized authority on arthritis; and he has listed four of the commonest conditions that bring on arthritis:

1. Marital shipwreck.
2. Financial disaster and grief.
3. Loneliness and worry.
4. Long-cherished resentments.

Naturally, these four emotional situations are far from being the only causes of arthritis. There are many different kinds of arthritis—due to various causes. But, to repeat, the commonest conditions that bring on arthritis are the four listed by Dr Russell L. Cecil.

Worry can even cause tooth decay. Dr William I.L. McGonigle said in an address before the American Dental Association that 'unpleasant emotions such as those caused by worry, fear, nagging …may upset the body's calcium balance and cause tooth decay.' Dr McGonigle told of a patient of his who had always had a perfect set of teeth until he began to worry over his wife's sudden illness. During the three weeks she was in the hospital, he developed nine cavities—cavities brought on by worry.

Have you ever seen a person with an acutely overactive thyroid?

A short time ago I went to Philadelphia with a friend of mine who has this disease. We consulted Dr Israel Bram, 1633 Spruce Street—a famous specialist who has been treating this type of ailment for thirty-eight years. Here is the advice he had hanging on the wall of his waiting room—painted on a large wooden sign. I copied it down on the back of an envelope while I was waiting:

Relaxation and recreation

The most relaxing recreating forces are a healthy religion, sleep, music and laughter.

Have faith in God—learn to sleep well—
Love good music—see the funny side of life—
And health and happiness will be yours.

When I interviewed Merle Oberon, she told me that she refused to worry because she knew that worry would destroy her chief asset on the motion-picture screen: her good looks.

'When I first tried to break into the movies,' she told me, 'I was worried and scared. I had just come from India, and I didn't know anyone in London, where I was trying to get a job. I saw a few producers, but none of them hired me; and the little money I had began to give out. For two weeks I lived on nothing but crackers and water. I was not only worried now. I was hungry. I said to myself, "Maybe you're a fool. Maybe you will never break into the movies. After all, you have no experience, you've never acted at all—what have you to offer but a rather pretty face?"'

'I went to the mirror. And when I looked in that mirror, I saw what worry was doing to my looks! I saw the lines it was forming.

'I saw the anxious expression. So I said to myself, "You've got to stop this at once! You can't afford to worry. The only thing you have to offer at all is your looks, and worry will ruin them!"'

Few things can age and sour a woman and destroy her looks as quickly as worry. Worry curdles the expression. It makes us clench our jaws and lines our faces with wrinkles. It forms a permanent scowl. It may turn the hair gray, and, in some cases, even make it fall out. It can ruin the complexion—it can bring on all kinds of skin rashes, eruptions, and pimples.

Heart disease is the number-one killer in America today. During the Second World War, almost a third of a million men were killed in combat; but during that same period, heart disease killed two million civilians—and one million of those casualties were caused by the kind of heart disease that is brought on by worry and high- tension living.

Here is a startling and almost incredible fact: more Americans commit suicide each year than die from the five most common communicable diseases.

Why? The answer is largely: Worry.

When the cruel Chinese war lords wanted to torture their prisoners, they would tie their prisoners hand and foot and put them under a bag of water that constantly dripped...dripped...dripped... day and night. These drops of water constantly falling on the head finally became like the sound of hammer blows—and drove men insane. This same method of torture was used during the Spanish Inquisition and in German concentration camps under Hitler.

Worry is like the constant drip, drip, drip of water; and the constant drip, drip, drip of worry often drives men to insanity and suicide.

Do you love life? Do you want to live long and enjoy good health? Can you keep the peace of your inner self in the midst of the tumult of a modern city? If you are a normal person, the answer is 'Yes.

Emphatically, yes.' Most of us are stronger than we realize. We have inner resources that we have probably never tapped.

> *Some of us think holding on makes us strong;*
> *but sometimes it is letting go.*
> —Herman Hesse

> *Worry is interest paid on trouble before it comes due.*
> —William Ralph Inge

PART 3

6

HOW TO CROWD WORRY OUT OF YOUR MIND

I shall never forget the night, a few years ago, when Marion J. Douglas was a student in one of my classes. (I have not used his real name. He requested me, for personal reasons, not to reveal his identity.) But here is his real story as he told it before one of our adult-education classes. He told us how tragedy had struck at his home, not once, but twice. The first time he had lost his five-year-old daughter, a child he adored. He and his wife thought they couldn't endure that first loss; but, as he said, 'Ten months later God gave us another little girl—and she died in five days.'

This double bereavement was almost too much to bear. 'I couldn't take it,' this father told us. 'I couldn't sleep, I couldn't eat, I couldn't rest or relax. My nerves were utterly shaken and my confidence gone.' At last he went to doctors; one recommended sleeping pills and another recommended a trip. He tried both, but neither remedy helped. He said, 'My body felt as if it were encased in a vise, and the jaws of the vise were being drawn tighter and tighter.' The tension of grief—if you have ever been paralysed by sorrow, you know what he meant.

'But thank God, I had one child left—a four-year-old son. He gave me the solution to my problem. One afternoon as I sat around feeling sorry for myself, he asked: "Daddy, will you build a boat for me?" I was in no mood to build a boat; in fact, I was in no mood to do anything. But my son is a persistent little fellow! I had to give in."

'Building that toy boat took about three hours. By the time it was finished, I realized that those three hours spent building that boat were the first hours of mental relaxation and peace that I had had in months!

'That discovery jarred me out of my lethargy and caused me to do a bit of thinking—the first real thinking I had done in months. I realized that it is difficult to worry while you are busy doing something that requires planning and thinking. In my case, building the boat had knocked worry out of the ring. So I resolved to keep busy.

'The following night, I went from room to room in the house, compiling a list of jobs that ought to be done. Scores of items needed to be repaired: bookcases, stair steps, storm windows, window shades, knobs, locks, leaky faucets. Astonishing as it seems, in the course of two weeks I had made a list of 242 items that needed attention.

'During the last two years I have completed most of them. Besides, I have filled my life with stimulating activities. Two nights per week I attend adult-education classes in New York. I have gone in for civic activities in my home town and I am now chairman of the school board. I attend scores of meetings. I help collect money for the Red Cross and other activities. I am so busy now that I have no time for worry.'

No time for worry! That is exactly what Winston Churchill said when he was working eighteen hours a day at the height of the war. When he was asked if he worried about his tremendous responsibilities, he said, 'I'm too busy. I have no time for worry.'

The great scientist, Pasteur, spoke of 'the peace that is found in libraries and labouratories.' Why is peace found there? Because the men in libraries and labouratories are usually too absorbed in their tasks to worry about themselves. Research men rarely have nervous breakdowns. They haven't time for such luxuries.

Why does such a simple thing as keeping busy help to drive out anxiety? Because of a law—one of the most fundamental laws ever revealed by psychology. And that law is: that it is utterly impossible for any human mind, no matter how brilliant, to think of more than one thing at any given time. You don't quite believe it? Very well, then, let's try an experiment.

Suppose you lean back right now, close your eyes, and try, at the same instant, to think of the Statue of Liberty and of what you plan to do tomorrow morning. (Go ahead, try it.)

You found out, didn't you, that you could focus on either thought in turn, but never on both simultaneously? Well, the same thing is true in the field of emotions. We cannot be pepped up and enthusiastic about doing something exciting and feel dragged down by worry at the very same time. One kind of emotion drives out the other. And it was that simple discovery that enabled Army psychiatrists to perform such miracles during the war.

When men came out of battle so shaken by the experience that they were called 'psychoneurotic,' Army doctors prescribed 'Keep 'em busy' as a cure.

Every waking minute of these nerve-shocked men was filled with activity—usually outdoor activity, such as fishing, hunting, playing ball, golf, taking pictures, making gardens, and dancing. They were given no time for brooding over their terrible experiences.

'Occupational therapy' is the term now used by psychiatry when work is prescribed as though it were a medicine. It is not new. The old Greek physicians were advocating it five hundred years before Christ was born!

Any psychiatrist will tell you that work—keeping busy—is one of the best anesthetics ever known for sick nerves. Henry W. Longfellow found that out for himself when he lost his young wife. His wife had been melting some sealing wax at a candle one day, when her clothes caught on fire. Longfellow heard her cries and tried to reach her in time; but she died from the burns. For a while, Longfellow was so tortured by the memory of that dreadful experience that he nearly went insane; but, fortunately for him, his three small children needed his attention. In spite of his own grief, Longfellow undertook to be father and mother to his children. He took them for walks, told them stories, played games with them, and immortalized their companionship in his poem 'The Children's Hour'. He also translated Dante; and all these duties combined kept him so busy that he forgot himself entirely, and regained his peace of mind.

Most of us have little trouble 'losing ourselves in action' while we have our noses to the grindstone and are doing our day's work. But the hours after work—they are the dangerous ones. Just when we're free to enjoy our own leisure, and ought to be happiest—that's when the blue devils of worry attack us. That's when we begin to wonder whether we're getting anywhere in life; whether we're in a rut; whether the boss 'meant anything' by that remark he made today; or whether we're getting bald.

When we are not busy, our minds tend to become a near-vacuum. Every student of physics knows that 'nature abhors a vacuum'. The nearest thing to a vacuum that you and I will probably ever see is the inside of an incandescent electric-light bulb. Break that bulb—and nature forces air in to fill the theoretically empty space.

Nature also rushes in to fill the vacant mind. With what? Usually with emotions. Why? Because emotions of worry, fear, hate, jealousy, and envy are driven by primeval vigor and the dynamic energy of the jungle. Such emotions are so violent that they tend to drive out of our minds all peaceful, happy thoughts and emotions.

Osa Johnson, the world's most famous woman explorer, recently told me how she found release from worry and grief. You may have read the story of her life. It is called I Married Adventure. If any woman ever married adventure, she certainly did. Martin Johnson married her when she was sixteen and lifted her feet off the sidewalks of Chanute, Kansas, and set them down on the wild jungle trails of Borneo. For a quarter of a century, this Kansas couple travelled all over the world, making motion pictures of the vanishing wild life of Asia and Africa. Back in America nine years ago, they were on a lecture tour, showing their famous films. They took a plane out of Denver, bound for the Coast. The plane plunged into a mountain. Martin Johnson was killed instantly. The doctors said Osa would never leave her bed again. But they didn't know Osa Johnson. Three months later, she was in a wheel chair, lecturing before large audiences. In fact, she addressed over a hundred audiences that season—all from a wheel chair. When I asked her why she did it, she replied: "I did it so that I would have no time for sorrow and worry."

If you and I are worried, let's remember that we can use good old-fashioned work as a medicine. If you and I don't keep busy—if we sit around and brood—we will hatch out a whole flock of what Charles Darwin used to call the 'wibber gibbers'. And the 'wibber gibbers' are nothing but old-fashioned gremlins that will run us hollow and destroy our power of action and our power of will.

To break the worry habit, here is

Rule 1: Keep busy. The worried person must lose himself in action, lest he wither in despair.

You can only lose what you cling to.
—Buddha

Don't worry about being a star,
worry about doing good work, and all that will come to you.
—Ice Cube

7

DON'T LET THE BEETLES GET YOU DOWN

Here is a dramatic story that I'll probably remember as long as I live. It was told to me by Robert Moore, of 14 Highland Avenue, Maplewood, New Jersey.

I learned the biggest lesson of my life in March, 1945. I learned it under 276 feet of water off the coast of Indo-China. I was one of eighty-eight men aboard the submarine Baya S.S. 318. We had discovered by radar that a small Japanese convoy was coming our way. As daybreak approached, we submerged to attack. I saw through the periscope a Jap destroyer escort, a tanker, and a mine layer. We fired three torpedoes at the destroyer escort, but missed. Something went haywire in the mechanics of each torpedo. The destroyer, not knowing that she had been attacked, continued on. We were getting ready to attack the last ship, the mine layer, when suddenly she turned and came directly at us. (A Jap plane had spotted us under sixty feet of water and had radioed our position to the Jap mine layer.) We went down to 150 feet, to avoid detection, and rigged for a depth charge. We put extra bolts on the hatches; and, in order to make our sub absolutely silent, we turned off the fans, the cooling system, and all electrical gear.

Three minutes later, all hell broke loose. Six depth charges exploded all around us and pushed us down to the ocean floor—a depth of 276 feet. We were terrified. To be attacked in less than a thousand feet of water is dangerous—less than five hundred feet is almost always fatal. And we were being attacked in a trifle more than half of five hundred feet of water—just about knee-deep, as far as safety was concerned. For fifteen hours, that Jap mine layer kept dropping depth charges. If a depth charge explodes within seventeen feet of a sub, the concussion will blow a hole in it. Scores of these depth charges exploded within fifty feet of us. We were ordered 'to secure'—to lie quietly in our bunks and remain calm.

I was so terrified I could hardly breathe. 'This is death,' I kept saying to myself over and over. 'This is death!... This is death!' With the fans and cooling system turned off, the air inside the sub was over a hundred degrees; but I was so chilled with fear that I put on a sweater and a fur-lined jacket; and still I trembled with cold. My teeth chattered. I broke out in a cold, clammy sweat. The attack continued for fifteen hours. Then ceased suddenly. Apparently the Jap mine layer had exhausted its supply of depth charges, and steamed away. Those fifteen hours of attack seemed like fifteen million years. All my life passed before me in review. I remembered all the bad things I had done, all the little absurd things I had worried about. I had been a bank clerk before I joined the Navy. I had worried about the long hours, the poor pay, the poor prospects of advancement. I had worried because I couldn't own my own home, couldn't buy a new car, couldn't buy my wife nice clothes. How I had hated my old boss, who was always nagging and scolding! I remembered how I would come home at night sore and grouchy and quarrel with my wife over trifles. I had worried about a scar on my forehead—a nasty cut from an auto accident.

How big all those worries seemed years ago! But how absurd they seemed when depth charges were threatening to blow me to kingdom come. I promised myself then and there that if I ever saw the sun and the stars again, I would never, never worry again. Never! Never!! Never! I learned more about the art of living in those fifteen terrible hours in that submarine than I had learned by studying books for four years in Syracuse University.

We often face the major disasters of life bravely—and then let the trifles, the 'pains in the neck,' get us down. For example, Samuel Pepys tells in his Diary about seeing Sir Harry Vane's head chopped off in London. As Sir Harry mounted the platform, he was not pleading for his life, but was pleading with the executioner not to hit the painful boil on his neck!

That was another thing that Admiral Byrd discovered down in the terrible cold and darkness of the polar nights—that his men fussed more about the 'pains in the neck' than about the big things. They bore, without complaining, the dangers, the hardships, and the cold that was often eighty degrees below zero. 'But,' says Admiral Byrd, 'I know of bunkmates who quit speaking because each suspected the other of inching his gear into the other's allotted space; and I knew of one who could not eat unless he could find a place in the mess hall out of sight of the Fletcherist who solemnly chewed his food twenty-eight times before swallowing.'

'In a polar camp,' says Admiral Byrd, 'little things like that have the power to drive even disciplined men to the edge of insanity.'

And you might have added, Admiral Byrd, that 'little things' in marriage drive people to the edge of insanity and cause 'half the heartaches in the world.'

At least, that is what the authorities say. For example, Judge Joseph Sabath of Chicago, after acting as arbiter in more than forty thousand unhappy marriages, declared: 'Trivialities are at the bottom of most marital unhappiness'; and Frank S. Hogan, District Attorney of New York County, says, 'Fully half the cases in our criminal courts originate in little things. Barroom bravado, domestic wrangling, an insulting remark, a disparaging word, a rude action—those are the little things that lead to assault and murder. Very few of us are cruelly and greatly wronged. It is the small blows to our self-esteem, the indignities, the little jolts to our vanity, which cause half the heartaches in the world.'

Mrs Carnegie and I had dinner at a friend's house in Chicago. While carving the meat, he did something wrong. I didn't notice it; and I wouldn't have cared even if I had noticed it. But his wife saw it and jumped down his throat right in front of us. 'John,' she cried, 'watch what you are doing! Can't you ever learn to serve properly!' Then she said to us: 'He is always making mistakes. He just doesn't try.' Maybe he didn't try to carve; but I certainly give him credit for trying to live with her for twenty years. Frankly, I would rather have eaten a couple of hot dogs with mustard—in an atmosphere of peace—than to have dined on Peking duck and shark fins while listening to her scolding.

Shortly after that experience, Mrs Carnegie and I had some friends at our home for dinner. Just before they arrived, Mrs Carnegie found that three of the napkins didn't match the table-cloth.

'I rushed to the cook,' she told me later, 'and found that the other three napkins had gone to the laundry. The guests were at the door. There was no time to change. I felt like bursting into tears! All I could think was, "Why did this stupid mistake have to spoil my whole evening?" Then I thought—well—why let it? I went in to dinner, determined to have a good time. And I did. I would much rather our friends think I was a sloppy housekeeper,' she told me, 'than a nervous, bad-tempered one. And anyhow, as far as I could make out, no one noticed the napkins!'A well-known legal maxim says: De minimis non curat lex—'the law does not concern itself with trifles.' And neither should the worrier—if he wants peace of mind.

Even so illustrious a figure as Rudyard Kipling forgot at times that "Life is too short to be little." The result? He and his brother-in-law fought the most famous court battle in the history of Vermont—a battle so celebrated that a book has been written about it: Rudyard Kipling's Vermont Feud.

The story goes like this: Kipling married a Vermont girl, Caroline Balestier, built a lovely home in Brattleboro, Vermont; settled down and expected to spend the rest of his life there. His brother-in-law, Beatty Balestier, became Kipling's best friend. The two of them worked and played together.

Then Kipling bought some land from Balestier, with the understanding that Balestier would be allowed to cut hay off it each season. One day, Balestier found Kipling laying out a flower garden on this hayfield. His blood boiled. He hit the ceiling. Kipling fired right back. The air over the Green Mountains of Vermont turned blue!

A few days later, when Kipling was out riding his bicycle, his brother-in-law drove a wagon and a team of horses across the road suddenly and forced Kipling to take a spill. And Kipling—the man who wrote,'If you can keep your head when all about you are losing theirs and blaming it on you'—he lost his own head, and swore out a warrant for Balestier's arrest! A sensational trial followed. Reporters from the big cities poured into the town. The news flashed around the world. Nothing was settled. This quarrel caused Kipling and his wife to abandon their American home for the rest of their lives. All that worry and bitterness over a mere trifle! A load of hay.

To break the worry habit before it breaks you, here is

Rule 2: Let's not allow ourselves to be upset by small things. We should despise and forget. Remember 'life is too short to be little.'

When I let go of what I am, I become what I might be. When I let go of what I have, I receive what I need.

—Tao Te Ching

I never worry about the problem. I worry about the solution.

—Shaquille O'Neal

8

A LAW THAT WILL OUTLAW
MANY OF YOUR WORRIES

As a child, I grew up on a Missouri farm; and one day, while helping my mother pit cherries, I began to cry. My mother said, 'Dale, what in the world are you crying about?' I blubbered, 'I'm afraid I am going to be buried alive!'

I was full of worries in those days. When thunderstorms came, I worried for fear I would be killed by lightning. When hard times came, I worried for fear we wouldn't have enough to eat. I worried for fear I would go to hell when I died. I was terrified for fear an older boy, Sam White, would cut off my big ears—as he threatened to do. I worried for fear girls would laugh at me if I tipped my hat to them. I worried for fear no girl would ever be willing to marry me. I worried about what I would say to my wife immediately after we were married. I imagined that we would be married in some country church, and then get in a surrey with fringe on the top and ride back to the farm ...but how would I be able to keep the conversation going on that ride back to the farm? How? How? I pondered over that earth-shaking problem for many an hour as I walked behind the plow.

As the years went by, I gradually discovered that ninety-nine per cent of the things I worried about never happened.

For example, as I have already said, I was once terrified of lightning; but I now know that the chances of my being killed by lightning in any one year are, according to the National Safety Council, only one in three hundred and fifty thousand.

My fear of being buried alive was even more absurd: I don't

imagine that—even back in the days before embalming was the rule—that one person in ten million was buried alive; yet I once cried for fear of it.

One person out of every eight dies of cancer. If I had wanted something to worry about, I should have worried about cancer—instead of being killed by lightning or being buried alive.

To be sure, I have been talking about the worries of youth and adolescence. But many of our adult worries are almost as absurd. You and I could probably eliminate nine tenths of our worries right now if we would cease our fretting long enough to discover whether, by the law of averages, there was any real justification for our worries.

I wrote several chapters of this book at James Simpson's Num-Ti-Gah Lodge, on the shore of Bow Lake in the Canadian Rockies. While stopping there one summer, I met Mr and Mrs Herbert H. Salinger, of 2298 Pacific Avenue, San Francisco. Mrs Salinger, a poised, serene woman, gave me the impression that she had never worried. One evening in front of the roaring fireplace, I asked her if she had ever been troubled by worry. 'Troubled by it?' she said.

My life was almost ruined by it. Before I learned to conquer worry, I lived through eleven years of self-made hell. I was irritable and hot-tempered. I lived under terrific tension. I would take the bus every week from my home in San Mateo to shop in San Francisco. But even while shopping, I worried myself into a dither: maybe I had left the electric iron connected on the ironing board. Maybe the house had caught fire. Maybe the maid had run off and left the children. Maybe they had been out on their bicycles and been killed by a car. In the midst of my shopping, I would often worry myself into a cold perspiration and rush out and take the bus home to see if everything was all right. No wonder my first marriage ended in disaster.

My second husband is a lawyer—a quiet, analytical man who never worries about anything. When I became tense and anxious, he would say to me, 'Relax. Let's think this out…. What are you really worrying about? Let's examine the law of averages and see whether or not it is likely to happen.'

For example, I remember the time we were driving from Albuquerque, New Mexico, to the Carlsbad Caverns—driving on a dirt road—when we were caught in a terrible rainstorm. The car was slithering and sliding. We couldn't control it. I was positive we would slide off into one of the ditches that flanked the road; but my husband kept repeating to me: 'I am driving very slowly. Nothing serious is likely to happen. Even if the car does slide into the ditch, by the law of averages, we won't be hurt.' His calmness and confidence quieted me.

A few years ago an infantile-paralysis epidemic swept over our part of California. In the old days, I would have been hysterical. But my husband persuaded me to act calmly. We took all the precautions we could: we kept our children away from crowds, away from school and the movies. By consulting the Board of Health, we found out that even during the worst infantile-paralysis epidemic that California had ever known up to that time, only 1835 children had been stricken in the entire state of California. And that the usual number was around two hundred or three hundred. Tragic as those figures are, we nevertheless felt that, according to the law of averages, the chances of any one child being stricken were remote.

'By the law of averages, it won't happen.' That phrase has destroyed ninety per cent of my worries; and it has made the past twenty years of my life beautiful and peaceful beyond my highest expectations.

The United States Navy used the statistics of the law of averages to buck up the morale of their men. One ex-sailor told me that when he and his shipmates were assigned to high-octane tankers, they were worried stiff. They all believed that if a tanker loaded with high-octane gasoline was hit by a torpedo, it exploded and blew everybody to kingdom come.

But the U.S. Navy knew otherwise; so the Navy issued exact figures, showing that out of one hundred tankers hit by torpedoes, sixty stayed afloat; and of the forty that did sink, only five sank in less than ten minutes. That meant time to get off the ship—it also meant casualties were exceedingly small. Did this help morale? 'This knowledge of the law of averages wiped out my jitters,' said Clyde W. Maas, of 1969 Walnut Street, St. Paul, Minnesota—the man who told this story. 'The whole crew felt better. We knew we had a chance; and that, by the law of averages, we probably wouldn't be killed.'

To break the worry habit before it breaks you—here is

Rule 3: Let's examine the record. Let's ask ourselves: 'what are the chances, according to the Law of Averages, that this event I am worrying about will ever occur?'

The greatest weapon against stress is our
ability to choose one thought over another.
—William James

When you begin to worry, go find something to do.
—Joyce Meyer

9

CO-OPERATE WITH THE INEVITABLE

When I was a little boy, I was playing with some of my friends in the attic of an old, abandoned log house in northwest Missouri. As I climbed down out of the attic, I rested my feet on a window sill for a moment—and then jumped. I had a ring on my left forefinger; and as I jumped, the ring caught on a nailhead and tore off my finger. I screamed. I was terrified. I was positive I was going to die. But after the hand healed, I never worried about it for one split second. What would have been the use?... I accepted the inevitable.

Now I often go for a month at a time without even thinking about the fact that I have only three fingers and a thumb on my left hand.

A few years ago, I met a man who was running a freight elevator in one of the downtown office buildings in New York. I noticed that his left hand had been cut off at the wrist. I asked him if the loss of that hand bothered him. He said, 'Oh, no, I hardly ever think about it. I am not married; and the only time I ever think about it is when I try to thread a needle.'

It is astonishing how quickly we can accept almost any situation—if we have to—and adjust ourselves to it and forget about it.

I often think of an inscription on the ruins of a fifteenth-century cathedral in Amsterdam, Holland. This inscription says in Flemish: 'It is so. It cannot be otherwise.'

As you and I march across the decades of time, we are going to meet a lot of unpleasant situations that are so. They cannot be otherwise. We have our choice. We can either accept them as inevitable and adjust ourselves to them, or we can ruin our lives with rebellion and maybe end up with a nervous breakdown.

Here is a bit of sage advice from one of my favorite philosophers, William James. 'Be willing to have it so,' he said. 'Acceptance of what has happened is the first step to overcoming the consequences of any misfortune.' Elizabeth Connley, of 2840 NE 49th Avenue, Portland, Oregon, had to find that out the hard way. Here is a letter that she wrote to me recently: 'On the very day that America was celebrating the victory of our armed forces in North Africa,' the letter says, "I received a telegram from the War Department: my nephew—the person I loved most—was missing in action. A short time later, another telegram arrived saying he was dead."

'I was prostrate with grief. Up to that time, I had felt that life had been very good to me. I had a job I loved. I had helped to raise this nephew. He represented to me all that was fine and good in young manhood. I had felt that all the bread I had cast upon the waters was coming back to me as cake! ... Then came this telegram. My whole world collapsed. I felt there was nothing left to live for. I neglected my work; neglected my friends. I let everything go. I was bitter and resentful. Why did my loving nephew have to be taken? Why did this good boy—with life all before him—why did he have to be killed? I couldn't accept it. My grief was so overwhelming that I decided to give up my work, and go away and hide myself in my tears and bitterness.

'I was clearing out my desk, getting ready to quit, when I came across a letter that I had forgotten—a letter from this nephew who had been killed, a letter he had written to me when my mother had died a few years ago. "Of course, we will all miss her," the letter said, "and especially you. But I know you'll carry on. Your own personal philosophy will make you do that. I shall never forget the beautiful truths you taught me. Wherever I am, or how far apart we may be, I shall always remember that you taught me to smile, and to take whatever comes, like a man."

'I read and reread that letter. It seemed as if he were there beside me, speaking to me. He seemed to be saying to me: "Why don't you do what you taught me to do? Carry on, no matter what happens.

Hide your private sorrows under a smile and carry on."

'So, I went back to my work. I stopped being bitter and rebellious. I kept saying to myself: 'It is done. I can't change it. But I can and will carry on as he wished me to do. I threw all my mind and strength into my work. I wrote letters to soldiers—to other people's boys. I joined an adult-education class at night—seeking out new interests and making new friends. I can hardly believe the change that has come over me. I have ceased mourning over the past that is forever gone. I am living each day now with joy—just as my nephew would have wanted me to do. I have made peace with life. I have accepted my fate. I am now living a fuller and more complete life than I have ever known.'

Elizabeth Connley, out in Portland, Oregon, learned what all of us will have to learn sooner or later: namely, that we must accept and co-operate with the inevitable. 'It is so. It cannot be otherwise.' That is not an easy lesson to learn. Even kings on their thrones have to keep reminding themselves of it. The late George V had these framed words hanging on the wall of his library in Buckingham Palace: 'Teach me neither to cry for the moon nor over spilt milk.'

I spent twelve years working with cattle; yet I never saw a Jersey cow running a temperature because the pasture was burning up from a lack of rain or because of sleet and cold or because her boyfriend was paying too much attention to another heifer. The animals confront night, storms, and hunger calmly; so they never have nervous breakdowns or stomach ulcers; and they never go insane.

Am I advocating that we simply bow down to all the adversities that come our way? Not by a long shot! That is mere fatalism. As long as there is a chance that we can save a situation, let's fight! But when common sense tells us that we are up against something that is so—and cannot be otherwise—then, in the name of our sanity, let's not 'look before and after and pine for what is not.'

No one living has enough emotion and vigor to fight the inevitable and, at the same time, enough left over to create a new life. Choose one or the other. You can either bend with the inevitable sleet storms of life—or you can resist them and break!

I saw that happen on a farm I own in Missouri. I planted a score of trees on that farm. At first, they grew with astonishing rapidity. Then a sleet storm encrusted each twig and branch with a heavy coating of ice. Instead of bowing gracefully to their burden, these trees proudly resisted and broke and split under the load—and had to be destroyed. They hadn't learned the wisdom of the forests of the North. I have travelled hundreds of miles through the evergreen forests of Canada, yet I have never seen a spruce or a pine broken by sleet or ice. These evergreen forests know how to bend, how to bow down their branches, how to co-operate with the inevitable.

The masters of jujitsu teach their pupils to 'bend like the willow; don't resist like the oak.'

To break the worry habit before it breaks you,

Rule 4: Co-operate with the Inevitable.

Stress is the trash of modern life—we all generate it but if you don't
dispose of it properly, it will pile up and overtake your life.
—Terri Guillemets

By forgetting the past and by throwing myself into other interests,
I forget to worry.
—Jack Dempsey

PART 4

10

HOW TO ADD ONE HOUR
A DAY TO YOUR WAKING LIFE

Why am I writing a chapter on preventing fatigue in a book on preventing worry? That is simple: fatigue often produces worry, or, at least, it makes you susceptible to worry. Any medical student will tell you that fatigue lowers physical resistance to the common cold and hundreds of other diseases; and any psychiatrist will tell you that fatigue also lowers your resistance to the emotions of fear and worry. So preventing fatigue tends to prevent worry.

Did I say 'tends to prevent worry'? That is putting it mildly. Dr Edmund Jacobson goes much further. Dr Jacobson has written two books on relaxation: Progressive Relaxation and You Must Relax; and as director of the University of Chicago Labouratory for Clinical Physiology, he has spent years conducting investigations in using relaxation as a method in medical practice. He declares that any nervous or emotional state 'fails to exist in the presence of complete relaxation.' That is another way of saying: You cannot continue to worry if you relax.

So, to prevent fatigue and worry, the first rule is: Rest often. Rest before you get tired.

Why is that so important? Because fatigue accumulates with astonishing rapidity. The United States Army has discovered by repeated tests that even young men—men toughened by years of

Army training—can march better, and hold up longer, if they throw down their packs and rest ten minutes out of every hour. So the Army forces them to do just that. Your heart is just as smart as the U.S. Army. Your heart pumps enough blood through your body every day to fill a railway tank car. It exerts enough energy every twenty-four hours to shovel twenty tons of coal onto a platform three feet high. It does this incredible amount of work for fifty, seventy, or maybe ninety years. How can it stand it? Dr Walter B. Cannon, of the Harvard Medical School, explains it. He says, 'Most people have the idea that the heart is working all the time. As a matter of fact, there is a definite rest period after each contraction. When beating at a moderate rate of seventy pulses per minute, the heart is actually working only nine hours out of the twenty-four. In the aggregate its rest periods total a full fifteen hours per day.'

During World War II, Winston Churchill, in his late sixties and early seventies, was able to work sixteen hours a day, year after year, directing the war efforts of the British Empire. A phenomenal record. His secret? He worked in bed each morning until eleven o'clock, reading reports, dictating orders, making telephone calls, and holding important conferences. After lunch, he went to bed again and slept for an hour. In the evening, he went to bed once more and slept for two hours before having dinner at eight. He didn't cure fatigue. He didn't have to cure it. He prevented it. Because he rested frequently, he was able to work on, fresh and fit, until long past midnight.

In his excellent book, Why Be Tired ? Daniel W. Josselyn observes, 'Rest is not a matter of doing absolutely nothing. Rest is repair.' There is so much repair power in a short period of rest that even a five-minute nap will help to forestall fatigue! Connie Mack, the grand old man of baseball, told me that if he doesn't take an afternoon nap before a game, he is all tuckered out at around the fifth inning. But if he does go to sleep, if for only five minutes, he can last throughout an entire double-header without feeling tired.

When I asked Eleanor Roosevelt how she was able to carry such an exhausting schedule during the twelve years she was in the White

House, she said that before meeting a crowd or making a speech, she would often sit in a chair or davenport, close her eyes, and relax for twenty minutes.

How does this apply to you? If you are a stenographer, you can't take naps in the office as Mrs Roosevelt did; and if you are an accountant, you can't stretch out on the couch while discussing a financial statement with the boss. But if you live in a small city and go home for lunch, you may be able to take a ten-minute nap after lunch. That is what General George C. Marshall used to do. He felt he was so busy directing the U.S. Army in wartime that he had to rest at noon. If you are over fifty and feel you are too rushed to do it, then buy immediately all the life insurance you can get. Funerals come high—and suddenly—these days; and the little woman may want to take your insurance money and marry a younger man!

Let me repeat: do what the Army does—take frequent rests. Do what your heart does—rest before you get tired, and you will add one hour a day to your waking life.

> *Nothing in the universe can stop you from*
> *letting go and starting over.*
> —Guy Finley

> *I believe that you are only in control of so much.*
> *So whatever you are not in control of you can't worry about.*
> —Elizabeth Olsen

11

AVOID FATIGUE AND LOOK YOUNG

One day last autumn, my associate flew up to Boston to attend a
session of one of the most unusual medical classes in the world.
Medical? Well, yes. It meets once a week at the Boston Dispensary,
and the patients who attend it get regular and thorough medical
examinations before they are admitted. But actually this class is a
psychological clinic. Although it is officially called the Class in Applied
Psychology (formerly the Thought Control Class—a name suggested
by the first member), its real purpose is to deal with people who are
ill from worry. And many of these patients are emotionally disturbed
housewives.

How did such a class for worriers get started? Well, in 1930,
Dr Joseph H. Pratt—who, by the way, had been a pupil of Sir William
Osier—observed that many of the outpatients who came to the
Boston Dispensary apparently had nothing wrong with them at all
physically; yet they had practically all the symptoms that flesh is heir
to. One woman's hands were so crippled with 'arthritis' that she had
lost all use of them. Another was in agony with all the excruciating
symptoms of 'cancer of the stomach'. Others had backaches, headaches,
were chronically tired, or had vague aches and pains. They actually
felt these pains. But the most exhaustive medical examinations
showed that nothing whatever was wrong with these women—in
the physical sense. Many old-fashioned doctors would have said it
was all imagination—'all in the mind'.

But Dr Pratt realized that it was no use to tell these patients to
'go home and forget it.' He knew that most of these women didn't
want to be sick; if it was so easy to forget their ailments, they would

do so themselves. So what could be done?

He opened this class—to a chorus of doubts from the medical doubters on the sidelines. And the class worked wonders! In the eighteen years that have passed since it started, thousands of patients have been 'cured' by attending it. Some of the patients have been coming for years—as religious in their attendance as though going to church. My assistant talked to a woman who has hardly missed a session in more than nine years. She said that when she first went to the clinic, she was thoroughly convinced she had a floating kidney and some kind of heart ailment. She was so worried and tense that she occasionally lost her eyesight and had spells of blindness. Yet today she is confident and cheerful and in excellent health. She looked only about forty, yet she held one of her grandchildren asleep in her lap. 'I used to worry so much about my family troubles,' she said, 'that I wished I could die. But I learned at this clinic the futility of worrying. I learned to stop it. And I can honestly say now that my life is serene.'

Dr Rose Hilferding, the medical adviser of the class, said that she thought one of the best remedies for lightening worry is 'talking your troubles over with someone you trust. We call it catharsis,' she said. 'When patients come here, they can talk their troubles over at length, until they get them off their minds. Brooding over worries alone, and keeping them to oneself, causes great nervous tension. We all have to share our troubles. We have to share worry. We have to feel there is someone in the world who is willing to listen and able to understand.'

My assistant witnessed the great relief that came to one woman from talking out her worries. She had domestic worries, and when she first began to talk, she was like a wound-up spring. Then gradually, as she kept on talking, she began to calm down. At the end of the interview, she was actually smiling. Had the problem been solved? No, it wasn't that easy. What caused the change was talking to someone, getting a little advice and a little human sympathy. What had really worked the change was the tremendous healing value that lies in—words!

Psychoanalysis is based, to some extent, on this healing power of words. Ever since the days of Freud, analysts have known that a patient could find relief from his inner anxieties if he could talk, just talk. Why is this so? Maybe because by talking, we gain a little better insight into our troubles, get a better perspective. No one knows the whole answer. But all of us know that 'spitting it out' or 'getting it off our chests' brings almost instant relief.

So the next time we have an emotional problem, why don't we look around for someone to talk to? I don't mean, of course, to go around making pests of ourselves by whining and complaining to everyone in sight. Let's decide on someone we can trust, and make an appointment. Maybe a relative, a doctor, a lawyer, a minister, or priest. Then say to that person, 'I want your advice. I have a problem, and I wish you would listen while I put it in words. You may be able to advise me. You may see angles to this thing that I can't see myself. But even if you can't, you will help me tremendously if you will just sit and listen while I talk it out.'

Talking things out, then, is one of the principle therapies used at the Boston Dispensary Class. But here are some other ideas we picked up at the class—things you can do in your home.

Keep a notebook or scrapbook for 'inspirational' reading. Into this book you can paste all the poems, or short prayers, or quotations, which appeal to you personally and give you a lift. Then, when a rainy afternoon sends your spirits plunging down, perhaps you can find a recipe in this book for dispelling the gloom. Many patients at the Dispensary have kept such notebooks for years. They say it is a spiritual 'shot in the arm.'

Don't dwell too long on the shortcomings of others! Sure, your husband has faults! If he had been a saint, he never would have married you. Right? One woman at the class who found herself developing into a scolding, nagging, and haggard-faced wife, was brought up short with the question: 'What would you do if your husband died?' She was so shocked by the idea that she immediately sat down and drew up a list of all her husband's good points. She made quite a list. Why don't you try the same thing the next time you feel you married a tight-fisted tyrant? Maybe you'll find, after reading his virtues, that he's a man you'd like to meet!

Get interested in your neighbours! Develop a friendly, healthy interest in the people who share the life on your street. One ailing woman who felt herself so 'exclusive' that she hadn't any friends, was told to try to make up a story about the next person she met. She began, in the streetcar, to weave backgrounds and settings for the people she saw. She tried to imagine what their lives had been like. First thing you know, she was talking to people everywhere—and today she is happy, alert, and a charming human being, cured of her 'pains.'Make up a schedule for tomorrow's work before you go to bed tonight. The class found that many wives feel driven and harassed by the unending round of housework and things they must do. They never got their work finished. They were chased by the clock. To cure this sense of hurry, and worry, the suggestion was made that they draw up a schedule each night for the following day. What happened? More work accomplished; much less fatigue; a feeling of pride and achievement; and time left over to rest and to 'primp.' (Every woman ought to take some time out in the course of the day to primp and look pretty. My own guess is that when a woman knows she looks pretty, she has little use for 'nerves.')

Finally—avoid tension and fatigue. Relax! Relax! Nothing will make you look old sooner than tension and fatigue. Nothing will work such havoc with your freshness and looks! My assistant sat for an hour in the Boston Thought Control Class, while Professor Paul E. Johnson, the director, went over many of the principles we have already discussed—the rules for relaxing. At the end of ten minutes of these relaxing exercises, which my assistant did with the others, she was almost asleep sitting upright in her chair! Why is such stress laid on this physical relaxing? Because the clinic knows—as other doctors know—that if you're going to get the worry-kinks out of people, they've got to relax!

Yes, you, as a housewife, have got to relax! You have one great advantage—you can lie down whenever you want to, and you can lie on the floor! Strangely enough, a good hard floor is better to relax on than an inner-spring bed. It gives more resistance. It is good for the spine.

All right, then, here are some exercises you can do in your home. Try them for a week—and see what you do for your looks and disposition!

Lie flat on the floor whenever you feel tired. Stretch as tall as you can. Roll around if you want to. Do it twice a day.

Close your eyes. You might try saying, as Professor Johnson recommended, something like this: 'The sun is shining overhead. The sky is blue and sparkling. Nature is calm and in control of the world—and I, as nature's child, am in tune with the Universe.' Or—better still—pray!

If you cannot lie down, because the roast is in the oven and you can't spare the time, then you can achieve almost the same effect sitting down in a chair. A hard, upright chair is the best for relaxing. Sit upright in the chair like a seated Egyptian statue, and let your hands rest, palms down, on the tops of your thighs.

Now, slowly tense your toes—then let them relax. Tense the muscles in your legs—and let them relax. Do this slowly upward, with all the muscles of your body, until you get to the neck. Then let your head roll around heavily, as though it were a football. Keep saying to your muscles, 'Let go...let go...' Quiet your nerves with slow, steady breathing. Breathe from deep down. The yogis of India were right: rhythmical breathing is one of the best methods ever discovered for soothing the nerves.

Think of the wrinkles and frowns in your face, and smooth them all out. Loosen up the worry-creases you feel between your brows, and at the sides of your mouth. Do this twice a day, and maybe you won't have to go to a beauty parlor to get a massage. Maybe the lines will disappear from the inside out!

I know but one freedom and that is the freedom of the mind.
—Antoine de Saint-Exupéry

Instead of fretting about getting everything done, why not simply accept that being alive means having things to do? Then drop into full engagement with whatever you're doing, and let the worry go.
—Martha Beck

12

HOW TO KEEP FROM WORRYING ABOUT INSOMNIA

Do you worry when you can't sleep well? Then it may interest you to know that Samuel Untermyer—the famous international lawyer—never got a decent night's sleep in his life.

When Sam Untermyer went to college, he worried about two afflictions—asthma and insomnia. He couldn't seem to cure either, so he decided to do the next best thing—take advantage of his wakefulness. Instead of tossing and turning and worrying himself into a breakdown, he would get up and study. The result? He began ticking off honours in all of his classes, and became one of the prodigies of the College of the City of New York.

Even after he started to practice law, his insomnia continued. But Untermyer didn't worry. 'Nature,' he said, 'will take care of me.' Nature did. In spite of the small amount of sleep he was getting, his health kept up and he was able to work as hard as any of the young lawyers of the New York Bar. He even worked harder, for he worked while they slept!

At the age of twenty-one, Sam Untermyer was earning seventy-five thousand dollars a year; and other young attorneys rushed to courtrooms to study his methods. In 1931, he was paid—for handling one case—what was probably the highest lawyer's fee in all history: a cool million dollars—cash on the barrelhead.

Still he had insomnia—read half the night—and then got up at 5 a.m. and started dictating letters. By the time most people were just starting work, his day's work would be almost half done. He lived to the age of eighty-one, this man who had rarely had a sound night's sleep; but if he had fretted and worried about his insomnia, he would probably have wrecked his life.

We spend a third of our lives sleeping—yet nobody knows what sleep really is. We know it is a habit and a state of rest in which nature knits up the raveled sleeve of care, but we don't know how many hours of sleep each individual requires. We don't even know if we have to sleep at all!

Fantastic? Well, during the First World War, Paul Kern, a Hungarian soldier, was shot through the frontal lobe of his brain. He recovered from the wound, but, curiously enough, couldn't fall asleep. No matter what the doctors did—and they tried all kinds of sedatives and narcotics, even hypnotism—Paul Kern couldn't be put to sleep or even made to feel drowsy.

The doctors said he wouldn't live long. But he fooled them. He got a job, and went on living in the best of health for years. He would lie down and close his eyes and rest, but he got no sleep whatever. His case was a medical mystery that upset many of our beliefs about sleep.

Worrying about insomnia will hurt you far more than insomnia.

Dr Nathaniel Kleitman, professor at the University of Chicago, has done more research work on sleep than has any other living man. He is the world's expert on sleep. He declares that he has never known anyone to die from insomnia. To be sure, a man might worry about insomnia until he lowered his vitality and was swept away by germs. But it was the worry that did the damage, not the insomnia itself.

Dr Kleitman also says that the people who worry about insomnia usually sleep far more than they realize. The man who swears 'I never slept a wink last night' may have slept for hours without knowing it. For example, one of the most profound thinkers of the nineteenth century, Herbert Spencer, was an old bachelor, lived in a boardinghouse, and bored everyone with his talk about his insomnia. He even put 'stoppings' in his ears to keep out the noise and quiet his nerves. Sometimes he took opium to induce sleep. One night he and Professor Sayce of Oxford shared the same room at a hotel. The next morning Spencer declared he hadn't slept a wink all night. In reality, it was Professor Sayce who hadn't slept a wink. He had been kept awake all night by Spencer's snoring!

The first requisite for a good night's sleep is a feeling of security. We need to feel that some power greater than ourselves will take care of us until morning. Dr Thomas Hyslop, of the Great West Riding Asylum, stressed that point in an address before the British Medical Association. He said: 'One of the best sleep-producing agents which my years of practice have revealed to me is—prayer. I say this purely as a medical man. The exercise of prayer, in those who habitually exert it, must be regarded as the most adequate and normal of all the pacifiers of the mind and calmers of the nerves.'

'Let God—and let go.'

One of the best cures for insomnia is making yourself physically tired by gardening, swimming, tennis, golf, skiing, or by just plain physically exhausting work. If we get tired enough, nature will force us to sleep even while we are walking. To illustrate, when I was thirteen years old, my father shipped a carload of fat hogs to Saint Joe, Missouri. Since he got two free railroad passes, he took me along with him. Up until that time, I had never been in a town of more than four thousand. When I landed in Saint Joe—a city of sixty thousand—I was agog with excitement. I saw skyscrapers six stories high and—wonder of wonders—I saw a streetcar. I can close my eyes now and still see and hear that streetcar. After the most thrilling and exciting day of my life, Father and I took a train back to Raven-wood, Missouri. Arriving there at two o'clock in the morning, we had to walk four miles home to the farm. And here is the point of the story: I was so exhausted that I slept and dreamed as I walked.

I have often slept while riding horseback. And I am alive to tell it!

So, to keep from worrying about insomnia, here are five rules:

If you can't sleep, do what Samuel Untermyer did. Get up and work or read until you do feel sleepy.

Remember that no one was ever killed by lack of sleep. Worrying about insomnia usually causes far more damage than sleeplessness.

Try prayer.

Relax your body.

Exercise. Get yourself so physically tired you can't stay awake.

You'll never find a rainbow if you're looking down.

—Charlie Chaplin

The Lord is my shepherd; I shall not want. He maketh me to lie down in green pastures: he leadeth me beside the still waters...

—Psalm XXIII

PART 5

13

REMEMBER THAT NO ONE EVER KICKS
A DEAD DOG

An event occurred in 1929 that created a national sensation in educational circles. Learned men from all over America rushed to Chicago to witness the affair. A few years earlier, a young man by the name of Robert Hutchins had worked his way through Yale, acting as a waiter, a lumberjack, a tutor, and a clothesline salesman. Now, only eight years later, he was being inaugurated as president of the fourth richest university in America, the University of Chicago. His age? Thirty. Incredible! The older educators shook their heads. Criticism came roaring down upon this "boy wonder" like a rockslide. He was this and he was that—too young, inexperienced—his educational ideas were cockeyed. Even the newspapers joined in the attack.

The day he was inaugurated, a friend said to the father of Robert Maynard Hutchins: 'I was shocked this morning to read that newspaper editorial denouncing your son.'

'Yes,' the elder Hutchins replied, 'it was severe, but remember that no one ever kicks a dead dog.'

Yes, and the more important a dog is, the more satisfaction people get in kicking him. So when you are kicked and criticized, remember that it is often done because it gives the kicker a feeling of importance. It often means that you are accomplishing something and are worthy of attention. Many people get a sense of savage satisfaction out of denouncing those who are better educated than they are or more successful.

One hardly thinks of the president of Yale as a vulgar man; yet a former president of Yale, Timothy Dwight, apparently took huge delight in denouncing a man who was running for President of the United States. The president of Yale warned that if this man were elected President, 'we may see our wives and daughters the victims of legal prostitution, soberly dishonoured, speciously polluted; the outcasts of delicacy and virtue, the loathing of God and man.'

Sounds almost like a denunciation of Hitler, doesn't it? But it wasn't. It was a denunciation of Thomas Jefferson. Which Thomas Jefferson? Surely not the immortal Thomas Jefferson, the author of the Declaration of Independence, the patron saint of democracy? Yea, verily, that was the man.

What American do you suppose was denounced as a 'hypocrite,' 'an impostor,' and as 'little better than a murderer'? A newspaper cartoon depicted him on a guillotine, the big knife ready to cut off his head. Crowds jeered at him and hissed him as he rode through the streets. Who was he? George Washington.

If we are tempted to be worried about unjust criticism, here is

Rule 1: Remember that unjust criticism is often a disguised compliment. Remember that no one ever kicks a dead dog.

In this hour, I do not believe that any darkness will endure.
—J.R.R. Tolkien

Worry is the interest paid by those who borrow trouble.
—George Washington

14

DO THIS—AND CRITICISM CAN'T HURT YOU

I once interviewed Major General Smedley Butler—old 'Gimlet-Eye.' Old 'Hell-Devil' Butler! Remember him? The most colourful, swashbuckling general who ever commanded the United States Marines.

He told me that when he was young, he was desperately eager to be popular, wanted to make a good impression on everyone. In those days the slightest criticism smarted and stung. But he confessed that thirty years in the Marines had toughened his hide. 'I have been berated and insulted,' he said, 'and denounced as a yellow dog, a snake, and a skunk. I have been cursed by the experts. I have been called every possible combination of unprintable cuss words in the English language. Bother me? Huh! When I hear somebody cussing me now, I never turn my head to see who is talking.'

Maybe old 'Gimlet-Eye' Butler was too indifferent to criticism; but one thing is sure: most of us take the little jibes and javelins that are hurled at us far too seriously. I remember the time, years ago, when a reporter from the New York Sun attended a demonstration meeting of my adult-education classes and lampooned me and my work. Was I burned up? I took it as a personal insult. I telephoned Gil Hodges, the Chairman of the Executive Committee of the Sun, and practically demanded that he print an article stating the facts—instead of ridicule. I was determined to make the punishment fit the crime.

I am ashamed now of the way I acted. I realize now that half the people who bought the paper never saw that article. Half of those who read it regarded it as a source of innocent merriment. Half of those who gloated over it forgot all about it in a few weeks.

I realize now that people are not thinking about you and me or caring what is said about us. They are thinking about themselves—before breakfast, after breakfast, and right on until ten minutes past midnight. They would be a thousand times more concerned about a slight headache of their own than they would about the news of your death or mine.

Even if you and I are lied about, ridiculed, double-crossed, knifed in the back, and sold down the river by one out of every six of our most intimate friends—let's not indulge in an orgy of self-pity. Instead, let's remind ourselves that that's precisely what happened to Jesus. One of His twelve most intimate friends turned traitor for a bribe that would amount, in our modern money, to about nineteen dollars. Another one of His twelve most intimate friends openly deserted Jesus the moment He got into trouble, and declared three times that he didn't even know Jesus—and he swore as he said it. One out of six! That is what happened to Jesus. Why should you and I expect a better score?

I discovered years ago that although I couldn't keep people from criticizing me unjustly, I could do something infinitely more important: I could determine whether I would let the unjust condemnation disturb me.

Let's be clear about this: I am not advocating ignoring all criticism. Far from it. I am talking about ignoring only unjust criticism. I once asked Eleanor Roosevelt how she handled unjust criticism—and Allah knows she's had a lot of it. She probably has more ardent friends and more violent enemies than any other woman who ever lived in the White House.

She told me that as a young girl she was almost morbidly shy, afraid of what people might say. She was so afraid of criticism that one day she asked her aunt, Theodore Roosevelt's sister, for advice. She said, 'Auntie Bye, I want to do so-and-so. But I'm afraid of being criticized.'

Teddy Roosevelt's sister looked her in the eye and said, 'Never be bothered by what people say, as long as you know in your heart you are right.' Eleanor Roosevelt told me that that bit of advice proved to be her Rock of Gibraltar years later, when she was in the White House. She told me that the only way we can avoid all criticism is to be like a Dresden-china figure and stay on a shelf. 'Do what you feel in your heart to be right—for you'll be criticized, anyway. You'll be "damned if you do, and damned if you don't."' That is her advice.

When you and I are unjustly criticized, let's remember

Rule 2: Do the very best you can; and then put up your old umbrella and keep the rain of criticism from running down the back of your neck.

Choose to be optimistic, it feels better.

—Dalai Lama XIV

It's not the work which kills people, it's the worry. It's not the revolution that destroys machinery it's the friction.

—Henry Ward Beecher

15

HOW MY MOTHER AND FATHER CONQUERED WORRY

As I have said, I was born and brought up on a Missouri farm. Like most farmers of that day, my parents had pretty hard scratching. My mother had been a country schoolteacher and my father had been a farmhand working for twelve dollars a month. Mother made not only my clothes, but also the soap with which we washed our clothes.

We rarely had any cash—except once a year when we sold our hogs. We traded our butter and eggs at the grocery store for flour, sugar, coffee. When I was twelve years old, I didn't have as much as fifty cents a year to spend on myself. I can still remember the day we went to a Fourth-of-July celebration and Father gave me ten cents to spend as I wished. I felt the wealth of the Indies was mine.

I walked a mile to attend a one-room country school. I walked when the snow was deep and the thermometer shivered around twenty-eight degrees below zero. Until I was fourteen, I never had any rubbers or overshoes. During the long, cold winters, my feet were always wet and cold. As a child I never dreamed that anyone had dry, warm feet during the winter.

My parents slaved sixteen hours a day, yet we were constantly oppressed by debts and harassed by hard luck. One of my earliest memories is watching the flood waters of the 102 River rolling over our corn and hay fields, destroying everything. The floods destroyed our crops six years out of seven. Year after year, our hogs died of cholera and we burned them. I can close my eyes now and recall the pungent odor of burning hog flesh.

One year, the floods didn't come. We raised a bumper corn crop, bought feed cattle, and fattened them with our corn. But the floods might just as well have drowned our corn that year, for the price of fat cattle fell on the Chicago market; and after feeding and fattening the cattle, we got only thirty dollars more for them than what we had paid for them. Thirty dollars for a whole year's work!

No matter what we did, we lost money. I can still remember the mule colts that my father bought. We fed them for three years, hired men to break them, then shipped them to Memphis, Tennessee—and sold them for less than what we had paid for them three years previously.

After ten years of hard, grueling work, we were not only penniless; we were heavily in debt. Our farm was mortgaged. Try as hard as we might, we couldn't even pay the interest on the mortgage. The bank that held the mortgage abused, and insulted my father, and threatened to take his farm away from him. Father was forty-seven years old. After more than thirty years of hard work, he had nothing but debts and humiliation. It was more than he could take. He worried. His health broke. He had no desire for food; in spite of the hard physical work he was doing in the field all day, he had to take medicine to give him an appetite. He lost flesh. The doctor told my mother that he would be dead within six months. Father was so worried that he no longer wanted to live. I have often heard my mother say that when Father went to the barn to feed the horses and milk the cows, and didn't come back as soon as she expected, she would go out to the barn, fearing that she would find his body dangling from the end of a rope. One day as he returned home from Maryville, where the banker had threatened to foreclose the mortgage, he stopped his horses on a bridge crossing the 102 River, got off the wagon, and stood for a long time looking down at the water, debating with himself whether he should jump in and end it all.

Years later, Father told me that the only reason he didn't jump was because of my mother's deep, abiding, and joyous belief that if we loved God and kept His commandments, everything would come

out all right. Mother was right. Everything did come out all right in
the end. Father lived forty-two happy years longer, and died in 1941,
at the age of eighty-nine.

During all those years of struggle and heartache, my mother
never worried. She took all her troubles to God in prayer. Every night
before we went to bed, Mother would read a chapter from the Bible;
frequently Mother or Father would read these comforting words of
Jesus: "In my Father's house are many mansions... I go to prepare a
place for you...that where I am, there ye may be also." Then we all
knelt down before our chairs in that lonely Missouri farmhouse and
prayed for God's love and protection.

My mother wanted me to devote my life to religious work. I
thought seriously of becoming a foreign missionary. Then I went away
to college; and gradually, as the years passed, a change came over me.
I studied biology, science, philosophy, and comparative religions. I
read books on how the Bible was written. I began to question many
of its assertions. I began to doubt many of the narrow doctrines
taught by the country preachers of that day. I was bewildered. Like
Walt Whitman, I 'felt the curious, abrupt questionings stir within me.'
I didn't know what to believe. I saw no purpose in life. I stopped
praying. I became an agnostic. I believed that all life was planless and
aimless. I believed that human beings had no more divine purpose
than had the dinosaurs that roamed the earth two hundred million
years ago. I felt that someday the human race would perish—just as
the dinosaurs had. I knew that science taught that the sun was slowly
cooling, and that when its temperature fell even ten per cent, no
form of life could exist on earth. I sneered at the idea of a beneficent
God who had created man in His own likeness. I believed that the
billions upon billions of suns whirling through black, cold, lifeless
space had been created by blind force. Maybe they had never been
created at all. Maybe they had existed forever—just as time and space
have always existed.

Do I profess to know the answers to all those questions now? No.
No man has ever been able to explain the mystery of the universe—

the mystery of life. We are surrounded by mysteries. The operation of your body is a profound mystery. So is the electricity in your home. So is the flower in the crannied wall. So is the green grass outside your window. Charles F. Kettering, the guiding genius of General Motors Research Labouratories, has been giving Antioch College thirty thousand dollars a year out of his own pocket to try to discover why grass is green. He declares that if we knew how grass is able to transform sunlight, water, and carbon dioxide into food sugar, we could transform civilization.

Even the operation of the engine in your car is a profound mystery. General Motors Research Labouratories have spent years of time and millions of dollars trying to find out how and why a spark in the cylinder sets off an explosion that makes your car run; and they don't know the answer.

The fact that we don't understand the mysteries of our bodies or electricity or a gas engine doesn't keep us from using and enjoying them. The fact that I don't understand the mysteries of prayer and religion, no longer keeps me from enjoying the richer, happier life that religion brings. At long last, I realize the wisdom of Santayana's words: 'Man is not made to understand life, but to live it.'

I have gone back—well, I was about to say that I had gone back to religion; but that would not be accurate. I have gone forward to a new concept of religion. I no longer have the faintest interest in the differences in creeds that divide the churches. But I am tremendously interested in what religion does for me, just as I am interested in what electricity and good food and water do for me. They help me to lead a richer, fuller, happier life. But religion does far more than that. It brings me spiritual values. It gives me, as William James put it, 'a new zest for life…more life, a larger, richer, more satisfying life.' It gives me faith, hope, and courage. It banishes tensions, anxieties, fears, and worries. It gives purpose to my life—and direction. It vastly improves my happiness. It gives me abounding health. It helps me to create for myself 'an oasis of peace amidst the whirling sands of life.'

Today, even psychiatrists are becoming modern evangelists. They are not urging us to lead religious lives to avoid hell-fires in the next world, but they are urging us to lead religious lives to avoid the hell-fires of this world—the hell-fires of stomach ulcer, angina pectoris, nervous breakdowns, and insanity.

On the average, someone commits suicide in the United States every thirty-five minutes. On the average, someone goes insane every hundred and twenty seconds. Most of these suicides—and probably many of the tragedies of insanity—could have been prevented if these people had only had the solace and peace that are found in religion and prayer.

One of the most distinguished psychiatrists living, Dr Carl Jung, says on page 264 of his book Modern Man in Search of a Soul, 'During the past thirty years, people from all the civilized countries of the earth have consulted me. I have treated many hundreds of patients. Among all my patients in the second half of life—that is to say, over thirty-five—there has not been one whose problem in the last resort was not that of finding a religious outlook on life. It is safe to say that every one of them fell ill because he had lost that which the living religions of every age have given to their followers, and none of them has been really healed who did not regain his religious outlook.'

The late Mahatma Gandhi, the greatest Indian leader since Buddha, would have collapsed if he had not been inspired by the sustaining power of prayer. How do I know? Because Gandhi himself said so. 'Without prayer,' he wrote, 'I should have been a lunatic long ago.'

Thousands of people could give similar testimony. My own father—well, as I have already said, my own father would have drowned himself had it not been for my mother's prayers and faith. Probably thousands of the tortured souls who are now screaming in our insane asylums could have been saved if they had only turned to a higher power for help instead of trying to fight life's battles alone.

When we are harassed and reach the limit of our own strength, many of us then turn in desperation to God—'There are no atheists in foxholes.' But why wait till we are desperate? Why not renew our strength every day? Why wait even until Sunday? For years I have had the habit of dropping into empty churches on weekday afternoons. When I feel that I am too rushed and hurried to spare a few minutes to think about spiritual things, I say to myself: 'Wait a minute, Dale Carnegie, wait a minute. Why all the feverish hurry and rush, little man? You need to pause and acquire a little perspective.' At such times, I frequently drop into the first church that I find open. Although I am a Protestant, I frequently, on weekday afternoons, drop into St. Patrick's Cathedral on Fifth Avenue, and remind myself that I'll be dead in another thirty years, but that the great spiritual truths that all churches teach are eternal. I close my eyes and pray. I find that doing this calms my nerves, rests my body, clarifies my perspective, and helps me revalue my values. May I recommend this practice to you?

During the past six years that I have been writing this book, I have collected hundreds of examples and concrete cases of how men and women conquered fear and worry by prayer. I have in my filing cabinet folders bulging with case histories.

I know men who regard religion as something for women and children and preachers. They pride themselves on being 'he-men' who can fight their battles alone.

How surprised they might be to learn that some of the most famous 'he-men' in the world pray every day. For example, 'he-man' Jack Dempsey told me that he never goes to bed without saying his prayers. He told me that he never eats a meal without first thanking God for it. He told me that he prayed every day when he was training for a bout, and that when he was fighting, he always prayed just before the bell sounded for each round. 'Praying,' he said, 'helped me fight with courage and confidence.'

'He-man' J. Pierpont Morgan, the greatest financier of his age, often went alone to Trinity Church, at the head of Wall Street, on Saturday afternoons and knelt in prayer.

When 'he-man' Eisenhower flew to England to take supreme

command of the British and American forces, he took only one book on the plane with him—the Bible.

'He-man' General Mark Clark told me that he read his Bible every day during the war and knelt down in prayer. So did Chiang Kai-shek, and General Montgomery—'Monty of El Alamein.' So did Lord Nelson at Trafalgar. So did General Washington, Robert E. Lee, Stonewall Jackson, and scores of other great military leaders.

A lot of 'he-men' are discovering that. If we are worried and anxious—why not try God? Why not, as Immanuel Kant said, 'accept a belief in God because we need such a belief?' Why not link ourselves now 'with the inexhaustible motive power that spins the universe?'

Even if you are not a religious person by nature or training—even if you are an out-and-out skeptic—prayer can help you much more than you believe, for it is a practical thing. What do I mean, practical? I mean that prayer fulfills these three very basic psychological needs which all people share, whether they believe in God or not:

Prayer helps us to put into words exactly what is troubling us. Praying, in a way, is very much like writing our problem down on paper. If we ask help for a problem—even from God—we must put it into words.

Prayer gives us a sense of sharing our burdens, of not being alone. Few of us are so strong that we can bear our heaviest burdens, our most agonizing troubles, all by ourselves. Sometimes our worries are of so intimate a nature that we cannot discuss them even with our closest relatives or friends. Then prayer is the answer. Any psychiatrist will tell us that when we are pent-up and tense, and in an agony of spirit, it is therapeutically good to tell someone our troubles. When we can't tell anyone else—we can always tell God.

Prayer puts into force an active principle of doing. It's a first step towards action. I doubt if anyone can pray for some fulfillment, day after day, without benefiting from it—in other words, without taking some steps to bring it to pass. The world-famous scientist, Dr Alexis Carrel, said: 'Prayer is the most powerful form of energy one can generate.' So why not make use of it? Call it God or Allah or

Spirit—why quarrel with definitions as long as the mysterious powers of nature take us in hand?

> *Some people grumble that roses have thorns;*
> *I am grateful that thorns have roses.*
>
> —Alphonse Karr

> *We never worry about the big things, just the small things.*
>
> —Travis Barker

16

EIGHT WORDS THAT CAN TRANSFORM YOUR LIFE

A few years ago, I was asked to answer this question on a radio program: 'What is the biggest lesson you have ever learned?'

That was easy: by far the most vital lesson I have ever learned is the importance of what we think. If I knew what you think, I would know what you are. Our thoughts make us what we are. Our mental attitude is the X factor that determines our fate. Emerson said: 'A man is what he thinks about all day long.' How could he possibly be anything else?

I now know with a conviction beyond all doubt that the biggest problem you and I have to deal with—in fact, almost the only problem we have to deal with—is choosing the right thoughts. If we can do that, we will be on the highroad to solving all our problems. The great philosopher who ruled the Roman Empire, Marcus Aurelius, summed it up in eight words—eight words that can determine your destiny: 'Our life is what our thoughts make it.'

Yes, if we think happy thoughts, we will be happy. If we think miserable thoughts, we will be miserable. If we think fear thoughts, we will be fearful. If we think sickly thoughts, we will probably be ill. If we think failure, we will certainly fail. If we wallow in self-pity, everyone will want to shun us and avoid us. 'You are not,' said Norman Vincent Peale, 'you are not what you think you are; but what you think, you are.'

Am I advocating a habitual Pollyanna attitude towards all our problems? No, unfortunately, life isn't so simple as all that. But I am advocating that we assume a positive attitude instead of a negative attitude. In other words, we need to be concerned about our problems, but not worried. What is the difference between concern and worry? Let me illustrate. Every time I cross the traffic-jammed streets of New York, I am concerned about what I am doing—but not worried. Concern means realizing what the problems are, and calmly taking steps to meet them. Worrying means going around in maddening, futile circles.

A man can be concerned about his serious problems and still walk with his chin up and a carnation in his buttonhole. I have seen Lowell Thomas do just that. I once had the privilege of being associated with Lowell Thomas in presenting his famous films on the Allenby-Lawrence campaigns in World War I. He and his assistants had photographed the war on half a dozen fronts; and, best of all, had brought back a pictorial record of T.E. Lawrence and his colourful Arabian army, and a film record of Allenby's conquest of the Holy Land. His illustrated talks entitled 'With Allenby in Palestine and Lawrence in Arabia' were a sensation in London—and around the world. The London opera season was postponed for six weeks so that he could continue telling his tale of high adventure, and showing his pictures at Covent Garden Royal Opera House. After his sensational success in London came a triumphant tour of many countries. Then he spent two years preparing a film record of life in India and Afghanistan. After a lot of incredibly bad luck, the impossible happened: he found himself broke in London. I was with him at the time. I remember we had to eat cheap meals at the Lyons' Corner House restaurants. We couldn't have eaten even there if Mr Thomas had not borrowed money from a Scotsman—James McBey, the renowned artist. Here is the point of the story: even when Lowell Thomas was facing huge debts and severe dis- appointments, he was concerned, but not worried. He knew that if he let his reverses get him down, he would be worthless to everyone, including his creditors.

So each morning before he started out, he bought a flower, put it in his buttonhole, and went swinging down Oxford Street with his head high and his step spirited. He thought positive, courageous thoughts and refused to let defeat defeat him. To him, being licked was all a part of the game—the useful training you had to expect if you wanted to get to the top.

Our mental attitude has an almost unbelievable effect even on our physical powers. The famous British psychiatrist, J.A. Hadfield, gives a striking illustration of that fact in his splendid 54-page booklet: The Psychology of Power. 'I asked three men,' he writes, 'to submit themselves to test the effect of mental suggestion on their strength, which was measured by gripping a dynamometer.' He told them to grip the dynamometer with all their might. He had them do this under three different sets of conditions.

When he tested them under normal waking conditions, their average grip was 101 pounds.

When he tested them after he had hypnotized them and told them that they were very weak, they could grip only 29 pounds—less than a third of their normal strength. (One of these men was a prize fighter; and when he was told under hypnosis that he was weak, he remarked that his arm felt 'tiny, just like a baby's.')

When Captain Hadfield then tested these men a third time, telling them under hypnosis that they were very strong, they were able to grip an average of 142 pounds. When their minds were filled with positive thoughts of strength, they increased their actual physical powers almost five hundred per cent.

Such is the incredible power of our mental attitude.

To illustrate the magic power of thought, let me tell you one of the most astounding stories in the annals of America. I could write a book about it; but let's be brief. On a frosty October night, shortly after the close of the Civil War, a homeless, destitute woman, who was little more than a wanderer on the face of the earth, knocked at the door of 'Mother' Webster, the wife of a retired sea captain, living in Amesbury, Massachusetts.

Opening the door, 'Mother' Webster saw a frail little creature, 'scarcely more than a hundred pounds of frightened skin and bones.' The stranger, a Mrs Glover, explained she was seeking a home where she could think and work out a great problem that absorbed her day and night.

'Why not stay here?' Mrs Webster replied. 'I'm all alone in this big house.'

Mrs Glover might have remained indefinitely with 'Mother' Webster if the latter's son-in-law, Bill Ellis, hadn't come up from New York for a vacation. When he discovered Mrs Glover's presence, he shouted: 'I'll have no vagabonds in this house;' and he shoved this homeless woman out of the door. A driving rain was falling. She stood shivering in the rain for a few minutes, and then started down the road, looking for shelter.

Here is the astonishing part of the story. That 'vagabond' whom Bill Ellis put out of the house was destined to have as much influence on the thinking of the world as any other woman who ever walked this earth. She is now known to millions of devoted followers as Mary Baker Eddy—the founder of Christian Science.

Yet, until this time, she had known little in life except sickness, sorrow, and tragedy. Her first husband had died shortly after their marriage. Her second husband had deserted her and eloped with a married woman. He later died in a poorhouse. She had only one child, a son; and she was forced, because of poverty, illness, and jealousy, to give him up when he was four years old. She lost all track of him and never saw him again for thirty-one years.

Because of her own ill health, Mrs Eddy had been interested for years in what she called 'the science of mind healing.' But the dramatic turning point in her life occurred in Lynn, Massachusetts. Walking downtown one cold day, she slipped and fell on the icy pavement— and was knocked unconscious. Her spine was so injured that she was convulsed with spasms. Even the doctor expected her to die. If by some miracle she lived, he declared that she would never walk again.

Lying on what was supposed to be her deathbed, Mary Baker

Eddy opened her Bible, and was led, she declared, by divine guidance to read these words from Saint Matthew: 'And, behold, they brought to him a man sick of the palsy, lying on a bed: and Jesus...said unto the sick of the palsy; Son, be of good cheer; thy sins be forgiven thee.... Arise, take up thy bed, and go unto thine house. And he arose, and departed to his house.'

These words of Jesus, she declared, produced within her such a strength, such a faith, such a surge of healing power, that she 'immediately got out of bed and walked.'

'That experience,' Mrs Eddy declared, 'was the falling apple that led me to the discovery of how to be well myself, and how to make others so... I gained the scientific certainty that all causation was Mind, and every effect a mental phenomenon.'

Such was the way in which Mary Baker Eddy became the founder and high priestess of a new religion: Christian Science—the only great religious faith ever established by a woman—a religion that has encircled the globe.

You are probably saying to yourself by now: 'This man, Carnegie, is proselytizing for Christian Science.' No. You are wrong. I am not a Christian Scientist. But the longer I live, the more deeply I am convinced of the tremendous power of thought. As a result of thirty-five years spent in teaching adults, I know men and women can banish worry, fear, and various kinds of illnesses, and can transform their lives by changing their thoughts. I know! I know!! I know!' I have seen such incredible transformations performed hundreds of times. I have seen them so often that I no longer wonder at them.

For example, one of these incredible transformations, which illustrate the power of thought, happened to one of my students. He had a nervous breakdown. What brought it on? Worry. This student told me, 'I worried about everything: I worried because I was too thin; because I thought I was losing my hair; because I feared I would never make enough money to get married; because I felt I would never make a good father; because I feared I was losing the girl I wanted to marry; because I felt I was not living a good life.

I worried about the impression I was making on other people. I worried because I thought I had stomach ulcers. I could no longer work; I gave up my job. I built up tension inside me until I was like a boiler without a safety valve. The pressure got so unbearable that something had to give—and it did. If you have never had a nervous breakdown, pray God that you never do, for no pain of the body can exceed the excruciating pain of an agonized mind.

'My breakdown was so severe that I couldn't talk even to my own family. I had no control over my thoughts. I was filled with fear. I would jump at the slightest noise. I avoided everybody. I would break out crying for no apparent reason at all.

'Every day was one of agony. I felt that I was deserted by everybody—even God. I was tempted to jump into the river and end it all.

'I decided instead to take a trip to Florida, hoping that a change of scene would help me. As I stepped on the train, my father handed me a letter and told me not to open it until I reached Florida. I landed in Florida during the height of the tourist season. Since I couldn't get in a hotel, I rented a sleeping room in a garage. I tried to get a job on a tramp freighter out of Miami, but had no luck. So I spent my time at the beach. I was more wretched in Florida than I had been at home; so I opened the envelope to see what Dad had written. His note said, "Son, you are 1,500 miles from home, and you don't feel any different, do you? I knew you wouldn't, because you took with you the one thing that is the cause of all your trouble, that is, yourself. There is nothing wrong with either your body or your mind. It is not the situations you have met that have thrown you; it is what you think of these situations. 'As a man thinketh in his heart, so is he.' When you realize that, son, come home, for you will be cured."

'Dad's letter made me angry. I was looking for sympathy, not instruction. I was so mad that I decided then and there that I would never go home. That night as I was walking down one of the side streets of Miami, I came to a church where services were going on. Having no place to go, I drifted in and listened to a sermon on the text: "He who conquers his spirit is mightier than he who taketh a city." Sitting in the sanctity of the house of God and hearing the same thoughts that my Dad had written in his letter—all this swept the accumulated litter out of my brain. I was able to think clearly and sensibly for the first time in my life. I realized what a fool I had been. I was shocked to see myself in my true light: here I was, wanting to change the whole world and everyone in it—when the only thing that needed changing was the focus of the lens of the camera, which was my mind.

'The next morning I packed and started home. A week later I was back on the job. Four months later I married the girl I had been afraid of losing. We now have a happy family of five children. God has been good to me both materially and mentally. At the time of the breakdown I was a night foreman of a small department handling eighteen people. I am now superintendent of carton manufacture in charge of over four hundred and fifty people. Life is much fuller and friendlier. I believe I appreciate the true values of life now. When moments of uneasiness try to creep in (as they will in everyone's life), I tell myself to get that camera back in focus, and everything is O.K.

'I can honestly say that I am glad I had the breakdown, because I found out the hard way what power our thoughts can have over our mind and our body. Now I can make my thoughts work for me instead of against me. I can see now that Dad was right when he said it wasn't outward situations that had caused all my suffering, but what I thought of those situations. And as soon as I realized that, I was cured—and stayed cured.' Such was the experience of this student.

I am deeply convinced that our peace of mind and the joy we get out of living depends not on where we are, or what we have, or who we are, but solely upon our mental attitude. Outward conditions have very little to do with it. For example, let's take the case of old John Brown, who was hanged for seizing the United States arsenal at Harpers Ferry and trying to incite the slaves to rebellion. He rode away to the gallows, sitting on his coffin. The jailer who rode beside him was nervous and worried. But old John Brown was calm and cool.

Looking up at the Blue Ridge mountains of Virginia, he exclaimed, "What a beautiful country! I never had an opportunity to really see it before."

Or take the case of Robert Falcon Scott and his companions—the first Englishmen ever to reach the South Pole. Their return trip was probably the cruelest journey ever undertaken by man. Their food was gone—and so was their fuel. They could no longer march because a howling blizzard roared down over the rim of the earth for eleven days and nights—a wind so fierce and sharp that it cut ridges in the polar ice. Scott and his companions knew they were going to die; and they had brought a quantity of opium along for just such an emergency. A big dose of opium, and they could all lie down to pleasant dreams, never to wake again. But they ignored the drug, and died 'singing ringing songs of cheer.' We know they did because of a farewell letter found with their frozen bodies by a searching party, eight months later.

Yes, if we cherish creative thoughts of courage and calmness, we can enjoy the scenery while sitting on our coffin, riding to the gallows; or we can fill our tents with 'ringing songs of cheer,' while starving and freezing to death.

If half a century of living has taught me anything at all, it has taught me that 'nothing can bring you peace but yourself.' What do I mean? Have I the colossal effrontery to tell you to your face—when you are mowed down by troubles, and your nerves are sticking out like wires and curling up at the ends—have I the colossal effrontery to tell you that, under those conditions, you can change your mental attitude by an effort of the will? Yes, I mean precisely that! And that is not all. I am going to show you how to do it. It may take a little effort, but the secret is simple.

William James, who has never been topped in his knowledge of practical psychology, once made this observation: 'Action seems to follow feeling, but really action and feeling go together; and by regulating the action, which is under the more direct control of the will, we can indirectly regulate the feeling, which is not.'

In other words, William James tells us that we cannot instantly change our emotions just by 'making up our minds to'—but that we can change our actions. And that when we change our actions, we will automatically change our feelings.

Does that simple trick work? Try it yourself. Put a big, broad, honest-to-God smile on your face; throw back your shoulders; take a good, deep breath; and sing a snatch of song. If you can't sing, whistle. If you can't whistle, hum. You will quickly discover what William James was talking about—that it is physically impossible to remain blue or depressed while you are acting out the symptoms of being radiantly happy!

This is one of the little basic truths of nature that can easily work miracles in all of our lives. I know a woman in California—I won't mention her name—who could wipe out all of her miseries in twenty-four hours if only she knew this secret. She's old, and she's a widow—that's sad, I admit—but does she try to act happy? No; if you ask her how she is feeling, she says, 'Oh, I'm all right'—but the expression on her face and the whine in her voice say, 'Oh, God, if you only knew the troubles I've seen!' She seems to reproach you for being happy in her presence. Hundreds of women are worse off than she is: her husband left her enough insurance to last the rest of her life, and she has married children to give her a home. But I've rarely seen her smile. She complains that all three of her sons-in-law are stingy and selfish—although she is a guest in their homes for months at a time. And she complains that her daughters never give her presents—although she hoards her own money carefully, 'for my old age.' She is a blight on herself and her unfortunate family! But does it have to be so? That is the pity of it—she could change herself from a miserable, bitter, and unhappy old woman into an honoured and beloved member of the family—if she wanted to change. And all she would have to do to work this transformation would be to start acting cheerful; start acting as though she had a little love to give away—instead of squandering it all on her own unhappy and embittered self.

I know a man in Indiana—H.J. Englert, of 1335 11th Street, Tell City, Indiana—who is still alive today because he discovered this secret. Ten years ago Mr Englert had a case of scarlet fever; and when he recovered, he found he had developed nephritis, a kidney disease. He tried all kinds of doctors, 'even quacks,' he informs me, but nothing could cure him.

Then, a short time ago, he got other complications. His blood pressure soared. He went to a doctor, and was told that his blood pressure was hitting the top at 214. He was told that it was fatal—that the condition was progressive, and he had better put his affairs in order at once.

'I went home,' he says, 'and made sure that my insurance was all paid up, then I apologized to my Maker for all my mistakes, and settled down to gloomy meditations. I made everyone unhappy. My wife and family were miserable, and I was buried deep in depression myself. However, after a week of wallowing in self-pity, I said to myself, "You're acting like a fool! You may not die for a year yet, so why not try to be happy while you're here?" I threw back my shoulders, put a smile on my face, and attempted to act as though everything were normal. I admit it was an effort at first—but I forced myself to be pleasant and cheerful; and this not only helped my family, but it also helped me.

'The first thing I knew, I began to feel better—almost as well as I pretended to feel! The improvement went on. And today—months after I was supposed to be in my grave—I am not only happy, well, and alive, but my blood pressure is down! I know one thing for certain: the doctor's prediction would certainly have come true if I had gone on thinking "dying" thoughts of defeat. But I gave my body a chance to heal itself, by nothing in the world but a change of mental attitude!'

Let me ask you a question: If merely acting cheerful and thinking positive thoughts of health and courage could save this man's life, why should you and I tolerate for one minute more our minor glooms and depressions? Why make ourselves, and everyone around us, unhappy and blue, when it is possible for us to start creating happiness by merely acting cheerful?

Let's fight for our happiness!

Let's fight for our happiness by following a daily program of cheerful and constructive thinking. Here is such a program. It is entitled "Just for Today." I found this program so inspiring that I gave away hundreds of copies. It was written thirty-six years ago by the late Sibyl F. Partridge. If you and I follow it, we will eliminate most of our worries and increase immeasurably our portion of what the French call la ioie de vivre.

JUST FOR TODAY

Just for today I will be happy. This assumes that what Abraham Lincoln said is true, that 'most folks are about as happy as they make up their minds to be.' Happiness is from within; it is not a matter of externals.

Just for today I will try to adjust myself to what is, and not try to adjust everything to my own desires. I will take my family, my business, and my luck as they come and fit myself to them.

Just for today I will take care of my body. I will exercise it, care for it, nourish it, not abuse it nor neglect it, so that it will be a perfect machine for my bidding.

Just for today I will try to strengthen my mind. I will learn something useful. I will not be a mental loafer. I will read something that requires effort, thought and concentration.

Just for today I will exercise my soul in three ways; I will do somebody a good turn and not get found out. I will do at least two things I don't want to do, as William James suggests, just for exercise.

Just for today I will be agreeable. I will look as well as I can, dress as becomingly as possible, talk low, act courteously, be liberal with praise, criticize not at all, nor find fault with anything and not try to regulate nor improve anyone.

Just for today I will try to live through this day only, not to tackle my whole life problem at once. I can do things for twelve hours that would appall me if I had to keep them up for a lifetime.

Just for today I will have a program. I will write down what I expect to do every hour. I may not follow it exactly, but I will have it. It will eliminate two pests, hurry and indecision.

Just for today I will have a quiet half-hour all by myself and relax. In this half-hour sometimes I will think of God, so as to get a little more perspective into my life.

Just for today I will be unafraid, especially I will not be afraid to be happy, to enjoy what is beautiful, to love, and to believe that those I love, love me.

If we want to develop a mental attitude that will bring us peace and happiness, here is

Rule 1: Think and act cheerfully, and you will feel cheerful.

I am so far from being a pessimist...on the contrary, in spite of my scars, I am tickled to death at life.
—Eugene O'Neill

If you look into your own heart, and you find nothing wrong there, what is there to worry about? What is there to fear?
—Confucius

17

NEVER WORRY ABOUT INGRATITUDE

I recently met a businessman in Texas who was burned up with indignation. I was warned that he would tell me about it within fifteen minutes after I met him. He did. The incident he was angry about had occurred eleven months previously, but he was still burned up about it. He couldn't talk of anything else. He had given his thirty-four employees ten thousand dollars in Christmas bonuses— approximately three hundred dollars each—and no one had thanked him. 'I am sorry,' he complained bitterly, 'that I ever gave them a penny!'

'An angry man,' said Confucius, 'is always full of poison.' This man was so full of poison that I honestly pitied him. He was about sixty years old. Now, life-insurance companies figure that, on the average, we will live slightly more than two thirds of the difference between our present age and eighty. So this man—if he was lucky—probably had about fourteen or fifteen years to live. Yet he had already wasted almost one of his few remaining years by his bitterness and resentment over an event that was past and gone. I pitied him.

Instead of wallowing in resentment and self-pity, he might have asked himself why he didn't get any appreciation. Maybe he had underpaid and overworked his employees. Maybe they considered a Christmas bonus not a gift, but something they had earned. Maybe he was so critical and unapproachable that no one dared or cared to thank him. Maybe they felt he gave the bonus because most of the profits were going for taxes anyway.

On the other hand, maybe the employees were selfish, mean, and ill-mannered. Maybe this. Maybe that. I don't know any more about it than you do. But I do know that Dr Samuel Johnson said:

'Gratitude is a fruit of great cultivation. You do not find it among gross people.'

Here is the point I am trying to make: this man made the human and distressing mistake of expecting gratitude. He just didn't know human nature.

If you saved a man's life, would you expect him to be grateful? You might—but Samuel Leibowitz, who was a famous criminal lawyer before he became a judge, saved seventy-eight men from going to the electric chair! How many of these men, do you suppose, stopped to thank Samuel Leibowitz, or ever took the trouble to send him a Christmas card? How many? Guess.... That's right—none.

Christ healed ten lepers in one afternoon—but how many of those lepers even stopped to thank Him? Only one. Look it up in Saint Luke. When Christ turned around to His disciples and asked, 'Where are the other nine?' they had all run away. Disappeared without thanks! Let me ask you a question: Why should you and I—or this businessman in Texas—expect more thanks for our small favors than was given to Jesus Christ?

And when it comes to money matters! Well, that is even more hopeless. Charles Schwab told me that he had once saved a bank cashier who had speculated in the stock market with funds belonging to the bank. Schwab put up the money to save this man from going to the penitentiary. Was the cashier grateful? Oh, yes, for a little while. Then he turned against Schwab and reviled him and denounced him—the very man who had kept him out of jail!

If you gave one of your relatives a million dollars, would you expect him to be grateful? Andrew Carnegie did just that. But if Andrew Carnegie had come back from the grave a little while later, he would have been shocked to find this relative cursing him! Why? Because Old Andy had left 365 million dollars to public charities—and had 'cut him off with one measly million,' as he put it.

That's how it goes. Human nature has always been human nature—and it probably won't change in your lifetime. So why not accept it? Why not be as realistic about it as was old Marcus Aurelius, one of the wisest men who ever ruled the Roman Empire. He wrote in his diary one day: 'I am going to meet people today who talk too much—people who are selfish, egotistical, ungrateful. But I won't be surprised or disturbed, for I couldn't imagine a world without such people.'

That makes sense, doesn't it? If you and I go around grumbling about ingratitude, who is to blame? Is it human nature—or is it our ignorance of human nature? Let's not expect gratitude. Then, if we get some occasionally, it will come as a delightful surprise. If we don't get it, we won't be disturbed.

Here is the first point I am trying to make in this chapter: It is natural for people to forget to be grateful; so, if we go around expecting gratitude, we are headed straight for a lot of heartaches.

I know a woman in New York who is always complaining because she is lonely. Not one of her relatives wants to go near her—and no wonder. If you visit her, she will tell you for hours what she did for her nieces when they were children: she nursed them through the measles and the mumps and the whooping cough; she boarded them for years; she helped to send one of them through business school, and she made a home for the other until she got married.

Do the nieces come to see her? Oh, yes, now and then, out of a spirit of duty. But they dread these visits. They know they will have to sit and listen for hours to half-veiled reproaches. They will be treated to an endless litany of bitter complaints and self-pitying sighs. And when this woman can no longer bludgeon, browbeat, or bully her nieces into coming to see her, she has one of her 'spells.' She develops a heart attack.

Is the heart attack real? Oh, yes. The doctors say she has 'a nervous heart,' suffers from palpitations. But the doctors also say they can do nothing for her—her trouble is emotional.

What this woman really wants is love and attention. But she calls it 'gratitude.' And she will never get gratitude or love, because she demands it. She thinks it's her due.

There are thousands of women like her, women who are ill from 'ingratitude,' loneliness, and neglect. They long to be loved; but the only way in this world that they can ever hope to be loved is to stop asking for it and to start pouring out love without hope of return.

Does that sound like sheer, impractical, visionary idealism? It isn't. It is just horse sense. It is a good way for you and me to find the happiness we long for. I know. I have seen it happen right in my own family. My own mother and father gave for the joy of helping others. We were poor—always overwhelmed by debts. Yet, poor as we were, my father and mother always managed to send money every year to an orphans' home. The Christian Home in Council Bluffs, Iowa. Mother and Father never visited that home. Probably no one thanked them for their gifts—except by letter—but they were richly repaid, for they had the joy of helping little children—without wishing for or expecting any gratitude in return.

After I left home, I would always send Father and Mother a check at Christmas and urge them to indulge in a few luxuries for themselves. But they rarely did. When I came home a few days before Christmas, Father would tell me of the coal and groceries they had bought for some 'widder woman' in town who had a lot of children and no money to buy food and fuel. What joy they got out of these gifts—the joy of giving without expecting anything whatever in return!

I believe my father would almost have qualified for Aristotle's description of the ideal man—the man most worthy of being happy. 'The ideal man,' said Aristotle, 'takes joy in doing favours for others; but he feels ashamed to have others do favours for him. For it is a mark of superiority to confer a kindness; but it is a mark of inferiority to receive it.'

Here is the second point I am trying to make in this chapter: If we want to find happiness, lets stop thinking about gratitude or ingratitude and give for the inner joy of giving.

Parents have been tearing their hair about the ingratitude of children for ten thousand years.

Even Shakespeare's King Lear cried out, 'How sharper than a

serpent's tooth it is to have a thankless child!'

But why should children be thankful—unless we train them to be? Ingratitude is natural—like weeds. Gratitude is like a rose. It has to be fed and watered and cultivated and loved and protected.

If our children are ungrateful, who is to blame? Maybe we are. If we have never taught them to express gratitude to others, how can we expect them to be grateful to us?

I know a man in Chicago who has cause to complain of the ingratitude of his stepsons. He slaved in a box factory, seldom earning more than forty dollars a week. He married a widow, and she persuaded him to borrow money and send her two grown sons to college. Out of his salary of forty dollars a week, he had to pay for food, rent, fuel, clothes, and also for the payments on his notes. He did this for four years, working like a coolie, and never complaining.

Did he get any thanks? No; his wife took it all for granted—and so did her sons. They never imagined that they owed their step-father anything—not even thanks!

Who was to blame? The boys? Yes; but the mother was even more to blame. She thought it was a shame to burden their young lives with 'a sense of obligation.' She didn't want her sons to 'start out under debt.' So she never dreamed of saying: 'What a prince your stepfather is to help you through college!' Instead, she took the attitude: 'Oh, that's the least he can do.'

She thought she was sparing her sons, but, in reality, she was sending them out into life with the dangerous idea that the world owed them a living. And it was a dangerous idea—for one of those sons tried to 'borrow' from an employer, and ended up in jail!

We must remember that our children are very much what we make them. For example, my mother's sister—Viola Alexander, of 144 West Minnehaha Parkway, Minneapolis—is a shining example of a woman who has never had cause to complain about the 'ingratitude' of children. When I was a boy, Aunt Viola took her own mother into her home to love and take care of; and she did the same thing for her husband's mother. I can still close my eyes and see those two old ladies sitting before the fire in Aunt Viola's farmhouse. Were they any 'trouble' to Aunt Viola? Oh, often, I suppose. But you would never have guessed it from her attitude. She loved those old ladies—so she pampered them, and spoiled them, and made them feel at home. In addition, Aunt Viola had six children of her own; but it never occurred to her that she was doing anything especially noble, or deserved any halos for taking these old ladies into her home. To her, it was the natural thing, the right thing, the thing she wanted to do.

Where is Aunt Viola today? Well, she has now been a widow for twenty-odd years, and she has five grown-up children—five separate households—all clamouring to share her, and to have her come and live in their homes! Her children adore her; they never get enough of her. Out of 'gratitude'? Nonsense! It is love—sheer love. Those children breathed in warmth and radiant human-kindness all during their childhoods. Is it any wonder that, now that the situation is reversed, they give back love?

So let us remember that to raise grateful children, we have to be grateful. Let us remember 'little pitchers have big ears'—and watch what we say. To illustrate—the next time we are tempted to belittle someone's kindness in the presence of our children, let's stop. Let's never say: 'Look at these dishcloths Cousin Sue sent for Christmas. She knit them herself. They didn't cost her a cent!' The remark may seem trivial to us—but the children are listening. So, instead, we had better say: 'Look at the hours Cousin Sue spent making these for Christmas! Isn't she nice? Let's write her a thank-you note right now.' And our children may unconsciously absorb the habit of praise and appreciation.

To avoid resentment and worry over ingratitude, here is

Rule 3: Instead of worrying about ingratitude, let's expect it. Let's remember that Jesus healed ten lepers in one day—and only one thanked him. Why should we expect more gratitude than Jesus got?

Let's remember that the only way to find happiness is not to expect gratitude, but to give for the joy of giving.

Let's remember that gratitude is a 'cultivated' trait; so if we want our children to be grateful, we must train them to be grateful.

Don't let your mind bully your body into believing it must carry the burden of its worries.

—Astrid Alauda

Worry and reasoning are two of Satan's most successful tools.

—Joyce Meyer

18

WOULD YOU TAKE A MILLION DOLLARS
FOR WHAT YOU HAVE?

I have known Harold Abbott for years. He lives at 820 South Madison Avenue, Webb City, Missouri. He used to be my lecture manager. One day he and I met in Kansas City and he drove me down to my farm at Belton, Missouri. During that drive, I asked him how he kept from worrying; and he told me an inspiring story that I shall never forget.

'I used to worry a lot,' he said, 'but one spring day in 1934, I was walking down West Dougherty Street in Webb City when I saw a sight that banished all my worries. It all happened in ten seconds, but during those ten seconds I learned more about how to live than I had learned in the previous ten years. For two years I had been running a grocery store in Webb City,' Harold Abbott said, as he told me the story. 'I had not only lost all my savings, but I had incurred debts that took me seven years to pay back. My grocery store had been closed the previous Saturday; and now I was going to the Merchants and Miners Bank to borrow money so I could go to Kansas City to look for a job. I walked like a beaten man. I had lost all my fight and faith. Then suddenly I saw coming down the street a man who had no legs. He was sitting on a little wooden platform equipped with wheels from roller skates. He propelled himself along the street with a block of wood in each hand. I met him just after he had crossed the street and was starting to lift himself up a few inches over the curb to the sidewalk. As he tilted his little wooden platform to an angle, his eyes met mine. He greeted me with a grand smile. 'Good morning, sir. It is a fine morning, isn't it?' he said with spirit. As I stood looking at him, I realized how rich I was. I had two legs. I could walk. I felt ashamed of my self-pity. I said to myself if he can be happy, cheerful, and confident without legs, I certainly can with legs. I could already feel my chest lifting. I had intended to ask the Merchants and Miners Bank for only one hundred dollars. But now I had courage to ask for two hundred. I had intended to say that I wanted to go to Kansas City to try to get a job. But now I announced confidently that I wanted to go to Kansas City to get a job. I got the loan; and I got the job.

'I now have the following words pasted on my bathroom mirror, and I read them every morning as I shave:

I had the blues because I had no shoes,

Until upon the street, I met a man who had no feet.'

I once asked Eddie Rickenbacker what was the biggest lesson he had learned from drifting about with his companions in life rafts for twenty-one days, hopelessly lost in the Pacific. 'The biggest lesson I learned from that experience,' he said, 'was that if you have all the fresh water you want to drink and all the food you want to eat, you ought never to complain about anything.'

Time ran an article about a sergeant who had been wounded on Guadalcanal. Hit in the throat by a shell fragment, this sergeant had had seven blood transfusions. Writing a note to his doctor, he asked: 'Will I live?' The doctor replied: 'Yes.' He wrote another note, asking: 'Will I be able to talk?' Again the answer was yes. He then wrote another note, saying: 'Then what in the hell am I worrying about?'

Why don't you stop right now and ask yourself: 'What in the hell am I worrying about?' You will probably find that it is comparatively unimportant and insignificant.

About ninety per cent of the things in our lives are right and about ten per cent are wrong. If we want to be happy, all we have to do is to concentrate on the ninety per cent that are right and ignore the ten per cent that are wrong. If we want to be worried and bitter and have stomach ulcers, all we have to do is to concentrate on the ten per cent that are wrong and ignore the ninety per cent that are glorious.

The words 'Think and Thank' are inscribed in many of the Cromwellian churches of England. These words ought to be inscribed on our hearts, too: 'Think and Thank.' Think of all we have to be grateful for, and thank God for all our boons and bounties.

Jonathan Swift, author of Gulliver's Travels, was the most devastating pessimist in English literature. He was so sorry that he had been born that he wore black and fasted on his birthdays; yet, in his despair, this supreme pessimist of English literature praised the great health-giving powers of cheerfulness and happiness. 'The best doctors in the world,' he declared, 'are Doctor Diet, Doctor Quiet, and Doctor Merryman.'

You and I may have the services of 'Doctor Merryman' free every hour of the day by keeping our attention fixed on all the incredible riches we possess—riches exceeding by far the fabled treasures of Ali Baba. Would you sell both your eyes for a billion dollars? What would you take for your two legs? Your hands? Your hearing? Your children? Your family? Add up your assets, and you will find that you won't sell what you have for all the gold ever amassed by the Rockefellers, the Fords, and the Morgans combined.

But do we appreciate all this? Ah, no. As Schopenhauer said: 'We seldom think of what we have but always of what we lack.' Yes, the tendency to 'seldom think of what we have but always of what we lack' is the greatest tragedy on earth. It has probably caused more misery than all the wars and diseases in history.

It caused John Palmer to turn 'from a regular guy into an old grouch,' and almost wrecked his home. I know because he told me so.

Mr Palmer lives at 30, 19th Avenue, Paterson, New Jersey. 'Shortly after I returned from the Army,' he said, 'I started in business for myself. I worked hard day and night. Things were going nicely. Then trouble started. I couldn't get parts and materials. I was afraid I would have to give up my business. I worried so much that I changed from a regular guy into an old grouch. I became so sour and cross that— well, I didn't know it then; but I now realize that I came very near to losing my happy home. Then one day a young, disabled veteran who works for me said, "Johnny, you ought to be ashamed of yourself. You take on as if you were the only person in the world with troubles. Suppose you do have to shut up shop for a while—so what? You can start up again when things get normal. You've got a lot to be thankful for. Yet you are always growling. Boy, how I wish I were in your shoes! Look at me. I've got only one arm, and half of my face is shot away, and yet, I am not complaining. If you don't stop your growling and grumbling, you will lose not only your business, but also your health, your home, and your friends!'

'Those remarks stopped me dead in my tracks. They made me realize how well off I was. I resolved then and there that I would change and be my old self again—and I did.'

A friend of mine, Lucile Blake, had to tremble on the edge of tragedy before she learned to be happy about what she had instead of worrying over what she lacked.

I met Lucile years ago, when we were both studying short-story writing in the Columbia University School of Journalism. Nine years ago, she got the shock of her life. She was living then in Tucson, Arizona. She had—well, here is the story as she told it to me:

'I had been living in a whirl: studying the organ at the University of Arizona, conducting a speech clinic in town, and teaching a class in musical appreciation at the Desert Willow Ranch, where I was staying. I was going in for parties, dances, horseback rides under the stars. One morning I collapsed. My heart! "You will have to lie in bed for a year of complete rest," the doctor said. He didn't encourage me to believe I would ever be strong again.'

'In bed for a year! To be an invalid—perhaps to die! I was terrorstricken! Why did all this have to happen to me? What had I done to deserve it? I wept and wailed. I was bitter and rebellious. But I did go to bed as the doctor advised. A neighbour of mine, Mr Rudolf, an artist, said to me, "You think now that spending a year in bed will be a tragedy. But it won't be. You will have time to think and get acquainted with yourself. You will make more spiritual growth in these next few months than you have made during all your previous life." I became calmer, and tried to develop a new sense of values. I read books of inspiration. One day I heard a radio commentator say: "You can express only what is in your own consciousness." I had heard words like these many times before, but now they reached down inside me, and took root. I resolved to think only the thoughts I wanted to live by: thoughts of joy, happiness, health. I forced myself each morning, as soon as I awoke, to go over all the things I had to be grateful for. No pain. A lovely young daughter. My eyesight. My hearing. Lovely music on the radio. Time to read.

Good food. Good friends. I was so cheerful and had so many visitors that the doctor put up a sign saying that only one visitor at a time would be allowed in my cabin—and only at certain hours.

'Nine years have passed since then, and I now lead a full, active life. I am deeply grateful now for that year I spent in bed. It was the most valuable and the happiest year I spent in Arizona. The habit I formed then of counting my blessings each morning still remains with me. It is one of my most precious possessions. I am ashamed to realize that I never really learned to live until I feared I was going to die.'

My dear Lucile Blake, you may not realize it, but you learned the same lesson that Dr Samuel Johnson learned two hundred years ago. 'The habit of looking on the best side of every event,' said Dr Johnson, 'is worth more than a thousand pounds a year.'

Those words were uttered, mind you, not by a professional optimist, but by a man who had known anxiety, rags, and hunger for twenty years—and finally became one of the most eminent writers of his generation and the most celebrated conversationalist of all time.

Logan Pearsall Smith packed a lot of wisdom into a few words when he said: 'There are two things to aim at in life: first, to get what you want; and, after that, to enjoy it. Only the wisest of mankind achieve the second.'

Would you like to know how to make even dishwashing at the kitchen sink a thrilling experience? If so, read an inspiring book of incredible courage by Borghild Dahl. It is called I Wanted to See. You may borrow it from your public library or purchase it from your local bookstore or from the publisher, The Macmillan Company, 60 Fifth Avenue, New York City.

This book was written by a woman who was practically blind for half a century. 'I had only one eye,' she writes, 'and it was so covered with dense scars that I had to do all my seeing through one small opening in the left of the eye. I could see a book only by holding it up close to my face and by straining my one eye as hard as I could to the left.'

But she refused to be pitied, refused to be considered 'different.' As a child, she wanted to play hopscotch with other children, but she couldn't see the markings. So after the other children had gone home, she got down on the ground and crawled along with her eyes near to the marks. She memorized every bit of the ground where she and her friends played and soon became an expert at running games. She did her reading at home, holding a book of large print so close to her eyes that her eyelashes brushed the pages. She earned two college degrees: an A.B. from the University of Minnesota and a Master of Arts from Columbia University.

She started teaching in the tiny village of Twin Valley, Minnesota, and rose until she became professor of journalism and literature at Augustana College in Sioux Falls, South Dakota. She taught there for thirteen years, lecturing before women's clubs and giving radio talks about books and authors. 'In the back of my mind,' she writes, 'there had always lurked a fear of total blindness. In order to overcome this, I had adopted a cheerful, almost hilarious, attitude towards life.'

Then in 1943, when she was fifty-two years old, a miracle happened: an operation at the famous Mayo Clinic. She could now see forty times as well as she had ever been able to see before.

A new and exciting world of loveliness opened before her. She now found it thrilling even to wash dishes in the kitchen sink. 'I begin to play with the white fluffy suds in the dishpan,' she writes. 'I dip my hands into them and I pick up a ball of tiny soap bubbles. I hold them up against the light, and in each of them I can see the brilliant colours of a miniature rainbow.'

As she looked through the window above the kitchen sink, she saw 'the flapping gray-black wings of the sparrows flying through the thick, falling snow.'

She found such ecstasy looking at the soap bubbles and sparrows that she closed her book with these words: "'Dear Lord,' I whisper, "Our Father in Heaven, I thank Thee. I thank Thee".'

Imagine thanking God because you can wash dishes and see rainbows in bubbles and sparrows flying through the snow!

You and I ought to be ashamed of ourselves. All the days of our years we have been living in a fairyland of beauty, but we have been too blind to see, too satiated to enjoy.

If we want to stop worrying and start living,

Rule 4: Count your blessings—not your troubles!

I promise you, nothing is as chaotic as it seems. Nothing is worth your health. Nothing is worth poisoning yourself into stress, anxiety, and fear.
—Steve Maraboli

There is nothing that wastes the body like worry, and one who has any faith in God should be ashamed to worry about anything whatsoever.
—Mahatma Gandhi

19

FIND YOURSELF AND BE YOURSELF: REMEMBER THERE IS NO ONE ELSE ON EARTH LIKE YOU

I have a letter from Mrs Edith Allred, of Mount Airy, North Carolina: 'As a child, I was extremely sensitive and shy,' she says in her letter. 'I was always overweight and my cheeks made me look even fatter than I was. I had an old-fashioned mother who thought it was foolish to make clothes look pretty. She always said: "Wide will wear while narrow will tear"; and she dressed me accordingly. I never went to parties; never had any fun; and when I went to school, I never joined the other children in outside activities, not even athletics. I was morbidly shy. I felt I was "different" from everybody else, and entirely undesirable.

'When I grew up, I married a man who was several years my senior. But I didn't change. My in-laws were a poised and self-confident family. They were everything I should have been but simply was not. I tried my best to be like them, but I couldn't. Every attempt they made to draw me out of myself only drove me further into my shell. I became nervous and irritable. I avoided all friends. I got so bad, I even dreaded the sound of the doorbell ringing! I was a failure. I knew it; and I was afraid my husband would find it out. So, whenever we were in public, I tried to be gay, and overacted my part. I knew I overacted; and I would be miserable for days afterwards. At last I became so unhappy that I could see no point in prolonging my existence. I began to think of suicide.'

What happened to change this unhappy woman's life? Just a chance remark!

'A chance remark,' Mrs Allred continued, 'transformed my whole life. My mother-in-law was talking one day of how she brought her children up, and she said, "No matter what happened, I always insisted on their being themselves. On being them-selves." That remark is what did it! In a flash, I realized I had brought all this misery on myself by trying to fit myself into a pattern to which I did not conform.

'I changed overnight! I started being myself. I tried to make a study of my own personality. Tried to find out what I was. I studied my strong points. I learned all I could about colours and styles, and dressed in a way that I felt was becoming to me. I reached out to make friends. I joined an organization—a small one at first—and was petrified with fright when they put me on a program. But each time I spoke, I gained a little courage. It took a long while—but today I have more happiness than I ever dreamed possible. In rearing my own children, I have always taught them the lesson I had to learn from such bitter experience: No matter what happens, always be yourself!'

This problem of being willing to be yourself is 'as old as history,' says Dr James Gordon Gilkey, 'and as universal as human life.' This problem of being unwilling to be yourself is the hidden spring behind many neuroses and psychoses and complexes. Angelo Patri has written thirteen books and thousands of syndicated newspaper articles on the subject of child training, and he says: 'Nobody is so miserable as he who longs to be somebody and something other than the person he is in body and mind.'

This craving to be something you are not is especially rampant in Hollywood. Sam Wood, one of Hollywood's best-known directors, says the greatest headache he has with aspiring young actors is exactly this problem: to make them be themselves. They all want to be second-rate Lana Turners or third-rate Clark Gables. 'The public has already had that flavour,' Sam Wood keeps telling them; 'now it wants something else.'

Before he started directing such pictures as Goodbye, Mr Chips and For Whom the Bell Tolls, Sam Wood spent years in the real-estate business, developing sales personalities. He declares that the same principles apply in the business world as in the world of moving pictures. You won't get anywhere playing the ape. You can't be a parrot. 'Experience has taught me,' says Sam Wood, 'that it is safest to drop, as quickly as possible, people who pretend to be what they aren't.'

I recently asked Paul Boynton, employment director for the Socony-Vacuum Oil Company, what is the biggest mistake people make in applying for jobs. He ought to know: he has interviewed more than sixty thousand job seekers; and he has written a book entitled 6 Ways to Get a Job. He replied: 'The biggest mistake people make in applying for jobs is in not being themselves. Instead of taking their hair down and being completely frank, they often try to give you the answers they think you want.' But it doesn't work, because nobody wants a phony. Nobody ever wants a counterfeit coin.

A certain daughter of a streetcar conductor had to learn that lesson the hard way. She longed to be a singer. But her face was her misfortune. She had a large mouth and protruding buck teeth. When she first sang in public—in a New Jersey night club—she tried to pull down her upper lip to cover her teeth. She tried to act 'glamorous.' The result? She made herself ridiculous. She was headed for failure.

However, there was a man in this night club who heard the girl sing and thought she had talent. 'See here,' he said bluntly, 'I've been watching your performance and I know what it is you're trying to hide. You're ashamed of your teeth!' The girl was embarrassed, but the man continued, 'What of it? Is there any particular crime in having buck teeth? Don't try to hide them! Open your mouth, and the audience will love you when they see you're not ashamed. Besides,' he said shrewdly, 'those teeth you're trying to hide may make your fortune!'

Cass Daley took his advice and forgot about her teeth. From that time on, she thought only about her audience. She opened her mouth wide and sang with such gusto and enjoyment that she became a top star in movies and radio. Other comedians are now trying to copy her!

The renowned William James was speaking of men who had never found themselves when he declared that the average man develops only ten per cent of his latent mental abilities. "Compared to what we ought to be,' he wrote, 'we are only half awake. We are making use of only a small part of our physical and mental resources. Stating the thing broadly, the human individual thus lives far within his limits. He possesses powers of various sorts which he habitually fails to use.'

You and I have such abilities, so let's not waste a second worrying because we are not like other people. You are something new in this world. Never before, since the beginning of time, has there ever been anybody exactly like you; and never again throughout all the ages to come will there ever be anybody exactly like you again. The new science of genetics informs us that you are what you are largely as a result of twenty-four chromosomes contributed by your father and twenty-four chromosomes contributed by your mother. These forty-eight chromosomes comprise everything that determines what you inherit. In each chromosome there may be, says Amran Scheinfeld, 'anywhere from scores to hundreds of genes—with a single gene, in some cases, able to change the whole life of an individual.' Truly, we are 'fearfully and wonderfully' made.

Even after your mother and father met and mated, there was only one chance in 300,000 billion that the person who is specifically you would be born! In other words, if you had 300,000 billion brothers and sisters, they might have all been different from you. Is all this guesswork? No. It is a scientific fact. If you would like to read more about it, go to your public library and borrow a book entitled You and Heredity, by Amran Scheinfeld.

I can talk with conviction about this subject of being yourself because I feel deeply about it. I know what I am talking about. I know from bitter and costly experience. To illustrate: when I first came to New York from the cornfields of Missouri, I enrolled in the American Academy of Dramatic Arts. I aspired to be an actor. I had what I thought was a brilliant idea, a short cut to success, an idea so simple, so foolproof, that I couldn't understand why thousands of ambitious people hadn't already discovered it. It was this: I would study how the famous actors of that day—John Drew, Walter Hampden, and Otis Skinner—got their effects. Then I would imitate the best points of each one of them and make myself into a shining, triumphant combination of all of them. How silly! How absurd! I had to waste years of my life imitating other people before it penetrated through my thick Missouri skull that I had to be myself, and that I couldn't possibly be anyone else.

That distressing experience ought to have taught me a lasting lesson. But it didn't. Not me. I was too dumb. I had to learn it all over again. Several years later, I set out to write what I hoped would be the best book on public speaking for businessmen that had ever been written. I had the same foolish idea about writing this book that I had formerly had about acting: I was going to borrow the ideas of a lot of other writers and put them all in one book—a book that would have everything. So I got scores of books on public speaking and spent a year incorporating their ideas into my manuscript. But it finally dawned on me once again that I was playing the fool. This hodgepodge of other men's ideas that I had written was so synthetic, so dull, that no businessman would ever plod through it. So I tossed a year's work into the wastebasket, and started all over again. This time I said to myself: 'You've got to be Dale Carnegie, with all his faults and limitations. You can't possibly be anybody else.' So I quit trying to be a combination of other men, and rolled up my sleeves and did what I should have done in the first place: I wrote a textbook on public speaking out of my own experiences, observations, and convictions as a speaker and a teacher of speaking. I learned—for all time, I hope—the lesson that Sir Walter Raleigh learned. (I am not talking about the Sir Walter who threw his coat in the mud for the Queen to step on. I am talking about the Sir Walter Raleigh who was professor of English literature at Oxford back in 1904.) 'I can't write a book commensurate with Shakespeare,' he said, 'but I can write a book by me.'

Be yourself. Act on the sage advice that Irving Berlin gave the late George Gershwin. When Berlin and Gershwin first met, Berlin was famous but Gershwin was a struggling young composer working for thirty-five dollars a week in Tin Pan Alley. Berlin, impressed by Gershwin's ability, offered Gershwin a job as his musical secretary at almost three times the salary he was then getting. 'But don't take the job,' Berlin advised. 'If you do, you may develop into a second-rate Berlin. But if you insist on being yourself, someday you'll become a first-rate Gershwin.'

Gershwin heeded that warning and slowly transformed himself into one of the significant American composers of his generation.

Charlie Chaplin, Will Rogers, Mary Margaret McBride, Gene Autry, and millions of others had to learn the lesson I am trying to hammer home in this chapter. They had to learn the hard way—just as I did.

When Charlie Chaplin first started making films, the director of the pictures insisted on Chaplin's imitating a popular German comedian of that day. Charlie Chaplin got nowhere until he acted himself. Bob Hope had a similar experience: spent years in a singing-and-dancing act—and got nowhere until he began to wisecrack and be himself. Will Rogers twirled a rope in vaudeville for years without saying a word. He got nowhere until he discovered his unique gift for humour and began to talk as he twirled his rope.

When Mary Margaret McBride first went on the air, she tried to be an Irish comedian and failed. When she tried to be just what she was—a plain country girl from Missouri—she became one of the most popular radio stars in New York.

When Gene Autry tried to get rid of his Texas accent and dressed like city boys and claimed he was from New York, people merely laughed behind his back. But when he started twanging his banjo and singing cowboy ballads, Gene Autry started out on a career that made him the world's most popular cowboy, both in pictures and on the radio.

You are something new in this world. Be glad of it. Make the most of what nature gave you. In the last analysis, all art is autobiographical. You can sing only what you are. You can paint only what you are. You must be what your experiences, your environment, and your heredity have made you. For better or for worse, you must cultivate your own little garden. For better or for worse, you must play your own little instrument in the orchestra of life.

To cultivate a mental attitude that will bring us peace and freedom from worry, here is

Rule 5: Let's not imitate others.

Let's find ourselves and be ourselves.

> *There must be quite a few things that a hot bath won't cure,*
> *but I don't know many of them.*
> —Sylvia Plath

> *There is something at work that's bigger than us. It's about having a trust in life and being at peace that things are happening the way they should. You do what you do as well as you can do it, and then you don't worry or agonize about the outcome.*
> —Sherilyn Fenn

20

IF YOU HAVE A LEMON, MAKE LEMONADE

While writing this book, I dropped in one day at the University of Chicago and asked the Chancellor, Robert Maynard Hutchins, how he kept from worrying. He replied, 'I have always tried to follow a bit of advice given to me by the late Julius Rosenwald, President of Sears, Roebuck and Company: "When you have a lemon, make lemonade."'

That is what a great educator does. But the fool does the exact opposite. If he finds that life has handed him a lemon, he gives up and says, 'I'm beaten. It is fate. I haven't got a chance.' Then he proceeds to rail against the world and indulge in an orgy of self-pity. But when the wise man is handed a lemon, he says: 'What lesson can I learn from this misfortune? How can I improve my situation? How can I turn this lemon into lemonade?'

After spending a lifetime studying people and their hidden reserves of power, the great psychologist, Alfred Adler, declared that one of the wonder-filled characteristics of human beings is 'their power to turn a minus into a plus.'

Here is an interesting and stimulating story of a woman I know who did just that. Her name is Thelma Thompson, and she lives at 100 Morningside Drive, New York City. 'During the war,' she said, as she told me of her experience, 'during the war, my husband was stationed at an Army training camp near the Mojave Desert, in California. I went to live there in order to be near him. I hated the place. I loathed it. I had never before been so miserable. My husband was ordered out on maneuvers in the Mojave Desert, and I was left in a tiny shack alone. The heat was unbearable—125 degrees in the shade of a cactus. Not a soul to talk to but Mexicans and Indians, and they couldn't speak English. The wind blew incessantly, and all the food I ate, and the very air I breathed, were filled with sand, sand, sand!

'I was so utterly wretched, so sorry for myself, that I wrote to my parents. I told them I was giving up and coming back home. I said I couldn't stand it one minute longer. I would rather be in jail! My father answered my letter with just two lines—two lines that will always sing in my memory—two lines that completely altered my life:

Two men looked out from prison bars,
One saw the mud, the other saw the stars.

'I read those two lines over and over. I was ashamed of myself. I made up my mind I would find out what was good in my present situation; I would look for the stars.

'I made friends with the natives, and their reaction amazed me. When I showed interest in their weaving and pottery, they gave me presents of their favorite pieces which they had refused to sell to tourists. I studied the fascinating forms of the cactus and the yuccas and the Joshua trees. I learned about prairie dogs, watched for the desert sunsets, and hunted for seashells that had been left there millions of years ago when the sands of the desert had been an ocean floor.

'What brought about this astonishing change in me? The Mojave Desert hadn't changed. The Indians hadn't changed. But I had. I had changed my attitude of mind. And by doing so, I transformed a wretched experience into the most exciting adventure of my life. I was stimulated and excited by this new world that I had discovered. I was so excited I wrote a book about it—a novel that was published under the title Bright Ramparts.... I had looked out of my self-created prison and found the stars.'

Thelma Thompson, you discovered an old truth that the Greeks taught five hundred years before Christ was born: 'The best things are the most difficult.'

Harry Emerson Fosdick repeated it again in the twentieth century: 'Happiness is not mostly pleasure; it is mostly victory. Yes, the victory that comes from a sense of achievement, of triumph, of turning our lemons into lemonades.

'I once visited a happy farmer down in Florida who turned even a poison lemon into lemonade. When he first got this farm, he was discouraged. The land was so wretched he could neither grow fruit nor raise pigs. Nothing thrived there but scrub oaks and rattlesnakes. Then he got his idea. He would turn his liability into an asset: he would make the most of these rattlesnakes. To everyone's amazement, he started canning rattlesnake meat. When I stopped to visit him a few years ago, I found that tourists were pouring in to see his rattlesnake farm at the rate of twenty thousand a year. His business was thriving. I saw poison from the fangs of his rattlers being shipped to labouratories to make antivenom toxin; I saw rattlesnake skins being sold at fancy prices to make women's shoes and handbags. I saw canned rattlesnake meat being shipped to customers all over the world. I bought a picture postcard of the place and mailed it at the local post office of the village, which had been re-christened 'Rattlesnake, Florida,' in honour of a man who had turned a poison lemon into a sweet lemonade.

'As I have travelled up and down and back and forth across this nation time after time, it has been my privilege to meet dozens of men and women who have demonstrated "their power to turn a minus into a plus."

The late William Bolitho, author of Twelve Against the Gods, put it like this: 'The most important thing in life is not to capitalize on your gains. Any fool can do that. The really important thing is to profit from your losses. That requires intelligence; and it makes the difference between a man of sense and a fool.'

Bolitho uttered those words after he had lost a leg in a railway accident. But I know a man who lost both legs and turned his minus into a plus. His name is Ben Fortson. I met him in a hotel elevator in Atlanta, Georgia. As I stepped into the elevator, I noticed this cheerful-looking man, who had both legs missing, sitting in a wheel chair in a corner of the elevator. When the elevator stopped at his floor, he asked me pleasantly if I would step to one corner, so he could manage his chair better. 'So sorry,' he said, 'to inconvenience you'—and a deep, heart-warming smile lighted his face as he said it. When I left the elevator and went to my room, I could think of nothing but this cheerful cripple. So I hunted him up and asked him to tell me his story.

'It happened in 1929,' he told me with a smile. 'I had gone out to cut a load of hickory poles to stake the beans in my garden. I had loaded the poles on my Ford and started back home. Suddenly one pole slipped under the car and jammed the steering apparatus at the very moment I was making a sharp turn. The car shot over an embankment and hurled me against a tree. My spine was hurt. My legs were paralysed.

'I was twenty-four when that happened, and I have never taken a step since.'

Twenty-four years old, and sentenced to a wheel chair for the rest of his life! I asked him how he managed to take it so courageously, and he said, 'I didn't.' He said he raged and rebelled. He fumed about his fate. But as the years dragged on, he found that his rebellion wasn't getting him anything except bitterness. 'I finally realized,' he said, 'that other people were kind and courteous to me. So the least I could do was to be kind and courteous to them.'

I asked if he still felt, after all these years, that his accident had been a terrible misfortune, and he promptly said, 'No.' He said, 'I'm almost glad now that it happened.' He told me that after he got over the shock and resentment, he began to live in a different world. He began to read and developed a love for good literature. In fourteen years, he said, he had read at least fourteen hundred books; and those books had opened up new horizons for him and made his life richer than he ever thought possible. He began to listen to good music; and he is now thrilled by great symphonies that would have bored him before. But the biggest change was that he had time to think. 'For the first time in my life," he said, "I was able to look at the world and get a real sense of values. I began to realize that most of the things

I had been striving for before weren't worthwhile at all.'

As a result of his reading, he became interested in politics, studied public questions, made speeches from his wheel chair! He got to know people and people got to know him. Today Ben Fortson—still in his wheelchair—is Secretary of State for the state of Georgia!

During the last thirty-five years, I have been conducting adult-education classes in New York City, and I have discovered that one of the major regrets of many adults is that they never went to college. They seem to think that not having a college education is a great handicap. I know that this isn't necessarily true because I have known thousands of successful men who never went beyond high school. So I often tell these students the story of a man I knew who had never finished even grade school. He was brought up in blighting poverty. When his father died, his father's friends had to chip in to pay for the coffin in which he was buried. After his father's death, his mother worked in an umbrella factory ten hours a day and then brought piecework home and worked until eleven o'clock at night.

The boy brought up in these circumstances went in for amateur dramatics put on by a club in his church. He got such a thrill out of acting that he decided to take up public speaking. This led him into politics. By the time he reached thirty, he was elected to the New York State legislature. But he was woefully unprepared for such a responsibility. In fact, he told me that frankly he didn't know what it was all about. He studied the long, complicated bills that he was supposed to vote on—but, as far as he was concerned, those bills might as well have been written in the language of the Choctaw Indians. He was worried and bewildered when he was made a member of the committee on forests before he had ever set foot in a forest. He was worried and bewildered when he was made a member of the State Banking Commission before he had ever had a bank account. He himself told me that he was so discouraged that he would have resigned from the legislature if he hadn't been ashamed to admit defeat to his mother. In despair, he decided to study sixteen hours a day and turn his lemon of ignorance into a lemonade of knowledge.

By doing that, he transformed himself from a local politician into a national figure and made himself so outstanding that The New York Times called him "the best-loved citizen of New York."

I am talking about Al Smith.

Ten years after Al Smith set out on his program of political self-education, he was the greatest living authority on the government of New York State. He was elected Governor of New York for four terms—a record never attained by any other man. In 1928, he was the Democratic candidate for President. Six great universities—including Columbia and Harvard—conferred honorary degrees upon this man who had never gone beyond grade school.

Al Smith himself told me that none of these things would ever have come to pass if he hadn't worked hard sixteen hours a day to turn his minus into a plus.

Nietzsche's formula for the superior man was 'not only to bear up under necessity but to love it.'

The more I have studied the careers of men of achievement the more deeply I have been convinced that a surprisingly large number of them succeeded because they started out with handicaps that spurred them on to great endeavor and great rewards. As William James said: 'Our very infirmities help us unexpectedly.' Yes, it is highly probable that Milton wrote better poetry because he was blind and that Beethoven composed better music because he was deaf.

Helen Keller's brilliant career was inspired and made possible because of her blindness and deafness.

If Tchaikovsky had not been frustrated—and driven almost to suicide by his tragic marriage—if his own life had not been pathetic, he probably would never have been able to compose his immortal 'Symphonie Pathétique.'

If Dostoevsky and Tolstoy had not led tortured lives, they would probably never have been able to write their immortal novels.

'If I had not been so great an invalid,' wrote the man who changed the scientific concept of life on earth—'if I had not been so great an invalid, I should not have done so much work as I have accomplished.'

That was Charles Darwin's confession that his infirmities had helped him unexpectedly.

'The same day that Darwin was born in England, another baby was born in a log cabin in the forests of Kentucky. He, too, was helped by his infirmities. His name was Lincoln—Abraham Lincoln. If he had been reared in an aristocratic family and had had a law degree from Harvard and a happy married life, he would probably never have found in the depths of his heart the haunting words that he immortalized at Gettysburg, nor the sacred poem that he spoke at his second inauguration—the most beautiful and noble phrases ever uttered by a ruler of men: "With malice towards none; with charity for all..."

Harry Emerson Fosdick says in his book, The Power to See it Through, 'There is a Scandinavian saying which some of us might well take as a rallying cry for our lives: 'The north wind made the Vikings.' Wherever did we get the idea that secure and pleasant living, the absence of difficulty, and the comfort of ease, ever of themselves made people either good or happy? Upon the contrary, people who pity themselves go on pitying themselves even when they are laid softly on a cushion, but always in history character and happiness have come to people in all sorts of circumstances, good, bad, and indifferent, when they shouldered their personal responsibility. So, repeatedly the north wind has made the Vikings.'

Suppose we are so discouraged that we feel there is no hope of our ever being able to turn our lemons into lemonade—then here are two reasons why we ought to try, anyway—two reasons why we have everything to gain and nothing to lose.

Reason one: We may succeed.

Reason two: Even if we don't succeed, the mere attempt to turn our minus into a plus will cause us to look forward instead of backward; it will replace negative thoughts with positive thoughts; it will release creative energy and spur us to get so busy that we won't have either the time or the inclination to mourn over what is past and forever gone.

Once when Ole Bull, the world-famous violinist, was giving a concert in Paris, the A string on his violin suddenly snapped. But Ole Bull simply finished the melody on three strings. 'That is life," says Harry Emerson Fosdick, "to have your A string snap and finish on three strings.'

That is not only life. It is more than life. It is life triumphant!

If I had the power to do so, I would have these words of William Bolitho carved in eternal bronze and hung in every schoolhouse in the land:

The most important thing in life is not to capitalize on your gains. Any fool can do that. The really important thing is to profit from your losses. That requires intelligence; and it makes the difference between a man of sense and a fool.

So, to cultivate a mental attitude that will bring us peace and happiness, let's do something about

Rule 6: When fate hands us a lemon, let's try to make lemonade.

People have a hard time letting go of their suffering. Out of a fear or the unknown, they prefer suffering that is familiar.
—Thich Nhat Hanh

Worry does not empty tomorrow of its sorrow.
It empties today of its strength.
—Corrie Ten Boom

21

HOW TO CURE MELANCHOLY IN FOURTEEN DAYS

When I started writing this book, I offered a two-hundred-dollar prize for the most helpful and inspiring true story on 'How I Conquered Worry.'

The three judges for this contest were: Eddie Rickenbacker, president, Eastern Air Lines; Dr Stewart W. McClelland, president, Lincoln Memorial University; H.V. Kaltenborn, radio news analyst. However, we received two stories so superb that the judges found it impossible to choose between them. So we divided the prize. Here is one of the stories that tied for first prize—the story of C.R. Burton (who works for Whizzer Motor Sales of Missouri, Inc.), 1067 Commercial Street, Springfield, Missouri.

'I lost my mother when I was nine years old, and my father when I was twelve,' Mr Burton wrote me. 'My father was killed, but my mother simply walked out of the house one day nineteen years ago; and I have never seen her since. Neither have I ever seen my two little sisters that she took with her. She never even wrote me a letter until after she had been gone seven years. My father was killed in an accident three years after Mother left. He and a partner had bought a café in a small Missouri town; and while Father was away on a business trip, his partner sold the café for cash and skipped out. A friend wired Father to hurry back home; and in his hurry, Father was killed in a car accident at Salinas, Kansas. Two of my father's sisters, who were poor and old and sick, took three of the children into their homes. Nobody wanted me and my little brother. We were left at the mercy of the town. We were haunted by the fear of being called orphans and treated as orphans. Our fears soon materialized, too. I lived for a little while with a poor family in town. But times were hard and the head of the family lost his job, so they couldn't afford to feed me any longer. Then Mr and Mrs Loftin took me to live with them on their farm eleven miles from town. Mr Loftin was seventy years old, and sick in bed with shingles. He told me I could stay there "as long as I didn't lie, didn't steal, and did as I was told." Those three orders became my Bible. I lived by them strictly. I started to school, but the first week found me at home, bawling like a baby. The other children picked on me and poked fun at my big nose and said I was dumb and called me an 'orphan brat.' I was hurt so badly that I wanted to fight them; but Mr Loftin, the farmer who had taken me in, said to me: "Always remember that it takes a bigger man to walk away from a fight than it does to stay and fight." I didn't fight until one day a kid picked up some chicken manure from the schoolhouse yard and threw it in my face. I beat the hell out of him; and made a couple of friends. They said he had it coming to him.

'I was proud of a new cap that Mrs Loftin had bought me. One day one of the big girls jerked it off my head and filled it with water and ruined it. She said she filled it with water so that "the water would wet my thick skull and keep my popcorn brains from popping."

'I never cried at school, but I used to bawl it out at home. Then one day Mrs Loftin gave me some advice that did away with all troubles and worries and turned my enemies into friends. She said, "Ralph, they won't tease you and call you an 'orphan brat' any more if you will get interested in them and see how much you can do for them." I took her advice. I studied hard; and though I soon headed the class, I was never envied because I went out of my way to help them.

'I helped several of the boys write their themes and essays. I wrote complete debates for some of the boys. One lad was ashamed to let his folks know that I was helping him. So he used to tell his mother he was going possum hunting. Then he would come to Mr Loftin's farm and tie his dogs up in the barn while I helped him with his lessons. I wrote book reviews for one lad and I spent several evenings helping one of the girls on her math.

'Death struck our neighbourhood. Two elderly farmers died and one woman was deserted by her husband. I was the only male in four families. I helped these widows for two years. On my way to and from school, I stopped at their farms, cut wood for them, milked their cows, and fed and watered their stock. I was now blessed instead of cursed. I was accepted as a friend by everyone. They showed me their real feelings when I returned home from the Navy. More than two hundred farmers came to see me the first day I was home. Some of them drove as far as eighty miles, and their concern for me was really sincere. Because I have been busy and happy trying to help other people, I have few worries; and I haven't been called an "orphan brat" now for thirteen years.'

Hooray for C.R. Burton! He knows how to win friends! And he also knows how to conquer worry and enjoy life.

So did the late Dr Frank Loope, of Seattle, Washington. He was an invalid for twenty-three years. Arthritis. Yet Stuart Whithouse of the Seattle Star wrote me, saying, 'I interviewed Dr Loope many times; and I have never known a man more unselfish or a man who got more out of life.'

How did this bed-ridden invalid get so much out of life? I'll give you two guesses. Did he do it by complaining and criticizing? No... By wallowing in self-pity and demanding that he be the center of attention and everyone cater to him? No... Still wrong. He did it by adopting as his slogan the motto of the Prince of Wales: 'Ich dien—I serve.' He accumulated the names and addresses of other invalids and cheered both them and himself by writing happy, encouraging letters. In fact, he organized a letter-writing club for invalids and got them writing letters to one another. Finally, he formed a national organization called The Shut-in Society.

As he lay in bed, he wrote an average of fourteen hundred letters a year and brought joy to thousands of invalids by getting radios and books for shut-ins.

What was the chief difference between Dr Loope and a lot of other people? Just this: Dr Loope had the inner glow of a man with a purpose, a mission. He had the joy of knowing that he was being used by an idea far nobler and more significant than himself, instead of being, as Shaw put it, 'a self-centered, little clod of ailments and grievances complaining that the world would not devote itself to making him happy.'

Here is the most astonishing statement that I ever read from the pen of a great psychiatrist. This statement was made by Alfred Adler. He used to say to his melancholia patients: 'You can be cured in fourteen days if you follow this prescription. Try to think every day how you can please someone.'

That statement sounds so incredible that I feel I ought to try to explain it by quoting a couple of pages from Dr Adler's splendid book, What Life Should Mean to You.

'Melancholia,' says Adler on page 258 of *What Life Should Mean to You*:

> Melancholia is like a long-continued rage and reproach against others, though for the purpose of gaining care, sympathy and support, the patient seems only to be dejected about his own guilt. A melancholiac's first memory is generally something like this: 'I remember I wanted to lie on the couch, but my brother was lying there. I cried so much that he had to leave.'

Melancholiacs are often inclined to revenge themselves by committing suicide, and the doctor's first care is to avoid giving them an excuse for suicide. I myself try to relieve the whole tension by proposing to them, as the first rule in treatment, 'Never do anything you don't like.' This seems to be very modest, but I believe that it goes to the root of the whole trouble. If a melancholiac is able to do anything he wants, whom can he accuse? What has he got to revenge himself for? 'If you want to go to the theater,' I tell him, 'or to go on a holiday, do it. If you find on the way that you don't want to, stop it.' It is the best situation any one could be in. It gives a satisfaction to his striving for superiority. He is like God and can do what he pleases. On the other hand, it does not fit very easily into his style of life.

He wants to dominate and accuse others and if they agree with him there is no way of dominating them. This rule is a great relief and I have never had a suicide among my patients.

Generally the patient replies, 'But there is nothing I like doing.' I have prepared for this answer, because I have heard it so often. 'Then refrain from doing anything you dislike,' I say. Sometimes, however, he will reply, 'I should like to stay in bed all day.' I know that, if I allow it, he will no longer want to do it. I know that, if I hinder him, he will start a war. I always agree.

This is one rule. Another attacks their style of life still more directly. I tell them, 'You can be cured in fourteen days if you follow this prescription. Try to think every day how you can please some one.' See what this means to them. They are occupied with the thought, 'How can I worry some one.' The answers are very interesting. Some say, 'This will be very easy for me. I have done it all my life.' They have never done it. I ask them to think it over. They do not think it over. I tell them, 'You can make use of all the time you spend when you are unable to go to sleep by thinking how you can please some one, and it will be a big step forward in your health.' When I see them next day, I ask them, 'Did you think over what I suggested?' They answer, 'Last night I went to sleep as soon as I got into bed. All this must be done, of course, in a modest, friendly manner, without a hint of superiority.

Others will answer, 'I could never do it. I am so worried.' I tell them, 'Don't stop worrying; but at the same time you can think now and then of others'. I want to direct their interest always towards their fellows. Many say, 'Why should I please others? Others do not try to please me.' 'You must think of your health,' I answer. 'The others will suffer later on.' It is extremely rare that I have found a patient who said, 'I have thought over what you suggested.' All my efforts are devoted towards increasing the social interest of the patient. I know that the real reason for his malady is his lack of co-operation and I want him to see it too. As soon as he can connect himself with his fellow men on an equal and co-operative footing, he is cured... The most important task imposed by religion has always been 'Love thy neighbour'... It is the individual who is not interested in his fellow man who has the greatest difficulties in life and provides the greatest injury to others. It is from among such individuals that all human failures spring... All that we demand of a human being, and the highest praise we can give him, is that he should be a good fellow worker, a friend to all other men, and a true partner in love and marriage.

Dr Adler urges us to do a good deed every day. And what is a good deed? 'A good deed,' said the prophet Mohammed, 'is one that brings a smile of joy to the face of another.'

Why will doing a good deed every day produce such astounding effects on the doer? Because trying to please others will cause us to stop thinking of ourselves: the very thing that produces worry and fear and melancholia.

Mrs William T. Moon, who operates the Moon Secretarial School, 521 Fifth Avenue, New York, didn't have to spend two weeks thinking how she could please someone in order to banish her melancholy. She went Alfred Adler one better—no, she went Adler thirteen better. She banished her melancholy, not in fourteen days, but in one day, by thinking how she could please a couple of orphans.

It happened like this: 'In December, five years ago,' said Mrs Moon, 'I was engulfed in a feeling of sorrow and self-pity. After several years of happy married life, I had lost my husband. As the Christmas holidays approached, my sadness deepened. I had never spent a Christmas alone in all my life; and I dreaded to see this Christmas come. Friends had invited me to spend Christmas with them. But I did not feel up to any gaiety. I knew I would be a wet blanket at any party. So, I refused their kind invitations. As Christmas Eve approached, I was more and more overwhelmed with self-pity. True, I should have been thankful for many things, as all of us have many things for which to be thankful. The day before Christmas, I left my office at three o'clock in the afternoon and started walking aimlessly up Fifth Avenue, hoping that I might banish my self-pity and

melancholy. The avenue was jammed with gay and happy crowds—
scenes that brought back memories of happy years that were gone. I
just couldn't bear the thought of going home to a lonely and empty
apartment. I was bewildered. I didn't know what to do. I couldn't
keep the tears back. After walking aimlessly for an hour or so, I found
myself in front of a bus terminal. I remembered that my husband and
I had often boarded an unknown bus for adventure, so I boarded the
first bus I found at the station. After crossing the Hudson River and
riding for some time, I heard the bus conductor say, "Last stop, lady."
I got off. I didn't even know the name of the town. It was a quiet,
peaceful little place. While waiting for the next bus home, I started
walking up a residential street. As I passed a church, I heard the
beautiful strains of "Silent Night." I went in. The church was empty
except for the organist. I sat down unnoticed in one of the pews. The
lights from the gaily decorated Christmas tree made the decorations
seem like myriads of stars dancing in the moonbeams. The long-
drawn cadences of the music—and the fact that I had forgotten to
eat since morning—made me drowsy. I was weary and heavy-laden,
so I drifted off to sleep.

'When I awoke, I didn't know where I was. I was terrified. I
saw in front of me two small children who had apparently come in
to see the Christmas tree. One, a little girl, was pointing at me and
saying "I wonder if Santa Claus brought her." These children were
also frightened when I awoke. I told them that I wouldn't hurt them.
They were poorly dressed. I asked them where their mother and daddy
were. "We ain't got no mother and daddy," they said.

'Here were two little orphans much worse off than I had ever been.
They made me feel ashamed of my sorrow and self-pity. I showed
them the Christmas tree and then took them to a drugstore and we
had some refreshments, and I bought them some candy and a few
presents. My loneliness vanished as if by magic. These two orphans
gave me the only real happiness and self-forgetfulness that I had had
in months. As I chatted with them, I realized how lucky I had been.
I thanked God that all my Christmases as a child had been bright

with parental love and tenderness. Those two little orphans did far more for me than I did for them. That experience showed me again the necessity of making other people happy in order to be happy ourselves. I found that happiness is contagious. By giving, we receive. By helping someone and giving out love, I had conquered worry and sorrow and self-pity, and felt like a new person. And I was a new person—not only then, but in the years that followed.'

I could fill a book with stories of people who forgot themselves into health and happiness. For example, let's take the case of Margaret Tayler Yates, one of the most popular women in the United States Navy.

Mrs Yates is a writer of novels, but none of her mystery stories is half so interesting as the true story of what happened to her that fateful morning when the Japanese struck our fleet at Pearl Harbor. Mrs Yates had been an invalid for more than a year: bad heart. She spent twenty-two out of every twenty-four hours in bed. The longest journey that she undertook was a walk into the garden to take a sunbath. Even then, she had to lean on the maid's arm as she walked. She herself told me that in those days she expected to be an invalid for the balance of her life. 'I would never have really lived again,' she told me, 'if the Japs had not struck Pearl Harbor and jarred me out of my complacency.'

'When this happened,' Mrs Yates said, as she told her story, 'everything was chaos and confusion. One bomb struck so near my home, the concussion threw me out of bed. Army trucks rushed out to Hickam Field, Scofield Barracks, and Kaneohe Bay Air Station, to bring Army and Navy wives and children to the public schools. There the Red Cross telephoned those who had extra rooms to take them in. The Red Cross workers knew that I had a telephone beside my bed, so they asked me to be a clearinghouse of information. So I kept track of where Army and Navy wives and children were being housed, and all Navy and Army men were instructed by the Red Cross to telephone me to find out where their families were.

'I soon discovered that my husband, Commander Robert Raleigh Yates, was safe. I tried to cheer up the wives who did not know whether their husbands had been killed; and I tried to give consolation to the widows whose husbands had been killed—and they were many. Two thousand, one hundred and seventeen officers and enlisted men in the Navy and Marine Corps were killed and 960 were reported missing.

'At first I answered these phone calls while lying in bed. Then I answered them sitting up in bed. Finally, I got so busy, so excited, that I forgot all about my weakness and got out of bed and sat by a table. By helping others who were much worse off than I was, I forgot all about myself; and I have never gone back to bed again except for my regular eight hours of sleep each night. I realize now that if the Japs had not struck at Pearl Harbor, I would probably have remained a semi-invalid all my life. I was comfortable in bed. I was constantly waited on, and I now realize that I was unconsciously losing my will to rehabilitate myself.

'The attack on Pearl Harbor was one of the greatest tragedies in American history, but as far as I was concerned, it was one of the best things that ever happened to me. That terrible crisis gave me strength that I never dreamed I possessed. It took my attention off myself and focused it on others. It gave me something big and vital and important to live for. I no longer had time to think about myself or care about myself.'

A third of the people who rush to psychiatrists for help could probably cure themselves if they would only do as Margaret Yates did: get interested in helping others. My idea? No, that is approximately what Carl Jung said. And he ought to know—if anybody does. He said: 'About one third of my patients are suffering from no clinically definable neurosis, but from the senselessness and emptiness of their lives.' To put it another way, they are trying to thumb a ride through life—and the parade passes them by. So they rush to a psychiatrist with their petty, senseless, useless lives.

Having missed the boat, they stand on the wharf, blaming everyone except themselves and demanding that the world cater to their self-centered desires.

You may be saying to yourself now: 'Well, I am not impressed by these stories. I myself could get interested in a couple of orphans I met on Christmas Eve; and if I had been at Pearl Harbor, I would gladly have done what Margaret Tayler Yates did. But with me things are different: I live an ordinary humdrum life. I work at a dull job eight hours a day. Nothing dramatic ever happens to me. How can I get interested in helping others? And why should I? What is there in it for me?'

A fair question. I'll try to answer it. However humdrum your existence may be, you surely meet some people every day of your life. What do you do about them? Do you merely stare through them, or do you try to find out what it is that makes them tick? How about the postman, for example—he walks hundreds of miles every year, delivering mail to your door; but have you ever taken the trouble to find out where he lives, or ask to see a snapshot of his wife and his kids? Did you ever ask him if his feet get tired, or if he ever gets bored?

What about the grocery boy, the newspaper vendor, the chap at the corner who polishes your shoes? These people are human—bursting with troubles, and dreams, and private ambitions. They are also bursting for the chance to share them with someone. But do you ever let them? Do you ever show an eager, honest interest in them or their lives? That's the sort of thing I mean. You don't have to become a Florence Nightingale or a social reformer to help improve the world—your own private world; you can start tomorrow morning with the people you meet!

What's in it for you? Much greater happiness! Greater satisfaction, and pride in yourself! Aristotle called this kind of attitude 'enlightened selfishness.' Zoroaster said, 'Doing good to others is not a duty. It is a joy, for it increases your own health and happiness.' And Benjamin Franklin summed it up very simply—'When you are good to others,' said Franklin, 'you are best to yourself.'

'No discovery of modern psychology,' writes Henry C. Link, director of the Psychological Service Center in New York, 'no discovery of modern psychology is, in my opinion, so important as its scientific proof of the necessity of self-sacrifice or discipline to self-realization and happiness.'

Thinking of others will not only keep you from worrying about yourself; it will also help you to make a lot of friends and have a lot of fun. How? Well, I once asked Professor William Lyon Phelps, of Yale, how he did it; and here is what he said:

'I never go into a hotel or a barbershop or a store without saying something agreeable to everyone I meet. I try to say something that treats them as an individual—not merely a cog in a machine. I sometimes compliment the girl who waits on me in the store by telling her how beautiful her eyes are—or her hair. I will ask a barber if he doesn't get tired standing on his feet all day. I'll ask him how he came to take up barbering—how long he has been at it and how many heads of hair he has cut. I'll help him figure it out. I find that taking an interest in people makes them beam with pleasure. I frequently shake hands with a redcap who has carried my grip. It gives him a new lift and freshens him up for the whole day. One extremely hot summer day, I went into a dining car of the New Haven Railway to have lunch. The crowded car was almost like a furnace and the service was slow. When the steward finally got around to handing me the menu, I said: "The boys back there cooking in that hot kitchen certainly must be suffering today." The steward began to curse. His tones were bitter. At first, I thought he was angry. "Good God Almighty," he exclaimed, "people come in here and complain about the food. They kick about the slow service and growl about the heat and the prices. I have listened to their criticisms for nineteen years and you are the first person and the only person that has ever expressed any sympathy for the cooks back there in the boiling kitchen. I wish to God we had more passengers like you".'

'The steward was astounded because I had thought of the coloured cooks as human beings, and not merely as a cog in the organization of a great railway. What people want,' continued Professor Phelps, 'is a little attention as human beings. When I meet a man on the street with a beautiful dog, I always comment on the dog's beauty.

As I walk on and glance back over my shoulder, I frequently see the man petting and admiring the dog. My appreciation has renewed his appreciation.'

'One time in England, I met a shepherd, and expressed my sincere admiration for his big, intelligent sheep dog. I asked him to tell me how he trained the dog. As I walked away, I glanced back over my shoulder and saw the dog standing with his paws on the shepherd's shoulders and the shepherd was petting him. By taking a little interest in the shepherd and his dog, I made the shepherd happy. I made the dog happy and I made myself happy.'

Can you imagine a man who goes around shaking hands with porters and expressing sympathy for the cooks in the hot kitchen—and telling people how much he admires their dogs—can you imagine a man like that being sour and worried and needing the services of a psychiatrist? You can't, can you? No, of course not. A Chinese proverb puts it this way: 'A bit of fragrance always clings to the hand that gives you roses.'

You didn't have to tell that to Billy Phelps of Yale. He knew it. He lived it.

If you are a man, skip this paragraph. It won't interest you. It tells how a worried, unhappy girl got several men to propose to her. The girl who did that is a grandmother now. A few years ago, I spent the night in her and her husband's home. I had been giving a lecture in her town; and the next morning she drove me about fifty miles to catch a train on the main line of the New York Central. We got to talking about winning friends, and she said: 'Mr Carnegie, I am going to tell you something that I have never confessed to anyone before—not even to my husband.' (By the way, this story isn't going to be half so interesting as you probably imagine.) She told me that she had been reared in a social-register family in Philadelphia. 'The tragedy of my girlhood and young woman-hood,' she said, 'was our poverty. We could never entertain the way the other girls in my social set entertained. My clothes were never of the best quality. I outgrew them and they didn't fit and they were often out of style.

I was so humiliated, so ashamed, that I often cried myself to sleep. Finally, in sheer desperation, I hit upon the idea of always asking my partner at dinner parties to tell me about his experience, his ideas, and his plans for the future. I didn't ask these questions because I was especially interested in the answers. I did it solely to keep my partner from looking at my poor clothes. But a strange thing happened: as I listened to these young men talk and learned more about them, I really became interested in listening to what they had to say. I became so interested that I myself sometimes forgot about my clothes. But the astounding thing to me was this: since I was a good listener and encouraged the boys to talk about themselves, I gave them happiness and I gradually became the most popular girl in our social group and three of these men proposed marriage to me.'

(There you are, girls: that is the way it is done.)

Some people who read this chapter are going to say: 'All this talk about getting interested in others is a lot of damn nonsense! Sheer religious pap! None of that stuff for me! I am going to put money in my purse. I am going to grab all I can get—and grab it now—and to hell with the other dumb clucks!'

Well, if that is your opinion, you are entitled to it; but if you are right, then all the great philosophers and teachers since the beginning of recorded history—Jesus, Confucius, Buddha, Plato, Aristotle, Socrates, Saint Francis—were all wrong. But since you may sneer at the teachings of religious leaders, let's turn for advice to a couple of atheists. First, let's take the late A.E. Housman, professor at Cambridge University, and one of the most distinguished scholars of his generation. In 1936, he gave an address at Cambridge University on 'The Name and Nature of Poetry.' In that address, he declared that 'the greatest truth ever uttered and the most profound moral discovery of all time were these words of Jesus: "He that findeth his life shall lose it: and he that loseth his life for my sake shall find it".'

We have heard preachers say that all our lives. But Housman was an atheist, a pessimist, a man who contemplated suicide; and yet he felt that the man who thought only of himself wouldn't get much out of life. He would be miserable. But the man who forgot himself in service to others would find the joy of living.

If you are not impressed by what A. E. Housman said, let's turn for advice to the most distinguished American atheist of the twentieth century: Theodore Dreiser. Dreiser ridiculed all religions as fairy tales and regarded life as 'a tale told by an idiot, full of sound and fury, signifying nothing.' Yet Dreiser advocated the one great principle that Jesus taught—service to others. 'If he [man] is to extract any joy out of his span,' Dreiser said, 'he must think and plan to make things better not only for himself but for others, since joy for himself depends upon his joy in others and theirs in him." If we are going "to make things better for others"—as Dreiser advocated—"let's be quick about it. Time is a-wastin". I shall pass this way but once. Therefore any good that I can do or any kindness that I can show—let me do it now. Let me not defer nor neglect it, for I shall not pass this way again.'

So if you want to banish worry and cultivate peace and happiness, here is

Rule 7: Forget yourself by becoming interested in others. Do every day a good deed that will put a smile of joy on someone's face.

Worry never robs tomorrow of its sorrow,
it only saps today of its joy.
—Leo Buscaglia

All right, every day ain't going to be the best day of your life, don't worry about that. If you stick to it you hold the possibility open that you will have better days.
—Wendell Berry

22

ONE OF THE TWO MAJOR DECISIONS OF YOUR LIFE

If you are under eighteen, you will probably soon be called upon to make the two most important decisions of your life—decisions that will profoundly alter all the days of your years; decisions that may have far-reaching effects upon your happiness, your income, your health; decisions that may make or break you.

What are these two tremendous decisions?

First: How are you going to make a living? Are you going to be a farmer, a mail carrier, a chemist, a forest ranger, a stenographer, a horse doctor, a college professor, or are you going to run a hamburger stand?

Second: Whom are you going to select to be the father or mother of your children?

Both of those great decisions are frequently gambles. 'Every boy,' says Harry Emerson Fosdick in his book, The Power to See It Through, 'every boy is a gambler when he chooses a vocation. He must stake his life on it.' How can you reduce the gamble in selecting a vocation? Read on; we will tell you as best we can. First, try, if possible, to find work that you enjoy. I once asked David M. Goodrich, Chairman of the Board, B. F. Goodrich Company—tire manufacturers—what he considered the first requisite of success in business, and he replied—'Having a good time at your work. If you enjoy what you are doing,' he said, 'you may work long hours, but it won't seem like work at all. It will seem like play.'

Edison was a good example of that. Edison—the unschooled newsboy who grew up to transform the industrial life of America—Edison, the man who often ate and slept in his labouratory and toiled there for eighteen hours a day. But it wasn't toil to him. 'I never did a day's work in my life,' he exclaimed. 'It was all fun.'

No wonder he succeeded!

I once heard Charles Schwab say much the same thing. He said: 'A man can succeed at almost anything for which he has unlimited enthusiasm.'

But how can you have enthusiasm for a job when you haven't the foggiest idea of what you want to do? 'The greatest tragedy I know of,' said Mrs Edna Kerr, who once hired thousands of employees for the Dupont Company, and is now assistant director of industrial relations for the American Home Products Company—'The greatest tragedy I know of,' she told me, 'is that so many young people never discover what they really want to do. I think no one else is so much to be pitied as the person who gets nothing at all out of his work but his pay.' Mrs Kerr reports that even college graduates come to her and say, 'I have a B.A. degree from Dartmouth [or an M.A. from Cornell]. Have you some kind of work I can do for your firm?' They don't know themselves what they are able to do, or even what they would like to do. Is it any wonder that so many men and women who start out in life with competent minds and rosy dreams end up at forty in utter frustration and even with a nervous breakdown? In fact, finding the right occupation is important even for your health. When Dr Raymond Pearl, of Johns Hopkins, made a study, together with some insurance companies, to discover the factors that make for a long life, he placed "the right occupation" high on the list. He might have said, with Thomas Carlyle, 'Blessed is the man who has found his work. Let him ask no other blessedness.'

I recently spent an evening with Paul W. Boynton, employment supervisor for the Socony-Vacuum Oil Company. During the last twenty years he has interviewed more than seventy-five thousand people looking for jobs, and he has written a book entitled 6 Ways to Get a Job. I asked him: 'What is the greatest mistake young people make today in looking for work?' 'They don't know what they want to do,' he said. 'It is perfectly appalling to realize that a man will give more thought to buying a suit of clothes that will wear out in a few years than he will give to choosing the career on which his whole future depends—on which his whole future happiness and peace of mind are based!'

And so what? What can you do about it? You can take advantage of a new profession called vocational guidance. It may help you—or harm you—depending on the ability and character of the counselor you consult. This new profession isn't even within gunshot of perfection yet. It hasn't even reached the Model T stage. But it has a great future. How can you make use of this science? By finding out where, in your community, you can get vocational tests and vocational advice. All the larger cities and thousands of smaller communities throughout the United States have this kind of service. If you are a veteran, the Veterans Administration will tell you where to apply. If you're not a veteran, then ask your public library or your local board of education where you may get vocational guidance. Hundreds of high schools and colleges have vocational-guidance bureaus. If you live in the country, write to your State Supervisor, Occupational Information and Guidance Service, in care of your state capitol. Many states have supervisors to give this sort of advice. In addition to the public agencies, a number of nation-wide organizations, such as the YMCA, YWCA, American Red Cross, B'nai B'rith, Boys' Clubs of America, Kiwanis Clubs, and the Salvation Army, have counselors to help you solve your vocational problems.

They can only suggest. You have to make the decisions. Remember that these counselors are far from infallible. They don't always agree with one another. They sometimes make ridiculous mistakes. For example, a vocational-guidance counselor advised one of my students to become a writer solely because she had a large vocabulary. How absurd! It isn't as simple as that. Good writing is the kind that transfers your thoughts and emotions to the reader—and to do that, you don't need a large vocabulary, but you do need ideas, experience, convictions, and excitement. The vocational counselor who advised this girl with a large vocabulary to become an author succeeded in doing only one thing: he turned an erstwhile happy stenographer into a frustrated, would-be novelist.

The point I am trying to make is that vocational-guidance experts, even as you and I, are not infallible. Perhaps you had better consult several of them—and then interpret their findings in the sunlight of common sense.

You may think it strange that I am including a chapter like this in a book devoted to worry. But it isn't strange at all, when you understand how many of our worries, regrets, and frustrations are spawned by work we despise. Ask your father about it—or your neighbour or your boss. No less an intellectual giant than John Stuart Mill declared that industrial misfits are 'among the heaviest losses of society.' Yes, and among the unhappiest people on this earth are those same 'industrial misfits' who hate their daily work!

Do you know the kind of man who 'cracked up' in the Army? The man who was misplaced! I'm not talking about battle casualties, but about the men who cracked up in ordinary service. Dr William Menninger, one of our greatest living psychiatrists, was in charge of the Army's neuropsychiatric division during the war, and he says: 'We learned much in the Army as to the importance of selection and of placement, of putting the right man in the right job... A conviction of the importance of the job at hand was extremely important. Where a man had no interest, where he felt he was misplaced, where he thought he was not appreciated, where he believed his talents were being misused, invariably we found a potential if not an actual psychiatric casualty.'

Yes—and for the same reasons, a man may "crack up" in industry. If he despises his business, he can crack it up, too.

Take, for example, the case of Phil Johnson. Phil Johnson's father owned a laundry, so he gave his son a job, hoping the boy would work into the business. But Phil hated the laundry, so he dawdled, loafed, did what he had to do and not a lick more. Some days he was 'absent.' His father was so hurt to think he had a shiftless, ambitionless son that he was actually ashamed before his employees.

One day Phil Johnson told his father he wanted to be a mechanic—work in a machine shop. What? Go back to overalls? The old man was shocked. But Phil had his way. He worked in greasy dungarees. He did much harder work than was required at the laundry. He worked longer hours, and he whistled at his job! He took up engineering, learned about engines, puttered with machines—and when Philip Johnson died, in 1944, he was president of the Boeing Aircraft Company, and was making the Flying Fortresses that helped to win the war! If he had stuck with the laundry, what would have happened to him and the laundry—especially after his father's death? My guess is he would have ruined the business—cracked it up and run it into the ground.

Even at the risk of starting family rows, I would like to say to young people: Don't feel compelled to enter a business or trade just because your family wants you to do it! Don't enter a career unless you want to do it! However, consider carefully the advice of your parents. They have probably lived twice as long as you have. They have gained the kind of wisdom that comes only from much experience and the passing of many years. But, in the last analysis, you are the one who has to make the final decision. You are the one who is going to be either happy or miserable at your work.

Now, having said this, let me give you the following suggestions—some of them warnings—about choosing your work:

Read and study the following five suggestions about selecting a vocational-guidance counselor. These suggestions are right from the horse's mouth. They were made by one of America's leading vocational-guidance experts, Professor Harry Dexter Kitson.

'Don't go to anyone who tells you that he has a magic system that will indicate your "vocational aptitude." In this group are phrenologists, astrologers, "character analysts," handwriting experts. Their "systems" do not work.'

'Don't go to anyone who tells you that he can give you a test that will indicate what occupation you should choose. Such a person violates the principle that a vocational counselor must take into account the physical, social, and economic conditions surrounding the counselee; and he should render his service in the light of the occupational opportunities open to the counselee.'

'Seek a vocational counselor who has an adequate library of information about occupations and uses it in the counseling process.'

'A thorough vocational-guidance service generally requires more than one interview.'

'Never accept vocational guidance by mail.'

Keep out of business and professions that are already jam-packed and overflowing! There are more than twenty thousand different ways of making a living in America. Think of it! Over twenty thousand. But do young people know this? Not unless they hire a swami to gaze into a crystal ball. The result? In one school, two thirds of the boys confined their choices to five occupations—five out of twenty thousand—and four fifths of the girls did the same. Small wonder that a few businesses and professions are overcrowded—small wonder that insecurity, worry, and 'anxiety neuroses' are rampant at times among the white-collar fraternity! Beware especially of trying to elbow your way into such overcrowded fields as law, journalism, radio, motion pictures, and the 'glamour occupations.'

Stay out of activities where the chances are only one out of ten of your being able to make a living. As an example, take selling life insurance. Each year countless thousands of men—frequently unemployed men—start out trying to sell life insurance without bothering to find out in advance what is likely to happen to them! Here is approximately what does happen, according to Franklin L. Bettger, Real Estate Trust Building, Philadelphia. For twenty years Mr Bettger was one of the outstandingly successful insurance salesmen in America. He declares that ninety per cent of the men who start selling life insurance get so heartsick and discouraged that they give it up within a year. Out of the ten who remain, one man will sell ninety per cent of all the insurance sold by the ten and the remaining nine men will sell only ten per cent of the insurance. To put it another way: if you start selling life insurance, the chances are nine to one that you will fail and quit within twelve months; and the chances are only one in a hundred that you will make ten thousand a year out of it. Even if you remain at it, the chances are only one out of ten that you will be able to do anything more than barely scratch out a living.

Spend weeks—even months, if necessary—-finding out all you can about an occupation before deciding to devote your life to it! How? By interviewing men and women who have already spent ten, twenty, or forty years in that occupation.

These interviews may have a profound effect on your future. I know that from my own experience. When I was in my early twenties, I sought the vocational advice of two older men. As I look back now, I can see that those two interviews were turning points in my career. In fact, it would be difficult for me even to imagine what my life would have been like had I not had those two interviews.

How can you get these vocational-guidance interviews? To illustrate, let's suppose that you are thinking about studying to be an architect. Before you make your decision, you ought to spend weeks interviewing the architects in your city and in adjoining cities. You can get their names and addresses out of a classified telephone directory. You can call at their offices either with or without an appointment. If you wish to make an appointment, write them something like this:

Won't you please do me a little favor? I want your advice. I am eighteen years old, and I am thinking about studying to be an architect. Before I make up my mind, I would like to ask your advice.

If you are too busy to see me at your office, I would be most grateful if you would grant me the privilege of seeing you for half an hour at your home.

Here is a list of questions I would like to ask you:

If you had your life to live over, would you become an architect again?

After you have sized me up, I want to ask you whether you think I have what it takes to succeed as an architect.

Is the profession of architecture overcrowded?

If I studied architecture for four years, would it be difficult for me to get a job? What kind of job would I have to take at first?

If I had average ability, how much could I hope to earn during the first five years?

What are the advantages and disadvantages of being an architect?

If I were your son, would you advise me to become an architect?

If you are timid, and hesitate to face a 'big shot' alone, here are two suggestions that will help.

First, get a lad of your own age to go with you. The two of you will bolster up one another's confidence. If you haven't someone of your own age to go with you, ask your father to go with you.

Second, remember that by asking his advice you are paying this man a compliment. He may feel flattered by your request. Remember that adults like to give advice to young men and women. The architect will probably enjoy the interview.

If you hesitate to write letters asking for an appointment, then go to a man's office without an appointment and tell him you would be most grateful if he would give you a bit of advice.

Suppose you call on five architects and they are all too busy to see you (which isn't likely), call on five more. Some of them will see you and give you priceless advice—advice that may save you years of lost time and heartbreak.

Remember that you are making one of the two most vital and far-reaching decisions of your life. So, take time to get the facts before you act. If you don't, you may spend half a lifetime regretting it.

If you can afford to do so, offer to pay a man for a half-hour of his time and advice.

Get over the mistaken belief that you are fitted for only a single occupation! Every normal person can succeed at a number of occupations, and every normal person would probably fail in many occupations. Take myself, for example: if I had studied and prepared myself for the following occupations, I believe I would have had a good chance of achieving some small measure of success—and also of enjoying my work. I refer to such occupations as farming, fruit growing, scientific agriculture, medicine, selling, advertising, editing a country newspaper, teaching, and forestry. On the other hand, I am sure I would have been unhappy, and a failure, at bookkeeping, accounting, engineering, operating a hotel or a factory, architecture, all mechanical trades, and hundreds of other activities.

A day of worry is more exhausting than a week of work.
—John Lubbock

If you ask what is the single most important key to longevity, I would have to say it is avoiding worry, stress and tension. And if you didn't ask me, I'd still have to say it.
—George Burns

HOW TO ENJOY YOUR LIFE AND YOUR JOB

PART 1
Stop Worrying

1

FOUR GOOD WORKING HABITS THAT WILL HELP PREVENT FATIGUE AND WORRY

GOOD WORKING HABIT NO. 1

Clear your desk of all papers except those relating to the immediate problem at hand.

Roland L. Williams, President of the Chicago and Northwestern Railway, once said, 'A person with his desk piled high with papers on various matters will find his work much easier and more accurate if he clears that desk of all but the immediate problem on hand. I call this good housekeeping, and it is the number-one step towards efficiency.'

If you visit the Library of Congress in Washington, D.C., you will find five words painted on the ceiling—five words written by the poet Pope:

'Order is Heaven's first law.'

Order ought to be the first law of business, too. But is it? No, the average desk is cluttered up with papers that haven't been looked at for weeks. In fact, the publisher of a New Orleans newspaper once told me that his secretary cleared up one of his desks and found a typewriter that had been missing for two years!

The mere sight of a desk littered with unanswered mail and reports and memos is enough to breed confusion, tension, and worries. It is much worse than that. The constant reminder of 'a million things to do and no time to do them' can worry you not only into tension and fatigue, but also into high blood pressure, heart trouble, and stomach ulcers.

Dr John H. Stokes, professor, Graduate School of Medicine, University of Pennsylvania, read a paper before the National Convention of the American Medical Association—a paper entitled "Functional Neuroses as Complications of Organic Disease." In that paper, Dr Stokes listed eleven conditions under the title: 'What to Look for in the Patient's State of Mind.' Here is the first item on that list:

The sense of must or obligation; the unending stretch of things ahead that simply have to be done.

But how can such an elementary procedure as clearing your desk and making decisions help you avoid this high pressure, this sense of must, this sense of an 'unending stretch of things ahead' that simply have to be done? Dr William L. Sadler, the famous psychiatrist, told of a patient who, by using this simple device, avoided a nervous breakdown. The man was an executive in a big Chicago firm. When he came to Dr Sadler's office, he was tense, nervous, worried. He knew he was heading for a tailspin, but he couldn't quit work. He had to have help.

'While this man was telling me his story,' Dr Sadler says, 'my telephone rang. It was the hospital calling; and instead of deferring the matter, I took time right then to come to a decision. I always settle questions, if possible, right on the spot. I had no sooner hung up than the phone rang again. Again an urgent matter, which I took time to discuss. The third interruption came when a colleague of mine came to my office for advice on a patient who was critically ill. When I had finished with him, I turned to my caller and began to apologize for keeping him waiting. But he had brightened up. He had a completely different look on his face.'

'Don't apologize, doctor!' this man said to Sadler. 'In the last ten minutes, I think I've got a hunch as to what is wrong with me. I'm going back to my office and revise my working habits... But before I go, do you mind if I take a look in your desk?'

Dr Sadler opened up the drawers of his desk. All empty—except for supplies. 'Tell me,' said the patient, 'where do you keep your unfinished business?'

'Finished!' said Sadler.

'And where do you keep your unanswered mail?'

'Answered!' Sadler told him. 'My rule is never to lay down a letter until I have answered it. I dictate the reply to my secretary at once.'

Six weeks later, this same executive invited Dr Sadler to come to his office. He was changed—and so was his desk. He opened the desk drawers to show there was no unfinished business inside of the desk. 'Six weeks ago,' this executive said, 'I had three different desks in two different offices—and was snowed under by my work. I was never finished. After talking to you, I came back here and cleared out a wagonload of reports and old papers. Now I work at one desk, settle things as they come up, and don't have a mountain of unfinished business nagging at me and making me tense and worried. But the most astonishing thing is I've recovered completely. There is nothing wrong anymore with my health!'

Charles Evans Hughes, former Chief Justice of the United States Supreme Court, said: 'Men do not die from overwork. They die from dissipation and worry.' Yes, from dissipation of their energies—and worry because they never seem to get their work done.

GOOD WORKING HABIT NO. 2

Do things in the order of their importance.

Henry L. Doherty, founder of the nationwide Cities Service Company, said that regardless of how much salary he paid, there were two abilities he found it almost impossible to find.

Those two priceless abilities: first, the ability to think. Second, the ability to do things in the order of their importance.

Charles Luckman, the lad who started from scratch and climbed in twelve years to president of the Pepsodent Company, got a salary of a hundred thousand dollars a year, and made a million dollars besides—

that lad declared that he owed much of his success to developing the two abilities that Henry L. Doherty said he found almost impossible to find. Charles Luckman said: 'As far back as I can remember, I have gotten up at five o'clock in the morning because I can think better then than any other time—I can think better then and plan my day, plan to do things in the order of their importance.'

Frank Bettger, one of America's most successful insurance salesmen, didn't wait until five o'clock in the morning to plan his day. He planned it the night before—set a goal for himself—a goal to sell a certain amount of insurance that day. If he failed, that amount was added to his next day—and so on.

I know from long experience that one is not always able to do things in the order of their importance, but I also know that some kind of plan to do first things first is infinitely better than extemporizing as you go along.

If George Bernard Shaw had not made it a rigid rule to do first things first, he would probably have failed as a writer and might have remained a bank cashier all his life. His plan called for writing five pages each day for nine heartbreaking years, even though he made a total of thirty dollars in those nine years—about a penny a day. Even Robinson Crusoe wrote out a schedule of what he would do each hour of the day.

GOOD WORKING HABIT NO. 3

When you face a problem, solve it then and there if you have the facts necessary to make a decision. Don't keep putting off decisions.

One of my former students, the late H.P. Howell, told me that when he was a member of the board of directors of U.S. Steel, the meetings of the board were often long-drawn-out affairs—many problems were discussed, few decisions were made. The result: each member of the board had to carry home bundles of reports to study.

Finally, Mr Howell persuaded the board of directors to take up one problem at a time and come to a decision. No procrastination—no putting off. The decision might be to ask for additional facts; it might be to do something or to do nothing. But a decision was reached on each problem before passing on to the next. Mr Howell told me that the results were striking and salutary: the docket was cleared. The calender was clean. No longer was it necessary for each member to carry home a bundle of reports. No longer was there a worried sense of unresolved problems.

A good rule, not only for the board of directors of U.S. Steel, but for you and me.

GOOD WORKING HABIT NO. 4

Learn to organize, deputize and supervise.

Many business persons are driving themselves to premature graves because they have never learned to delegate responsibility to others, insisting on doing everything themselves. Result: details and confusion overwhelm them. They are driven by a sense of hurry, worry, anxiety and tension. It is hard to learn to delegate responsibilities. I know. It was hard for me, awfully hard. I also know from experience the disasters that can be caused by delegating authority to the wrong people. But difficult as it is to delegate authority, executives must do it if they are to avoid worry, tension and fatigue.

Executives who build up big businesses and don't learn to organize, deputize and supervise usually pop off with heart trouble in their fifties or early sixties—heart trouble caused by tension and worries. Want a specific instance? Look at the death notices in your local paper.

Our fatigue is often caused not by work,
but by worry, frustration and resentment.
—Dale Carnegie

Only the prepared speaker deserves to be confident.
—Dale Carnegie.

2

HOW TO BANISH THE BOREDOM THAT PRODUCES FATIGUE, WORRY AND RESENTMENT

One of the chief causes of fatigue is boredom. To illustrate, let's take the case of Alice, an executive who lives on your street. Alice came home one night utterly exhausted. She acted fatigued. She was fatigued. She had a headache. She had a backache. She was so exhausted she wanted to go to bed without waiting for dinner. Her mother pleaded... She sat down at the table. The telephone rang. The boy friend! An invitation to a dance! Her eyes sparkled. Her spirits soared. She rushed upstairs, put on her Alice-Blue gown, and danced until three o'clock in the morning; and when she finally did get home, she was not the slightest bit exhausted. She was, in fact, so exhilarated she couldn't fall asleep.

Was Alice really and honestly tired eight hours earlier, when she looked and acted exhausted? Sure she was. She was exhausted because she was bored with her work, perhaps bored with life. There are millions of Alices. You may be one of them.

It is a well-known fact that your emotional attitude usually has far more to do with producing fatigue than has physical exertion. A few years ago, Joseph E. Barmack, Ph.D., published in the Archives of Psychology a report of some of his experiments, showing how boredom produces fatigue. Dr Barmack put a group of students through a series of tests in which, he knew, they could have little interest. The result? The students felt tired and sleepy, complained of headaches and eyestrain, felt irritable. In some cases, even their stomachs were upset. Was it all 'imagination'? No. Metabolism tests were taken of these students. These tests showed that the blood pressure of the body and the consumption of oxygen actually decrease when a person is bored, and that the whole metabolism picks up immediately as soon as he begins to feel interest and pleasure in his work!

We rarely get tired when we are doing something interesting and exciting. For example, I recently took a vacation in the Canadian Rockies up around Lake Louise. I spent several days trout fishing along Corral Creek, fighting my way through brush higher than my head, stumbling over logs, struggling through fallen timber—yet after eight hours of this, I was not exhausted. Why? Because I was excited, exhilarated. I had a sense of high achievement: six cut-throat trout. But suppose I had been bored by fishing, then how do you think I would have felt? I would have been worn out by such strenuous work at an altitude of seven thousand feet.

Even in such exhausting activities as mountain climbing, boredom may tire you far more than the strenuous work involved. For example, Mr S.H. Kingman, president of the Farmers and Mechanics Savings Bank of Minneapolis, told me of an incident that is a perfect illustration of that statement. In July, 1953, the Canadian government asked the Canadian Alpine Club to furnish guides to train the members of the Prince of Wales Rangers in mountain climbing. Mr Kingman was one of the guides chosen to train these soldiers. He told me how he and the other guides—men ranging from forty-two to fifty-nine years of age—took these young army men on long hikes across glaciers and snow fields and up a sheer cliff of forty feet, where they had to climb with ropes and tiny footholds and precarious handholds. They climbed Michael's Peak, the Vice-President Peak, and other unnamed peaks in the Little Yoho Valley in the Canadian Rockies. After fifteen hours of mountain climbing, these young men, who were in the pink of condition (they had just finished a six-week course in tough Commando training), were utterly exhausted.

Was their fatigue caused by using muscles that had not been hardened by Commando training? Anyone who had ever been through Commando training would hoot at such a ridiculous question! No, they were utterly exhausted because they were bored by mountain climbing. They were so tired that many of them fell asleep without waiting to eat. But the guides—men who were two and three times as old as the soldiers—were they tired? Yes, but not exhausted. The guides ate dinner and stayed up for hours, talking about the day's experiences. They were not exhausted because they were interested.

When Dr Edward Thorndike of Columbia was conducting experiments in fatigue, he kept young men awake for almost a week by keeping them constantly interested. After much investigation, Dr Thorndike is reported to have said: 'Boredom is the only real cause of diminution of work.'

If you are a mental worker, it is seldom the amount of work you do that makes you tired. You may be tired by the amount of work you do not do. For example, remember the day last week when you were constantly interrupted. No letters answered. Appointments broken. Trouble here and there. Everything went wrong that day. You accomplished nothing whatever, yet you went home exhausted—and with a splitting head.

The next day everything clicked at the office. You accomplished forty times more than you did the previous day. Yet you went home fresh as a snowy-white gardenia. You have had that experience. So have I.

The lesson to be learned? Just this: our fatigue is often caused not by work, but by worry, frustration, and resentment.

While writing this chapter, I went to see a revival of Jerome Kern's delightful musical comedy Show Boat. Captain Andy, captain of the Cotton Blossom, says in one of his philosophical interludes: 'The lucky folks are the ones that get to do things they enjoy doing.' Such folk are lucky because they have more energy, more happiness, less worry and less fatigue. Where your interests are, there is your energy also. Walking ten blocks with a nagging wife or husband can be more fatiguing than walking ten miles with an adoring sweetheart.

And so what? What can you do about it? Well, here is what one stenographer did about it—a stenographer working for an oil company in Tulsa, Oklahoma. For several days each month, she had one of the dullest jobs imaginable: filling out printed forms for oil leases, inserting figures and statistics. This task was so boring that she resolved, in self-defense, to make it interesting. How? She had a daily contest with herself. She counted the number of forms she filled out each morning, and then tried to excel that record in the afternoon. She counted each day's total and tried to better it the next day. Result? She was soon able to fill out more of these dull printed forms than any other stenographer in her division. And what did all this get her? Praise? No... Thanks? No... Promotion? No... Increased pay? No... But it did help to prevent the fatigue that is spawned by boredom. It did give her a mental stimulant. Because she had done her best to make a dull job interesting, she had more energy, more zest, and got far more happiness out of her leisure hours.

I happen to know this story is true, because I married that girl.

Here is the story of another stenographer who found it paid to act as if her work were interesting. She used to fight her work. But no more. She is Miss Vallie G. Golden, of Elmhurst, Illinois. Here is her story, as she wrote it to me:

'There are four stenographers in my office and each of us is assigned to take letters from several men. Once in a while we get jammed up in these assignments. One day, when an assistant department head insisted that I do a long letter over, I started to rebel. I tried to point out to him that the letter could be corrected without being retyped—and he retorted that if I didn't do it over, he would find someone else who would! I was absolutely fuming! But as I started to retype this letter, it suddenly occurred to me that there were a lot of other people who would jump at the chance to do the work I was doing. Also, that I was being paid a salary to do just that work. I began to feel better. I suddenly made up my mind to do my work as if I actually enjoyed it—even though I despised it. Then I made this important discovery: if I do my work as if I really enjoy it, then I do enjoy it to some extent. I also found I can work faster when I enjoy my work. So there is seldom any need now for me to work overtime. This new attitude of mine gained me the reputation of being a good worker. And when one of the department superintendents needed a private secretary, he asked for me for the job—because, he said, I was willing to do extra work without being sulky! This matter of the power of a changed mental attitude,' wrote Miss Golden, 'has been a tremendously important discovery to me. It has worked wonders!'

Miss Golden used the wonder-working 'as if' philosophy of Professor Hans Vaihinger. He taught us to act 'as if' we were happy—and so on.

If you act 'as if' you are interested in your job, that bit of acting will tend to make your interest real. It will also tend to decrease your fatigue, your tensions, and your worries.

A few years ago, Harlan A. Howard made a decision that completely altered his life. He resolved to make a dull job interesting—and he certainly had a dull one: washing plates, scrubbing counters, and dishing out ice cream in the high-school lunchroom while the other boys were playing ball or kidding the girls. Harlan Howard despised his job—but since he had to stick to it, he resolved to study ice cream—how it was made, what ingredients were used, why some ice creams were better than others. He studied the chemistry of ice cream, and became a whiz in the high-school chemistry course. He was so interested now in food chemistry that he entered the Massachusetts State College and majored in the field of 'food technology.' When the New York Cocoa Exchange offered a hundred-dollar prize for the best paper on uses of cocoa and chocolate—a prize open to all college students—who do you suppose won it? ...That's right. Harlan Howard.

When he found it difficult to get a job, he opened a private labouratory in the basement of his home in Amherst, Massachusetts. Shortly after that, a new law was passed. The bacteria in milk had to be counted. Harlan A. Howard was soon counting bacteria for the fourteen milk companies in Amherst—and he had to hire two assistants.

Where will he be twenty-five years from now? Well, the men who are now running the business of food chemistry will be retired then, or dead; and their places will be taken by young lads who are now radiating initiative and enthusiasm. Twenty-five years from now, Harlan A. Howard will probably be one of the leaders in his profession, while some of his classmates to whom he used to sell ice cream over the counter will be sour, unemployed, cussing the government, and complaining that they never had a chance. Harlan A. Howard might never have had a chance, either, if he hadn't resolved to make a dull job interesting.

Years ago, there was another young man who was bored with his dull job of standing at a lathe, turning out bolts in a factory. His first name was Sam. Sam wanted to quit, but he was afraid he couldn't find another job. Since he had to do this dull work, Sam decided he would make it interesting. So he ran a race with the mechanic operating a machine beside him. One of them was to trim off the rough surfaces on his machine, and the other was to trim the bolts down to the proper diameter. They would switch machines occasionally and see who could turn out the most bolts. The foreman, impressed with Sam's speed and accuracy, soon gave him a better job. That was the start of a whole series of promotions. Thirty years later, Sam—Samuel Vauclain—was president of the Baldwin Locomotive Works. But he might have remained a mechanic all his life if he had not resolved to make a dull job interesting.

H.V. Kaltenborn—the famous radio news analyst—once told me how he made a dull job interesting. When he was twenty-two years old, he worked his way across the Atlantic on a cattle boat, feeding and watering the steers. After making a bicycle tour of England, he arrived in Paris, hungry and broke. Pawning his camera for five dollars, he put an ad in the Paris edition of The New York Herald and got a job selling stereopticon machines. I can remember those old-fashioned stereoscopes that we used to hold up before our eyes to look at two pictures exactly alike. As we looked, a miracle happened. The two lenses in the stereoscope transformed the two pictures into a single scene with the effect of a third dimension. We saw distance. We got an astounding sense of perspective.

Well, as I was saying, Kaltenborn started out selling these machines from door to door in Paris—and he couldn't speak French. But he earned five thousand dollars in commissions the first year, and made himself one of the highest-paid salesmen in France that year. H. V. Kaltenborn told me that this experience did as much to develop within him the qualities that make for success as did any single year of study at Harvard. Confidence? He told me himself that after that experience, he felt he could have sold The Congressional Record to French housewives.

That experience gave him an intimate understanding of French life that later proved invaluable in interpreting, on the radio, European events.

How did he manage to become an expert salesman when he couldn't speak French? Well, he had his employer write out his sales talk in perfect French, and he memorized it. He would ring a doorbell, a housewife would answer, and Kaltenborn would begin repeating his memorized sales talk with an accent so terrible it was funny. He would show the housewife his pictures, and when she asked a question, he would shrug his shoulders and say, 'An American ... an American.' He would then take off his hat and point to a copy of the sales talk in perfect French that he had pasted in the top of his hat. The housewife would laugh, he would laugh—and show her more pictures. When H. V. Kaltenborn told me about this, he confessed that the job had been far from easy. He told me that there was only one quality that pulled him through: his determination to make the job interesting. Every morning before he started out, he looked into the mirror and gave himself a pep talk: 'Kaltenborn, you have to do this if you want to eat. Since you have to do it—why not have a good time doing it? Why not imagine every time you ring a doorbell that you are an actor before the footlights and that there's an audience out there looking at you? After all, what you are doing is just as funny as something on the stage. So why not put a lot of zest and enthusiasm into it?'

Mr Kaltenborn told me that these daily pep talks helped him transform a task that he had once hated and dreaded into an adventure that he liked and made highly profitable.

When I asked Mr Kaltenborn if he had any advice to give to the young men of America who are eager to succeed, he said: 'Yes, go to bat with yourself every morning. We talk a lot about the importance of physical exercise to wake us up out of the half-sleep in which so many of us walk around. But we need, even more, some spiritual and mental exercises every morning to stir us into action. Give yourself a pep talk every day.'

Is giving yourself a pep talk every day silly, superficial, childish? No, on the contrary, it is the very essence of sound psychology. 'Our life is what our thoughts make it.' These words are just as true today as they were eighteen centuries ago when Marcus Aurelius first wrote them in his book on Meditations: 'Our life is what our thoughts make it.'

By talking to yourself every hour of the day, you can direct yourself to think thoughts of courage and happiness, thoughts of power and peace. By talking to yourself about the things you have to be grateful for, you can fill your mind with thoughts that soar and sing.

By thinking the right thoughts, you can make any job less distasteful. Your boss wants you to be interested in your job so that he or she will make more money. But let's forget about what the boss wants. Think only of what getting interested in your job will do for you. Remind yourself that it may double the amount of happiness you get out of life, for you spend about one half of your waking hours at your work, and if you don't find happiness in your work, you may never find it anywhere. Keep reminding yourself that getting interested in your job will take your mind off your worries, and, in the long run, will probably bring promotion and increased pay. Even if it doesn't do that, it will reduce fatigue to a minimum and help you enjoy your hours of leisure.

People rarely succeed unless they have fun in what they are doing.
—Dale Carnegie

Remember happiness doesn't depend upon who you are or what you have; it depends solely on what you think.
—Dale Carnegie

3

HOW TO OVERCOME TIREDNESS

Here is an astounding and significant fact: Mental work alone can't make you tired. Sounds absurd. But a few years ago, scientists tried to find out how long the human brain could labour without reaching 'a diminished capacity for work,' the scientific definition of fatigue. To the amazement of these scientists, they discovered that blood passing through the brain, when it is active, shows no fatigue at all! If you took blood from the veins of a day labourer while he was working, you would find it full of 'fatigue toxins' and fatigue products. But if you took a drop of blood from the brain of an Albert Einstein, it would show no fatigue toxins whatever at the end of the day.

So far as the brain is concerned, it can work 'as well and as swiftly at the end of eight or even twelve hours of effort as at the beginning.' The brain is utterly tireless...So what makes you tired?

Psychiatrists declare that most of our fatigue derives from our mental and emotional attitudes. One of England's most distinguished psychiatrists, J.A. Hadfield, says in his book The Psychology of Power: 'The greater part of the fatigue from which we suffer is of mental origin; in fact exhaustion of purely physical origin is rare.'

One of America's most distinguished psychiatrists, Dr A.A. Brill, goes even further. He declares, 'One hundred percent of the fatigue of the sedentary worker in good health is due to psychological factors, by which we mean emotional factors.'

What kinds of emotional factors tire the sedentary (or sitting) worker? Joy? Contentment? No! Never! Boredom, resentment, a feeling of not being appreciated, a feeling of futility, hurry, anxiety, worry—those are the emotional factors that exhaust the sitting worker, make him susceptible to colds, reduce his output, and send him home with a nervous headache. Yes, we get tired because our emotions produce nervous tensions in the body.

The Metropolitan Life Insurance Company pointed that out in a leaflet on fatigue: 'Hard work by itself,' said this great life insurance company, 'seldom causes fatigue which cannot be cured by a good sleep or rest... Worry, tenseness, and emotional upsets are three of the biggest causes of fatigue. Often they are to blame when physical or mental work seems to be the cause... Remember that a tense muscle is a working muscle. Ease up! Save energy for important duties.'

Stop now, right where you are, and give yourself a checkup. As you read these lines, are you scowling at the book? Do you feel a strain between the eyes? Are you sitting relaxed in your chair? Or are you hunching up your shoulders? Are the muscles of your face tense? Unless your entire body is as limp and relaxed as an old rag doll, you are at this very moment producing nervous tensions and muscular tensions. You are producing nervous tensions and nervous fatigue!

Why do we produce these unnecessary tensions in doing mental work? Daniel W. Josselyn said, 'I find that the chief obstacle...is the almost universal belief that hard work requires a feeling of effort, else it is not well done.' So we scowl when we concentrate. We hunch up our shoulders. We call on our muscles to make the motion of effort, which in no way assists our brain in its work.

Here is an astonishing and tragic truth: millions of people who wouldn't dream of wasting dollars go right on wasting and squandering their energy with the recklessness of seven drunken sailors in Singapore.

What is the answer to this nervous fatigue? Relax! Relax! Relax! Learn to relax while you are doing your work!

Easy? No. You will probably have to reverse the habits of a lifetime. But it is worth the effort, for it may revolutionize your life! William James said, in his essay 'The Gospel of Relaxation': 'The American overtension and jerkiness and breathlessness and intensity and agony of expression...are bad habits, nothing more or less.' Tension is a habit.

Relaxing is a habit. And bad habits can be broken, good habits formed.

How do you relax? Do you start with your mind, or do you start with your nerves? You don't start with either. You always begin to relax with your muscles!

Let's give it a try. To show how it is done, suppose we start with your eyes. Read this paragraph through, and when you've reached the end, lean back, close your eyes, and say to your eyes silently, 'Let go. Let go. Stop straining, stop frowning. Let go. Let go.' Repeat that over and over very slowly for a minute...

Didn't you notice that after a few seconds the muscles of the eyes began to obey? Didn't you feel as though some hand had wiped away the tension? Well, incredible as it seems, you have sampled in that one minute the whole key and secret to the art of relaxing. You can do the same thing with the jaw, with the muscles of the face, with the neck, with the shoulders, the whole of the body. But the most important organ of all is the eye. Dr Edmund Jacobson of the University of Chicago has gone so far as to say that if you can completely relax the muscles of the eyes, you can forget all your troubles! The reason the eyes are so important in relieving nervous tension is that they burn up one fourth of all the nervous energies consumed by the body. That is also why so many people with perfectly sound vision suffer from 'eyestrain.' They are tensing the eyes.

Vicki Baum, the famous novelist, said that when she was a child, she met an old man who taught her one of the most important lessons she ever learned. She had fallen down and cut her knees and hurt her wrist. The old man picked her up. He had once been a circus clown, and as he brushed her off, he said, 'The reason you injured yourself was because you don't know how to relax. You have to pretend you are as limp as a sock, as an old crumpled sock. Come, I'll show you how to do it.'

That old man taught Vicki Baum and the other children how to fall, how to do flip-flops, and how to turn somersaults. And always he insisted, 'Think of yourself as an old crumpled sock. Then you've got to relax!'

You can relax in odd moments, almost anywhere you are. Only don't make an effort to relax. Relaxation is the absence of all tension and effort. Think ease and relaxation. Begin by thinking relaxation of the muscles of your eyes and your face, saying over and over, 'Let go ...let go ...let go and relax.' Feel the energy flowing out of your facial muscles to the center of your body. Think of yourself as being as free from tension as a baby.

That is what Galli-Curci, the great soprano, used to do. Helen Jepson told me that she used to see Galli-Curci before a performance, sitting in a chair with all her muscles relaxed and her lower jaw so limp it actually sagged. An excellent practice—it kept her from becoming too nervous before her stage entrance; it prevented fatigue.

Here are four suggestions that will help you learn to relax:

1. Relax in odd moments. Let your body go limp like an old sock. I keep an old, maroon-coloured sock on my desk as I work—keep it there as a reminder of how limp I ought to be. If you haven't got a sock, a cat will do. Did you ever pick up a kitten sleeping in the sunshine? If so, both ends sagged like a wet newspaper. Even the yogis in India say that if you want to master the art of relaxation, study the cat. I never saw a tired cat, a cat with a nervous breakdown, or a cat suffering from insomnia, worry, or stomach ulcers. You will probably avoid these disasters if you learn to relax as the cat does.

2. Work, as much as possible, in a comfortable position. Remember that tensions on the body produce aching shoulders and nervous fatigue.

3. Check yourself four or five times a day, and say to yourself, 'Am I making my work harder than it actually is? Am I using muscles that have nothing to do with the work I am doing?' This will help you form the habit of relaxing, and as Dr David Harold Fink says, 'Among those who know psychology best, it is habits two to one.'

4. Test yourself again at the end of the day, by asking yourself, 'Just how tired am I? If I am tired, it is not because of the mental work I have done, but the way I have done it.' 'I measure my accomplishments,' said Daniel W. Josselyn, 'not by how tired I am at the end of the day, or when irritability proves that my nerves are tired, I know beyond question that it has been an inefficient day both as to quantity and quality.' If every businessperson in America would learn that same lesson, our death rate from 'hypertension' diseases would drop overnight. And we would stop filling up our sanitariums and asylums with people who have been broken by fatigue and worry.

Take a chance! All life is a chance. The man who goes farthest is generally the one who is willing to do and dare.

—Dale Carnegie

www.ingramcontent.com/pod-product-compliance
Lightning Source LLC
Chambersburg PA
CBHW011741010726
47498CB00012B/2889